David Livingstone: The Wayward Vagabond

AFRICAN CLASSICS SERIES

1. *Secret Lives* – Ngugi wa Thiong'o
2. *Matigari* – Ngugi wa Thiong'o
3. *A Grain of Wheat* – Ngugi wa Thiong'o
4. *Weep Not, Child* – Ngugi wa Thiong'o
5. *The River Between* – Ngugi wa Thiong'o
6. *Devil on the Cross* – Ngugi wa Thiong'o
7. *Petals of Blood* – Ngugi wa Thiong'o
8. *Wizard of the Crow* – Ngugi wa Thiong'o
9. *Homing In* – Marjorie Oludhe Macgoye
10. *Coming to Birth* – Marjorie Oludhe Macgoye
11. *Street Life* – Marjorie Oludhe Macgoye
12. *The Present Moment* – Marjorie Oludhe Macgoye
13. *Chira* – Marjorie Oludhe Macgoye
14. *A Farm Called Kishinev* – Marjorie Oludhe Macgoye
15. *No Longer at Ease* – Chinua Achebe
16. *Arrow of God* – Chinua Achebe
17. *A Man of the People* – Chinua Achebe
18. *Things Fall Apart* – Chinua Achebe
19. *Anthills of the Savannah* – Chinua Achebe
20. *The Strange Bride* – Grace Ogot
21. *Land Without Thunder* – Grace Ogot
22. *The Promised Land* – Grace Ogot
23. *The Other Woman* – Grace Ogot
24. *The Minister's Daughter* – Mwangi Ruheni
25. *The Future Leaders* – Mwangi Ruheni
26. *White Teeth* – Okot P'Bitek
27. *Horn of My Love* – Okot P'Bitek
28. *God's Bits of Wood* – Sembene Ousmane
29. *Emperor Shaka the Great* – Masizi Kunene
30. *No Easy Walk to Freedom* – Nelson Mandela
31. *Mine Boy* – Peter Abrahams
32. *Takadini* – Ben Hanson
33. *Myths and Legends of the Swahili* – Jan Knappert
34. *Mau Mau Author in Detention* – Gakaara wa Wanjau
35. *Igereka and Other African Narratives* – John Ruganda
36. *Kill Me Quick* – Meja Mwangi
37. *Going Down River Road* – Meja Mwangi
38. *Striving for the Wind* – Meja Mwangi
39. *Carcase for Hounds* – Meja Mwangi
40. *The Last Plague* – Meja Mwangi
41. *The Big Chiefs* – Meja Mwangi
42. *The Slave* – Elechi Amadi
43. *The Concubine* – Elechi Amadi
44. *The Great Ponds* – Elechi Amadi
45. *The African Child* – Camara Laye

PEAK LIBRARY SERIES

1. *Without a Conscience* – Barbara Baumann
2. *The Herdsman's Daughter* – Bernard Chahilu
3. *Hearthstones* – Kekelwa Nyaywa
4. *Of Man and Lion* – Beatrice Erlwanger
5. *My Heart on Trial* – Genga Idowu
6. *Kosiya Kifefe* – Arthur Gakwandi
7. *Return to Paradise* – Yusuf K Dawood
8. *Mission to Gehenna* – Karanja wa Kang'ethe
9. *Goatsmell* – Nevanji Madanhire
10. *Sunset in Africa* – Peter M Nyarango
11. *The Moon Also Sets* – Osi Ogbu
12. *Breaking Chains* – Dorothea Holi
13. *The Missing Links* – Tobias O Otieno
14. *I Shall Walk Alone* – Paul Nakitare
15. *A Season of Waiting* – David Omowale
16. *Before the Rooster Crows* – Peter Kimani
17. *A Nose for Money* – Francis B Nyamnjoh
18. *The Travail of Dieudonné* – Francis B Nyamnjoh
19. *A Journey Within* – Florence Mbaya
20. *The Doomed Conspiracy* – Barrack O Muluka and Tobias O Otieno
21. *The Lone Dancer* – Joe Kiarie
22. *Eye of the Storm* – Yusuf K Dawood
23. *Animal Farm* – George Orwell
24. *Stillborn* – Diekoye Oyeyinka
25. *Ugandan Affairs* – Sira Kiwana
26. *African Quilt* – Harshi Syal Gill and Parvin D. Syal
27. *The Dolphin Catchers and other stories*
28. *Black Ghost* – Ken N. Kamoche
29. *The Guardian Angels* – Issa Noor
30. *David Livingstone: The Wayward Vagabond* – M. G. Kahende

David Livingstone:
The Wayward Vagabond

M. G. N. Kahende

East African Educational Publishers

Nairobi • Kampala • Dar es Salaam • Kigali • Lusaka • Lilongwe

Published by
East African Educational Publishers Ltd.
Elgeyo Marakwet Close, off Elgeyo Marakwet Road, Kilimani, Nairobi
P.O. Box 45314, Nairobi - 00100, KENYA
Tel: +254 20 2324760
Mobile: +254 722 205661 / 722 207216 / 733 677716 / 734 652012
Email: eaep@eastafricanpublishers.com
Website: www.eastafricanpublishers.com

East African Educational Publishers also has offices or is represented in the following countries: Uganda, Tanzania, Rwanda, Malawi, Zambia, Botswana and South Sudan.

© M. G. N. Kahende, 2019

First published 2019

ISBN 978-9966-56-434-4

DEDICATION

To:

My father

My mother

&

Timothy

Ciiru

Alex

Wambui

Njoroge and

Grace.

ACKNOWLEDGEMENT

I would like to acknowledge Grace, who typed the manuscript, and my editor, Benson Shiholo, for his invaluable technical guidance.

NOTE FROM THE AUTHOR

In the 19th Century, the greatest explorer and missionary on African soil was a Scotsman by the name Dr. David Livingstone. A Surgeon, he did not bring with him a scalpel, scissors, stitching kit or any anaesthetic drugs, the basic tools of a surgeon. He carried pens and notebooks.

Livingstone transformed himself from a doctor to a spy.

Sponsored by the Royal Geographical Society which was controlled by the British Foreign Office, he made three epic journeys to Africa. In his reports, he detailed the wealth and natural resources of the land and the navigability of Zambezi River. He was also obsessed with finding the source of the River Nile. His works facilitated the colonisation of Africa.

Why a qualified Surgeon devoted his entire existence to the life of a wayward vagabond, roaming a "Dark Continent" inhabited by "savages", "cannibals", "uncivilised" and "backward" natives is truly a mystery.

His adventures changed the course of history in Africa, to the detriment of the lives of natives and indeed his own. This is a historical novel.

NOBODY WINS

So it has been
since creation
that tragedy is closely linked
to wanton greed,
and so it shall be
till the end of time.

For the human mind is askew
Driven by pleasure or pain
into a foggy world
where reason is submerged
in murky incomprehensibles
nurtured by dreams
in which we all live
as heroes and winners
victims and villains
of diabolical illusions in turns!

The carnage of destruction
and the stench of death
fill the void of our existence
to give empty life meaning
in which nobody wins
both the powerful and the powerless.

For we all are damned
Hapless wayward vagabonds, singing
"This world is not my home"
For pain, hatred and chaos
rule our lives.

Why not make this world
OUR SWEET HOME
in true brotherhood of man,
Regardless of race, creed or colour.

CONTENTS

CHAPTER 1

I AM WIRED

It was a warm tropical afternoon, when I took a walk to the edge of the forest, just before the sun retired from its laborious long lazy drift across the skies. I yearned to enjoy the serene tropical sunset and the myriad sounds of birds and animals which reach a crescendo as dusk draws near. It was hard to distinguish which sound came from which beak or mouth, as they mellowed into each other like the smoothness of beats in music of a good orchestra, conducted by a seasoned maestro.

The deep roar of lions in the savannah grassland came, riding on the waves of the wind, to join the trumpet sound of elephants in the hills, as guinea fowls, swallows, weaver birds, zebras, donkeys, cows, sheep and goats rendered their acts in the crescendo. It was moments like these which gave meaning to life, of uninhibited and undiluted joy. I lay under a fig tree which had yielded prodigious clusters of fruits which clung to branches and hung on vines, challenging birds, animals and humans to have their fill. Overripe fruits had fallen to the ground and the aroma was intoxicating. Bees, birds, ants and squirrels had assembled for a rich harvest. I swept a patch and stretched myself on the ground to fully inhale the heavenly atmosphere.

It was at that time when I was contemplating retirement from my special vocation of studying the frailty of human nature. I had hoped my findings could be useful to save the human race from assured self-destruction. Alas, I had come to the sad irrevocable conclusion that the future of man is irretrievably doomed. I was thinking of a new occupation in which to direct my energy, while enjoying nature. The Year was 1828.

As I lay under the fig tree, I cannot tell when sleep overtook me.

Into the heavenly atmosphere at my disposal, St. Peter intruded, descending from high above. At first, I thought kites, eagles and hawks were flapping their wings around me, but all of a sudden, I was blinded by the brilliance of light and beautiful colours like those of a thousand diamonds and rainbows, dancing together, as he landed.

"Don't be afraid, and do no open your eyes," he said to me.

At once, I noticed it was the voice of St. Peter, who guards the Pearly Gates in Heaven.

"What do you want Peter, have you come to summon me to Heaven?" I asked him.

You see, my name is Everywhere, the free soul who escaped from Heaven before my scheduled flight to earth. I was impatient. I wanted to live in Kuzania, the former Garden of Eden. I could not imagine living in India or China. And there was no guarantee that I would not be sent there. I am a soul in exile, a refugee, an internally displaced person. Lately, Heaven has elevated me to the status of special envoy on earth, an ambassador at large, but not plenipotentiary and extraordinary. My powers are limited, but I am honoured.

"I have come to deliver a message. You have been selected by Heaven to undertake a special assignment," St. Peter continued.

"Not again! All my past assignments have flopped. Man is an incorrigible fool," I protested.

"Dare you defy the Lord?" he asked me in a harsh and threatening voice.

"At your command!" I acquiesced.

"Good! We knew we could count on you. In the town of Blantyre in Scotland lives a lad of humble birth who goes by the name, David Livingstone. He was born in 1813. He is a boy with a troubled spirit which in the future will lead him to undertake missions in which the history of man will be altered. In the process, the peaceful and prosperous Kingdom of Monomotapa in Central Africa will be targeted. Momentous tidings on a global scale are about to be unleashed and Livingstone will be in the thick and thin of it. Your mission is of crucial importance. As you know, there are very few things which can move God to tears; like Lucifer's attempted coup in Heaven and the betrayal by Adam and Eve in the Garden of Eden.

"In our estimation, another disaster of a great magnitude is in the offing in the manner of the fall of the Kingdom of Monomotapa. You are commanded to keep a tab on the saga. You will carefully follow Livingstone henceforth and record your findings carefully. You will not interfere in any way, however tempting, but keep your findings confidential until the Day of Judgment. You are free to choose and design the manner and means of executing your mandate. Be warned that a lot is at stake and God is concerned. You will only

hear from us should the need for the readjustment of your mission arise. Just a small hint; Satan in his eternal recklessness reckons conditions are ripe to sow seeds of chaos, confusion, terror and catastrophes in the world, and in Africa in particular, beginning with the strongest Kingdom, Monomotapa. The clamour for empires is about to begin. We fear the worst for the natives. Good luck."

In a whiff, St. Peter was gone before I could engage him further. I felt like a blind man, marching to the unknown; a condemned man with a noose on his neck. When I opened my eyes, dusk had set in. Birds were back in their nests and the animals in their lairs. Like a man carrying a heavy burden, I walked slowly back to the village with the name David Livingstone and the Kingdom of Monomotapa ringing incessantly and discordantly in my head. The names had come to replace the soothing sweet sound of the natural orchestra at the edge of the forest at dusk. I had been ushered into the dark uncertainty of the unknown, by a heavenly command.

I had contemplated a new vocation without burdens only to be rewarded with what looked to me like a task of gigantic proportions, one over which I had no control.

Aware that a single mistake in the execution of my mission could bring the wrath of the Almighty upon me, thereby jeopardising my freedom and existence, I had to be as assiduous as possible in my undertaking.

I was moving into unchartered territory, as blind as a bat. It was then that I sent a text message to the chief Celestial librarian to furnish me with information on Scotland and its people. The response was instantaneous and it read as follows;

Scotland is in the northern reaches of the earth. It is an uneasy member of the United Kingdom which came into existence in 1712 under the tutelage of the English. It is divided into two regions namely, the Northern Highlands and the Southern Highlands or Uplands. The Handrian Wall which was built by the Romans in the South separates Scotland from England. In the days gone by, it was said the wall marked the end of civilisation and the beginning of savagery.

The Highlands are sparsely populated because when the Union was founded, the English sent three hundred (300) dukes, earls, lairds and landlords to teach the Scots proper farming methods. In a policy labelled Clearance, Scottish peasants were forcefully and brutally thrown out of their ancestral land, paving the way for large scale estates or enclosures.

The English plough was introduced to till the land. The settlers introduced foreign grasses: rye grass, clover, turnips, cabbages and potatoes. Ayshire cattle and Borders of sheep were also brought. The Scottish highlands were now the new bread basket for England. After many attempts by England to conquer Scotland by the sword, the final blow was delivered by a pen on a piece of paper, the Act of the Union.

The influx of English settlers resulted in the complete disorganisation of the traditional Scottish set up. The peasants moved into cities and towns and became drunkards and slum dwellers. A lucky few went into fishing, spinning of linen, coal mining and military service.

There were many who could not stand the presence of the English on their soil and opted to migrate to Canada and the United States of America. You are warned that the present docility of Scotsmen is disturbing because history talks of a gallant people, proud and unconquerable.

The History of Scotland can be described as exciting, complex, fascinating and turbulent. The original natives of the land were known as the Picts. They painted their faces like Red Indians. They were mortal enemies of the English tribes comprising the Angloi, the Frisones, and the Britons who the Picts referred to as Sasanach, a most derogatory term. So insulted, the English tried repeatedly to conquer the Picts, but to no avail. That is why they enlisted the help of the Anglo-Saxons from Continental Europe in an attempt to conquer the Picts. They did not succeed, but in a new twist of history, the Anglo-Saxons refused to return to the Continent, opting for assimilation.

It was funny how the Picts warmly welcomed other tribes to settle on their land like the Celts from Bohemia in Austria or the Vikings from the Scandinavian countries. But they could not stand the English and the Romans! Maybe they knew something about the two that the rest of the world did not know, that they were never to be trusted and they were cruel, hungry for power and greedy for material wealth.

It was the Celtic blood which had united the people of Scotland, Ireland and Wales. It is this fraternity which had driven the Romans from England.

After the Union, the Scots became second class citizens in their own country and their language, Gaelic, was displaced by English. The English overlords had decided to sit on the Scots and to civilise them through the exploitation of their land, labour and other resources.

The situation is not any different from that of slaves and masters.

The brief ended.

What did it have to do with my mission?

I searched for Blantyre in the Herodotus' Atlas, *Mappo Mundo*. After a long and arduous comb, I located the tiny dot with small letters, which looked light years from Kuzania, my adopted and lovely home.

I embarked on my mission at once. I set the compass and rode on the wind heading north, following the course of the majestic and picturesque Great Rift Valley, with great herds of animals and dotted with great lakes, some with steam swirling from geothermal wells. Way beyond the boundaries of Kuzania, I came across the sight of billows of smoke rising to the skies. As the area is a semi-desert, my curiosity was aroused; I hovered closer to the ground below. Lo and behold! The smoke was rising from thousands of grass thatched huts in villages which were on fire in the Kingdom of Donyiro.

To my consternation, I saw a new strange breed of men of a fair complexion with curly hair, riding on horses and camels carrying long swords, sharp lances, axes and cudgels. They were chasing and butchering the black natives of the Kingdom and setting houses on fire. For miles, the ground was strewn with bodies of dead warriors, some still clutching their spears, while vultures swooped down to pluck out eyes from their lifeless bodies.

The Arab foreign invaders had crossed the Red Sea in their thousands determined to conquer and occupy the Donyiro Kingdom. Against the new weapons and brute determination of the invaders, the Kingdom stood no chance and was easily subdued. Since St. Peter had not mentioned this genocide, I judged it was of minor significance to Heaven. Then I shuddered. If this arson, carnage and pillage could not move God to tears, then how horrible were the events in Monomotapa going to be? With a heavy heart, I headed north again.

When I encountered the River Nile, I was fascinated by the extensive irrigation along its banks. This was the land of Egypt or Misri where a similar carnage like the one I had just witnessed in Donyiro had taken place years back. The native population had been decimated by invaders from across the Red Sea.

I crossed the Mediterranean Sea and came to the Alps Mountains where Hannibal the Carthagian had been stopped by a harsh winter from conquering Europe. His was a clear case of madness. How did he expect elephants to lead the charge on snow? What were they going to eat? Ice?

The mind of man is truly demented, especially when driven by dreams of conquest, booty, grandeur and power. I hoped David Livingstone would not suffer such folly as I did not want to see a repeat of what I had witnessed in Donyiro. It had been nauseating.

Crossing the English Channel, I admired the majestic beauty of the White Cliffs of Dover, whose serene calmness and angelic softness to the eye eased the burden and agony in my heart.

Traversing England heading northwards, I marvelled at the pace of the agricultural and industrial revolutions. Vast areas of land were under cultivation and I concluded the peasants must have been driven out of their land as I had been informed was the case in Scotland. I cursed the demi-gods of Lords and others for their heartlessness.

Steel mills and textile factories had been set up and black smoke was billowing from their massive chimneys painting the sky black. Connecting the factories to the sea port were the railway lines. On the rails, steam engines were puffing black smoke, dragging along wagons heavily loaded with goods for export or import. Some wagons were carrying coal and I suspected it was from Scotland.

The new class of industrialists and commercial farmers lived in great affluence while the workers lived a life of squalor, like animals, in a human zoo. The uplifting of the heart which had been engendered by the Cliffs of Dover was replaced by a morbid hatred of the English class system, and I longed to be in Scotland sooner.

As I crossed the Cheviot Hills, the Southern Highlands came into view. My heart was pulsating with anxiety.

Drifting in the calm afternoon breeze, I decided to explore the land before seeking my quarry.

The country was amazingly beautiful with forested highlands. In the north, the majestic Grampian Mountains looked just like Nyandarua Mountains in Kuzania. I felt homesick.

These mountains were the source of the Loch Ness River, which had a fabled monster. Undeterred by the legend, there were many Scottish fishermen pulling out salmons from its waters, whose fillet would end up in the homes of the wealthy in England.

Throughout the land, there were few wild animals. I saw red deers, bats, pine martens, red squirrels, badgers, foxes, hares and wild pigs. They must have killed all their giraffes, buffaloes, elephants, lions and hyenas a long time ago for reasons best known to themselves.

"What a pity," I remarked.

I hovered down to espy on people in the towns. There was some kind of celebration in one town and I took interest in the proceedings. The penurious settings at once revealed they were Scotsmen, drunk and rowdy. Lo and behold! Men were wearing heavy skirts or kilts, dancing to the music of the most amazing musical instruments on earth, which had pipes jutting upwards in many directions. They were huge heavy instruments laboriously played by blowing air into one pipe, squeezing the air bag and pressing the fingers up and down on some keys and the music would come out of the other pipes! It was the craziest thing I had ever seen, and I bet no other people on earth will ever attempt to play the thing or dance to its cacophony. Whether it was the Picts, the Celts or the Scandinavians or a combination of all three which had come up with the bag pipe, I couldn't tell, but it was not attractive both in sight and sound.

The food they were eating looked awful. There was one pot which attracted everybody. It was serving a dish called Haggis, the most popular meal in Scotland. It contained sheep lungs, liver, heart and other throw-away parts, all cooked together. I couldn't stand the sight and so I moved on.

It was then that I saw black men coming out of ground-like moles leaving burrows. At first I thought they were Africans, but my brief from the celestial library had made no mention of Africans in Scotland, not even black slaves!

There were pails of water outside the holes and every time the men washed their faces and hands, they became white men! There were heaps of black solid stones and at once, I realised these were Scottish coal miners coming from underground shafts covered in black soot. Many came out coughing, sneezing and blowing black mucus from their noses. They all looked malnourished, sick and most unhappy. I doubted if they would wear skirts and go to the towns to eat Haggis, dance to the strange music of bag pipes and drink themselves silly. My heart went out to them. I moved on as I had other urgent mattes to discharge.

Blantyre, whose meaning is "Top of the Land" was a small town divided by the river Clyde. On one side of the river lived poor Scottish workers while the other housed, the civilised rich Englishmen, owners of coal mines, factories and commercial farms, who dictated life in Scotland. They lived in mansions with lawns and flowers gardens, swimming pools, and tennis courts while a well-manicured golf course stood at the edge of the forest for their exclusive use. Scotsmen were caddies, not players, though the game had been invented in Scotland.

The town had four roads. One headed to the mines, another to the industrial area, the third to Mount Pleasant where the English lived, and finally the last one to the ugly tenements or slums where the miserable workers lived. The tenements were separated from the rest by River Clyde, like an outcast, the undesirable. Tenements were blocks of buildings; each block had many single rooms, bedsitters so to speak and each housed a family. They were owned by English landlords and once a Scot lost his job, he was thrown out. Those who lived in the tenements were considered privileged as they were the employed, assured of a salary at month end, however meagre, and above all a roof over their heads.

The rest of the population lived in the countryside looking after sheep and they had not been touched and soiled by modernity or what the English called civilisation. They lived like Stone Age men. This is the lot which was witnessing the grabbing of their pasture land as towns and factories expanded. Occasionally, the peasants drifted to towns in the evening and over the weekend for a drink and to enjoy the vices of urbanization like prostitution. They discussed with the workers the growing concern with the oppressive Union which was threatening their lives from all directions. This was the totality of Blantyre and its surroundings, a forlorn place in the middle of nowhere where everybody except the English looked miserable and lost, where the only release from anger was through alcohol and prostitution and, where women either joined in or shouted themselves hoarse at home, cursing.

I learnt that young Livingstone returned from work every evening riding at the back of his father's bicycle, the only one in Blantyre, the one they called 'the Boneshaker' on account of how it rattled and rocked the rider up and down. Livingstone's father had been enterprising in the past selling fish heads and fish bones to the workers for soup in Blantyre which he carried on the Boneshaker.

Times had changed and he was now in the rut of the miserable, who could only be relieved from the pain of living by death.

I was dying to be connected with my quarry. Positioning myself on the road which they would follow home, I waited. After a lengthy while, along came father and son on the Boneshaker, speeding down the hill heading home.

The father was on the pedals with young Livingstone at the back holding tightly to his waist with both arms. I was shocked at the miserable site of both of them. Livingstone looked awful, bonny and ungraceful. He reminded me of the remains of an unfinished attempt in the construction of a scarecrow. He was sneezing, whizzing and coughing, which was punctuated by the squeaking and rattling of different parts of the frame of the Boneshaker.

The weather was chilly and windy as it was just before the onset of winter. Trees had shed all the leaves and they looked dry and lifeless. Everywhere, the land was bare and barren and both the land and its inhabitants looked cursed and condemned by some supernatural force.

The father, whose name was McDougal, was kicking the Boneshaker as fast as he could to exert maximum speed to cheat the threatening darkness.

Below the hill and across the shaky wooden bridge sat the blocks of tenements where coal and factory workers lived.

Suddenly, the bicycle chain snapped and the father struggled to control the shaking beast which was threatening to scatter father and son on the hard ground.

"Stop, I can't breathe!" cried Livingstone.

"Just hold on!" shot back the father.

"I am going to vomit," declared Livingstone in desperation.

"Hold it back," shouted the father at the top of his voice.

As the Boneshaker was brought to a halt, Livingstone fell off with a thud, face first. He was vomiting and bleeding from the nose, the result of the knock. After a few morsels of the remains of what he had eaten earlier were violently dislodged from his stomach, air in spurts and spasms came gushing wildly through his mouth and nostrils. The sounds accompanying were neither a sneeze nor a cough or a belch, but something close to a combination of all of them. It was a most horrible, unnatural, scary and frightening noise, one you can only probably get by squeezing the balls of an old chimpanzee.

All the while, his father had his hands on the shoulders of the lad.

"Cough it out! Cough it out!" he urged the boy as Livingstone did his best to clear his clogged lungs.

David marshalled supernatural efforts and made a most determined attempt to free himself from the suffocating demon. His efforts were rewarded with the expulsion of thick yellow phlegm laced with blood and coal soot from his lungs. His father was alarmed at the sight of the ugly mixture spat on the ground.

"Oh my God! Oh my God! You have contracted Black Death!" he cried.

Black Death was the name given to tuberculosis by coal miners. The disease consumed many at a very early age because of the poor working conditions. Livingstone understood, but did not answer. He was suffering from delirium. After a while, Livingstone attempted to stand up, but immediately slumped to the ground again. No strength was left in him. They rested a little while longer as his father's thoughts raced wildly from the huge medical bill coming for his son's treatment to an early rest in the grave if things got worse. Both were harrowing.

"I feel much better now father," declared Livingstone.

"Then let's go home," said the father.

As the bicycle chain could not be repaired, the father was pushing the Boneshaker with one hand while holding Livingstone by the wrist with the other. After a short walk in which nothing was said, the father felt the hand of Livingstone grow limp.

"Father, I can't walk anymore," he cried.

"Hang on, I will take you home," declared the father.

He lifted Livingstone and hoisted him on his shoulder, supporting him with one arm while he pushed the Boneshaker, the family's most valued treasure in their miserable lives, with the other. The Boneshaker had done its duty in the earlier days; delivering fish heads and fish bones as a faithful bread winner does. It was yearning for a well-deserved rest. As darkness descended upon Blantyre, the sorry figure of a tired, bonny and unkempt man carrying the bundle of an equally unhealthy and sick son while at the same time pushing a broken down bicycle was a pitiable sight indeed. The son looked like he had little or no life in him. They were cold, extremely dirty and very hungry.

As soon as his father put David down in the house, his mother asked, "And what is the matter with him?"

"He has Black Death," his father replied.

"Oh my little boy! Oh my little boy! God forbid! Heaven help us," cried the mother.

The mother sobbed uncontrollably while holding David in her arms, as though she was exorcising the demon apparently lodged in her "little boy". At last, she wiped away her tears and heaved a deep sigh of relief.

"It is the English who have brought the curse to Scotland! More coal for their factories while we die like worthless things. They should pack their bags and go away; leave us alone!" she asserted in defiance.

This outburst seemed to bring Livingstone back to life. He lifted his head and shook it in approval of his mother's pronouncement on the source of all ills in Scotland. They were of the same mind with so many others in Scotland.

"Tomorrow, you take him to the doctor," his father told his mother.

"No, you take him on the bicycle. I have other children to look after!" she objected.

"The bicycle broke down; we will need extra money to pay the doctor and to buy medicine. Tomorrow, I will not work on the surface; I will go down the shaft to earn extra money," his father expounded.

"Not again! The foul air will kill you!" argued his mother alarmed.

"Do I have a choice?" asked the father, much more addressing himself, aware that the extra income earned by David would not be forthcoming for a long time. If times were tough, they were going to be tougher.

"Tell the doctor I will settle the bill in instalments," he said.

He took a pail and filled it with cold water and proceeded to the communal bathroom outside. Soon, he was splashing his body with ice cold water cupped in the palms of his hands. There was no soap; soot always remained on the body, and so it had been in all his working days as a coal miner. The soot and his white skin blended to give him a ghostly look, like a clown in a play, depicting a tragedy.

I watched the family eat and retire to bed. It was a chilly night like I had never experienced. Poverty like this I had never imagined. Were these living human beings or objects, robot tools of production in service of the English investors?

As the family retired to bed, I hung around to eavesdrop on anything of interest in the room. The family lived in a filthy single room which was in dire need of repairs and paint. It was poorly furnished with wooden stools and double decked beds. There were three cooking pots, all black on the outside, lying by the coal stove, unwashed. The few items of clothing the family possessed were hanging by nails on walls. On top of an old cupboard were some books which attracted my curiosity. One was the Holy Bible and from its tattered condition, I could tell it had been much overused. Beneath the Bible was Herodotus' Histories of the World, equally weather beaten.

The other was The Travels of Mungo Park, the story of a Scottish explorer, a hero of some sort. Under them was a folded map of the world which had been inherited from Mungo Park, Livingstone's uncle. It was Herodotus' Mappo Mundo. I spread the single sheet atlas and was presently dumbfounded to find the Kingdom of Monomotapa encircled in red. I did not know who had inked it because Mungo Park had been a great traveller in West not Central Africa. The coincidence with my mission was most curious. At that point, I threw a glance at Livingstone who was cuddled up, covered in a tattered old miners overall. He was still whizzing and coughing terribly and I at once dismissed any connection between him and the person who had encircled the kingdom in red. I concluded he was too young and too naive to have thoughts stretching that far. But then, if not him, who else had done it?

It then occurred to me that the ways of the divine and those of Lucifer are most mysterious. I recalled that there was nothing special or outstanding about a legendary Biblical youth called David before he used a sling to put a pebble into Goliaths skull, killing him instantly. And likewise, there was nothing extraordinary about another lad called Jesus until he mesmerised chief priests in a Synagogue in a theological debate in Jerusalem, at the age of twelve! Wonders will never cease and if I could bring myself to believe St. Peter, there before me was the next youngster chosen to play a great role in reshaping the history of the world. But my heart was still troubled. Livingstone was sickly with one foot in the grave; in my humble judgement, another bout of coughing could easily put paid to St. Peter's predictions.

At that point, there was a stir in the bed hosting the parents. The father was urging the mother to turn because the children were deep in sleep and it was time to make love. The woman was not yielding and instead she replied, "At a time like this, as we watch one child die, it is not proper to think about making another baby."

"Who said David is going to die? Are you God to dictate how long he should live? I am simply asking for the only one pleasure left in our lives and yet you deny me?"

"Okay then, have it your way," then she turned.

I did not want to witness the making of another Scottish baby, soon to be thrown into child labour in coal mines and textile factories, so I sneaked out.

The following day in the evening, I visited the tenement again. Livingstone and his siblings were listening to their father most attentively.

"It has not always been like this. In the beginning, the Scots and their Celtic cousins; the Irish and the Welsh, were a prosperous and proud people. But we have always had our struggles with the English.

When the Romans conquered England and attempted to move northwards, they found Scottish defences impregnable. Not only that, we harassed them so much that they had to build walls to thwart our incursions southwards. Finally, it was us, the Celtic fraternity who drove out the Romans and liberated England. Then came the Union, and the crown was first in Scotland, with Wales and Ireland in the fold. That was the architecture which marked the beginning of our end."

McDougal paused, deep in troubled thoughts.

"Then why can't we get out of the Union?" asked Livingstone.

"Good question son, good question. In fact, it has been done before. The English had tried to lord it over us before the Union, but a great warrior by the name Robert Bruce freed Scotland," said the father.

"If we ever needed another Robert Bruce, time is now," said the mother.

"I wish God could save us from the English like he saved the Israelites from Philistines," said Livingstone.

"Time for bed," said the father and they retired. I ran out of the house not to hear the father demand from the mother once again for "the only pleasure left" in their lives.

I was fascinated with the debate on the need for a gallant leader to liberate Scotland from the English. It is stuff like this which brings out heroes to spice history, or to add misery to the short life of man. It was out of the question, in my estimation, that David Livingstone would have any role to play in the game. But then, who knows, the ways of the supernatural are very mysterious.

Anxiously, I waited for the events to unfold.

CHAPTER 2

"KING DAVID"

God in his infinite wisdom gave the miserable creature called Man a lifespan of three score years and ten. In the same vein, he allocated the tortoise three hundred years and the crow one hundred and fifty. One wonders why man was less favoured in this respect. The answer is to be found in the behaviour of the other creatures. The tortoise and the crow live a harmless life. In all their days, they inflict no harm to their kind, to others or to nature. The creature called man, however, is forever behaving like a bull in a China shop or a loose monkey in an orchard with ripe fruits! In three score years and ten, a single man turns the world upside down and moves his creator to tears.

If the life of man had been extended to say two hundred years, imagine what damage he would cause, given he would have enough time to perfect his folly! If such had been the case, the world would have long ceased to exist. We must therefore give praise to the Lord that in His wisdom he gave the miserable and irresponsible creature no more than three score years and ten. This is Divine wisdom at its best. Nowhere is it better illustrated than in the lives of deranged minds of men who seek to play heroes, championing this or that cause. Hypocrites, self-seekers who invoke the name of God or their country, to justify their nefarious schemes!

In the small head of man, wild dreams germinate the seeds of chaos, cruelty and destruction in the name of nationalism, liberation, salvation, democracy and civilisation. Greed and power are camouflaged by high sounding good intentions such as the word of God, friendship, protection and philanthropy. The more callous the schemer, the greater his rewards and conversely the more acute the suffering of those gullible, his victims. Wonders will never cease as long as man lives! And yet I do not think it would have served any purpose for the life of man to have been reduced to lesser years, like the lifespan of chicken because the gods would not have had anybody to blame for their own shortcomings and amusement. Three score years and ten is just perfect for man to prove his worthlessness and for the gods to have their fill!

These thoughts were foremost on my mind as I embarked on my assignment, for the history of man is the history of heroism, hypocrisy, betrayal, cruelty and exploitation since the beginning. I was sure it was not bound to change ever!

Early in the afternoon of the following day, I visited the tenement. The children were eating the remains of the previous night: turnips, tatties and chicken liver. The food was cold and tasteless. Livingstone had come from the hospital where he had received a jab in his fight against tuberculosis. As he downed the last morsel, he looked miserable, downcast and deep in thought. He stood up, went to the shelf and picked the Bible, *Mappo Mundo* and *The Travels of Mungo Park*. As he was stepping outside, his mother intercepted him.

"And where do you think you are going?" she asked.

"I am going up the hill. I need some peace and quiet as I read these books," he said.

"You should take the children with you. I could do with some sleep," said the mother.

"No mother, I want to be alone. I have to be alone," he emphasized.

Livingstone spoke with a firm voice and a tone of maturity his mother had not heard before. She did not say a word, but waved Livingstone away with her left hand. Livingstone went up the hill, found a quiet spot and sat down.

Every house in Scotland boasted of two books; the Bible and *The Travels of Mungo Park*. The Bible stories provided entertainment, which gave rise to hope and salvation. They were sources of solace and inspiration to the poor living a life of misery in a desolate nation. Indeed, it is in hard times that people turn to God, when life for the oppressed, the downtrodden becomes a daily nightmare, incomprehensible. The stories are capped with hymns which are in themselves a catharsis to ease the pangs of pain, albeit momentarily before reality dawns again. They are like morphine or opium; painkillers, which never address the root cause of the problem.

Countless times, Livingstone had heard his father discussing with other workers about the ills of the Union. His mother had also remarked, and most convincingly so, that what Scotland needed was another Robert Bruce to drive out the English, end the Union and stop the exploitation and suffering in Scotland. These words lit a fire in Livingstone's soul. He began thinking about solutions to these problems. It was in this context that he fell in love with his namesake, David in the Bible. He marvelled at how the young boy, armed with a sling and a pebble saved the Israelites from the Philistines. "Who was to save the Scots?" he asked himself.

Folklore had it that the Scots were men of valour and in the past, they had defeated all invaders including the English and the Romans. What was so different this time? What happened to the mighty Celtic warriors? His father had told him the balance of terror had shifted in favour of the English with the advent of the gun and the cannon. The Celts had been good with lances and swords, but that era was gone. He did not believe his father because he thought every strong point must have a weakness. Goliath was a giant, wearing iron armour, but his helmet had an opening for wiping his brow through which David had driven the pebble!

Equally so, the English had an Achilles heel. He found it in their arrogance, pomposity, greed and the hunger for power! He had found the answer, but the means to exploit them had to be found. As he read the story of David and Goliath one more time, he felt warmth engulf him. It was as if some power had entered into him with a voice crying, "David save the people of Scotland." He was scared and he put the Bible away. He took *The Travels of Mungo Park*.

Mungo Park was a national hero. Had it not been sacrilegious, the Scots could have added his book to other books in the Bible. It would have found a resting place somewhere between the Old and the New Testament. His name would be immortalised alongside those of Solomon, Moses, John the Baptist and other saints. They believed he was a seer, a dreamer, an explorer and most of all, a man chosen by God. Had he amassed the wealth he had gone to seek in Africa, he would have returned to smash the English Monarchy and break up the Union. Unfortunately, he had died prematurely. So, someone else had to rise up and liberate Scotland from the tyranny of the English. An uncle to Livingstone, it was him who had left the *Mappo Mundo* on their house in one of his visits, together with *Histories of the World*.

The press had been fed with the lies that Mungo Park had drowned when his boat shot a waterfall on the Niger only to land on jagged rocks.

"It was a cover up because the monarchy desperately needed people to explore the world to map out natural resources in readiness for the expansion of the empire," his father had told Livingstone.

"What exactly happened to Mungo Park?" Livingstone had asked.

"He died of the disease of the heart," came the reply.

"He died of a heart attack? Then why did the English have to lie about it?" the young lad asked.

"No, he did not die of a heart attack. You see, Mungo Park paid a courtesy call on the King of Mali Kingdom. While in the palace, he laid his eyes on a stunningly beautiful princess who won his heart immediately. Unfortunately, the princess was betrothed to the Prince of the Kingdom of Niger. Mungo Park did not heed the warnings from the warriors not to make passes at her. Every day, he returned with ever more beautiful gifts for the princess. Your uncle was warned that he was abusing the hospitality extended to him by the gracious and kind people of Mali, but he was too deep in love to listen. His body was found floating in the river Niger trapped between rocks after the Great Rapids. A spear was sticking firmly in his chest. The English made a legend out of him with lies. They were enticing more Scots to explore the world in the hope that they too would become heroes like Mungo Park. Beware of beautiful women and the caprice of the English," his father warned him at the end.

Livingstone was recollecting these memories on the hill as he fingered *The Travels of Mungo Park*, which had been written by a German paid by the Royal Geographical Society. He drifted into deep slumber and the same voice came to him, "Rise and liberate Scotland, yours is a divine mission."

With his eyes half open, he saw the whole of Scotland transformed. It looked beautiful and full of life, with happy, vibrant and rich people singing "Hosanna to the King", but instead of singing to God, they were singing praises to "King David" the Saviour, the liberator. He saw Scots at dinner eating fish and chips, steak, mutton, apples, grapes, bananas and mangoes. He rubbed his eyes vigorously and when he came to, he saw thick and dark smoke rising from coal factories in the distance below and the shabby slums of tenements where lives of Scots were miserably spent, wasted and lost. He was angry and determined to embark on his mission someday, if only he could find a way. His dream bothered him as he descended the hill, on the rocky path leading to his wretched home.

Fate has a habit of arranging things in a very mysterious way beyond human understanding. For once, I was convinced that my trip to Scotland was not in vain; for indeed I had witnessed a most extraordinary transformation in Livingstone. I was a witness to the command for a "divine mission". Only I could not tell whether it came from Heaven or from hell. If the English, to suit their ends, can turn ordinary men into heroes, surely so, can the Devil. I was concerned.

In all my days, I had never seen a people as miserable as these. I concluded that the greatest sin in the world is greed out of which is born man's inhumanity to man. It transforms those who have into demi-gods, oblivious of the suffering of the poor. The rich become arrogant and in that state they misuse the tools of power and statecraft to further their nefarious insatiable appetite for more wealth and power. These are the vices which give rise to slavery, genocide, all forms of corruption and dictatorship. When you add the superiority of arms, the future of man and the very foundation of humanity is threatened by the powerful, the superpowers. It is a conditioned vice which benefits a few – the heartless. The oppressed became radicalised, rebellion follows and gives rise to heroes, at the cost of many lives. But the more things change, the more they remain the same. Today's celebrated heroes become tomorrow's villains. The Celts who had liberated England from the Romans were now slaves.

I came to the conclusion that the life of the creature called man is one hell of a circus; it is a mess at its very best and an ever present and threatening catastrophe at its worst. It defies logic and is the most tragic of all God's creations. It revolves around an inescapable trap to do wrong and to suffer the consequences as was in the Garden of Eden, and forever thereafter.

The creature called man boasts that he was created in the image of God! Nothing could be further from the truth for God is perfect in all ways. Man is the very opposite. The truth of the matter is that God created man from an experiment which went awry. To His amusement, when He abandoned the experiment, the creatures developed a new life of their own. They kept on evolving into higher forms and He decided to give them a chance to develop into whatever, hence the current mess on earth. The tragicomedy show has never ceased to either amuse or anger The Creator.

Earth is nothing more than a huge laboratory inhabited by all sorts of creatures large and small, some most beautiful, some very ugly. Man has arrogated himself the position of the master of this creation, but incrementally, he is decimating everything with voracious greed and speed.

Many species of animals are gone, as dead as the dodo and with time, some of the human communities will be gone. Africans, Red Indians, Aborigines have come close to suffering the fate of the dodos and the Neanderthals. The game is not over yet and if St. Peter is to be believed, the worst is yet to come and David Livingstone is earmarked to play a leading role in this theatre of the absurd.

In this megalomania, the plans are disguised and complicated, lost in hallucinations of grandeur. These are the miscalculations which are stifling the lives of millions as they serve goblins of demons, which Livingstone claims he has been charged to fight, and he has sworn to march forward gallantly when the time comes.

* * *

The plot was thickening and I decided to stick around to watch the transformation of the young lad who though frail physically, was now hell bent on a "divine mission". As I told you before, in all my days, I had been a humble citizen of Kuzania, living incognito. I had judged that God's tolerance of my disappearance from Heaven gave me reason to believe that He had a mission for me on earth. On my own, I had embarked on the study of the frailty of the creature called man, with a view to contributing to positive changes on earth, once I understood the causality of the weaknesses and how they could be addressed. My self-appointed mission and that of God in the Garden of Eden or Jesus in Palestine was doomed. I came to the conclusion that the creature called Man is irredeemable and mired in a rut of misery, pain and self-destruction. Each community fashions tools for its demise, like pelicans peck their breasts and nibble their own hearts to death. It is weird and unnatural, but it's the truth. The choice of self-assured destruction is a quest beyond my comprehension.

At this juncture I decided to visit England to see for myself the lives of the authors of the misery in Scotland. I descended on the city of London, which the huge river Thames had sliced into two, connected by a massive bridge. Besides the burgess and boats, the river had no natural attractions. Fish, foliage and birds had died because of pollution from industrial refuse, only a few weeping willow trees were growing drooping towards the waters like they were in prayer, mourning the state of affairs in England. I was to learn with time that the early European cities had been built along river banks to facilitate transport and trade.

London had a huge population of workers who went about their business like robots. There was no human feeling or warmth and the jostle and bustle was a cut-throat fight for survival. Throughout the land, people were engaged in factories, farming, shipping and services such as banking and insurance. They were slightly better fed, housed and clothed than any other lot I had ever seen, but seething underneath was bitter anger generated by the inhuman exploitation of workers on all fronts. In the countryside, fences were everywhere with boards reading "PRIVATE, TRESPASSERS WILL BE PROSECUTED". These were farms owned by Lords and the rich. The Lords even had their own chamber in the House of Parliament through which they advanced and protected their selfish interests.

I gathered that the land had previously been well tilled by serfs and peasants who were unceremoniously thrown out by an act of parliament to create the enclosures which facilitated the mechanisation of farming and the agriculture revolution. The peasants became pools of labour for the budding cotton, woollen, steel, fertilizer, chemical and packaging industries. From then on, two classes of citizens had emerged, that of the owners of land and capital and that of workers. While the wealthy lived in castles and mansions, the poor were huddled in great concentrations in towns, where they lived and died with no sense of belonging. The same had been replicated in Scotland, which had been turned into what the English called a "domestic colony".

In this misery, people were marrying young and there was a huge population explosion. A wiseacre by the name Malthus, who like me was interested in the welfare of the creature called Man, viewed the situation with concern. He warned the government in London that unless something was done, the population would soon outstrip resources and there would be a revolution. His solution was that the British Government should look for territories elsewhere to offload the excess population. The rich and the poor were paying great attention to his message. Smarting still from the defeat in America, the British Government was considering the proposal by Malthus with caution. The matter was under active consideration. The industrialists were adding their voice to Malthus' with a clamour for new sources of raw materials and markets for finished products. I found in England a momentum which was gaining strength by the day, the urgent need to conquer other lands in spite of the failure in America. The first victim was India.

I was much intrigued by this small nation which was now a leading world power with the agriculture and industrial revolutions. I looked into the evolution of the nation which revealed that the population had a cocktail of bloods from past conquests. Initially, the inhabitants were of a Germanic descent that was conquered by Viking giants, then by Normans and finally, by short and stout Romans. Each conquest had added new blood and fresh genes to the extent the English were a cocktail of bloods. From the Vikings, they had learnt that superior weapons win battles, while from the Romans they had learnt that war is an art which needs careful preparation and execution. Thus, they became masters of weaponry, strategy and tactics. I learnt that when the Celtic stock drove out the Romans from England, the English offered the crown to the King of Scotland as a reward for his wisdom and courage. The Union was thus founded on the ground that unity is strength, and the English felt that much more secure.

With changing circumstances, the crown eventually found its way to England and got stuck there forever. The English used the power at their disposal: political, economic and industrial to establish and enhance their dominance within the Union and beyond. In the changed scenario, the Celts found themselves reduced to workers: hewers of wood and drawers of water. The English had perfected the strategy of patience, callousness and deception. They had artificial smiles which disarmed the enemy while they prepared for the fatal blow.

In sum, I found the English cautious, methodical, and painstaking, which guaranteed that they always got what they wanted. It was therefore not surprising that caught unaware, the Scots and the Irish had been lured into the snare of the Union – and the result – exploitation, suffering and untold misery. The unequal relations had created such hatred that the matter was weighty and so volatile that it only needed a spark to explode. The English were handling the situation with their usual meticulous caution as though it was normal and God ordained. There were those born to rule others, they believed, the chosen race, like the children of Israel, and themselves.

In my estimation, I could not see Scotland extricating itself from the English stranglehold or how Livingstone could embark on the mission described by St. Peter. But the ways of the Lord are mysterious. He can turn water into wine with a whisper! More confused than assured, I returned to

Scotland, after spending a lengthy period of time in England, aware that Livingstone had a herculean, if not impossible task before him. The English were a tough nut to crack.

* * *

Lo and behold! Livingstone was jogging up and down the hills every day! His lanky form was wobbling ungainly up and down the paths, which reminded me of the Boneshaker. During the runs, he would stop, stoop, hiss and cough endlessly, his lungs expelling thick yellow phlegm, this time without traces of soot and blood. The boy was on the mend through sheer determination. The neighbours said he had been bewitched and gripped by a fit of madness as nobody could stop him from the demanding and fatal exercise.

"One of these days, you will run up the hill and your heart or lungs will give way. We will carry you down dead!" his father had warned him.

Livingstone smiled and said to him, "That won't happen!"

Indeed it did not happen and every passing day, the run became even more vigorous. It was as if the coughing was removing the remaining virus of tuberculosis in his body. Right before my eyes, I watched the physical transformation of David Livingstone into a much healthier and physically able young gentleman. Whether this ability to punish himself with great resolve into a different person had anything to do with his forthcoming mission, I could not tell. I concluded that he was going to grow into a resolute man, focused and determined to achieve whatever he set his mind on. In school as well, he was achieving high grades, like his uncle Mungo Park had done. After establishing that much about Livingstone and guessing there was a lot of time left before he embarked on his mission as foretold by St. Peter, I had a burning urge to visit the kingdom of Monomotapa. I set the compass south and took off.

CHAPTER 3

TO MONOMOTAPA AND DRUMS OF WAR

In the year 1829, after establishing the facts of life in Scotland in general and Blantyre in particular, with some background knowledge of the English and their government, I yearned to do the same for the Kingdom of Monomotapa, the reputed home to the fabled King Solomon's mines, which whether mythical or otherwise was not of concern to me. In my judgment, though premature, there was nothing to connect the two places, which had no similarity whatsoever. To me, there was a disconnect somewhere in my mission, a shot in the dark. A wide chasm divided the two distant lands, a vast gap which could not be bridged by any imagination.

Though I had wanted to get there in a whiff, my plans were interrupted by yet another command from St. Peter who instructed me to make stopovers in Lisbon and the Vatican. I was confused. Was I on another mission or was the plot getting thicker beyond my grasp?

In Portugal, I found the population very poor on account of lack of any tangible economic activities. The agriculture and industrial revolutions had passed them by. The country lay at the bottom of European economic league, though it had many good sailors and pirates. Many of its citizens were labourers all over Europe earning peanuts. Their King either did not care about the welfare of his subjects or he did not know what to do about the poverty surrounding him. He had a good friend in the Pope in the Vatican, his only friend. Taking advantage of the good Portuguese sailors, the Pope was establishing the Roman Catholic Church wherever they set anchor. The church had interest not only in the ecclesiastical, but also in the secular, especially land acquisition, cultivation agriculture, real estate and mining. A cult called the Mafia was providing the finance capital to the Vatican and the church was spreading its reach through the king of Portugal and his sailors and armed forces.

Even more confused, I flew to the Vatican. The Holy Roman Empire had disappeared with the Treaty of Westphalia. What remained was a tiny independent enclave called the Vatican surrounded by Italy, which had been given the status of an independent state. It was not even a micro-state, but a collection of buildings housing monks, cardinals and the Pope, of course. It was a male only establishment. That this was the nerve centre of an empire that once ruled the world was mind boggling. It was once again on the march to conquer by proxy, in the name of the Lord.

I did not understand what David Livingstone had to do with this triangle of the Mafia, the Pope and the King of Portugal. Livingstone was a Protestant, a rival denomination to Catholics which owed its origin to a marital feud involving the search for an heir to the English Monarchy. When the King of England and the Pope disagreed on the matter of a divorce, the King founded his own church, the Church of England, one which would do his bidding. While the Scots somehow joined the Anglican Church, the Irish did not; they remained staunch Catholics adding to complications in the Union.

The spirits told me all these tidings had something with my mission, how, we shall wait and see.

As I did not know what other surprise was in store, I slowed down. I flew over Cairo and enjoyed the configuration of the Nile Delta which marks the end of the journey for the Nile. As I moved South, I was fascinated by the majesty of the great river. Its source remained the greatest geographical mystery which Mungo Park had sworn to unravel before he met his death on River Niger. Thousands of miles south of Cairo, I came across great marshes covered with papyrus reeds. I realised that the Nile emerged from these marshes called Jonglei Swamp or the Sud.

Maybe I had discovered the source of the Nile or had I? On the Southern end of the Sud, there was a great river which entered the marshes! I followed the course of the river which led into a great lake. On the other side of the same lake, I saw the same great river, entering from an easterly direction. As the source of the Nile was playing hide and seek with me, I decided to leave the solving of the mystery to more patient men.

Before I could recollect my thoughts, I was flying over a great mountain called Kilimanjaro, and saw that it had a snow capped dome. To the north-west was the region of the Great Lakes and to the east was the Indian Ocean. I knew I was not far from Monomotapa as per Herodotus' *Mappo Mundo*. There was a range of high hills which descended steeply to form the Zambezi Valley, in the middle of which was the great Zambezi river, travelling across the heartland of the Kingdom of Monomotapa heading eastwards. My heart was palpitating with anxiety.

* * *

The natural beauty of the land was a sight to behold. Before entering the capital called Matapa, I circled the land, to familiarise myself with the place. What impressed me most was the organisation of the settlements of the inhabitants, and the economic activities therein. The land was fertile, yielding rich harvests and I could tell it was a very rich kingdom.

I established that there were several states which made the Kingdom just like the United Kingdom. These nationalities were later to be given the derogatory term of "tribes" by foreigners with all its negative connotations. Each state had its capital, which was the seat of the regional government as there was a devolved system of governance. The fields of corn, millet and beans were now bare as the harvesting season had just ended. Preparation of land for the new planting season had just begun. Vast fields of sugarcane, bananas, cassava and all sorts of fruits were most pleasing to the eye.

Beyond the farmlands were huge flat grazing grounds with countless numbers of fat cows, sheep and goats. These animals grazed at peace with wild animals such as gazelles, elands and impalas. Beyond these fields towards the hills was the land of the big game where, herds of elephants carried massive tusks which looked like enormous burdens, as they mowed grass and chewed branches of trees to whet their insatiable appetite. Nearby, herds of rhinos with big twin horns moved laboriously as their calves ran around playfully, oblivious of their neighbours including giant kudus, buffaloes, giraffes, zebras and hidden in the bushes, prides of lions, leopards and cheetahs basking on anthill mounds in the afternoon warm breeze. I was astounded by the sizes and the sheer numbers of these beasts. It was a marvel to see these things which no kingdom on earth could match, not even the Maasai Serengeti. In Europe, all I had seen were dogs, foxes and squirrels. They had killed their big games a long time ago and I shuddered to think what would happen to these wonderful animals should Europeans ever come to Africa.

The river Zambezi crisscrossing the land was home to a great variety of fish, crocodiles, hippos and water pythons. As the Zambezi cascades down, there were vast irrigations with rice, sugarcane and other crops, shielding the kingdom from hunger even in times of drought.

The kingdom was ruled by King Simba, the just and the benevolent. His leadership was the very epitome of excellence. He was a no-nonsense man though and very hard to please. As a perfectionist, he demanded the very best from his subjects and from himself. All government positions were filled on merit. Although he ruled with an iron fist, he was revered because he was magnanimous. The Kingdom enjoyed unprecedented prosperity, peace, security and cohesion. The burst of economic activities including diversification of export commodities and value addition had attracted traders from all over the world. The main trading partners were India and China. However, trading was undertaken in Sofala and Ngorofa, the main ports, as no foreigner was allowed in the interior for fear of diseases and bad habits spreading. Sofala was on the Indian Ocean while Ngorofa was an inland port on the Zambezi River.

The mines were owned by the men who worked in them. In many areas close to the hills were villages of miners and craftsmen. The industry of the Kingdom was the kind of stuff out of which fairy tales are made. Everything was neat and tidy and the future looked very rosy and secure. I agreed with Herodotus that the Kingdom had what it took to be a great power. Its armed forces comprised of thousands of fearsome warriors.

The Kingdom of Monomotapa was grandiose, strong and prosperous. It was the most advanced economically, politically, technologically and militarily south of the Sahara. Here, life was better than in the majority of the European states, I had visited.

The capital, Matapa, was surrounded by a great stone wall. In such a serene setting, I could not fathom what had necessitated the construction of a massive defence wall other than the hubris of snobbish show-off. The only danger which had existed around the Kingdom was slave trade. However, all the states under the kingdom were free from this scourge as the King did not condone it. He had a very powerful army to enforce his will on the matter. In Sofala, I was privileged to witness the off-loading of two giant pandas, gifts from the Emperor of China to the King of Monomotapa, who had earlier sent two giraffes to his friend the Emperor.

As Herodotus had rightly pointed out, the Kingdom was endowed with a strong breed of men most industrious, wealthy, happy and free. Its army was composed of giant warriors most fearsome and strong. They jealously protected the sovereignty, independence and territorial integrity of the

Kingdom, whose government was democratic and free. It was the envy of the other Kingdoms in Africa and beyond. Endowed with gold, gemstones, diamonds, silver, ivory, copper, tin, oak, ebony, cedar, bamboo and a variety of fish in the rivers and lakes, it could easily pass for the unspoilt Garden of Eden. River Zambezi drains into the Indian Ocean after a journey of 2,000 km. As one of the biggest rivers in Africa, it was a big blessing to the kingdom. Herodotus had predicted that one day, Monomotapa and Abyssinia would rule the world because they had all it took to be superpowers. The two giant kingdoms enjoyed most cordial ties, though they were separated by a long distance.

For religion, all the people in the Kingdom worshipped one God known as *Mwari*. They did not suffer division in spiritual guidance like in the United Kingdom, torn between Catholics and Protestants. They had a highly advanced priesthood and one creed. The spiritual head was the High Priest who lived and conducted business in the Holy Shrine located within the walls of the capital Matapa in the Hill of the Holy. Religion was a uniting factor in the kingdom though different nationalities had differing cultural peculiarities. All preachers and clergy were answerable to the High Priest who was a member of the King's Advisory Council which handled matters of defence, security, governance, trade and external relations.

In the valley outside the main gate of Matapa, I was attracted by a most eye-catching activity. Close to a hundred virgin girls were picking reeds splitting them into thin shreds, cutting them to size, stitching them together and tying them around their waists. They would then wriggle and gyrate their bodies in dancing motions. The reeds would shake around and flap up and down. After bathing and oiling their bodies, they looked angelic, beautiful and full of life. They were young, vibrant and well fed. Each and every one of them was a wonder to behold, an angel. Being of the spirit, I am not moved by the charms of the human flesh, but for once, I wished I was human to taste the wonders locked in those bodies. I envied the men who would marry them. The distraction took quite some while before I came to my senses. Reluctantly, I left them and entered the city wondering what kind of ritual they were preparing for. I was going to follow up the matter later even if it was for curiosity's sake.

The walled Matapa city had five majestic hills. There was something spiritual about the configuration of the hills which soothed my soul. At creation, God must have had something special in his mind about the place, for His exclusive enjoyment. He did not complete it, and therefore, left the setting to the enjoyment of man.

On the big hill in the centre sat the magnificent palace housing the royal household. Two hills flanking it were home to elite warriors. Farther back was the hill of blacksmiths who made weapons and jewels for the King and his family. The last hill was the Hill of the Holy which housed the High Priest in the Holy Shrine. It was a most secluded place. Unlike Blantyre, this was a place designed for gods. There were no gloomy faces, malnourished children or filthy dwellings.

Each hill had a gurgling well, and the crystal clear water ran downhill joining to form a huge pool, just outside the city. This is where I had found the girls clad in reeds. It is the source of River Mbuni, which drains into the Zambezi.

All hills were connected by a marvellous road network, with colourful boulevards planted with trees and flowers. The setting had mesmerised Herodotus so much so that, he gave it the name Magandox, whose meaning remains a mystery. Perhaps, if barbarians had not burnt the great library of Alexandria in Misri, I might have unearthed the meaning. Suffice it to say, I prefer Matapa to Magandox.

The mood in the city was one of festivities. After the Kingdom experienced a bumper harvest, the King had declared that it was time for the reed dance. Nothing was more precious to the Kingdom than the reed dance, which had a spiritual and a religious reverence. It was out of the reed dance that the royal lineage was propagated, by the King taking a wife each season. Every constituent nation hoped that one of its own would win the crown that season. As time went by, the King had many wives, each chosen from a reed dance.

All the constituent states had sent virgins, and cows, goats and farm produce for consumption, in the one week festival. The beautiful damsels I had found by the pool were the virgins to perform the reed dance. The capital had been cleaned, spruced and the hedges and boulevards trimmed. Fishermen, butchers and cooks were ready to discharge their duties.

Two days before the festival, King Simba received messengers from Emperor Theodore of Abyssinia. The message was most grave. It read,

> *Your Highness and Dear brother,*
> *I send to you warm and fraternal greetings.*
> *Be warned that the Sultan of Donyiro Kingdom in cahoots*

with slave traders and mercenaries from Oman, Arabia, Egypt, Yemen and Mesopotamia are making military preparations to invade your Kingdom. The pretext is that you have denied slave traders and Arab merchants free access to business in Monomotapa.

On my part, I have taken the necessary precautionary measures to protect Abyssinia from any misadventure by the lot. To assist you, I have taken tactical measures to delay and diminish the Donyiro army movement southwards by poisoning wells along the route.

Be warned that the upstart Sultan of Donyiro is most ruthless, reckless and irrationally destructive. If you need further assistance I will only be too glad to oblige.

Signed,

Emperor Theodore

The Empire of Abyssinia

Addis Ababa

I recalled that on my way to Scotland, I had witnessed the invasion of Donyiro by foreign forces that had destroyed the native kingdom and set up the Donyiro Sultanate.

I was confused, torn between whether I should wait to see the invasion and how Monomotapa would fare with its huge army or return to Scotland to see how Livingstone was doing.

At the back of my mind, I had misgivings about leaving Monomotapa. After witnessing the prosperity and happiness in the Kingdom, it had greatly uplifted my spirit. I had no wish to dampen my joy by returning to Scotland. If it had not been the wish of Heaven to subject me to this mission, I would have opted to spend my days in Kuzania with holidays in Monomotapa as a tourist to enjoy the many attractions the Kingdom had to offer including the wonderful virgins and reed dances.

Just then, news arrived that a strange tribe known as Boers who had migrated from Europe had grown into sizeable population in South Africa. They had been beefed up by French Huguenots Protestants running away from the wrath of one Emperor Louis XIV who had ordered their massacre on St. Bartholomew's Day. Together, they had decided to invade the hinterland of South Africa to secure fertile land from the natives by force of arms, with a vow never to return to oppression in Europe. I decided to visit the battlefield out of curiosity.

Sure enough many wagons loaded with men, cannons and muskets had moved far north. The Zulu *impis* or warriors, defenders of the land were armed with short swords called *assegais*. Although they were fearless and brave, they were no match for the superior arms of the Europeans. In the battlefield, the Europeans buried their dead while scores of Zulu warriors were left rotting, food for hyenas, jackals and vultures. They were killed in their thousands by guns. It was as if all vultures in the world had migrated there for the season of the feast. They followed the proceedings on the ground, hovering high and descending to fill their huge stomachs with the carrion.

I noted that they first gorged out the eyes either as a prized delicacy or so that the victim could not see what was coming next. My heart bled for the Zulus who had become disorganised, disoriented and hapless. Their fate was sealed. Their tongues would always click in anger, until they re-established their manhood and dignity. For now, like the Scots, their fertile land was gone and localities given strange names.

The Boers and Huguenots drove the natives from all the fertile land. The natives were huddled together in barren pieces of earth which could not support life. From these villages, they trekked for miles to work on the new lush farms, which were once their birth-right, but now out of bounds. The foreigners opened coal, gold and diamond mines and like the Scots, the Zulus became labourers, living on slave wages and conditions. In a flush, they had been reduced to paupers and beggars. Their gods had deserted them and so it would be, for ages to come. The invaders were allocating themselves tens of thousands of acres each, like they had done in America and Australia.

* * *

The wind brought news of yet another war raging in the neighbourhood. That was in the three adjoining kingdoms in Angola: the Ovibundu, the Bundu and the Bakongo. The Portuguese were trying to dislodge the natives from their fertile lands and diamond mines. In view of the impending threat by the Donyiros on the Kingdom of Monomotapa, I decided to visit there to further broaden my knowledge on war.

I found the Portuguese engaging the Kingdom of Bundu then under a Queen known as Nzinga. She was a very tough woman, very intelligent and a great war strategist. The Portuguese had thought that an African woman leader would not be a match for their army. It turned out to be a grave miscalculation.

Unlike the Zulu, the Bundu had better weapons than the short *assegai* spear. They too had muskets and bows and arrows.

I learnt that the arrows were tipped with deadly poison. All that was needed was a small glaze of the skin, and the victim would be agonisingly dead within the hour. The bows, arrows and the poisonous liquid were obtained from the Kingdom of Monomotapa in return for gold, diamonds and elephant tusks. It had an advanced defence industry.

These were the very items the Portuguese wanted to control. I concluded that the Bundu Kingdom was giving as much as it was getting and was safe, at least for now. I pondered why the King of Portugal, a good Roman Catholic, should send his army so far away to fight natives, who were only interested in living their lives peacefully. Then I recalled the relationship between the King, the Pope and the Mafia.

I also learnt that the slaves captured in these kingdoms were loaded into ships and sent to Brazil and the Caribbean Islands, to provide slave labour in coffee and sugarcane plantations. They were the same Portuguese I had visited in Europe: poor beyond measure, now on a mission of spreading Christianity, civilisation and commerce, through the destruction and conquest of peaceful and rich African kingdoms.

The creature called man is truly amazing. So, it was not only Arabs who were depopulating and dehumanizing Africans, but Europeans were deeply drawn into the vortex, making commodities out of their fellow human beings, and exploiting their resources mercilessly! Worse still, some African Kingdoms, which had succumbed to the Portuguese military onslaught, like the Kingdom of the Bakongo to the north of Bundu, had their Kings and subjects baptised and turned into zombies, obeying the will of their foreign masters. They were happily rendering their services raiding neighbours, to beef up the export of slaves.

In return, they got beads, tinklets, blankets and whisky. I questioned how a people could be so daft as to collaborate with foreign agents of the devil, to visit such grievous harm to a neighbour. I condemned and cursed the Bakongo and hoped that someday, they would realise their folly and join the Bundu Kingdom to drive out the invaders. I also realised how wise the King of Monomotapa was, because in aiding Nzinga and the Bundu Kingdom, he was also putting a buffer zone between his kingdom and the march of the Portuguese eastwards. What all this had to do with Livingstone and his relationship with Monomotapa, I could not tell. I reckoned that the momentous events predicted by St. Peter were already afoot.

I formed the picture of an Africa under siege from foreigners, recalling stories of hordes of Portuguese and Spanish Conquistadores who had laid bare Kingdoms of Aztecs, Mayas and Incas in Latin America and decimating the native population. The invaders had settled down changing names of places, rivers, lakes and mountains. The native population had been pushed into the wild where they fought with pumas, panthers, jaguars, anacondas and piranhas for survival.

I judged that in time, the fate of the Africans could be worse, given that many European capitals were incorporating global expansion in their foreign policy. Africa was a big fat offering made even more attractive by its natural wealth. Sad with this realisation, I came to the conclusion that the fate of many African Kingdoms could be worse than that of Scotland, Australia and Latin America if the English, the French, the Germans, the Italians, the Portuguese, the Belgians and the Spanish decided to have a piece of the huge and sweet African pie. I remembered Malthus and his crusade for overseas territories to avert a revolution in England which also went for other European States.

In this sullen mood, I set off for the Donyiro Sultanate which had decided to enter the fray in a pre-emptive move to outwit European schemers. Yes, events of momentous magnitude were afoot. I was now a most willing observer and witness. I thanked St. Peter and the Heavens for choosing me as a witness to these tidings.

In my long life in Kuzania, my adopted home, I had never thought of making a journey beyond the borders. I was contented living in a fool's paradise. I resolved to concern myself with matters internal in that country, so I shut out the world beyond. It was as if I had blinkers, obscuring the rest of the world. All that was behind me now! My mission which connected me to David Livingstone and Monomotapa, had catapulted me to the world of inter-state relations, of international trade and strategic concerns. I was confused and in a state of vertigo being a novice in international affairs. I was fascinated with what was going on, so I plunged headlong into the Donyiro threat.

As I headed for the Sultanate for first-hand information, I feared I would miss the parade of virgins in the reed dance, but I deemed the visit to Donyiro an urgent matter.

In the Sultanate, one thing which fascinated me was that there were two Niles, one called Blue, the other White, one coming from the east and the other from the south. They met at a place farther north before their final destination to Cairo and the Mediterranean. This, I argued to myself was the confusion why no one had ever found the source of the Nile since the time of the Greeks and Romans! The land was mainly a desert, but to the south, it was green and lush.

After the invaders from across the Red Sea conquered the Donyiro Kingdom, they castrated or slaughtered all the native males, and imposed their culture, language and religion on the population. Similar misfortune had befallen the native people of Misri and the Maghreb. The Sahel had been transformed in this manner from the Atlantic coast to the Red Sea and it appeared the push was now southwards. Worrisome was the fact that Zanzibar, Pemba and Mombasa had already fallen. Standing against this thrust were the Kingdoms of Abyssinia and Monomotapa.

The new Donyiro rulers had judged the Kingdom of Abyssinia too powerful to conquer, at least for now. The population was huge and the army was very powerful, armed with rifles and cannons. An invasion on Abyssinia was deemed suicidal and could even result in a reversal of the gains of the new rulers in Donyiro.

Slave traders and merchants convinced the Donyiro Sultan that the wealth and healthy population of potential slaves in Monomotapa was well worth an invasion. They talked of stashes of gold, diamonds, copper and silver in a vault called "King Solomon's Mines" guarded only by an old witch. They assured the Sultan that the warriors of Monomotapa were only armed with bows, arrows, spears and swords and they had no cavalry.

And so it was that the Sultan of Donyiro was convinced by greedy traders led by one, Tipu Tipu, the greatest slave trader in East and Central Africa to mount a military expedition on the Kingdom of Monomotapa. They also told him that with the booty from the Kingdom, mercenaries could be hired from anywhere in the world to invade Abyssinia. Their religion was destined to stretch from Cairo to the Zambezi and the Sultanate, together with the Sultan of Oman, would be masters of a vast empire comprising the eastern seaboard and the hinterland of Eastern Africa.

The Sultan was all smiles as he said "Inshallah!" He longed for the day when all infidels would worship Allah after his own fashion, facing Mecca, and speak Arabic, regardless of their mother tongue and the colour of their skin. This creed had been given the term "Arabisation and Islamisation of Africa". The natives would be slaves, labourers, drawers of water and hewers of wood. The more the matter was discussed the more it excited the Sultan of the Donyiro Sultanate.

As the military expedition was judged simple, but most rewarding, there was no reason for hesitation. Mercenaries from Egypt, Arabia, Yemen, Oman and Mesopotamia were recruited to beef up his soldiers for a swift victory. Quite a sizeable part of his army would be left behind because the Sultan did not trust the infidel Emperor of Abyssinia or the French who were moving eastwards across the Sahara desert for a destination unknown.

The world was changing, becoming dangerous and unpredictable. There was the urgency by those involved to strengthen the armed forces and acquire territories before others laid claims on them. The rampage involved Arabs, Portuguese, Spaniards, Italians, the French, the British, the Germans and the Belgians looking elsewhere after they were barred by the Americans from setting foot in the Western Hemisphere in the Monroe Decree. If only the general march by Europeans could be delayed, the Sultan thought, he could get his coveted price of Abyssinia. The snag was that the Emperor had acquired weapons of mass destruction from France and China with names such as cannons and muskets which used a substance called gun powder which he did not understand exactly how it worked. He was not a coward and one day he would find a way to neutralise the guns probably with a large army of mercenaries. There is strength in very large numbers as the Chinese saying goes.

When everything was in place, he gave the order for the army to embark on the march south.

"Don't leave anything valuable behind and above all, burn the capital. We shall build another one according to our taste all in good time."

Before the army left, news was received that Emperor Theodore of Abyssinia had mobilised his forces. The Sultan ordered all forces to stay put while he dispatched a high powered delegation to Addis Ababa to assure the Emperor that the Sultanate harboured no ill intentions against his kingdom and that the sensible thing to do in the face of threats from Europe was for the two neighbouring states to sign a mutual defence pact. The Emperor declined to go into an alliance with the Sultanate and told the head of the visiting delegation, "If you ever attack Abyssinia, you will be met with a response which will be massive and conclusive. We will teach you a lesson which will reverberate around the world including in European capitals. And by the way, if you are not planning to attack us, why have you mobilised and hired so many mercenaries?" Emperor Theodore asked the special envoy.

"The Sultan is planning a military expedition on Monomotapa to protect our business interests. We need certain assurances from King Simba."

"And you need such a huge military expedition to enforce concessions?" asked the Emperor.

"They are there just in case..." said the envoy.

"Tell the Sultan I have received his message and also tell him an attack on Monomotapa is an ill-conceived adventure," he did not elaborate.

Upon return, the special envoy gave a short report to the Sultan.

"Our mission was successful. We extracted the assurance of the Emperor that there will be no war between our two countries," he reported most convincingly.

"Good, then proceed with the execution of the mission to Monomotapa," said the Sultan. He was all smiles.

Leaders behave in a most reckless way when driven by wild dreams based on military might and economic greed. It does not matter how civilised humans will become, this will always remain so, a truism uncontestable. I told you about the curse of the creature called man, and you can substitute Monomotapa for Iraq with the Americans let loose, sniffing oil!

I had a good mind to return to Scotland to catch up with David Livingstone as the Donyiro army marched south. I guessed it was going to take quite some while before the two armies locked horns.

How Livingstone was to join this fray in whichever manner or capacity remained mind-boggling to me, but I had the assurance of St. Peter that Livingstone would be involved by and by. I was enjoying my mission, aware that my heart had to be steeled to withstand the looming carnage threatening from many directions and involving many actors on the stage, with conflicting interests and many lives at stake.

CHAPTER 4

THE REJECTION OF THE SAVIOUR

My long journeys traversing continents had left me frail, weary and drained. I yearned for some rest to recuperate. I also needed time to evaluate the information I had collected, the things I had seen and heard, to understand how they related to my mission. The appraisal was necessary in order to keep focused, lest I digress from my assignment which would invite a harsh retribution from the Almighty. The return to Scotland had to wait for a while.

The transformation of the world is a process, not an event. In my judgement, the actors had not finalised their plans.

My nostalgia for Kuzania, my adopted home, became immediate, urgent and welcome. I was going home for a busy working holiday.

As I landed, I felt relieved, relaxed and energised. The weather was wonderful, the land was lush with a rich green after the rains and the people were happy and healthy. I cursed those that denied the people of Scotland their rightful and God-given gift to be happy and enjoy their lives like the people of Kuzania. I also wondered if in the great tidings predicted by St. Peter, the people of Kuzania could ever find themselves victims of external nefarious forces. I shuddered. The hunger for colonies was a threat to many.

It was then that I recalled the words of Herodotus that: "If a man insisted always on being serious, and never allowed himself a bit of fun and relaxation, he would go mad or become unstable without knowing it." I had to try and relax a bit and in this context my sojourn in Kuzania was more justified.

In between fun and relaxation I went back to my data, but however much I juggled it, this way and that way, I could not detect a pattern. It made no sense. It was like working a jigsaw puzzle with several parts missing. I then realised the true meaning of the words of St. Peter, that my mission was "to follow, keep tab on things and to record my findings most carefully." An extrapolation of the situation was out of the question. Although my mind kept wandering far into the future, I drew a blank each time. As commanded,

I therefore recorded carefully what I had seen, in the manner of God's command, "Write these things". It took a long time to record all I had seen and heard in my travels across the world on my mission.

Satisfied that I was on the right track and having regained strength, I set off for Scotland to seek David Livingstone.

I returned to Scotland in summer as I did not want to experience the biting cold that covers the place in winter, when a thick coat of snow envelopes the land as snowflakes fall for days on end. Life becomes miserable and unbearable. Even the trees shed their leaves and they too carry snow on their branches. They look dead. Animals are locked up like prisoners and fed like sick people in hospitals, while in the wild, many of the creatures go into hibernation for months. I had long concluded that the northern hemisphere is a cursed land and that is why it produces people who are cruel, and who are masters of sardonic humour, in complete contrast to the blessed warm lands of the tropics and their happy people, who are never caged by the vagaries of the weather.

Livingstone did not grow up like a normal child and no Scottish child did. As I said before, the miners and their wives were the property of the mine owners. They were required to work in the mines daily. Mercifully, the children and women worked half day.

Livingstone worked in the morning and attended school in the afternoon. After school, boys rushed to the forest to trap hares to supplement their poor family diet. They set wires with nooses and when hares ran into the loop, they would be snared. Each boy knew his traps.

The English administrators had prohibited the killing of wild animals bigger than a hare, but they allowed themselves the preserve of hunting deers and foxes for food and sport, as the Scots watched.

The hares were a menace to the English vegetable farmers who gave wires and cords to the poor Scottish boys to eliminate the nuisance for them.

Livingstone never went to snare hares. He had more serious things to do. After school, he would change clothes and embark on his daily routine of jogging up and down the hills to strengthen his body. Boys ridiculed him that with his frail frame, he could never make an athlete of any repute. He ignored them. In time, the tuberculosis which had lodged itself in his lungs was gone and the coughing and hissing had stopped.

After the runs, he would take a shower in the communal bathroom before doing his homework and general reading. He had acquired wide knowledge on the world around him and beyond, thanks to the works of Mungo Park and others. The *Mappo Mundo* was his constant companion.

He completed high school as top student in science subjects, which earned him a scholarship to the Glasgow School of medicine, to study Medicine, just like Mungo Park.

Life in the University was settling and organised. He did not play games, but spent most of his time in the library and on the University athletics track jogging in the evenings. However, at night, he would join clandestine debates on the need to end the English occupation of Scotland.

Once again, he emerged top student in the final year. He hoped to join the London School of Medicine just like Mungo Park, to specialise in surgery.

I located him in the municipal park in Glasgow, in the company of three other students. He had grown into a tall mature boy with a thin physical frame, burning eyes and an unkempt hair and beard. He looked very serious. This was no longer the dying boy I had first encountered. He wore an oversize coat which made him look like a menacing scarecrow, one which would scare both man and beast. The coat was either borrowed from a man with much broader body frame or it was a "hand me down" from a friendly hand. He certainly could not have bought it. It exposed his state of penury. Still, it did not diminish the worth of the man, or seem to bother him a single bit.

On the forehead, he had developed deep furrows as would be found on faces of philosophers or deep thinkers.

I moved close to eavesdrop on the discussions. They were seated on a bench. Since I did not know their names, I labelled them first, second and third speaker.

The First Speaker, a bespectacled lad who also wore a long beard was driving home a point.

"I will never caddy for the English again. Yesterday, the manager of the textile factory called me an idiot and a stupid Scot simply because I could not find his ball in the tall grass. It was as if it was my fault the ball had landed there! It was his fault and yet I had to bear the brunt of his anger! They grow rich on our labour and resources yet they treat us like trash! I couldn't stand it anymore. They have to be driven out of here." he said.

"We have to take our land back," said the Second Speaker emphatically.

"We have to take up arms. The English only understand force. Our forefathers beat them in battle many times. Why can't we?" asked the Third Speaker.

"Yes, the Americans led the way and won their independence. The Irish have said enough is enough. What are we waiting for? No wonder they call us stupid Scots. We have become lily-livered! But, even if we pick arms, who will help us? The Irish have the Pope, the Italians and the French on their side in Catholic solidarity. They supply them with arms and money. Who can we count on, the rich Scottish Jacobites in Jamaica growing sugar? Do you think they care about the motherland anymore? Nobody cares about us," said the First Speaker.

At last, Livingstone spoke, "Believe you me, we have God on our side. Do you remember how God delivered the children of Israel from the mighty army of Philistines? Goliath was an invincible giant wearing iron armour, but there was an opening in his helmet for wiping sweat from his brow. Against such odds, all the Israelites had could be summed up in two words "fools' courage".

"But they had God on their side. Remember how the young boy David drove a pebble into the skull of Goliath with a sling and the mighty Philistines fled the battle field! It can be done, with God on your side, and I swear, God is on our side. I will find that opening in the armour of the English!"

There was something very captivating and convincing in the body language and the delivery of Livingstone's words. It took out words from the mouths of his friends. For a while, they remained transfixed. He was a man inspired, they concluded.

"But listen David, God had long declared the Israelites as his chosen people. Who are we? Stupid Scots, we sold our birth-right to the English, in a diabolical Union in return for servitude, poverty and diseases. We are nobody's chosen people. We are our own executioners," said another fellow student in the group. What he said rang true. It was sad and shameful, but it was the truth and nothing but the truth.

"I wish we were Catholics, because the Pope and the French and the Italians would come to our aid," lamented a bespectacled student who looked more like a potential preacher than a potential freedom fighter.

"Listen guys; God has a plan for Scotland. His ways are mysterious but perfect. All we have to find is the opening in the helmet of the English, their Achilles heel. And then we can deliver the blow, like the pebble which David fired into Goliath's forehead," said Livingstone whose posture was like that of the leader and spirit of the group planning rebellion and treason.

"There has to be a change. We have to end the Union," said Livingstone, in a firm tone with finality.

"With God for my country!" Livingstone found himself saying. The others in a chorus repeated the words. The words sounded powerful and offered a ray of hope, through divine intervention.

Livingstone smiled broadly and said, "No. We have to change that. It has to be, 'For God and my country!" Let's hold hands and swear an oath to liberate Scotland." They joined hands and Livingstone administered the oath.

"For God and my country!" he said.

"For God and my country!" they repeated.

With the group recharged in this solemn commitment, the meeting was adjourned. They marched to dinner with renewed vigour.

After I heard Livingstone speak, I began to believe that the man was indeed on a mission. I was not on a wild goose chase. Fascinated, I decided to stay close.

* * *

Many things had happened in Scotland while I was away, including a general political awakening. It was being fuelled by the Irish armed resistance, which was gaining momentum, and spreading like bushfire throughout the southern region of Ireland.

Aware of the dilemma the Scots were having with the Church of England, a rebel French Catholic priest thought he could take advantage of the situation. He went round the country talking to the clergy about the need to break away from the Archbishop of Canterbury who headed the Anglican Church. He succeeded and the Scots announced the birth of their own church, the Presbyterian Church.

Unfortunately, it was not affiliated with any other church or country and its limitation to garner support for an independence movement was obvious. Nevertheless, there was a general feeling that the Scots were now free in some regard.

Even more serious was the formation of a clandestine Scottish Liberation Movement. It had a huge following among the miners, factory workers and students. Unknown to me, Livingstone had been elected the leader of the "Youth Wing" because of his passion, eloquence and education. One of the first resolutions of the movement was never to sing the English national anthem with, "God save the Queen." A young lass, only 18 years old had been crowned Queen of England, to preside over the dreams and fortunes of the English. Her name was Alexandria Victoria. If a young girl five years his junior could preside over the affairs of Great Britain, why couldn't he play a mighty role in the affairs of Scotland? Livingstone argued with himself.

His mind was made to execute his "divine mission" to the end. Young Livingstone, as he went through transformation in the chaotic hell of life in Scotland, was a very bitter man, and he was not alone. He equated the English boastfulness and oppression with the arrogance of the Philistines.

While the English had many Goliaths in the ranks of their mighty army, the Scots lacked a David with the hand of God to guide him to the Achilles heel of the oppressor. However hard he tried to reason with himself, Livingstone could not find the weakest point of the English armour, but he thought it lay between arrogance, greed and the hunger for more power.

Either through hallucinations or hubris, Livingstone thought he was that special agent of the Lord, who would free his people from the trappings of the Union. His would be a mission based on divine guidance through which means he could not fathom, but not certainly with a sling and a pebble. As I looked at him, I wondered if I was not witnessing the beginning of madness, with the devil at the helm.

My instructions were very clear, to observe and not to intervene. I was deeply troubled by what I had seen of Livingstone. I concluded that the man had no sense of direction though it appeared there was purpose in his thoughts. What all this had to do with Monomotapa, I could not fathom at all. Why had he circled the Kingdom of Monomotapa on the *Mappo Mundo*? Still I saw no connection and I doubted my mission. But then I said to myself, who am I to fault the call of Heaven? Was I on a wild goose chase or would time inject twists and turns which would give my mission the ordained importance. I am of a very patient nature and my mind remained open, though I could see no connection whatsoever between Livingstone and the mighty Kingdom of Monomotapa, thousands of miles apart.

The Divine work in mysterious ways. I recalled that the Son of a carpenter had turned the world upside down with a simple message of the salvation of the soul. Exhausted, I caught some sleep.

Livingstone woke up very early next morning. There was a meeting of the Scottish Liberation Movement in the Pitlokry Castle in the mountains, deep in the woods beyond the eavesdropping of nosey Englishmen. If there were two things the English had failed to snatch from the Scots, it was the Pitlokry Castle which was a revered symbol of nationalism and the legendary Lockness monster, a creature said to reside in the waters to the far north and which was the subject of mythical tales. No two people had the same description of the monster, but all Scots swore it existed, as a loner.

I followed Livingstone to the meeting.

To us, celestial creatures and members of the Order of the Divine, whose lives stretch from the beginning of time to eternity, nothing comes as a complete surprise because we have seen it all. We recognise the fact that the frail creature called man was given a short life span of three-score years and ten, simply seventy years. It is a very short time in which to achieve anything meaningful except for those who move very fast. Livingstone was definitely moving in that direction. I will take some time to delve into how this came about.

Life is a trickster beyond our comprehension. It marches on, seeking those to elevate, those to humble and those to destroy. There is no scale to predetermine which person or category of people will be slotted where. Things just happen though some wiseacres term the proceedings as dictated by "God's Plan". Nothing could be further from the truth. I tell you in truth, you are the master of your own destiny, either singly or collectively.

For those elevated into leadership, heroism or whatever other form of success, it all begins with dreams which translate themselves into quests for achievement of goals in life. The more ambitious the vision, the greater the reward, or adversely, the punishment. There is no guarantee that great success today will not be reversed in the course of time, to a disaster! Heroes today will be tomorrow's villains and there are chapters of history giving vivid examples. One assurance I give you is that there always will be dreamers and some will succeed while others will fail.

May be it was the map and notes by Herodotus or *Travels in Africa* by Mungo Park or the stories in the Bible which triggered the imagination of

David Livingstone. But from a very early age, he saw himself as the chosen one to uplift the spirits of the hapless Scots. His dream had taken shape.

The struggle became an avenue for charting new dreams for many. The independence, sovereignty and territorial integrity of Scotland was the preserve of those who dared. The journey started in their minds and it was receiving special and specific attention in the castle of Pitlokry, including by David Livingstone. The trouble was the form the struggle was going to take. There were those who were advocating for armed struggle in line with what the Irish were doing. They called for the formation of an armed wing. There were others who were calling for civil disobedience with the boycott of English factories and products which they said would eventually lead to bilateral negotiations with London towards the goal of independence.

To my surprise, I saw Livingstone take to the podium. My heart skipped a beat. He began to speak, "Onward Christian soldiers marching onto war," he shouted and the whole membership replied in like manner most vigorously. He continued, "For God and my country, I stand before you to deliver an important message. First of all, I wish to thank you all most sincerely for the many messages of congratulations upon my graduation in medicine. I am most proud of my new title, Dr. David Livingstone ... (and the hall broke into cheers) and like Mungo Park, I promise to make Scotland proud..." (more cheers).

"I have been given a scholarship to further my studies, specializing in surgery at the University of London. It is an honour tinged with misgivings because although I cannot turn it down, I will be living in the heartland of our adversary. Secondly, it is with sadness that I announce that I have to relinquish the leadership of the youth wing of our Movement in the new circumstances, as I do not see myself available to travel back and forth from London, as often as would be necessary. Nevertheless, I promise to continue being a staunch and faithful member of the Movement and to make contributions in whatever form within my power.

"I have given much thought to the debate as to whether we should wage an armed struggle or stage civil disobedience. I wish to make my stand known before my departure. We are all in agreement that we should restore the dignity of our motherland and our people must enjoy unfettered freedom. We have arrived at a critical juncture in the struggle, a point of no return and a clear way forward acceptable to all is needed. The Irish have come to the conclusion that their way is the armed struggle. I wish them well. Our situation compared to theirs is similar in some aspects and very different in others. We cannot follow their example blindly. First, they are Catholics and we are not, and because of that, they can count on the French and the Vatican to give them support.

"When we broke away from the Church of England, I was elated, but did it have to take the efforts of a foreign rebel Roman Catholic Priest to found the Presbyterian Church of Scotland? What is wrong with us? That said and done, it is a giant leap forward, in our quest for disengagement with the English.

"Today, we sing a strange national anthem, "God save the Queen", in deference to a young lass called, "Queen Victoria", the Queen of England. Yet she does not care whether we live or perish. "Look at the Irish; they are dying of hunger because blight has destroyed their potatoes. What is the Queen and the English doing? Nothing! Instead, they are laughing, joking and jeering at the Irish. Next, it will be us! Had the Irish been an independent state, the French and the Vatican would have come to their assistance, but the English have declared the calamity an 'internal matter!'

"Is it a curse to be Irish or Catholic? Don't we all worship the same God? Didn't the English know that the Irish were Roman Catholics when they proposed the Union? Now the English are foaming in the mouth that the Irish are agitating against the Union and others are fleeing to America. Do these people have a heart? Don't the Irish have a choice?

"What about us in Scotland. What crime have we committed? All the coal mines and cotton factories are owned by the English. We play second fiddle in all matters, economic, social and political, in our own motherland! The conditions of work are deplorable, the salaries are slave wages and we are not permitted to have unions to fight for our rights. Our infrastructure, health services and education system are neglected. In the armed forces, how many Scots have risen above the rank of Captain? None! What do the English fear, a coup by a Scot General?

"In recent times, the main preoccupation we have been engaged in is the burial of our dead. Too many of us are dying from tuberculosis, and with no potatoes, from hunger. Do the English care? Not a hoot.

"Time has come for concrete action. Time has come to quit the Union. Let the leeches and bloodsuckers seek new victims because Scotland says with one voice, enough is enough!

"You might all wonder why I am saying these things on the eve of my departure. First, I want to assure you that I will never abandon the struggle. In my dreams I have found a solution to our problem. I call it the third way or "divine mission". It is such a simple plan that I marvelled why I took so long to see it! You all know the English lost face when they lost the war of independence against the American colonies. They also lost the supply of cheap materials and a market for their finished products. They have decided to redress the balance by acquiring a vast global empire. This is where we come in, to exploit their Achilles heel.

"Every Scotsman should abet and promote the English dream... (protests from the crowds). Please, hear me out. Let us help the English to scatter themselves to all corners of the globe and when they are embroiled in cut-throat struggles and wars with natives of distant lands and they do not have a man or a coin to spare, we will declare our independence!" he said triumphantly.

"Brilliant," said a member.

"Nonsense," differed another.

David Livingstone had sold the idea of the "divine mission" and though it generated much debate, the Movement did not buy it. It was dismissed by the majority as a non-starter. Livingstone was visibly shaken, crestfallen, in tears and deeply disappointed. He did not say another word.

At once, my eyes opened very wide. Was Livingstone sincere about helping the English acquire an empire? Would this vast global empire include Africa, and if so, would Monomotapa be targeted? What role was Livingstone to play? Doubtfully, I began to read some connection between Livingstone and Monomotapa, though in what fashion I could not tell. I recalled he had encircled the Kingdom in red in his *Mappo Mundo*! Like some members of the Movement, I had the feeling that Livingstone was not quite in control of his senses. He was acting like the agent of a higher force. For good or for bad, only time would tell. The essence of my mission had revealed itself somewhat. Though I was warned not to interfere, which I would not, I began to feel a deep revulsion for David Livingstone and his way of thinking, and I was not the only one.

At the end of the meeting, the chairman of the Movement summoned the top brass to a quick house-keeping meeting. David Livingstone was not included and as he was walking alone towards the exit, the chairman said, "I was taken aback by the words of Livingstone. He thinks that Scotsmen should don kilts and march to distant lands to die for the establishment of an English Empire! I do fear that he has been compromised. His scholarship must have come at a high prize. He has sold his soul and betrayed his country for a mere stipend. From now on, he should be regarded as an outsider, a traitor."

It was so decided. These were instructions to be followed by all members of the Movement.

I caught up with Livingstone as he walked to the road. He was deeply engrossed in thought, rationalising the situation thus; "When David marched forward armed with a sling and a pebble, even the Israelites laughed at him. Everybody thought he was crazy. In the end, they all marvelled at the hand of God and its wonders. In the same way, I will carry on with the "divine mission" even if the Movement and the whole of Scotland jeer at me. In the end, they too will marvel at the work of the hand of the Lord". So resolved, he packed and left for England.

I decided to accompany him, to the School of Medicine in the University of London, for his specialisation in surgery. If I had ever seen a stubborn man, David Livingstone topped the list. He had a one track mind, very resolute. Leaders, heroes and villains are known for such qualities, for better or for worse.

CHAPTER 5

THE ATTACK

In the short life of the frail creature called Man, time passes very fast. Within the span of only seventy years, he is born and dead, having encountered untold miseries; both man-made and the vagaries of nature, and the vicissitudes of the unexpected. It does not matter whether you are rich or poor, black or white or yellow, to all, life is incomprehensible. There are those who pretend to be powerful and knowledgeable and they call themselves civilised. But let me tell you, when the die is cast, they come tumbling down with a loud thud, leaving behind an unenviable legacy. For tell me which King or kingdom in the history of man is remembered for having been just? We remember them more for their faults than their goodness. Their fall or dethronement is celebrated with shouts of, "Good riddance", but their successors become even more tyrannical; and the world marches on, as we await the end. It is just as good because the experiment has outlived its usefulness. It is increasingly causing God more misery than joy.

As the Donyiro army set forth to conquer Monomotapa in the name of Allah and increased trade in slaves and ivory, two events which would have a huge impact on the kingdom were taking place. The Emperor of Abyssinia had dispatched a message to royalties in Europe warning that should the Donyiros succeed in their nefarious mission, it would spell doom for the future of Christianity in Africa. None of them responded to the warning save for the King of Portugal. He summoned the Commander of the Portuguese forces and told him, "The Pope and I have agreed that Southern and Central Africa is of strategic importance to the Roman Catholic Church and to Portugal in particular. The key in our strategy is the eventual conquest and control of the Kingdom of Monomotapa. It is God's wish that I chart the future of that part of the world. The Arab-Donyiro Sultanate is working against our interests by sending an army to conquer Monomotapa. This must be stopped!" he said, pacing up and down in anger.

"Your Highness, I am afraid we cannot spare any troops as our army is bogged down in Angola. What I know is that the Kingdom of Monomotapa possesses the most powerful war machine in Africa and no Arab army can defeat it. I assure you the kingdom is safe for now." said the Commander.

"Are you sure of your assessment?" the King asked.

"One can never be absolutely sure in war, but the odds are against the invaders," the Commander said.

"Well, in that case, I will offer military assistance to the king just to make sure. I will offer rifles to deal with the Donyiro Calvary of horses and camels." he said with a grin.

"That would be in order, Your Majesty, provided they are few in number, so that they do not pose a threat to us when we finally move against the kingdom."

"I am not naive, am I?" asked the king.

"No, you are not Your Majesty. Your wisdom is respected by all royalties in Europe and beyond." said the Commander, bowing to the King. It was on this understanding that the king of Portugal sent a message to the king of Monomotapa, which read; *I am disturbed, perplexed and angered by news that the Donyiro Sultanate is set to mount an attack on your kingdom. Noting that the forces of the Sultanate have a powerful Calvary, I am offering you assistance in guns and men to neutralise their prime advantage, to facilitate your quick victory. If you are agreeable, it will give me enormous pleasure.*

When king Simba of Monomotapa received the message, he laughed. He sent back a befitting response; *I believe your offer of military assistance is misplaced. Your military action in Angola portrays you in bad faith. Rest assured that the mighty warriors of my kingdom are more than capable of dealing with the Donyiro menace or any other foreign aggression, without assistance. This we will soon demonstrate to the world. If you want my friendship and cooperation, pull your troops out of Angola and cease trading in slaves.*

The king of Portugal felt very insulted. How could a King of savages behave in such a rude manner? "I will teach the native idiot a lesson in common decency at an appropriate time!" he swore. The second event which was to have an impact on the Kingdom was the birth of twins to King Simba, as the Donyiro army advanced. What happened was this: wise to the fact that war is an unpredictable thing, King Simba ordered the evacuation of his household to the Royal Caves in Vumba Mountains to the east of the Kingdom for safety.

Of critical importance was the fact that Simba's youngest and favourite wife was heavily pregnant. All his other wives had given him daughters but an heir was yet to be born. The heir had to be male. Indications and predictions were that this time round, a boy was on the way.

In the caves, the Queen gave birth to twins, both boys! However, the behaviour of the Queen thereafter completely changed for the worse. She did not want to see her husband at all or talk to anybody. She refused to explain her strange behaviour. King Simba became worried, unhappy and a recluse. Something must have gone awfully wrong in the caves, but the Queen would not reveal what.

Other subsequent events only confirmed the suspicion that something sinister had happened in the Royal Caves in the Vumba Mountains, which had something to do with the birth of the twins. It became known as the "curse of the caves", which was messing around with the issue of the heir to the throne, the sanity of the Queen and the ability of Simba to reason rationally.

Now, where was I? Yes, the threat by the Donyiros which necessitated the evacuation of the royal household to the caves in Vumba Mountains...and I was there when the twins were born...I went searching for the Donyiro army in the vast desert south of the Sultanate and Abyssinia. The search was proving very cumbersome to my surprise. How could such a vast army render itself invisible?

When I reached the region of the great lake which separates the Sultanate with Abyssinia, I knew I had overshot the target. However, as I hovered around, I saw many skeletons of men, camels, horses and donkeys, strewn in a straight line from north to the south. I followed the bones which led me to the opening of the Great Rift Valley.

At once, I knew why I had failed to locate the Donyiro army. The Rift Valley is vast and very deep.

All the wells south of the great lake had been poisoned by agents of Emperor Theodore to decimate and slow down the march of the invaders, as he had promised his good friend King Simba of Monomotapa. The number of carcasses on a long stretch indicated the measure had been effective.

The resourceful Commander of the Donyiro forces had adopted another strategy. He designed a new route leading the troops deep into the Rift

Valley, with many fresh water lakes which could not be poisoned due to their sheer size. The route proved treacherous. Great herds of wild animals; lions, slithering pythons and the terrain, brought the march almost to a halt. But they trudged on. When the army came to the border with Kuzania, home to the giant snow-capped mountain north-east of Kilimanjaro, a decision was made to move eastwards out of the Rift Valley to avoid the fearsome Maasai of whom Tipu Tipu had warned. I joined the march in the shadows of the gigantic mountain.

Here, there was less game meat, and so raids into villages of natives to empty the granaries were ordered. The massacres, arson and pillaging I witnessed was horrendous. Word spread in all directions that the army of the Donyiros was marching southward and destroying everything in its wake. Whole communities evacuated their villages and moved to the mountains. As a result, the army, short of provisions and granaries to raid, was starving.

Rebellion broke out as the mercenaries threatened to abandon the mission. It was only the realisation of the fact that the journey back was equally as treacherous as the journey forward that saved the expedition. The promise of mountains of gold and silver and the prayers of the Imams made the situation slightly bearable.

Then they came to the end of the semi-desert and entered the plains. Here, there was plenty of game to eat and time to recuperate. The guides who had previously taken part in slave raids told the Commander they would soon come to the mountains and forests which gave birth to the source of the great Zambezi River. It rekindled their spirits and the urge to move on. At night though, they were harassed by mosquitoes and shadowy figures who attacked them with poisoned arrows. Scores of soldiers and animals were lost to this menace which they could not deal with and which followed them as they marched south.

Apparently, the bitter pastoralists and peasants whose lives they had disorganised through looting and pillaging had sworn revenge and they were exacting it. It was a well-coordinated revenge and in the background, agents of Emperor Theodore of Abyssinia were involved. Their mission had been to poison the wells and to render whatever other assistance to the Kingdom of Monomotapa, in the face of the impeding attack by the loathsome Donyiros. The Imams kept the force moving with prayers and curses to savage infidels operating under the cover of darkness. They told the soldiers "remember ours is a sacred mission, and there will be suffering before we attain glory. For those who lose their lives, they will live forever as martyrs and a rich reward awaits them in Heaven. For those who live, they will be heroes and rich men. In the name of Allah, we march forward to conquer; no force on earth can stop us."

Considering the hell they had been through since they embarked on the long and treacherous adventure, many doubted the sanity of the mission, but there was no turning back.

The King of Monomotapa received information that the Donyiro army was approaching the mountains which marked the northern defence line of the Kingdom. His army which had long been mobilised was put on red alert. It was time to defend the Kingdom.

* * *

News of the looming battle had spread around the world. The Portuguese were particularly irked by the possibility of a Donyiro victory as it would dent their plans of an empire stretching from Angola on the west coast to Mozambique on the east coast. The King was in consultation with the Pope in a schema for an appropriate response to this threat which posed problems to their interests. The British, the French, the Belgians and the Boers in South Africa were also alarmed. However, it was not dawning on them that Monomotapa was not worthless carrion, but a proud and powerful Kingdom, capable of defending its sovereignty, independence and territorial integrity.

Intelligence reports furnished to King Simba indicated that the invading army was sizeable, but not overwhelming. He owed gratitude to the Emperor of Abyssinia and the pastoralists and farmers who had exacted telling blows to the invaders through water poisoning and night raids with poisonous arrows. Still, there was cause for alarm.

I need not dwell at length on the battle itself as this was not part of my mandate from Heaven. However, it would be a remiss on my part not to mention a number of issues critical in the engagement.

The Donyiro army had brought with it platoon bridges to facilitate the crossing of the Zambezi. The engineers contracted had come from Mesopotamia and they had mastered the art and engineering of river crossing on the Tigris and Euphrates rivers. However, with the whittling of the carrier corps and the death of camels and donkeys along the journey, much of the equipment had been lost or discarded. The engineers had assured the Commander that they would replenish the lost parts with the giant bamboos available on the banks of Zambezi and in the nearby mountains.

The pass through the mountains to the Zambezi was narrow, steep and treacherous. It was used by wild animals going to the river to quench their thirst.

The King of Monomotapa and the War Council had drawn their battle plans. The first and critical engagement would be when the Donyiro forces entered into the deep pass. Archers from all over the Kingdom had been ferried across the river and they were waiting in the mountains. As soon as the enemy was deep in the gorge, poisoned arrows rained on them from all sides. It was difficult to respond and impossible to hide. After countless salvos of arrows had been fired, boulders of rocks which had been placed on the slopes began to rain on them with such speed, noise and devastation that panic spread through the ranks of the invaders. There were cries of anguish from soldiers and loud brays from horses and donkeys as they tumbled and fell into the river below. The archers of Monomotapa and the forest hunters and gatherers were having a field day shooting at sitting ducks.

"Retreat! Retreat!" the Commander of the invaders ordered, but he might just as well have been addressing the deaf. In the scamper, there was no order. It was everybody for himself, in total disarray. The animals in fear and uncontrollable frenzy, some surging forward others jumping over the cliffs made the battle almost comical.

The Commander with his decorations and his big horse were smashed by a rolling boulder and they fell down a steep cliff to be welcomed by rocks many feet down below. There was a twitch here and a twitch there, and then all was still, both stone dead lying side by side with every bone in their bodies broken and blood flowing freely. The sad state of the Commander and his horse told the whole story of the invasion.

The lucky ones who managed to retreat were pursued and killed by the warriors and lynched by the pastoralists and peasants whose villages they had pillaged and burned. Only a miserable handful managed to return to the Sultanate, to tell the story of the debacle.

The news of the ignominious defeat of the Donyiro army was received with anger by the Sultan of the Donyiro Sultanate. When all the facts came to light, the chief envoy he had sent to Abyssinia to explain the purpose of the military mission to Monomotapa was hanged in the market square, accused of betraying the strategic interests of the state and aggravating the security of the Sultanate in cahoots with the Emperor of Abyssinia. He told his sad State that the Donyiro Sultanate reserved the right to exact a befitting revenge on Abyssinia at an appropriate moment of choosing in the future.

"We did not lose the war; we were betrayed by the Kafir Emperor of Abyssinia," he told his people.

In Lisbon, the victory was received with both shock and alarm. How could a Kingdom of rustic bumpkins so easily vanquish the fearful Donyiros with such ease? "If Monomotapa is to be conquered, new strategies and means, besides arms have to be devised," so the King of Portugal wrote to the Pope. He did not elaborate on, "new strategies and means".

David Livingstone read in the press the account of the great victory of the army of Monomotapa with joy. He was sure that his "divine mission" was on course. The British would get bogged down for ages trying to conquer the Kingdom! Like the Donyiros, they would lose many soldiers and the appetite for war! Scotland would gain independence without firing a shot. And those who had doubted and ridiculed him would come kneeling before him saying, "Hail King David, the Saviour".

He took the *Mappo Mundo* and again studied the location of the Kingdom of Monomotapa and smiled. It was well situated in Central Africa. God had shown him the solution and the way. He was sure that with time, he would be calling the shots, leading the British by the nose, to their destruction!

* * *

In the meantime, it was time to bring the Queen and the twins from the Vumba Mountains for the greatest celebrations the Kingdom had ever known. For indeed there was a lot to celebrate, and on top of the bill, the birth of an heir to the throne, but alas!

CHAPTER 6

TICKET TO AFRICA

Livingstone was devastated after the Scottish Liberation Movement rejected his alternative plan to liberate Scotland. He was dejected.

He was now back in Blantyre preparing to move to the London School of Medicine. He spent most of his time on the hills reading books, but in the evening, he would embark on his runs up and down the hill. While he was the envy of the town for his academic achievement, he did not show any signs of happiness or the desire to celebrate with others.

At home in the evening, while the family was assembled, he hardly said anything. His parents were concerned with his disposition which bordered on the melancholy.

"David, you are a great success in life, like your uncle Mungo Park and yet you do not look happy. Why?" his father asked.

"Half of me is happy and thankful to God while the other half is sad. The happy part is that I have not let you down. The sad part is that I am nothing if Scotland is not free," said Livingstone.

"I understand. You have the same blood as your great uncle Mungo Park. You want to achieve too many things at the same time. I will tell you what, you should complete your studies and think of other things thereafter. Sooner than later, Scotland will be free." said the mother.

"It had better be sooner than later," said Livingstone.

That night, Livingstone could not find sleep. As he tossed and turned in his bed, he prayed to God to give him strength to continue with his mission. He was convinced that time was on his side and he would prove his detractors wrong, all in good time.

A couple of days later, he was aboard a bus heading to London.

The Deity that shapes our lives had a mighty big surprise for Livingstone "the Saviour" when he arrived in London.

In 1836, he was received by the Rector which was a rare honour. In the briefing, the Rector called Livingstone a blessing to the people of Scotland and the general medical fraternity throughout the Union.

"You remind me of Mungo Park, a great Scot whom I had admired as a surgeon. But I will never fathom the madness which drove him to abandon a noble profession for a worthless cause such as exploring Africa! I'm sure you are more focused," said the Rector.

Livingstone could only reply with a "yes sir", but he hated the harsh judgement passed by the Rector on his uncle. To him, Mungo Park was one of the greatest heroes Scotland had ever produced. His one desire was to follow the footsteps of his uncle and to excel in that direction.

"How can a surgeon trained in the most prestigious school of medicine in the world choose to live the life of a savage in Africa? It was sheer and utter madness! I am sure that, though Scot, you will be wise and put knowledge to better use," said the Rector.

Livingstone hated every bit of the conversation. So, this was how the English derided Scottish heroes? Even though, in public, they had painted Mungo Park as a hero! The Rector had always remembered Mungo Park as a man with a wild nature, one which could not be tamed by reason. But in private, he would tell his friends; "The Scots have very little common sense and no sense of judgement. I was not surprised that Mungo Park became a wayward vagabond and met his death in unceremonious circumstances in the middle of nowhere."

The Rector was a senior member of the Royal Geographical Society, a hidden hand of the British Government charged with mapping the wealth of the world in unknown lands. It operated under the umbrella of the British Foreign Office and received funding from both the government and rich individuals in the government and in the private sector. It financed explorers and missionaries, in other words, spies who in turn furnished reports on their findings. Indeed Mungo Park had been funded by the same society whose membership was now deriding him as a "stupid Scot".

"You are on a full scholarship and we have found a two-bedroom apartment near the school, which you will be sharing with a fine young Englishman. He is a Master's student at the London School of Economics pursuing International Trade and Strategic Studies. Though your courses are not the same, you will find him most useful and affable. His name is John Kirk."

Just then, there was a knock on the door, and a young man, immaculately dressed stepped in.

"John, this is the brilliant student from Scotland I talked to you about. David, you are in safe hands and John will take you through the ropes. Enjoy your stay in London."

There was a wry smile on the Rector's face which Livingstone did not like. Anyway, the English never had any respect for the Scots. Brilliant or educated, they still remained "the stupid Scots", as the English called them, and Livingstone knew that.

Livingstone's five years stay was to yield mixed fortunes. In the short run, he came to fathom the operations of the Foreign Office through John Kirk. Kirk told him that the government was in full agreement with the economist and clergy Malthus, who had warned that the population was outstripping the resources, especially land. First, a solution had to be found by way of creating colonies overseas. Second, as long as African slaves were being exported, America enjoyed competitive advantage on the world market by producing cheaper goods. Therefore, the abolition of slave trade had become an urgent issue. Third, the supply of raw materials to British factories was of critical importance for the continued retention of the Kingdom as the top economic power in Europe. For these reasons, it had been decided that the conquest of India would be given priority. Britain wanted to control the world spice, silk, cotton and tea trade. Lastly, India with its huge population was a critical market for British finished products.

"Who knows? When the time to conquer the rest of Asia comes, we could use Indian soldiers to die on our behalf for a farthing!" said Kirk.

"What of Africa?" asked Livingstone.

"No, no, no, Africans are too wild, primitive and savage to conquer. Can you imagine doing business with cannibals? All we will do is to provide the natives with cheap meals of English merchants and settlers! Anybody who ventures into the interior will never be seen again. We have weighed the facts carefully and Africa is out of the question," said Kirk.

David Livingstone was alarmed. He had built his "divine mission" around the conquest of the Kingdom of Monomotapa and now he had been told that the only thing the English wanted was to stop slave trade and have nothing else to do with Africa. If his "divine mission" was to work, it was his duty to turn the foreign policy on its head. Africa had to feature as a priority in the British Foreign Policy if Scotland was to be saved. How he was going to do it remained a daunting task.

John Kirk was in his mid-twenties. He came from an aristocratic family in England which owned a huge farm with cows and horses. They also grew sugar beet on a large scale.

He was of an average built, not tall, not short. His eyes were sparkling blue and he had two mops for eyebrows, long and hideous looking. It was the eye brows which distinguished him most, as they gave him an air of a very cruel and tough man.

He took Livingstone around the city of London, to parties and pubs. Their relationship was not exactly warm but somehow, Kirk never let Livingstone out of his sight in the evenings and over the weekends, as if Livingstone would disappear or get lost without him.

Kirk wore suits all the time with a waist coat and a bow tie, making him one of the smartest young men Livingstone had ever seen. As a Foreign Service Officer, he was expected to be smart at all times, but he carried it to the limits, including on weekends. He gave one the impression that he was absolutely inflexible in his approach to life.

In contrast, Livingstone wore whatever he fancied as long as it was clean. One evening, John Kirk decided to give Livingstone "a real man's drink" in a pub. They started with Guinness lager, moved to ale and finally ended with whisky. Guinness, Kirk explained, was in honour of Ireland, ale in honour of England and whisky in honour of Scotland. They did not honour Wales, the fourth part of the Union.

Livingstone became visibly drunk, giving John Kirk the opportunity to strike: "I hear some people in Scotland want to break from the Union." said Kirk. Livingstone was caught completely by surprise.

"Yeah, I have heard the same rumour," replied Livingstone.

"What did you hear?"

"Exactly what you have just told me; that there are some in Scotland who are not happy with the Union."

"I suppose you have never heard of the Scottish Liberation Movement, have you?"

"No, never," said an alarmed Livingstone.

"Forgive me if I say some people are never satisfied or grateful. The English have pumped a lot of capital in Scotland giving opportunities for employment in coal mines, cotton factories and whisky distilleries!

This is what the Union is all about, free flow of capital, people and ideas!" said Kirk.

"I beg your pardon! I don't think the English investors give a damn about the welfare of the Scots. I have worked in the factories; you know the conditions are deplorable," said an irritated Livingstone.

"But still, it is better than nothing! Life will improve as the economy picks up with new sources of raw materials and new markets overseas. Just wait and see. The Scots have to be patient," said Kirk.

"They have been patient long enough," retorted Livingstone.

"In other words, you sympathise with the Scottish Liberation Movement's position?" asked Kirk.

"As I told you, I do not know of such a movement in Scotland," said Livingstone, beginning to show signs of anger.

"Ok. Let's drop the subject. Let's have one for the road," said Kirk.

"Not for me, I have had enough," said Livingstone.

From that day, Livingstone avoided Kirk as much as he could, unless it was absolutely necessary. Kirk was aware of the chill and he knew the reason. He was an intelligence officer and his assignment was to extract as much information as possible from his roommate on the Scottish Liberation Movement. He knew Livingstone's background like the palm of his hand, including his role in the Liberation Movement. He was on an assignment.

In the long run, the "friendship" between Livingstone and John Kirk would have disastrous consequences as time would reveal. Governments have a very long reach, especially on matters security.

Thus begun the long relationship between Livingstone and John Kirk, the Secret Service Officer attached to the Foreign Office, now a Masters student and Livingstone's housemate.

Livingstone was dreaming of the liberation of Scotland from the English. He was raking his mind on the way forward. In the footsteps of Mungo Park, he would first seek fame and attention and from this unassailable standpoint, he would execute the plan to liberate his motherland. England had to be brought to her knees. He had found the Achilles heel of the English, in greed, self-pride and the dream of a vast empire.

In Ireland, a revolutionary movement known as United Irishmen and later named Young Ireland was giving the English a big headache.

An armed rebellion was afoot and being Roman Catholics, the Irish were receiving support from the French, the Italians and the Vatican. The Scots were protestant and could not find a friendly foreign country to support their cause. To Livingstone, an armed uprising in Scotland was out of the question. He was praying hard to the Good Lord for assistance and guidance.

A conversation with John Kirk triggered another vision. Besides being an explorer like Mungo Park, he would also undertake missionary work like Dr. Robert Moffat, another Scotsman based in Bechuanaland. Moffat had become a darling of the Royal Geographical Society which had a keen interest in his knowledge of Africa South of the Limpopo River. He had written articles on fortunes to be made in gold, diamonds and silver in that area and beyond.

So, Livingstone decided to become a missionary "just in case things did not work out". This was a fall-back position, one he hoped would bring him wealth, just like Moffat, out of which he would finance the nationalist cause. He therefore took a course in missionary work and was ordained by the London Missionary Society and attached to the Ongar Church in Essex. His performance was so pathetic that the head of the church was contemplating asking for a replacement. What saved Livingstone was his unselfish assistance in the local clinic which was understaffed. In his final report to the London Missionary Society, the head of the church did not hesitate to point out that Livingstone was ill-suited for missionary work. Whether he was right or wrong, only time would tell. Maybe the church leader had read the wrong crystal ball!

It was John Kirk who informed Livingstone that Robert Moffat was in London to launch his book entitled "*Missionary labours and scenes in Southern Africa*". The venue was the Royal Geographical Society hall in 1840.

The Royal Geographical Society was a tool of the British Government charged with the responsibility of searching for new opportunities for British investors, and markets for industrial products. Alarmed by warnings by Malthus, an English economist and clergyman, that the fast growth of population would soon wreak havoc as land was not elastic, the Royal Geographical Society added the settlement of Britons overseas as a critical area of concern. Moffat was an important cog in this wheel turning.

How Moffat, a simple doctor and a clergyman from Scotland had risen from a jack to a King remained a great mystery to many.

Every Christmas, he would return to throw lavish parties in London, Glasgow and Edinburgh. Only those dealing with gold and diamonds knew where the money came from. His bank manager had labelled him "top priority customer". This mysterious man had the onerous task of translating the Bible into Sachwana, the language of the natives of Bechuanaland who spoke with a click of the tongue.

"They worship me! They think I have a direct line, a hot line to God! They come to church every Sunday and give diamonds for offerings! I am supposed to intercede with the Creator for their problems including impotence, barrenness, human and animal diseases, droughts which are lengthy, famine and you name it – all sorts of problems. You should hear their confessions ranging from theft of chicken, murder, adultery, fornication and envy. They are like little children who are wilfully naughty, but expect unending forgiveness and love. Life in Bechuanaland is very interesting, amusing and most of all, very rewarding," said an obviously drunk Moffat. He was drunk with his newly-found fame.

The famous poet, Rudyard Kipling, who had been listening to Moffat, commented: "The picture you paint of Africans is very much the same experience I have in India. I agree with you, these characters never grow up to full adulthood. They remain children throughout their lives. They must have an IQ not much higher than orangutans!"

"I couldn't agree with you more!" said Moffat amid great laughter.

"But where do they get the diamonds from?" asked Kipling.

"From all over the place, there is gold and diamonds from mines and dry river beds! The natives have no value for them except for decorating their mud huts. You can exchange a well-decorated hut for a blanket or two and pluck out the glittering stones for a song! They fetch a premium here. Because I am their special friend, their chiefs have given me a diamond mine!"

"Lucky bastard!" quipped Kipling.

"Seriously, you should come over and write your poetry in Bechuanaland. You can write about the animals, the land and the people," said Moffat.

"What is there to write about animals?" asked Kipling.

"You can write about the law of the jungle! You can tell about the hierarchy in animals eating habits! For example, the lion kills a zebra, eats the meat, leaves morsels between the bones for the vultures to clean-up and finally the hyenas crush the bones! A few minutes later, they have not only fed themselves but they have cleaned the place. The jungle has a lot to teach human beings," said Moffat to an attentive Kipling who then said,

"That will be the subject of my next poem, "*The Law of the Jungle*", why didn't I think of it?" Sure enough Kipling wrote a classic on the subject.

During the launch of Moffat's book, the first speaker was a German by the name Dr. Karl Gutzlaff, the author of the biography of Dr. Mungo Park. He talked of the challenges and dangers faced by explorers and heaped praise on Mungo Park who had drowned exploring River Niger. He left out the gory details, or the truth of how Mungo Park died. He lamented that Mungo Park had died prematurely before fulfilling his great dream which was the search for the source of the River Nile. He urged the Royal Geographical Society to honour Mungo Park by financing explorations in search of the world's greatest geographical mystery which lay in the heart of Africa. David Livingstone, who was sitting attentively taking notes lifted his head and looked at the speaker. He wanted to assure him that he was the man chosen by divine authority to continue with the work of Mungo Park especially in the search for the source of the Nile.

"Naturally, the glory of discovering the source of the Nile should fall upon a son of this land, not necessarily a Scotsman although they seem to have a great knack for the search of the unknown." This was greeted with laughter. The Scots took it as a compliment while the English thought it underlined the recklessness of the Scots.

Next on the podium was the Lord Mayor of London who thanked Moffat for his bravery as a trailblazer, his sacrifices and his continued investment in the city of London. "Your work is strengthening the standing of the United Kingdom in the eyes of the world and it goes a long way to create a new world to replace the loss of the colonies in America." This was greeted with applause.

Next on line was the curator of the London Museum who was full of praise for explorers and missionaries for retrieving from natives valuable works of art for safe keeping in the museum for the benefit of posterity.

"I particularly long for the day the legendary Casket in the Kingdom of Monomotapa will find a resting place on our shelves. The Casket is the most highly valued piece of art surpassing the Mona Lisa. We must bring it here before the French, the Portuguese or God forbid, the Arabs get hold of it".

"What on earth is the Casket in the Kingdom of Monomotapa?" David Livingstone asked himself. It raised a strong curiosity in his mind, one which would endure.

"The hunt for the Casket to me is more valuable than the search for the source of the River Nile," concluded the Curator. His speech raised a lot of interest as evidenced in the discussions that ensued.

With time, the Casket became the subject of imaginative stories in the tabloids in London and beyond. The Casket if priceless, they all said, should not be left under the care of careless, uncivilised and primitive natives who did not know its value. It should be preserved in the London Museum for posterity to enjoy. It was worth going to war for, but the United Kingdom was still smarting from the thrashing it had received in the hands of Americans. Another adventure was not in the offing…not just yet.

David Livingstone decided to add the Casket to his "divine mission".

During the reception, Livingstone met and talked to many missionaries, explorers and key figures of influential societies which sponsored expeditions. He learnt that as early as 1722, the Lutheran Church through a sect known as Moravian Society, had set in motion the training of missionaries to be sent to faraway places to convert heathens to Christianity. There was the London Missionary Society, Church Missionary Society, Methodist Missionary Society, Berlin Missionary Society, and the Roman Catholic Sacred Congregation of the Propaganda, Society of the Divine Word, Mary Hill Society of St. Joseph and above all, the Royal Geographical Society. With so many of them, he was convinced that he would not be short of a sponsor when his turn came. Explorers and Missionaries had become an important and special breed of men, sought after by governments through church organisations.

By the time he came face–to–face with the host, Dr. Robert Moffat, Livingstone was crystal clear in his mind that he wanted to be a missionary and an explorer. His "divine mission" was screaming in his head for activation.

Moffat's initial engagement with Livingstone was extraordinary. Livingstone told Moffat that Mungo Park was his uncle. Second, that he wanted to continue with the work of his late uncle and extend it all over Africa, especially the search for the source of the River Nile.

Moffat told Livingstone that the United Kingdom was in great need of such patriotic men. He informed him that the loss of American colonies had been a big blow to the prestige, integrity, the self-esteem of the United Kingdom and above all its economy.

"The calling goes beyond personal whims. We must do all we can," said Moffat.

David Livingstone told him he was ready to do that and more.

Moffat was touched by the seriousness and commitment shown by the young man. He invited him to his house over the weekend for more discussions.

That weekend, Livingstone also met Moffat's wife and daughter, Mary. Mary was a beautiful girl with sexy wild eyes as mysterious as Africa, though short and plump in stature. She too had wide knowledge of Africa though she had never been there. She wanted to visit the continent as an archaeologist with words such as, "I believe Africa is the birthplace of man and the Garden of Eden is hidden in there somewhere."

When Moffat offered the use of his private library to Livingstone, the latter had more than one reason to smile. He would be relishing Mary's seductive wild eyes. He was jolted back to reality by the voice of Moffat.

"It seems we Scots are destined for greatness. The trailblazer was your uncle Mungo Park, I haven't done too badly myself and now you enter into the fray! David, you will not regret your decision," he told him.

By the time Livingstone graduated as a surgeon, he had read everything on Africa in Moffat's library. In addition, he was madly in love with Mary which seemed to please Moffat to no end. Mary had been unruly and she had a passion for alcohol. He thought a love affair with a man as serious as Livingstone might tame her.

In 1844, Livingstone and Mary were married in a most colourful ceremony sponsored by Moffat. Those who graced the occasion were the influential members of the inner circle in London including representatives from the Royal family, the Archbishop of Canterbury, industrialists, merchants, farmers, shippers and publishers, among others. For a wedding present, Moffat offered an all-expenses paid trip to Bechuanaland for their honeymoon. The Royal Geographical Society and the London Missionary Society topped it up with offers to Livingstone to extend his stay beyond the honeymoon to embark on exploratory and missionary work. Livingstone was lost for words. Moffat had a hand in the offers. That evening, a very happy Moffat told Livingstone,

"Africa has wealth galore and it is up to you to dip your hand in the treasure stove and grab as much as you can for the United Kingdom, for Scotland, and above all, for yourself! You do not expose yourself to danger for nothing. You will become one of the most famous and rich men in the world, I assure you. What else can I do for a fellow Scot who is fired to succeed the hard way like Mungo Park and myself?" The self-praising Moffat was visibly drunk with Scotch whisky and pomposity.

As the newly-wed retired for the night, Livingstone was wondering how quickly fortunes change. His pipe dream was turning into a fairy-tale, powerful, tangible, exciting and potentially profitable. He swore to hold on to his "divine mission". He had no doubt that some dangers lay ahead in mysterious and primitive Africa, where animals and cannibals roamed the land freely.

"For God and my country," he swore.

The wheel of fortune was turning and the speed was increasing, heading in the right direction. Revenge is very sweet if it does not backfire, and he was doing it for Scotland. The English would be meals for the cannibals!

"Sweet Africa, the Dark Continent, the Black hole!" he whispered with a smile.

He then took the *Mappo Mundo* and looked at Monomotapa, right next to Bechuanaland! His prayers were being answered like those of Moses and David in the Bible. It all reinforced his belief that God was with him and his mission would succeed.

"Seek and you will find, ask and you will receive," so says the Bible! Then he reached out for Mary who had joined him in bed.

I bolted out of the room as the activities thereafter were not part of my mission from Heaven.

CHAPTER 7

THE DIFFERENCE

Shuttle diplomacy is the most sapping and engaging of all occupations in the world. In reward, it reveals both sides of the coin at the same time, giving the observer a great point of vantage. It puts you in a position to see what others cannot see as they concentrate on this or that aspect of a phenomenon. The other day, I heard a wise old man say, "A point of seeing is also a point of not seeing." It is not so for the envoy. He connects many sides of seemingly unconnected issues, be they of cooperation or competition, to the extent that he can predict what is to happen next. Shuttle diplomacy elevates you to a tin god. Enjoyable though it may be, it leaves you most drained. My trips all over the globe were having a toll on me. I was exhausted and badly in need of a long rest, but I was ahead of the world, like the man who saw tomorrow.

Judging that Livingstone was going to take some time longer in London and the King of Monomotapa was nowhere close to solving the mystery surrounding the birth of the twins in the Royal Caves in Vumba Mountains which made the Queen sad and incommunicable, I decided to go to my adopted home of Kuzania to take a well-deserved rest. I cannot tell you how long I rested as days are short yardsticks in calculating time for us of the Order of the Divine. Suffice it to say I rested long enough to recover from fatigue and move on.

Feeling much rejuvenated I moved to Monomotapa. King Simba the just, the benevolent and the magnanimous had aged beyond recognition. When a man has not enjoyed a single meal, the comfort of loving women and the joy of laughter for a long time, he becomes wasted. He was no longer in control of events around him. He was a pale shadow of the once invincible warrior and the jovial and wise king who was taking his Kingdom to lofty heights. In my long absence, three events had taken place in the kingdom which had added greatly to the misery of the King and the Kingdom. One was the national youth wrestling championship competition, the other was the circumcision of the twins and the third was the reed dance for the twins to choose wives.

Here, I wish to backtrack a bit. The twins, Ndovu and Taiwo, for those were their names, were not identical. Their body structure and manners were as different as day and night. A few months upon their departure from their mother's womb, the mother noticed that Ndovu, the older of the two, who wore the ribbon and the heir to the throne suckled until her breasts hurt. He slept for hours unlike his brother who was a light sleeper and who spent time gazing at everything. Taiwo was very alert.

Ndovu grew plump and the length of his limbs was shorter compared to Taiwo's. These traits became more pronounced as they grew up. What distinguished them even more was the fact that Ndovu exhibited slower mental development. His brother learnt how to walk and talk very quickly. It took a long while before Ndovu could stand on his own or utter a coherent sound. This glaring difference was of concern to the King. How could the heir to the throne be such a dullard? The King, who once harboured dreams of making Monomotapa the most powerful Kingdom on earth, was a worried man. While in the past he had frequently held counsel with his cabinet and the discussions had been on how to quadruple agriculture, mining and industrial output, no such meetings were being held because of the crisis on how to unravel the mystery or secrets of the Vumba Mountains surrounding the birth of the twins.

Plans for deeper shafts into the gold and diamond mines were shelved and so were blueprints for the expansion of irrigation farming. The great falls known as Mosi-O-Tunya or god's smoke due to the mist and vapour which resulted from the long drop of water had been identified as the source of water for irrigation. It had been estimated that if the falling water could be trapped into pipes, it could be moved more than one hundred miles in any direction on account of pressure. Some water could be sold to Bechuanaland which was a semi-desert in the middle of the Kalahari, and which was rich in diamonds.

Such had been the splendid vision of the future of the Kingdom but which was never to be, all because the Queen Mother would not speak and the King had lost sense of direction as a result. There was disquiet in the Kingdom. The king had pleaded with the Queen thus.

"For long, I had waited for an heir. You gave me one and for this I will always be grateful. My love for you is double, no, triple of what it used to be. As there is no end to the joy you brought me, I swore never to take another wife in the reed dance. I have lavished you with jewellery and the finest linen from India and China. If you asked for more, I will not hold back. Ask for anything.

"Since you came from the Royal Caves in Vumba Mountains, you have not been yourself. You used to be charming and warm. You have become aloof, cold and uncommunicative. You have lost your radiance and laughter. Your special qualities of a great heart and mind were cherished by all members of the Kingdom. What is the matter?

"You are destroying yourself, you are destroying me and in the end you will destroy the Kingdom. I beg you please my darling, speak to me," pleaded the King.

"My King, my love, my husband, your words are soothing and they make my heart mellow, and I thank you. Let me promise you that if I had an answer to this matter, I would not keep it away from you for even one minute. It is the gods and spirits of our Kingdom who chose me to make you happy for all my life. But it is the same gods and spirits who have conspired to spin my head so much so that I no longer know myself. I do not know what I have done to deserve this punishment. Have no fear that I was ever unfaithful to you. You are the father of the twins. Let us put it this way, what the gods and spirits give with one hand, they sometimes take away with the other. I am but their humble subject," replied the Queen.

The King pondered the message but could not make sense out of it. Were the lives of the twins in danger?

"My Queen, you talk like one bearing a heavy burden, whose nature you have not shared with me. What have the gods and spirits revealed to you?" the King asked, shaking and expecting the worst.

"What I have told you is enough and I have nothing else to add. Oh, how I wish they could release me or kill me!" said the Queen as she broke into sobs and tears.

"Come, come my dear, stop crying. If it is the premonition of a disaster you have seen in your dreams, dispel the fear for I will not let such a thing happen to Monomotapa as long as I live. So don't let bad dreams punish you anymore." assured the King.

"It is not a dream, it is more than a dream…" and she once again broke into tears. Finally, she said, "I have spoken enough," and the King did not

get another word out of her mouth on the grave issue which he did not understand. It was heart-breaking and most unnatural.

It is said that the gods and the spirits have a way of speaking to man in many forms and ways. What is done in the darkness ultimately comes to light. As I told you before, as the twins were growing up, great differences between them began to show: physical, mental and temperamental. The gods and the spirits were speaking to the King and the Kingdom, revealing what the mother had refused to tell. It came in bursts and spurts over time. As I told you, Ndovu was a glutton and he became plump and slow. His main preoccupation besides eating was sleeping. When he was unhappy, he would cry for a long time clinging to his mother's dress, yet this was the heir to the throne!

Taiwo, on the other hand, had a very fine physique. He was independent, very active, social and brave. He was the darling of everybody in the royal household including the King, and this troubled his father to no end. Taiwo enjoyed listening to stories about the Kingdom's past. He also enjoyed tales from fishermen, hunters, herdsmen and miners. He particularly boasted of the fact that he was born in a cave at a time when the Monomotapa army was vanquishing invaders. He called himself a child of victory. He told all who cared to listen that he would be a great archer and a champion wrestler. Frequently, he joined archers in the shooting range and it was remarkable how quickly he mastered the use of the bow and arrows. Quietly, he befriended the Kingdom's champion wrestler who gladly gave him private lessons. Soon, boys much older than him were no match for his prowess. They talked about the power of his grip and his very fast moves.

Every year, a national wrestling championship was held. It was divided into two categories namely the uncircumcised youth and the warriors. The King took particular interest in the spectacle, himself a champion wrestler in his heydays. When the day came, the King and the royal household went to the stadium. The twins sat on either side of their father. When the victor of the youth category was given the prize of a fat bull, he walked briskly and gave it to Taiwo, with a bow. Everybody was surprised! How could the champion surrender his cherished prize? Taiwo declined to take the bull and told the champion,

"I have many bulls and this is yours to keep. Congratulations," he shook the champion's hand warmly and genuinely.

The champion turned to the King and said, "Our King and the father of the Kingdom, your son Taiwo is the greatest wrestler in our age group. Had he taken part in the contest, the bull would have been his. We all know he is the champion and for this reason, I cannot accept the prize," said the champion.

Taiwo was in a fix. He prayed that the conversation would come to an end before his father learnt of his wild escapades.

"Taiwo, is it true that you are a fine wrestler?" asked the King.

"Yes father, I am," he replied.

"Then there is only one way to settle the issue. Both of you will get into the ring and settle the matter by yourselves!" roared the King.

After a long period in which the empire had not seen the King smile, they were treated to a broad smile. The King was reminiscing his past glory as a great wrestler. He had the pride that some of that fighting spirit had entered his son's blood. He called the referee and told him,

"I want a clean and tough fight. No fixing!" he said, in a firm voice.

The referee who was the nation's immediate former wrestling champion smiled back.

"Let the contest begin!" ordered the King.

Taiwo took off his royal robe and donned a wrestler's outfit. When he entered the ring, there were wild cheers. The King was holding his breath fearing of a royal humiliation. He had been taking so much pain of late that one more episode would not make a difference, he rationalised. The two boys gamely sized each other and then in a flash, Taiwo seized the champion by the neck and brought him down over his shoulders. The champion hit the canvas with a thud. Taiwo wrapped his arms around the upper part of his competitor while at the same time, he gripped the lower part of the body with his legs, and then he started twisting the body in different directions, like a python smothers a victim. When the bones, spine and muscles could take no more, the champion yelled out,

"I surrender!" Immediately, the referee tapped Taiwo's shoulder and ordered him to loosen the grip. He did as ordered and stood up in triumph. There had never been such a swift, decisive and memorable match in the history of the empire. The speed, grace and agility of Taiwo shocked all especially his father, who was ecstatic. He called Taiwo to his side and hugged him as wild cheers filled the air. Taiwo proudly took the bull and then gave it to the vanquished competitor.

"This is the prize for the runners-up!" Taiwo told the loser. The boy took the bull with pride.

News of the fight and Taiwo's victory spread like wildfire throughout the Kingdom. The name Taiwo was associated with kindness, bravery, grace, strength, decisiveness and victory. He became a legend at a tender age! All the way back to the palace, the King's right hand rested on Taiwo's shoulder as he cheerfully acknowledged greetings from his subjects lined along the road. Taiwo and his father were exchanging warm smiles. His brother, Ndovu, walked a distance behind totally forgotten. In the palace, a big feast was held in honour of Taiwo. As usual, his brother ate like a glutton and slept while Taiwo engaged the guests and charmed them with his maturity. His father's eyes followed him everywhere regretting why he was not the one wearing the bracelet. The gods and spirits at times are very unfair, he concluded or were they? Had the gods and spirits spoken and the King refused to hear their voice?

The second time the gods and the spirits intervened was not a laughing matter. It was in the other very special event that the Kingdom had eagerly waited for, the circumcision ceremony. Having decided that the twins had come of age, the King proclaimed the date of the event. The mature boys who had been waiting for the proclamation jumped with joy. Taiwo was particularly pleased that he would now pass the transition from boyhood to manhood, to a warrior. He could join the archers' elite brigade of the armed forces. Ndovu, his brother and the heir to the throne received the news with fear.

"Is it painful?" He prodded his mother.

"How would I know? I have never been circumcised. Go and ask your father." the mother replied sarcastically. Ndovu did not go to find out from his father. Instead, he went to his room and cried.

For the ceremony, temporary huts were constructed to house the boys as they recuperated. They were built in the forest nearby because the boys had to be isolated until they healed. It was in this temporary village that they would learn all things pertaining to adulthood including war, sex and how to handle women and children. They also learnt the history of the Kingdom and the need to protect it with their very lives.

Granaries were filled with food: cows, sheep and goats were brought for consumption by the circumcised lads. Good feeding, it was reckoned, promoted fast healing and always when the boys emerged from the forest, they were more robust than when they went in.

Before the cutting ceremony, each boy was required to fashion his special gear from head to toe, in which he would emerge from the forest after healing. So, after the King announced the date, boys went hunting for birds with bright feathers like ostriches and peacocks and leopards and lions for skins. Each hunted according to his strength though hunting in groups was allowed when the prey was big or dangerous. It is he who delivered the fatal blow that claimed the prize. Taiwo did not wait for the King to organise a hunting party for the twins. With his friend whom he had beaten in the wrestling match, they stole away and went into the bush. Each came back with the skin of a leopard and two skins of colobus monkeys. They left them with the Commander of the archers' brigade for treatment. The hunting continued for days.

A week later, the King summoned Ndovu and Taiwo to his sanctuary.

"Show me what you have gathered for your decorations!" he demanded. In a short while, Taiwo came with a leopard skin and two colourful colobus monkeys' skins all well treated and with countless bright feathers from all kinds of birds. His brother came with two chicken feathers he had collected in the yard. The King was raving mad at Ndovu.

"What an imbecile I have for a son! What an heir to the throne are you? Look at what your brother has achieved, he will be the most colourful on the day, and you? What are you going to wear? An old cow hide and old chicken feathers? You are a disgrace to yourself and to the royal household! Get out of here!" he scolded Ndovu as he turned to Taiwo.

"My son, you make me very proud. If it was not for fear of a curse, I would defy the will of the gods and the spirits…" he did not elaborate.

Taiwo didn't get the meaning of his father's words, but he took it as a great compliment.

Early the following morning, the Queen sent Ndovu to the bush in the company of hunters. They came back with the skin of a lion and ostrich feathers. When the story was told, everybody laughed at Ndovu.

"Where did you deliver the fatal blow to the lion, on the head or in the heart?" Taiwo asked him jeeringly. Ndovu bowed his head in shame as he had no answer.

In the village, boys to be cut with Ndovu and Taiwo were telling everybody; "In the future, I will tell all who care to listen, that I was cut with the same knife as Taiwo!" The name Ndovu was not mentioned. The boys were always cut with the same knife which was cleaned and sharpened every time a skin was severed.

On the eve of the ceremony, the boys to face the knife were clean shaven on their heads. That night, which was called "the Devil's Night" or the night when nobody slept, adults moved from homestead to homestead of the boys' parents, drinking beer and consuming food, while wishing the boys a happy and prosperous future. The revelling and eating parties moved in groups with men and women together. Between homesteads, they sang X-rated songs as had always been the tradition. Second, if a man and a woman fancied each other, the custom allowed for a fling in the bush. It was the only time promiscuity was socially and officially sanctioned. The argument was that it helped to spread genes, which was good for the survival of the households and the Kingdom. In case of a curse, the "outside blood" would be spared.

Early in the morning, all candidates were standing in the pool where I had found the virgins washing. The ice cold water numbed their bodies. They emerged to face the knife with Ndovu leading the procession. He would be the first to be cut. A warrior stood behind each candidate for support.

The surgeon came to Ndovu and fixed a cold gaze on him while sharpening the knife. Ndovu had to be cut first as he was heir to the throne and Taiwo would follow. All of a sudden, Ndovu let out a yell full of fear and bolted. Stunned, the crowd stayed glued to their feet watching the spectacle of the heir to the throne running as fast as his fat legs could carry him. He was heading for the nearby bush. Upon reaching there, he clambered up a tree. For quite some while, nobody spoke or moved. Finally, a senior member of the King's Council of the Wise ordered the warriors to bring Ndovu back. He came yelling, protesting that he did not want to be circumcised as it would be painful. He was pinned to the ground and the operation executed. The warrior who had been charged with supporting him took him aside. He was sobbing uncontrollably, calling for his mother.

Taiwo was next. When the surgeon looked at him straight in the eye with a cold stare, Taiwo did not blink. He smiled. Without flinching, he was cut.

He was given loud cheers by the crowd, whose echo reached the royal palace. It pleased the King thinking his boys had bravely become men, but soon word came to him of the cowardice demonstrated by Ndovu and the shame it brought to the royal household.

Throughout the Kingdom, the one theme that rent the air in every conversation was the story of the coward called Ndovu. It was openly being said that the boy was not fit to wear the crown.

The anger of the King like the wrath of the gods knew no bounds. He even contemplated putting Ndovu to death for disgracing the royal household. He would have done so without any qualms, but then he remembered that the Queen had a secret she would not reveal. He feared that his action might trigger the calamity the Queen had been privileged to see in advance, but whose nature she would not tell him. If he was a recluse before, he was even more reclusive now, anger boiling in his veins over the Queen and Ndovu. The victory over the Donyiros and Taiwo's brave exploits were not enough to remove the heavy burden in his heart. Sometimes the gods and the spirits conspire to protect idiots and cowards. The fact that Ndovu would remain in the recuperating village for a month was period enough for the King's anger to subside. The intensity and need to take strong action would ebb with time.

Then came the reed dance and the choosing of wives by the twins of which I will tell you about later.

My judgment was that the Kingdom was under siege from within, like it was consuming itself to nothingness. I looked into the crystal ball and I shuddered. Could Monomotapa be saved from itself? And what if there was another external threat? Could it master enough cohesion to face it? The Donyiro Sultanate had been defeated and in such a manner that another invasion from there was impossible, but the King of Portugal had threatened to conquer the Kingdom at a time of his choosing and Livingstone in his "divine mission" was contemplating clashes between British troops and the warriors of Monomotapa.

I was no longer in doubt that what St. Peter had seen would come to pass. I was becoming impatient. If I had had any say over the matter, I would have certainly accelerated the action to lessen the suspense I was suffering. I resigned myself to waiting, as events unfolded before my eyes, justifying St. Peter's concern, hence my mission. The image of Livingstone in the fray was looming larger and larger, but I could not fathom at what point he would enter into the scene or how. I waited.

CHAPTER 8

THE SAVIOUR IN SLAVERY

In the summer of 1844 while at the port of departure for Bechuanaland, as Livingstone was excitedly talking to Mary about the long journey, he was pleasantly surprised to see John Kirk.

"John, don't tell me you are going to Africa as well!" Livingstone remarked, stretching his hand for a good friendly handshake.

"No! Not just yet. I came to bid you farewell and to wish you all the best in your sojourn among the cannibals!" retorted Kirk amid laughter.

"It is most kind of you," said Livingstone.

"By the way, if you ever find the heaps of gold and diamonds which Moffat talks about, I will be your willing business partner," said Kirk.

"Sure, our friendship has been strong and it can be further deepened through business partnership. I owe you one John. You really took good care of me in London. If I ever find a fortune, you will be an equal beneficiary," said Livingstone, more in jest than honesty.

John Kirk sat at a vantage point on a platform in the dockyard pretending to enjoy the view of the harbour and the ships coming and going. In essence, he was on duty watching those that David Livingstone last made contact with, with a keen eye on those who might appear to be members of the Scottish Liberation Movement. He was disappointed as his watch yielded nothing.

A young lad of twelve was boarding the ship to Cape Town, under the care of Livingstone and Mary. His name was Cecil Rhodes, the son of an English clergyman, who was the Chaplain at Buckingham Palace and a senior member of both the Royal Geographical Society as well as the Church Missionary Society. The lad was suffering from arthritis and Moffat had suggested to his father that the hot weather in Bechuanaland might be the cure. For a fee, Moffat had offered to take care of Rhodes in Bechuanaland.

The ship was loaded with all sorts of characters – hunters, fortune seekers and harlots. As England was going through a lean economic spell, many were leaving for greener pastures. Cape Town was a favourite destination. Stories were abound of poor men who had left England only to return loaded with gold and diamonds and Moffat was one of them. Returning hunters had filled ships with game trophies some of which were show pieces in the British Museum as well as in the homes of the wealthy, including the palaces of royalties in Europe.

The stories on the ship were many, some out of this world as drunkards tried to outdo each other on their past exploits in Africa and what they hoped to achieve this time round. I detected criminal elements in the ship who thought their business would be made easy by the climate of lawlessness in Cape Town.

Eventually, after many weeks, the ship docked in Cape Town. Moffat had made excellent arrangement for Livingstone and his party to be transported to Bechuanaland, a couple of hundreds of miles to the north. There were ox-driven wagons at their disposal. As they drove north leaving the mountains behind, the weather became unbearably hot.

"We are now entering the southern fringes of the Kalahari Desert," announced the head of the caravan. The land was sparsely populated with naked natives with small squinty eyes and yellow teeth. David Livingstone recalled that Moffat had told him there were hundreds of villages full of natives waiting to receive Jesus Christ as their Saviour. He pondered how Jesus could ever be interested in such a primitive looking breed of the human race, if indeed they were human. To him, they more belonged to the animal kingdom or a retarded line of Homo erectus.

When they came to Gaborone which was a small village, they found Moffat and his wife waiting. Looking around, Livingstone counted a few structures which were built to European design. They included Moffat's house, a small church and what appeared to be two classrooms. There was no clinic. There was a fourth structure which was nearing completion, a short distance from Moffat's house.

Curious natives and miserable looking white men who looked like they had not seen water for ages gave them a warm reception.

"Where do these white people live?" asked Livingstone.

"They live among the natives in the huts. Some have even taken native wives! They claim life here is ten times better than in England," replied Moffat.

"And what do they do for a living?" enquired Livingstone.

"They work for me," replied Moffat with a broad grin.

Little did Livingstone and Rhodes know that they too would be added to this troop of white slaves working for Moffat in the diamond mines.

Dr. Robert Moffat was a cunning man. In the big book they call the Bible, there is a moving story of love which centres on a character called Jacob. He fell in love with a damsel called Rachel, daughter of a trickster who went by the name Laban. Now Laban made Jacob work for seven hard years before he could deliver Rachel. Late one night, after seven years, there was a knock on Jacob's door. When he opened, a woman was thrust to him in the dark by Laban with words such as "Congratulations, she is yours". Jacob was delighted and without as much as exchanging greetings, he made love to her most passionately. The lady enjoyed every minute of it. When he woke up in the morning, Jacob realised that he had been given Leah, the elder sister of Rachel! Leah was ungainly with squinty eyes. In protest, Jacob went to Laban and was told to work for another seven years for the hand of Rachel. He agreed.

Moffat had a lot in common with Laban, but Livingstone ended up with one woman, short and plump Mary, with her wild eyes, while Jacob ended up with two, one beautiful and the other ugly beyond measure. If Livingstone had thought that he had been given Mary on a silver platter, he was in for a rude shock. He had sunk further into the trap by accepting the offer of a honeymoon in Bechuanaland. However, for Livingstone, the whole arrangement seemed ordained from the deities as it brought him right on the door step of Monomotapa which was his prime target in the "divine mission". Nothing else mattered to him.

Livingstone was to work for Moffat for ten years in Bechuanaland. Monomotapa and Bechuanaland were only separated by the Ndebele Kingdom of Lobengula. The wide chasm I had seen between Livingstone and Monomotapa had been bridged and contact made that possible. I began to believe in the words of St. Peter and braced myself for what was in store.

Livingstone and Mary were lavished by Moffat with all manner of comfort including wine, whisky and cigars. Once the new house was completed, they moved in with Rhodes and then came the job offer. Livingstone was to be in charge of the diamond mines while Rhodes was put in charge of mail between Gaborone and Cape Town. It was Moffat who taught Rhodes how to open envelopes and read all mail before sealing them again. He was not to touch Moffat's mail of course. In this way, Moffat kept a tab on the entire goings around him.

Livingstone thought he would be in Bechuanaland for only a short while before he embarked on his "divine mission".

Soon Livingstone and Rhodes mastered the language of the savages though the clique gave them problems as it had given Moffat. Over the weekend, they went hunting game for food and trophies. Both became good marksmen.

Livingstone was astonished at how quickly young Rhodes was settling down as well as internalising the history of the natives and the land beyond Bechuanaland, from the stories he read in Moffat's library and from people around him. When Livingstone asked him what he wanted to be when he grew up, he replied, "A perfect Englishman".

Livingstone did not understand the meaning, but he took it as some sort of insult, which was the attitude of all the people from that part of the world towards Scotsmen. He swallowed hard and promised to deliver a befitting retort of his own at some future date. He liked the lad though.

Livingstone never asked Moffat about the one hundred villages of natives with souls ready for Christ. He had by now clearly understood that Moffat used the church and the school only to extract diamonds and gold from the natives who did not understand why he so much liked the useless shiny stones, and above all as references in his reports to the Church Missionary Society and the Royal Geographical Society. He was a pioneer! Nay, a philanthropist in the service of the Lord!

Moffat did not let anyone into the secrets of his "missionary work" including his wife, daughter or Livingstone. It was a private preserve of his, and so was the tally of all diamond and gold trade between the vast land of Bechuanaland and the outside world. How long this control would last, only time would tell.

By the eighth year, Livingstone had a bug biting him. Had he abandoned the "divine mission?" He told himself no, only that he had been busy serving Moffat like Jacob had served Laban, as a slave! When time came, Jacob had moved out of Laban's control. It was time for him to move, but where to? How was he going to activate the British invasion of Monomotapa when he had no plan? Had the Heavens led him this far only to abandon him as a slave to Moffat? He prayed fervently that just as David of the Bible had been empowered with a sling and a pebble in battle, he too would be shown the way forward.

Increasingly, Livingstone visited places far afield in Bechuanaland, to the north, towards Monomotapa. He was warned by the natives not to venture too far in case he fell into the hands of Lobengula who was powerful and cruel and who killed any foreigner who strayed into his kingdom.

He learnt that the Kingdom of Monomotapa was ruled by a powerful King, King Simba the just and the magnanimous. However, stories coming from the Kingdom were talking of uncertain times ahead, as the mother of the heir to the throne was silent about a curse from the gods and the spirits which she would not reveal. Also the heir to the throne had been born weak both in the body and in the head. His twin brother was very suitable, but then it was the first-born who would be king. To Livingstone, these were troubled waters, probably ready for fishing in.

He learnt about the mighty Kingdom of the Bundu under threat from the Portuguese. The Queen called Nzinga was repelling military adventurism by the Portuguese, but the latter had more powerful weapons. He was told that after Angola; the Portuguese planned to attack Monomotapa and claim the land between the Atlantic and the Indian Ocean. The last bit was alarming. Where would that leave his "divine mission" if they succeeded?

Livingstone read the story of Jacob in the Bible and learnt that by the time he left Laban, he was a very rich man, but for him, the little he had saved from his small salary from Moffat was worth nothing. He decided to pay Moffat back, by engaging in diamond and gold trade. He also brought Rhodes into the picture. Over time, they had also talked about the need for Britain to take over territories in African, but they did not know how to convince Queen Victoria. Malthus had given the warning, but the wrong target had been chosen, India of all places!

"I have this burning urge to go to Monomotapa," Livingstone told Rhodes.

"What for?" asked Rhodes.

"I feel it holds the key to British fortunes in Central and Southern Africa. It is vast, rich and fertile," said Livingstone who then added, "and it better be soon before the Portuguese move in." he looked damn serious.

"I'll go with you," said Rhodes.

Upon further enquiry, Livingstone was informed that besides the direct northern route to Monomotapa, there was an alternative route via Cape Town to Sofala and then the journey up the Zambezi. The snag was that Sofala was managed by the Portuguese who did not want other European nationalities around, unless they were dropping or picking goods at the port. The route by boat from Sofala up the Zambezi to the interior was controlled by Arabs who did not want to see intrusions in their area of control. They had been weakened after the Donyiro defeat but they were still a force to reckon with.

The other route possible was due north-west. There was a No Man's triangular land between Ndebele, Bundu and Monomotapa which was tacitly created to avoid war between the three Kingdoms. It was known as the demilitarised zone. From there, one could go eastwards to Monomotapa with some luck.

For the next two years, Livingstone and Rhodes stole diamonds from Moffat's mines. They also bought some from the natives in preparation for their adventure northwards. Time had come for them to extricate themselves from Moffat's slavery.

Mary Moffat, Livingstone's wife noted the tension growing between her husband and her father. By then, she was the mother of four and had acquired the habit of drinking too much. When Moffat suggested that she should go back to London so that the kids could get some decent education, Livingstone seconded the idea. It would give him the freedom he needed. So Mary and the kids were packed and shipped to London. She was surprised by the amount of gold and diamonds Livingstone gave her for the family upkeep. She was going to be very comfortable.

Moffat had planned that with Mary out of the way, he would deal with Livingstone and Rhodes with a firm hand. His business had shrunk substantially and he was painfully aware that the two were responsible. He was going to kick up a fuss on the issue at some opportune moment.

There are signs which point to the fact that a plan has the blessings of Our Maker. For Livingstone, first, it was the fact that Monomotapa had featured prominently in his dreams as the conduit through which Scotland would be liberated with the British Army pinned down by the mighty warriors of Monomotapa. Second, divine benevolence had landed him in Bechuanaland right next door to Monomotapa. If this was not a divine scheme, then what was?

Livingstone had digested the new thrust of the British Foreign Policy from John Kirk in the period they stayed together. The problem was the focus on India. He had also noted and internalised the warning by Malthus of the dangers of population pressure in Britain which could lead to a social upheaval or a revolution. He particularly liked the warning that since land is not elastic, a solution lay in immigration to other continents. Somehow, he had to bring Africa into focus in this equation.

Britain had too easily pushed the French and the Portuguese out of India much to Livingstone's disappointment. His schema was based on large scale wars between the British, the natives and other European powers. Africa remained his trump card and it had to happen on a grand scale, otherwise his mission was doomed. He would work through John Kirk to convince the British Government to focus particularly on Africa. He was going to use Kirk's proposal for a business partnership as bait!

It dawned on him that the answer to the question was closer than he had ever imagined! He had Cecil Rhodes in his grasp. Young, ambitious, energetic, self-assured and corky, he always achieved whatever he set his mind on. The fresh target, Rhodes, was tall, robust, and full of fire; his arthritis had long disappeared. He fitted perfectly in the mission. Livingstone smiled to himself. The script would be as follows: because young Cecil Rhodes had voiced his ambition to build a business empire in Africa, Livingstone was going to use the warning by Malthus to snare Rhodes. Rhodes would then sell the idea to the monarchy through his father who was the chaplain in Buckingham palace, and the deal would be sealed.

"To hell with John Kirk," Livingstone said to himself.

The purpose and motive for making as much money as possible for Livingstone and Rhodes had crystallized. For Livingstone, it was to finance his "divine mission" and for Rhodes, it was to accumulate enough capital to build a business empire. The thrust put them on a bruising collision course with Moffat, the master of the art of deceit, but there was no turning back.

"David, tell me, when we settle in Africa, what will happen to the Africans? I kind of like them, nice and generous. I would hate to see them go the way of the Red Indians in America or the Aborigines in Australia," asked an innocent looking Rhodes.

The innocent question sent Livingstone's mind racing to Scotland.

What had happened to the Scots when the agriculture "improvers" and the English industrialists settled in the land? Large tracks of land had been alienated and the natives of the land rendered homeless. They had found employment as workers in coal mines, textile industries, and fishermen while some had migrated to faraway lands never to return. He felt anger building, but he had to control himself because in essence, he was going to be the architect of English colonialism in Africa, his key plot for the independence of Scotland.

"Don't worry about the Africans. The name of the game is survival of the fittest. When the settlers, industrialists and miners arrive, they will need labour, won't they? Sure enough they will be second class citizens on their land, but such developments cannot be avoided. They are ordained from above," replied Livingstone, well aware that colonial imperialism was a condition engendered by greed rather than a command from above. Man's inhumanity to man was a vice which brought God to tears.

"Yeah! They are a strong breed of people and very hard working. We will take all the land and build the United States of Africa to rival the United States of America! I can't wait for that day!" said an excited Rhodes.

"Then you must start working on London to extend the empire to Africa before the French, Italians, Portuguese and God knows who else wants to gobble it up. If we get the Kingdom of Monomotapa, the rest will fall on our lap without too much of an effort. We will be the masters of the continent from Cape Town to Cairo," said Livingstone.

"What am I supposed to do?" asked Rhodes.

"Ask your father to convince the Queen that the answer to a prosperous Britain lies in acquiring territory in Africa. Secondly, tell him to convince William Wilberforce that if the export of slaves to America continues at the present rate, British settlers in Africa will be short of labour. Britain must work for the abolition of slave trade for her own survival," said Livingstone.

"It makes sense, I will write to my dad. He never lets me down. Let me tell you this. You have been like a big brother to me. I owe you for all I know about the world. Someday, I will pay you back, but I feel, our future is tied together and I am glad. You Scots have a God-given talent for reading the future. You saved the British Isles from the Romans and Mungo Park had talked about the great wealth in West Africa. Here we are once again, with a Scot leading the charge, charting the future for a prosperous and mighty

British Empire! The Empire is a question of bread and the survival of our great nation!" said Rhodes.

Livingstone smiled. Rhodes had swallowed the bait, hook, line and sinker at a go. The survival of the nation? Which nation? Livingstone asked himself. He felt very powerful, invincible. In this game, he was the master. He had many pawns including Queen Victoria, John Kirk, William Wilberforce, Cecil Rhodes, his father-in-law and hordes of Englishmen to sacrifice, all for the independence of Scotland! His "divine mission" was truly on course.

"Amen." He whispered to himself, his eyes fixed on the blue skies above, in what he considered to be the direction of Heaven, the home of the divine.

CHAPTER 9

VOICES FROM THE DARK

My shuttle diplomacy had been reduced to a hop across the border. Leaving Livingstone and Rhodes to finalise their grand scheme of conquest, I visited Monomotapa, the selected target of their malicious scheming.

I found a distraught King Simba in consultation with the Council of the Wise. It was composed of selected sages from different nationalities in the Kingdom. The King was addressing the Council,

"Rumours doing rounds in the kingdom are damaging the reputation of the royal family. Some say the twins are not my sons and that is why the Queen will not speak for fear of punishment, including the killing of the twins. Let me assure you, that nothing is further from the truth. The boys are from my loins; you can tell by looking at Taiwo. People also say that the mother is possessed by an evil spirit. This is also not true. When the Queen talks to me, she is humble, respectful and most coherent. However, she carries in her heart what she terms as a "heavy burden", but one she will not talk about.

"The burden, I am now convinced has something to do with the identity of the twins. I do not understand why Taiwo is not Ndovu and why Ndovu is not Taiwo. The difference is clear. The one who is fit to be King is not the heir and vice versa. I have contemplated having Ndovu killed to ease the problem, but I will not have it done until the Queen delivers the disturbing message from the gods. I have no wish to see a bigger calamity befall this Kingdom. In the meantime, I have noticed that the boys have become men. Time has come for them to take wives. In our customary way, I command that the reed dance be held at the end of the on-going harvest."

There and then, the meeting ended. King Simba was no longer brooking dialogue or lengthy discussions on any matter. He wanted to be left alone. I could not believe my ears. The reed dance I had long wished to witness was going to take place at last, with the parade of a hundred virgins wearing next to nothing, shaking their bodies and lifting their legs to the rhythm of the drums! I was going to feast my eyes on them starting from the moment they went to make the reed mini-skirts. I would then follow them to their bathing in the pool, to the oiling of their bodies and finally to the dancing arena. I was going to have a full voluptuous eye feast on them because for all I cared, this one could very well be the last reed dance in the Kingdom.

Soon, the harvest was over and the coveted event was in full swing! King Simba, with his sons Ndovu and Taiwo came riding on a marvellously decorated ox-driven cart, the same one that the Queen had ridden in to the Vumba Mountains. At the gates of the amphitheatre, they disembarked and walked side by side to the dais a hundred metres away. The only person most conspicuous by her absence was the Queen with a very heavy heart.

The King, a giant of a man walked with brisk steps, but his once upright and majestic posture was betrayed by a creeping stoop with sagging shoulders. Still, he was a most imposing figure. He had not shaved for years and his white beard was long and unkempt.

Taiwo had grown very tall, the same height as his father. He was muscular, strong, charming and handsome. His long strides and those of his father moved in tandem. Beside them was the clumsy fat and short Ndovu. He could not match their strides and his walk was more of a trot, most awkward.

The King waved to the cheering crowd, his raised giraffe-tail flywhisk swishing from right to left. He wore a splendid outfit of lion and leopard skins and on his head sat a hood made from the skin of a colobus monkey. Ndovu and Taiwo were equally majestically adorned.

The cheering of the crowd reached a crescendo when the King, after inspecting a guard of honour, mounted the dais. He had a broad smile and bright burning eyes. Although his brow revealed deep crease lines from old age and the anguish of the curse, one could tell he was genuinely happy. The problems facing the kingdom were not on his mind albeit for now.

As the royalty sat down, the crowd settled on the terraces. It was time for the show to begin.

The Monomotapa virgins came clad in next to nothing. If I had thought them most beautiful the first time I saw them by the pool as they made and fitted their reed skirts, this time they were angelic. Pure virgins, one hundred and more of them, more beautiful than King Solomon could have described in his songs. They entered the arena dancing to the beat of the drums.

Though young, none of them looked shy in their semi-nakedness. They halted before the King, seated on the raised platform, with Ndovu to his right and Taiwo to his left. With one voice, they hailed King Simba the great, the gracious and the magnanimous. Not that their eyes were fixed on the King, not at all. Their focus was on his two sons who today would choose their wives. The virgins knew very well that one of them would be the future Queen and, sooner or later, sire an heir to the throne. They were engaged in serious business.

Reading each virgin's mind, I was perturbed to see that none of them was focusing on Ndovu who would be the future King. Rather, their eyes and attention were trained on Taiwo, the living legend, but who it was said was born after Ndovu and therefore lost the crown by a few minutes. They all wished that Taiwo had been born first for what a king and husband he would have made! For all they cared, each wanted to be Taiwo's wife not Ndovu's, even if that would deny them the title of Queen. For once, in the reed dance, every virgin wanted to play second fiddle.

The virgins then formed a circle and began moving round in quick short steps, right left, and right left singing a melodious tune while shaking their shoulders and gyrating their hips. One part of the human anatomy which has always fascinated me is the breasts. Whoever selected the virgins had given priority to the shape and size of the breasts. They were full and nicely shaped, with protruding nipples that left the crowd gasping especially the young men. These were the mammaries which the King would cuddle at night, the very ones he would be putting his chest upon as he made babies, the very ones the babies would suckle including the future King. Breasts are pleasing organs; they deserve great reverence. The organs were bouncing buoyantly as the virgins made their moves. The buttocks, thighs and waistlines were sculptured in Heaven. In all my travels to Scotland, London, and Portugal I had never seen women as beautiful, provocative and desirable as these!

Then another arrangement of music bellowed out and the virgins formed a single file. They were moving from right to left. When each girl was directly before the King, she would do a solo dance, vibrating from head to toe as if she was possessed by demons-jumping, lifting this leg high and then the other and the crowd would respond with deafening cheers. It took some while before all the virgins had performed what I called the mad act after which they again returned in single file. In the solo act which followed, they came in slow motion. Again when they came close to the dais, each girl, detached herself from the group in turns, moved slowly turning around, her hands on the hips, her angelic face smiling and daring all who wanted to see that she was the best of the lot.

Each act and body frame was worth etching in the memory for ever but unfortunately, there were a hundred of them and the memory is not a video recorder or a camera. I could not judge which girl was the best, but there were a few differences here and there. Some were slightly taller or shorter, some darker, and some more gifted below the waist than others. Men are known to admire certain aspects of these features more than others and it was time for Ndovu and Taiwo to show their preferences.

When the parading of gorgeous bodies stopped, the King ordered Ndovu to move to the line of virgins and choose a wife. Looking down, Ndovu moved blindly in a straight line and held the hand of the damsel on his path. It was only then that he looked up. The woman in front of him was the tallest of the lot. One could not see any other aspect that distinguished her from the lot. He led the girl to the dais amid loud ululations from the women and the wild beating of drums. He had picked a wife but had he considered all the options wisely? It appeared not. The King then ordered Taiwo to move forward and choose a wife.

Taiwo was a natural actor. He moved from one end of the line to the other, looking straight in the eyes of the virgins who responded by posing invitingly and charming him with broad sweet smiles. Some even had the audacity to wink at him. As he turned around to inspect the line of virgins the second time, keeping them mesmerised, you could hear a pin drop. Everybody was enjoying the suspense. After the second inspection, he pulled back a whole thirty paces and cast his eyes upon all the virgins, then with deliberate long strides, and a charming smile, he walked to what I must confirm was the most beautiful of the lot. When he held her hand, a radiant dazzling smile spread on her face. Her eyes, welling with tears of joy, were like a thousand diamonds sparkling in the rays of the morning sun. Taiwo, the strong handsome warrior lifted her in his arms as she put her arms around his neck and this is the way she was brought to the dais.

The story of how Taiwo held the King and the crowd to a long spell of anxiety before choosing the most beautiful woman the world had ever seen, only added to his fame. The joy in the land was total.

In all animals, the instinct for procreation is paramount and it is no less in human beings. The hunt for the next heir to the throne began with the honeymoon, with Ndovu charged to keep the fire burning. Within a year, Taiwo had a bouncing baby boy with strong limbs. On the other hand, Ndovu's wife was not even pregnant. There were issues which went like this:

"When the spirits are displeased, they do not hide their anger. Their retribution is swift and harsh. If only the Queen Mother had spoken, the spirits and the gods would have come to the aid of Monomotapa, but women are stubborn creatures and they can destroy any Kingdom with whatever weapon they fancy. In the Garden of Eden, it was the apple, a simple sweet fruit; in the case of Samson and Delilah, it was scissors and a haircut in the case of Solomon, it was the sheer terror of numbers of women and concubines combined, while in the case of Monomotapa, it was silence, pure simple silence. Ndovu was now in the thick of the "curse of the caves."

The calls for procreation with all its pleasure were no less for Ndovu and the Princess. On their very first night of marriage, they were anticipating the beginning of a life of sheer bliss, pleasures untold and many children. They went to bed early, each with their expectations and fears. Ndovu had been ushered into unchartered territory with the burden of breaking virginity. For the Princess, it was the pain which she had been told comes with the first act of copulation which gave her shivers. She reckoned that the sooner she was done, the better.

As Ndovu caressed the naked Princess, he suddenly heard disturbing and strange noises.

"Did you hear that noise?" he asked the Princess.

"What noise, there is not a sound," said the Princess.

After a short while, Ndovu heard another sound.

"And that one?" he asked her.

"I heard nothing," she said.

Ndovu mounted courage and pulled the Princess close to him. She was a most willing partner and then hell broke loose. At first, he recognised the hooting of an owl which was followed by shrieking of bats, howling of jackals and the wicked laughter of hyenas.

"Surely, you can hear them," he told the Princess.

"As I told you, all is quiet," said the Princess, getting rather uneasy with Ndovu's behaviour. And it continued like that until dawn. The Princess was still a virgin. A week and a month passed by in the same confusion. Ndovu lost all interest in sexual intercourse. He was scared of going to bed, believing that evil creatures of the night had been released to torture him every time he tried to make love. There were a few times he tried to make love to the Princess in the daytime, but the cries of the creatures of darkness still came to haunt him.

After a couple of months, the Princess, now looking sad, angry and confused was confronted by the Queen Mother.

"My daughter, you do not look well at all. What is the matter?" she asked.

The Princess narrated to the Queen what had been happening.

"If he does not change his behaviour, I would rather go back home!" concluded the Princess.

This was a grave matter. At once, the Queen went to the King to report what she had been told.

"It is the 'curse of the caves!' It is now affecting my children! Speak woman, speak or you will ruin this Kingdom!" shouted the King.

"I leave you to deal with your son," said the cold voice of the Queen as she left.

The King decided to visit the chief witchdoctor because the High Priest had no answer to the question on the nature of the ominous curse.

The business of witchdoctors border on the eerie and the macabre, which is conducted with the same secrecy as that of mating cats; their exposure is taboo. One seeks the assistance of this breed of men with great caution and only in extreme cases. These mediums under the guidance of nefarious powers read things which no one else can; they are able to heal or destroy from a distance. They live like snakes; loathful of public limelight. They are like the creatures of darkness, hideous, fearsome, under the control of their powerful master, Lucifer.

When a King consults a witchdoctor, the matter at hand has to be extremely grave, such as bordering on a major threat to the survival of the state. Also, the King must have exhausted all other remedies. In all other cases, consultations are with the man of God, the High Priest but at times, we must recognise that there are other forces that dictate the affairs of men, and they are equally powerful. Had it not been so, the powerful domain ruled by Satan would have long collapsed. Witchdoctors are agents of Lucifer, portenders of doom and misfortunes. It is pathetic, comical and dangerous when a King disguises himself for the purpose of a visit to the witchdoctor, in the middle of the night. But that is what Simba did.

Sneaking stealthily like a thief, he arrived on the doorstep of the abode of the evil creature, at the edge of the forest on a hill opposite the Hill of the Holy.

The hut appeared empty, but before the King knocked on the door, the door opened, it appeared as if of its own accord. The King was frightened for once, then he noted a small frail creature standing behind the door which was ajar.

"Come in Your Highness, the spirits warned me of your visit tonight," said the voice of the creature.

"Did they mention to you the nature of my consultations?" asked the King.

"Yes they did, and I have prepared well," replied the frail creature.

The witchdoctor stoked the fire and added splinters of wood. Soon there was a glow, bright enough to reveal that the witchdoctor was wearing a facial mask. He had a small round head, clean shaven and his body was covered in a white substance, either ashes or lime.

He wore nothing between the neck and the waist, revealing a thin wrinkled body with layers of skin folds sitting on one another around the stomach.

A square flap from the skin of a snake, most probably a python, fastened to a string around his waist, covered his genitals.

His hands and legs were very thin. They were covered in what looked like scales instead of skin, like you would find on the body of a creature from the wild. Nails on his fingers and toes were long, curled, yellow and dirty. Had he proclaimed himself an alien from another planet, no one could have had cause to doubt him. He lived alone.

There was no seat so the King sat on the floor. Before him was an old cow hide on which the creature spread an assortment of articles. There were calabashes, two fly whisks – black and white, pebbles, shells, the tail of a rabbit, several skulls of all sorts of creatures and finally the rotting body of a lizard. The witchdoctor took what looked like powder from one of the calabashes and sprinkled it on the fire with an incantation, "Mighty one, mighty one, grant me the powers." Immediately, there was a blinding flame which rose five feet high for a split second. Its brightness was very oppressive to the naked eye. Before the King could regain his sight, he felt the cold hand of the witchdoctor on his forehead. It was an unnerving touch.

"Fear not Your Highness, for you have come to the right place. How shall I get paid?" asked the witchdoctor.

"In whatever form you ask," said the King.

"Three fat bulls and five heifers to be left at the edge of the forest tomorrow night!" demanded the witchdoctor.

"Granted," replied the King.

"The spirits have only one thing to say," said the witchdoctor.

"Speak, speak, what is it?" asked the King anxiously.

"They tell me that all good things must come to an end and so must our mighty Kingdom. You are not to blame; you will always be remembered as the greatest Changamire of all Changamires. You brought peace, unity, prosperity and great progress to our nation. As Man lives for a number of years before he dies, so must Kingdoms. They too have a beginning and an end. Brace yourself for many worse problems to come in the Kingdom and in the royal household, for it is so written in the big book of life. You are now free to leave," prophesied the witchdoctor.

"I did not come here to be told there are problems in the Kingdom and in the royal household, I came here for solutions!" shouted the King.

"You may raise your voice as much as you want, but you cannot force the spirits to reveal more than they want to. You may leave in peace," said the witchdoctor.

"At least ask them how I can force the Queen to speak; that might save the Kingdom," pleaded the King.

"As it was in the Garden of Eden, so it is here also. The woman will speak after the damage is done. I fear you might not even be there to hear it!" said the witchdoctor.

"Then I will kill her and with her will die the curse!" the King threatened.

"It is abominable to raise your hand against the Queen. And should you bring death to her prematurely, you will suffer agonies beyond human endurance. Let the spirits have their way," said the creature.

It was a distraught and angry King who set forth back to the palace through the bushes, in a cold and chilly night, one capable of springing mischief. Nothing stirred except a giant python which crossed the King's path harmlessly, forcing him to halt for a while. He returned to the palace undetected and summoned the chief night guard. You do not incur the wrath of the King and hope to get away with it. The King commanded,

"I want the chief witchdoctor dead and burnt in his hut tonight!"

In the morning, there were only smouldering ashes and the remains of a skeleton at the very place the King had been the night before. Lucifer would exact a befitting revenge for the death of his most faithful servant in the Kingdom of Monomotapa; this you can rest assured.

The King did not feel guilty whatsoever. If the spirits wanted a fight, he was going to give them one. He swore not to standby idly and watch Monomotapa disintegrate just to please evil spirits. What did the old prediction by Herodotus say – "Monomotapa and Abyssinia shall rise to be world powers." Changamire thought he was capable of reversing the curse including the problem Ndovu was facing, in one way or another; it was just a matter of time. The witchdoctor was to blame for all the misfortunes as the chief agent of evil spirits. Now that he was gone, then surely the Kingdom was safe once more, or was it?

CHAPTER 10

A BECKONING TARGET

Livingstone had worked as the manager of Moffat's mines for a long time. Once in a while, he had been allowed to conduct the church service when Moffat was not feeling well, most times with a hangover. Even Bushmen concluded, like others had done before, that Livingstone was ill-suited for the pulpit. He could not make a missionary. But there was a cripple who thought otherwise. Since Livingstone always preached about miracles in both the Old and the New Testament, he hoped that soon, he would witness one with himself as the beneficiary. He kept asking Livingstone when God would reveal himself to the people of Bechuanaland through a miracle.

"Soon, very soon," Livingstone would respond.

"Then let it be me. Let the first miracle make me walk," he always pleaded.

In time, the cripple could recite all the miracles performed by Jesus from the healing of the lepers, the resurrection of Lazarus, the turning of water into wine and the multiplication of fish and bread to feed a multitude, and so on and so forth.

"I hope that one day, your God, Jesus or yourself will have mercy on me and make me whole. I am a true believer," the cripple would say.

If Livingstone ever came close to converting anybody to Christianity, this was it. But when the miracle did not come, the cripple denounced Livingstone, his God and the Church and reverted to his Bushman faith.

Moffat did not once complain about Livingstone's lack of missionary zeal, but questioned why Livingstone ever enrolled in a missionary school. All he cared for was the output from the mines. And for quite some while, Livingstone had performed very well, before things began to change for the worse.

With Mary, who had produced children like a rat and who believed in the joy of alcohol out of the way, Livingstone tried to entice Moffat to extend his interests to Monomotapa but he was told, "I am satisfied with what I have in Bechuanaland; if everybody was trustworthy, I could be doing even better." Moffat then moved away from Livingstone. He had dropped a hint that he knew why his business was not doing as well as had been expected. Livingstone had received a very fair warning.

One of the miners had told Livingstone,

"Towards the Caprivi Strip to the north, there are lots of diamonds. The area borders Angola and the Bakongo Kingdoms, which are the main producers of diamond and gemstones. In Caprivi Strip, natives decorate their huts with diamonds. Inside the huts, the diamonds reflect the fire, like tiny light bulbs. Outside the huts, they reflect the sun. Since they have no other use for them, they don't understand the European craze with the stones! For a blanket or a calico sheet, you can pluck the diamonds from the walls or even bring a whole hut down, and the Bushmen would not take offence. Someday, we should visit the place if you are interested."

That evening, Livingstone removed the Herodotus' *Map of Africa* and located Caprivi Strip. To his surprise, it was very close to the border with the Kingdom of Monomotapa, which lay to the east. An urge build in him, to make the trip north without further delay. Rhodes came strolling in.

"Cecil, do you know what the boss told me this afternoon? He said if everybody was trustworthy, his business would be thriving!" They looked at each other and burst into laughter.

"You know David, I believe I have amassed enough to move on. I have this dream of establishing a vast business empire stretching from Cape Town to Cairo. Don't you have a dream yourself?" asked Rhodes.

"Oh my God, Yes I have!" said Livingstone.

"What is it?" asked Rhodes.

"Top secret for now, but let me promise you one thing, I swear I will help you build the empire!" said Livingstone.

"I am not joking, but first, I have to return to England, to take a degree in politics and International Finance. I want to become a prime mover in world affairs," said Rhodes.

Livingstone looked at the young man and he smiled to himself. He had floated the idea of extending imperialism to Africa and here was the tool to execute it! He thanked his stars. What lacked was just the trigger to blast the "divine mission" into orbit, the framework, the timing and the execution of the invasion of the kingdom of Monomotapa!

"You need a lot of money to see you through college and to set up your empire.

One of the guides tells me there are more diamonds to the north of here, more than the world can dream about. I intend to go there sooner than later. I need lots of money for the actualisation of my dream and for the upkeep of Mary and the children," said Livingstone.

"Count me in! When do we leave?" asked an excited Rhodes.

"As soon as we can extricate ourselves from Moffat," answered Livingstone.

To both, time was of essence and the sooner the better; they activated their individual dreams, or, were the dreams connected?

Moffat had been aware that the quantities and quality of diamonds from his mines and from the church collection had declined. He was pained that Livingstone and Rhodes were not treating him with the reverence he had gotten used to. His patience ran out. He summoned Livingstone for a dressing down.

"David, I brought you down here to open your eyes to what the world has to offer. I engaged you in my business hoping there would be mutual benefit, for you and for me. It appears I was wrong. Since Mary left, you have grown horns. The business has gone down. Instead of concentrating on your work, you have become a tourist, visiting villages all over the place and even worse, taking Rhodes with you! What are you up to? What are you searching for?" asked an incensed Moffat.

"You may recall that when we were in England, you told me there were a hundred villages full of natives waiting to receive Christ. I went looking for them and all I have found are small pockets of Bushmen. You were not sincere when you talked of the urgent need for missionaries. How can one ever trust you?" Livingstone asked Moffat.

Moffat fixed a murderous stare at Livingstone, who continued speaking:

"As for diamonds, I doubled your output. As time goes by, we all become wiser and judging that you did not possess God-given monopoly for diamonds, I decided to plunge into the trade as well. I have been to the countryside to acquire the stones! I see no conflict of interest. As for the mines, unless you discover new ones, the old ones are exhausted." said Livingstone.

Moffat opened his mouth:

"You have called me a liar, insincere and inconsiderate. This is the thanks I get for giving you a chance to be a man. I don't know what drove me into giving you my daughter or bringing you to Bechuanaland. I should have left you to rot in Scotland!" Moffat shouted.

"Two things Dr. Moffat, first, leave Mary out of this. And second, don't ever dare imagine that you are the master of my destiny!" shouted back Livingstone.

"So, we have now entered the territory of disrespect and insults! For the sake of Mary and the children, I will overlook your unfortunate attitude if you apologise," said Moffat suing for peace.

"I will do no such thing! Don't think that I am ungrateful for all you have done for me, but equally so, I expect you to understand that I am a man with a free will. I have been a burden to you long enough; I now wish to move on," Livingstone asserted.

"You intend to move on? Back to the United Kingdom? Back to miserable Scotland? You are a fool!" said Moffat.

"I loathe the United Kingdom more that you do Dr. Moffat, but I love Scotland! I have a mission to accomplish…" countered Livingstone.

He hated himself the moment he mentioned the mission.

In Scotland, Moffat was seen as a stooge of the English, but that is why he had been given a seat in the Royal Geographical Society, the only Scot in the organisation. The Scottish Liberation Movement had labelled him a traitor. Livingstone was aware that Moffat did not give a damn about the independence of Scotland. He was too self-centred to care, entangled in his own fortunes.

"What mission?" probed Moffat.

"To continue with the work of Mungo Park," said Livingstone.

"Leave that to wayward vagabonds! These days, explorers are ten a penny, characters of dubious reputation hungry for money and fame. Did you hear of the German idiot Ludwig Krapf who has claimed to have seen snow on a mountain on the equator? Is this the band of fellows you want to join? And where will Mary and the children be when you roam the jungle?" Moffat queried.

"Mary and the children will be well provided for," said Livingstone.

"You have bought and stolen enough of my diamonds to ensure that, haven't you?" asked Moffat with a sneer.

"You need the help of a psychiatrist," said Livingstone in a cool and controlled voice.

"No, I don't, but you do," replied Moffat. To him, Livingstone appeared quite normal one minute but outrageously insane the next. He gave up trying to dissuade him from his chosen course of what he thought was self-destruction.

"You are free to leave whenever you wish," concluded Moffat.

"I will be leaving within the week heading north through the desert; for your information, Rhodes is coming with me," said Livingstone.

"I told you, you are mad! If Lobengula doesn't skin you alive, the Portuguese will. And if they don't, King Simba of Monomotapa will!" said a furious Moffat.

At the mention of Monomotapa, Livingstone felt his blood boil with anxiety. He did not wish to engage Moffat anymore. There was a beckoning on the horizon, a beckoning target waiting to be shot at.

"Goodbye Dr. Moffat!" he blurted out as he rose to leave.

Moffat just stared at him, he did not respond.

* * *

Guides familiar with the region to the north were sought. Refugees from the Ndebele Kingdom, Angola as well as Bushmen offered their services. They were running away from the dull life in Gaborone and wanted some adventure. Livingstone and Rhodes had endeared themselves to the local population so much so that all they had to do was ask and offers would come pouring in. They were not as stingy or cold as Dr. Moffat.

The guides did not care to ask for the final destination of the journey or how long they would be gone. All they knew was that they were in good and trustworthy company and the pay was good.

When Rhodes as the postmaster in Gaborone had gone to Cape Town to deliver or collect mail, he had traded gold, diamonds and gemstones for himself and for Livingstone. Provisions including tents, guns and bullets were bought as well as gifts for village chiefs and for barter trade with gold and diamonds. So, the party was carrying a lot of valuables and mixed currencies.

Finally, wagons, bulls and donkeys were acquired and harnessed for the long torturous journey to the north. When the day of departure arrived, everybody came to witness the spectacle. No white man had gone to the far reaches of the north and returned. There had been Europeans on that trail in search of King Solomon's mines and they had all perished either in the desert or at the sharp edge of the sword or spear of a warrior. People said they were sad to see Livingstone and Rhodes so vigorously marching to their deaths, in the year 1854.

As the departing party waved goodbye, there was the angry figure of Dr. Moffat sitting on a stone under an acacia tree watching. He had made up his mind that Livingstone and Rhodes were the most ungrateful wretches who had ever crossed his life. They deserved what was coming to them; death! As the caravan began to move, he let out a curse and said, "May misfortunes accost you at every turn of your journey." Satisfied that he had delivered his final word on the matter, he retreated to his house and opened a bottle of whisky, not caring whether it was in celebration or in mourning. All he knew was that he needed a drink to calm his frayed nerves.

Most eager in the caravan was Cecil Rhodes who carried note books and pens to map out the natural wealth of the areas to the north. These notes would come in handy in his plans to establish his business empire stretching from Cape Town to Cairo. He was young, ambitious, energetic, visionary and most resolute. Equally enthusiastic was Livingstone who saw Rhodes as the Trojan horse to fulfil his "divine mission".

Like all deserts, Kalahari is most unfriendly and unbearably hot, so travelling was under the moonlight.

Although the party had carried a lot of water, it was running out fast. It became a major worry for Livingstone.

A couple of weeks later, they came across a lake in the middle of the desert.

"We will halt here, recuperate and quench our thirst to the full," declared Livingstone.

"No master," said the chief guide. "This is a salt lake, we call it Lake Ngami. The water you see is thick with salt and absolutely unpalatable. We will change course to the north-west to Okavango where there is plenty of fresh water. We will also be moving away from Lobengula's Kingdom and heading towards Caprivi Strip, the No Man's land, the demilitarised zone."

The chief guide was a Bushman from Namibia, one of the most famous trackers in the region.

"How long will it take?" asked Rhodes.

"About a week or so," said the guide.

They dismounted and went to the lake to harvest salt.

"Let us take a lot; we will sell it to the people in Caprivi Strip," said the guide. Then turning to Rhodes he said, "You can walk on the solid parts of the lake. See!"

Both Rhodes and the guide started walking on the lake to the amusement of all including Livingstone who promptly joined the walk "on water".

"Do you recall that in the Bible Jesus walked on water?" asked Livingstone.

"I do, it must have been a salt lake like this one, the Dead Sea! That's it!" said Rhodes bursting into laughter.

"Don't be sacrilegious!" warned Livingstone.

"We are performing a miracle!" continued Rhodes.

"Stop it before some calamity falls upon us," said Livingstone.

"I was only trying to cheer us up," said Rhodes. They sure needed a light moment to ease their minds and aching bodies.

They loaded the salt on the wagons and moved on. Here and there, they came across settlements of Bushmen who engaged them in friendly chats. The natives were happy to receive gifts in exchange for the worthless little shiny stones called diamonds for which they had no use but to decorate their mud huts.

They came to Okavango, a huge swamp with hundreds and thousands of animals and birds of all kinds. Around the swamp were giant trees under whose shade rested more animals including lions. The party chose a safe spot and pitched tent. They were going to rest for quite some while to recuperate and to replenish their meat stock with wild game. There were plenty of fruits to pick and fish to smoke. Rhodes wrote in his diary, "Okavango is a paradise in the desert. It should be turned into a major tourist attraction."

A week later, the party was marching along the banks of Cubango River, heading towards the mountains on the other side of which was the Caprivi Strip, the No Man's land which separated Angola from Lobengula's Matebeleland and Monomotapa Kingdom.

Caprivi was serene. Unlike Bechuanaland, the vegetation was lush; the streams had clean sparkling water, in which there was plenty of fish. There was plenty of game, fruits and honey all around.

"Why on earth should land as beautiful as this belong to nobody?" asked Rhodes.

"Because it is the island of peace, it is a demilitarised zone which keeps the armies of the three Kingdoms at bay. Any attempt to occupy this strip will result in war," said the head guide.

"This is very civilised conduct. We do not have an arrangement like this in Europe to keep the Germans from the French or the French from the English." said Livingstone, almost adding, "Or the English from the Scots!"

The party rested and hunted for some days. In the interlude, Livingstone was contemplating his next move. Until now, his life had been like a picnic. Looking eastwards, he could see the ground rising higher and higher to the mountains which marked the western borders of the Kingdom of Monomotapa, his quarry. He also had a feeling that all along, a spirit had guided his steps, but then all of a sudden, the spirit had deserted him. He was on his own.

As he pondered what to do next, he recalled the story in the Bible where Moses felt abandoned by God and went to the mountain to meditate. God found him there and gave him the Ten Commandments. He also recalled how Jesus had retreated to the wilderness for forty days and forty nights to seek answers to the many questions which lingered about his mission. As He was eating locusts and honey, it was not God who came to Him, but the Devil himself, with very tantalizing offers for a little show of faith, like throwing Himself from the roof of a tall building. There are therefore critical moments in any mission where the main actor is abandoned by the gods and the spirits to chart his next move, independently. This is the defining moment and that was where Livingstone stood, on the threshold of his mission.

Whether he walked to the stream alone or to the higher grounds, Livingstone did not encounter either God or the devil to guide him. He had no clue as to how to approach the Monomotapa issue.

Early one morning, the camp woke up to find itself surrounded by Portuguese soldiers. Livingstone picked up courage and confronted the Commander of the Portuguese contingent.

"Who are you and where are you going?" asked the Commander.

"I am Dr. David Livingstone from the United Kingdom. This here is Cecil Rhodes, the deputy leader of the expedition and the rest are porters. I am an explorer, a missionary and a trader. And who are you?" he inquired of him.

"I am the Commander of the eastern brigade of the Portuguese forces in Angola. I am also a trader dealing in diamonds, gold, ivory and slaves," he said, and then they shook hands.

"May I invite you for a cup of tea?" Livingstone proposed.

"By all means, yes! It is a long time since I had a cup of good tea," replied the Commander, ordering his soldiers to ease down their guns. The senior ones remained within ear-shot while the juniors retreated.

In the background, there were noises of people crying and the metallic sound of chains from slaves. They were being taken to the coast from the Congo and other adjacent areas. On their tired shoulders rested massive elephant tusks.

As the tea was cooking, the Commander engaged Livingstone thus:

"No Englishman has ever come this far. You are not a Protestant are you?" asked the Commander.

"Indeed, I am; but I am a Scot, not an Englishman," said Livingstone.

"Damn! Oh, I am sorry, about the issue of religion, I mean. We are all good Christians, all of us, but it was your King who rebelled against the Pope, not so?" said the Commander.

"That is true, but the Scots now have their own church, the Presbyterian Church of Scotland. We are not members of the Church of the English, the Anglican Church," said Livingstone as Rhodes looked on speculating where the conversation was heading to.

"We hate the English, they took India from us. All the hard work of Vasco da Gama came to nothing. They left for us a small enclave called Goa, as small as Caprivi Strip and you know what, it is landlocked with no right of passage to the outside world! The English are a crazy lot!" said the Commander, and it seemed to please Livingstone while it sent blushes on the face of Cecil Rhodes.

"If they ever try to encroach on any of our territories again, it will be war, and all the Roman Catholics in the world, including the Irish will be fighting on our side!" declared the Portuguese Commander.

Livingstone was praying within himself that God should grant this war quickly as part of his "divine mission". He kept quiet nodding his head, seemingly in agreement.

"Let's change the subject. And what are you exploring?" asked the Commander.

"The source of the River Nile," stated Livingstone.

"Are you out of your mind? Do you know how far you are from Egypt?" asked the Commander.

"You know, everybody from the days of the Greeks and the Romans tried to find the source of the Nile from Cairo and they all failed. That is why I have decided to start from the south and march northwards! The river must surely flow northwards from somewhere!" Livingstone explained.

"Hear him! Hear him! He will follow each and every river on this continent until he finds the one which flows towards Cairo! Sorry to tell you Mr. Scotsman or Englishman or whatever, I have never met a greater idiot than yourself!" said the Commander gleefully.

"You may think so, but I will prove you wrong with time. But tell me; how far are we from Cairo? I have walked many thousands of miles from Cape Town. I had thought by now, I would be reaching the journey's end, where are we?" asked Livingstone, laughing in the inside. The Portuguese soldiers were laughing uncontrollably with tears streaming down their cheeks. The question sounded ridiculous, most comical.

"Holy Moses, where are we?" asked the Commander still laughing as he continued:

"We are in the No Man's land in Southern Africa! You have not even covered a quarter of the journey! I can see why the English could never find the route to India! Good God Almighty, where are we?" And the party continued laughing.

"And you call yourself and explorer? Don't you have a map or a compass?" asked the Commander.

"No." said Livingstone with the mirth bordering on hysteria.

"But tell me," began the Commander in a very serious tone. "If you are a mad man who I believe you are, why do you have such an elaborate caravan? Something does not add up. Who are you?" He was now looking at Livingstone sternly.

"I am what I told you I am, no more, no less. I carry with me the blessings of Queen Victoria and her wishes for the spread of civilisation, Christianity and commerce in this Dark Continent. The Nile is important for this noble mission," Livingstone affirmed.

"Bullshit! Yours is a hopeless case; I have a mind to kill you and take your porters for slaves. What do you say to that?" threatened the Commander.

"Well, this here is Cecil Rhodes, who carries blue blood in his veins. He is a cousin to Queen Victoria. If anything should happen to him, be prepared for war with England," asserted Livingstone in a very serious tone.

The Commander thought for a while and then said, "I was only teasing you. Wars are bad things. You also declared yourself a trader. What do you buy or sell?" asked the Commander.

"I buy gold, diamonds and gemstones," said Livingstone.

"Do you have money?" asked the Commander.

"It depends," replied Livingstone.

"I have plenty of diamonds, gold and gemstones. You know, I had a hunch from the moment I saw you that something good would come out of our encounter. That is why I did not shoot you!" the Commander said with a warm smile on his face.

A soldier with a weighty pouch was summoned. The Commander poured the contents out of the bag on a spread cowhide, revealing glittering diamonds, gold and an assortment of gemstones. There was one diamond which was bigger than anything the world had ever seen. Holding it in his hand, the Commander said,

"Let's do business."

Livingstone and Rhodes bought all the pieces.

"We prefer doing business with you because when we arrive in Luanda, the big boys will snatch the fortune in the name of the crown. We get nothing. One day, after we defeat Queen Nzinga, we will settle in Angola as miners, ranchers, farmers growing coffee, and so forth. We will need capital. Then we will conquer Monomotapa and extend our empire to Sofala. You must return to do business with me wherever you find me!" said a very happy Commander.

"Sure, sure," said a most alarmed Livingstone.

"Let us celebrate," suggested the Commander. A big eland was killed and roasted.

As the parties ate and drank whisky, Livingstone asked for permission to inspect the slaves.

"You can buy as many as you want," the Commander assured Livingstone.

Indeed Livingstone bought two slave boys on whom he took pity. Their names were Chuma and Sutsi. He ordered them unchained.

"Englishman, I plead with you! Please, go home. Don't go north as the journey will kill you. You can't come with us to the west as I will not let you. Your best bet is to go back south or with a lot of luck, eastwards to Sofala through the Kingdom of Monomotapa. Good luck and may God bless your life abundantly."

The Portuguese left with their cargo of slaves and ivory, heading west.

Livingstone and his party headed east, towards the Kingdom of Monomotapa. It was now or never.

That evening, he recorded in his diary that he had come to the border with Angola and was now heading to Sofala through Monomotapa – the first white man to do so. If he was accomplishing nothing, at least he was gaining experience as an explorer. But most gratifying, over the mountains to the east, very near, was the Kingdom of Monomotapa, a beckoning target. The "divine mission" was truly on course.

CHAPTER 11

THE WALLS WON'T FALL

The journey out of Caprivi Strip, the No Man's land, was getting increasingly tougher as the party climbed to higher grounds. While the donkeys were at ease with the terrain, the bulls were not; slowing down the pace considerably.

Early on the morning of the third day, the party was surrounded by Monomotapa warriors who had been trailing the Portuguese brigade from the moment it entered the Caprivi Strip. They had witnessed the goings-on between Livingstone's team and the Portuguese from a vantage point on higher grounds. The warriors were particularly surprised to see two slave boys, Chuma and Sutsi, surrendered to Livingstone who unchained them and gave them food. If he was a slave trader, then he was of a kind they had never seen. Slave traders chained and flogged their captives.

Surprised and outnumbered, Livingstone told his party not to touch their guns. The head of the warriors, a majestic giant of a man with a big scar on his bare chest approached Livingstone.

"Your team is heading in the wrong direction. You are heading east out of the No Man's land towards the Monomotapa border. I suggest you turn back," he said.

"We are heading in the right direction. I am an Englishman and I carry a message of goodwill for the Changamire," lied Livingstone.

"The Changamire does not entertain foreigners," said the big warrior.

"This time he will. We want you to carry a message to him, that we are as friendly as the Abyssinians, Chinese and Indians and we hate the Portuguese. You will take to him gifts which will prove our high esteem, admiration and respect for his statesmanship in this land and beyond." The warrior consulted his colleagues before addressing Livingstone again.

"Who are these two boys and what do they mean to you?" he asked, pointing at Chuma and Sutsi.

"These boys were captured as slaves by the Portuguese. I took pity on them and bought them. They are now free," said Livingstone.

"You speak the truth white man. Indeed, we witnessed the transaction, though you did not know we were around. Don't you deal with slave trade?" asked the head warrior.

"I loathe it! The Queen's government is working hard towards its abolition. Why should human beings treat their fellow human beings like commodities for sale? It is wrong, immoral and inhuman," said Livingstone.

"I can see you have a kind heart like the Changamire! He hates slave traders. Bring the gifts, I will send a word to him."

Livingstone offloaded sheets of cloths, blankets, cowrie shells, a felt hat and salt from Lake Ngami.

"Take these to the Changamire and tell him I will bring more with me," said Livingstone.

A party of warriors left with the gifts while Livingstone's party was detained to await the answer from the capital.

It would be days before the warriors returned. In the meantime, Livingstone and his party were engaging the warriors in uneasy, but friendly conversations.

"I have heard much about your great kingdom," Livingstone was saying.

"Everybody in the world knows about our mighty kingdom. We are the greatest kingdom on earth – rich, powerful and happy," said the head warrior in a matter of fact way.

"This is why Queen Victoria wants to establish good relations with the Changamire. We have a lot to benefit from each other, for the mutual benefit of our peoples," said Livingstone.

"How big is your Kingdom and how far is it from here?" asked the head warrior.

"It is as far as India but nearer than China. It is made up of two islands but make no mistake, it is very powerful. We call it the United Kingdom," said Livingstone with pride.

"I see. And why does the Queen want to befriend Changamire. Doesn't she know that he is old and has enough wives?" Livingstone and Rhodes laughed heartily.

"It is not that she is looking for a husband, no! What she wants is the establishment of bilateral relations, exchange of goods and ideas you see, that sort of thing. This is the message I carry," Livingstone clarified.

"I see," said the warrior who did not fathom Livingstone's jargon. In as far as Monomotapa was concerned; there were a few countries which were worth befriending. They were China, India, Benin and Abyssinia, full stop. Anyone else was to be ignored or fought.

"Do you have good medicine men in your country?" asked the warrior.

"Of course, the best in the world, I am a doctor myself. I can treat very many diseases," said Livingstone.

"Can you deal with a curse?" asked the warrior.

"It depends, why?" Livingstone asked.

"There is a curse haunting our Kingdom. It came from the caves and it is ravaging the Changamire, the royal household and even threatening the Kingdom. Only the Queen knows the nature of the curse, but she will not reveal it. Can you deal with a situation like that one?" asked the big warrior.

"Wait. Let me consult with my God and I will give you an answer," replied Livingstone.

Livingstone called the porters and asked them if they knew about the curse. A man who had arrived in Bechuanaland from Angola volunteered some information:

"It appears that after the Queen gave birth to twins, both boys, something went wrong with her head. Most worrisome is that between the twins, the elder one, the heir to the throne is an idiot while his younger brother is brilliant and fit to be king. They say it all went wrong in the caves, but nobody knows what happened."

Livingstone took Rhodes aside and said,

"We have to take advantage of this situation. We need all the information we can lay our hands on before we meet the King." It was so agreed and they set about befriending the warriors and extracting as much information as they could on the situation in the Kingdom. By the time the warriors returned from the capital, both men knew as much as they needed to know. They had become instant consultants with answers and solutions to the problems in Monomotapa. This would be their point of entry into the affairs of the Kingdom. All that Livingstone prayed for was a chance to talk to the King, the great Changamire.

The warriors from the capital returned with their report.

"We have told the King that you have a special message from your Queen. We gave him the gifts. We told him you hate the Portuguese and that you abhor slave trade and that you rescued two young boys from the slave traders. He says you come to the capital," reported the mid-rank warrior who had carried Livingstone's message and gifts to King Simba.

David Livingstone was elated and sad at the same time. Here were happy and kind people who were at the very core of his "divine mission". For his mission to succeed they had to be destroyed and yet this had to happen for the sake of Scotland. He wondered how divinity worked and why some had to perish for others to live. Then he remembered what Darwin had said that the game was known as survival of the fittest by natural selection. He also recalled how God performed many miracles to save his chosen people, the Israelites. Didn't he drown the whole army of Misri in the Red Sea to save them? Now, the Scots were the chosen people and Monomotapa had to go, but at the cruel hands of the English, in the name of the British Empire.

Livingstone turned to Rhodes, "The journey of your business empire from Cape Town to Cairo has just begun!" Rhodes looked at him and smiled. He wasn't sure how the trip to Monomotapa was going to help him in his venture. However, it would accord him the opportunity to assess the natural wealth in the area.

They came to the top of the hill and lo and behold, snaking for miles in as far as the eye could see was the mighty Zambezi River. Towards the bottom of the hill, there was a huge cloud of vapour rising accompanied by thunderous noise. It was most baffling.

"What is that sound and why is there so much smoke over there?" asked Livingstone.

"That is Mosi-O-Tunya, the great falls, the home of the spirits." answered a warrior.

As the party descended the hill, the sound from the falls became louder and louder and then they were engulfed in mist.

"I have to see the Mosi-O-Tunya," said Livingstone.

"No problem," said the Commander of the warriors.

Soon, they were standing at the falls, which stretched for over four hundred metres in length, but the depth of the fall was unfathomable.

Livingstone turned to Rhodes and said, "The world has no equal to this majesty, not the Niagara Falls, the Pyramids of Egypt, the White Cliffs of Dover or the Hanging Gardens of Babylon. This is the greatest of all wonders in the world."

"I couldn't agree with you more," said Rhodes who had taken out his diary and was sketching the great falls.

"I name this wonder, Victoria Falls," said Livingstone.

"Why?" asked Rhodes.

"Because beautiful places deserve beautiful names; Mosi-O-Tunya sounds primitive!"

Rhodes did not say a word. He would write a most captivating report and present it to the Royal Geographical Society which fed the British Government with reports on the suitability of faraway lands for colonisation due to expected profitability. For example, he would inform that the Zambezi Valley could grow so much cotton, that it would not only satisfy the demand in Lancashire and other textile towns. "In fact", he would add, "it would outstrip the cotton production in America." This would be mouth-watering!

True, the land which the Zambezi River traversed was magnificent. The ground rose from the river valley to high hills with expanses of fertile plateaus where the population mainly lived and cultivated. In between were thick forests with hardwood, including teak, mahogany, ebony, podo and other types of trees. Livingstone estimated that one could become a billionaire in a relatively very short time exporting timber to Europe to build cathedrals, castles and ships.

The Shire Highlands were so lush unlike the land in Scotland. Here one could grow wheat, corn, fruits and also keep dairy herds in their thousands without too much of an effort.

There was no winter to bother about. He could see in his mind droves of Englishmen rushing to occupy the land and his dream coming closer to fruition.

He would tell the English about gold, copper, diamonds and silver to be mined in abundance with very minimal capital outlay. "Anybody and everybody who ventures into Africa will be a millionaire in the shortest period of time. Huge profits and big fortunes are guaranteed for those with a modicum spirit of adventure."

He was sure the words "huge profits" and "big fortunes" would be the magnets to entice and trap the English.

To camouflage his real intentions, his report would go under the innocuous title, *Missionary Travels in Africa*. Innocent sounding heading, but potent enough in content to send thousands of Englishmen, soldiers and civilians alike to their graves, in the hands of the mighty warriors of Monomotapa.

He thanked God for giving him wisdom to deceive with such simplicity, for the freedom of Scotland. As I watched, I almost shouted, "Leave God out of this!"

They were climbing another hill, truly exhausted. When they came to the top, another great surprise awaited them. In the distance, they beheld what looked like the most magnificent city on earth, surrounded by a stone wall.

"That is Matapa, the capital city of Monomotapa," announced the Commander of the warriors, proudly.

Livingstone and Rhodes stood still, spellbound. In their imagination, they had pictured Matapa as a huge village with mud huts. How on earth a capital so removed from European civilisation could rival European cities in beauty, architecture and masonry was beyond their comprehension. Then it dawned on them, were the Pyramids of Egypt not built by black people? The mysteries of the Dark Continent were a myriad, as secretive as the source of the Nile.

In the lowlands below the city were huge farms with varieties of crops. There were also thousands of animals grazing in the distance, both domestic and wild, side by side in harmony.

The city was surrounded by a long stone wall, much like the Great Wall of China. Livingstone noted that the wall enclosed not one hill but several. The capital was therefore built on these hills, with a huge palace standing on the highest of them. David Livingstone was lost for words. Was this city built by Africans or did other people build it, maybe aliens from outer space for indeed its layout, design and architecture were out of this world.

"This is the hand of God, not of man. I am tempted to believe we are entering the Garden of Eden!" Rhodes whispered to Livingstone.

"Don't be ridiculous. The King must have contracted Chinese or Indians to build the city. Africans are not capable of achieving such a feat," declared Livingstone.

"They built the Pyramids of Egypt though," said Rhodes.

"Who told you? The Pyramids were built by aliens. Africa has always been a backward and dark continent," retorted Livingstone.

"The Dark Continent! That is a good title for our journey's report," said Rhodes.

"Those are my words not yours," said Livingstone.

"I was only suggesting," said Rhodes perceiving what appeared to be an irritation from Livingstone's tone of voice. He decided not to talk anymore, unless talked to.

There they stood, inside the walls of the great and magnificent city of Matapa, the capital city of Monomotapa. Livingstone was transfixed and indeed so were all members of his party.

Livingstone was speaking to himself saying, "I am spellbound by the beauty, majesty and size of this city. Who could have ever thought of finding such ingenuity in the heartland of Africa! The architects, builders and craftsmen who built this city rival those of India, China and Europe; and they are more refined! These are civilised people. I shudder to think what we have to offer them if anything at all!" As he paused, the answer came to him, "What we have to offer them is death, destruction, dehumanisation and in a word, chaos and misery." It was as if the devil himself had spoken to him, like God used to speak to Moses!

"Who am I serving?" he asked himself surreptitiously.

"The King is waiting, we have to move faster," the Commander beckoned Livingstone.

They entered the city, moving along the broadest boulevard of all, which had trees and very well-trimmed hedges of flowers. All the hills were connected by huge roads. A rickshaw could have easily turned around on any of them.

Word had gone round that the King was to receive visitors and throngs of people paraded both sides of the road leading to the palace. They cheered and waved as the party advanced. They were a happy and friendly people, well fed and clothed.

Upon arrival at the palace yard, the party was surprised to find there were no outer gates. They came to the entrance to the King's palace; a huge door made of ebony and oak was swung open. There, right in the centre of the yard under a tree sat the stately figure of King Simba with members of the Council of the Wise. King Simba did not stand.

Although age was catching up with him, he was looking well and healthy, but he had deep creases on his forehead and looked tired. The curse had drained the shine from his face, mainly for lack of sleep and appetite. As he sat, he towered over the others because, by any standards, he was a giant of a man. In his heydays, he was a champion wrestler, the strongest and toughest warrior, but still gentle and kind. As King, his people regarded him as a gift from God. He had done so much to bring justice, peace and prosperity to the Kingdom.

However, together with the curse, old battle wounds, knocks and scars were sapping his agility and gaiety. But he was still a very imposing figure, with burning searching eyes which rarely blinked. He fixed a searching steady gaze on Livingstone as he walked towards him, like he had always assessed his opponents in both sports and battle. The tall thin figure in jungle uniform, a thick brown belt and an interesting looking hat was a puzzle to the King. Having shunned foreigners all his life, this was an interesting exposure.

When Livingstone came to the King, he stopped about five paces away and bowed. To the King, it was a pleasing gesture because the foreigner recognised his stature and respected his authority. He motioned to Livingstone to advance and offered his hand for a handshake. Stools were provided for Livingstone and Rhodes while the rest of Livingstone's party were taken to another part of the compound.

"Where you come from, is there no food?" the King asked Livingstone, who was taken by surprise.

"There is food Your Majesty," he replied.

"Then I assume you don't have much of an appetite! In this country, we do not trust thin people because they spend too much of their time scheming mischief. That is why they never have time to eat! Welcome to Monomotapa. Who are you and what do you want here?" he asked.

"My name is David Livingstone, a Scotsman, a British Citizen, an explorer, a missionary and a trader. With me here is Cecil Rhodes, my deputy," said Livingstone.

"I am Simba the Changamire, King of the Kingdom of Monomotapa."

"I am greatly honoured to meet you, Your Majesty, and we are grateful for the warm reception and wonderful hospitality accorded to us. I bring Your Majesty warm greetings and gifts from Queen Victoria of England," said Livingstone.

"How is she? I have heard much about Queen Victoria from Emperor Theodore of Abyssinia. He wants to marry her, " said King Simba.

"No! No! No! Not Queen Victoria! May be another Queen elsewhere," said Livingstone.

"The trouble with you common people is that you do not know the secrets which royal families share across the world. As I have told you, King Theodore has proposed marriage to Queen Victoria of England. Didn't Solomon propose marriage to the Queen of Sheba; and Julius Caesar to Cleopatra? Anyway, that is neither here nor there. As I said before, welcome to Monomotapa."

Livingstone and Rhodes were shocked that King Simba, living in the heart of dark Africa knew about the Queen of Sheba, King Solomon, Julius Caesar and Cleopatra! They would pursue the matter in the course of time. But certainly, Simba was not an ignorant man as they had supposed. Livingstone, with trembling hands unwrapped the gifts; they included blankets, towels, tinklets, cowrie shells and an assortment of jewellery.

With no much enthusiasm, the King said, "Thank you for your generosity. I wish you had added a hat and a belt like the one you are wearing!" he said as he smiled.

"Next time, I will bring you both items," said Livingstone

"Now tell me why you are here," said the King in a serious tone.

"First, I bring you wishes for a long and healthy life from Queen Victoria. Second, I bring you the good news of the gospel. Third, I come to explore the possibility of trade between our two nations." said Livingstone.

"When you told me you were an explorer, I thought you were like the Portuguese who are excited to find rivers and mountains. Our history says, there once came a Greek by the name Herodotus who drew mountains and rivers on paper, and that was all he was interested in. Strange people these, very strange people," said the King.

"Oh, you know about Herodotus? He drew the first map of the world, *Mappo Mundo* and your Kingdom is in his map! I am also an explorer like Herodotus, but my quest is very simple, to find the source of the River Nile!" said Livingstone.

The King fixed a gaze at Livingstone who was wearing a broad and friendly smile. With his unkempt beard and pronounced jaw, he looked like an ancient prophet, or a saint like those he had seen in the picture books which Emperor Theodore had read to him during his last visit to Monomotapa. He had learnt that most prophets ended in one tragedy or another. One called Moses had gone to the mountains and disappeared without trace. He must have been an explorer, King Simba concluded. That Livingstone would exhibit the same madness was beyond his comprehension. Anyway, a man who travels thousands of miles to bring blankets, a message from a woman and good news of the gospel must be mad or suicidal.

"When you return to your Kingdom, tell the Queen that friendship is earned not granted on the basis of a few gifts. But should she marry my best friend Emperor Theodore, then by extension, she will be a good friend of mine too. About trade, we trade in all things except slaves, and I am told you also abhor the trade. On the gospel, I have heard much from Emperor Theodore about God's chosen people and their prophets. I have told him to his face that such a God who selects one tribe upon whom he confers all kinds of favours at the expense of everyone else is not my God. My God is *Mwari* and he is kind and merciful to all without discrimination. On the search for the source of the Nile, you will have to look elsewhere as we do not have such a river in our Kingdom," said the King with finality.

"The river flows northwards to Misri," said Livingstone.

"If it is that far north, you should seek help from Emperor Theodore. All our rivers flow either to the east like the Zambezi or to the west like the Cubango and the Congo. Not a single river flows northwards or southwards. Well, you must be very tired," said the King.

"Yes, we are," replied Livingstone.

"One more thing, I was told you are a doctor with a wide knowledge of many diseases. You will be escorted to your quarters, freshen up and join me for a private dinner this evening," said the King.

Livingstone's party was escorted to their quarters. The King retired to the interior of the palace, to await his important meeting with the strange man called Livingstone, who looked like a prophet or a saint from some far away land. He knew he could trust him. He had a glimmer of hope that this alien might just be the man to solve the riddle of the curse. He was a godsend, he concluded.

Livingstone, once refreshed, sat on his bed and prayed to God for forgiveness in advance, because he was not going to relent on his strategy for the independence of Scotland however kind the people of Monomotapa were. It was going to be a hard task for the British to conquer the Kingdom because it was powerful and united. Unlike in Jericho where Joshua and his troops ran around the walls of the city and the walls came tumbling down, here, the walls won't fall as they were built with granite stones, with a very firm foundation by a resolute people.

He smiled to himself and said, "When the English are in the snare, they will face the wrath of King Simba and his people and they will be counting their dead in the thousands and then Scotland will be free!"

He was ready for the meeting with King Simba.

CHAPTER 12

MISPLACED TRUST

When Livingstone was escorted to the palace that evening, he found the King waiting in his private chamber. Dressed in his royal regalia, the King looked wonderful and powerful.

"Sit down doctor, sit down. First we talk and then we eat," said the King.

"I am honoured Your Majesty," said Livingstone.

"Do you think Queen Victoria will consider the proposal for marriage by Emperor Theodore favourably?" asked the King. Once again, the question caught Livingstone off guard.

"I don't think so," he said bluntly.

"It has taken long for her to make up her mind and Theodore is impatient. The British Ambassador in Addis Ababa Mr. Cameron seems very uneasy about the issue. If the Queen takes much longer, Theodore will lock up Mr. Cameron, and then she will be forced to reply," said the King.

"Frankly, if such a proposal has been made, the Queen will regard it as an insult," said Livingstone.

"Why?" asked a surprised Simba.

"Because they are not compatible or equals. If Theodore had been, say the Emperor of Germany, maybe she might have given it a thought," said Livingstone.

"What is the difference between the Emperor of Abyssinia and the Emperor of Germany? asked the King.

"Well, besides the fact that one is white, and one is black, Abyssinia does not appear anywhere on the English radar. It is only a small empire." said Livingstone.

"In other words, it is like trying to mate a giraffe and a hedgehog, is that what you mean? asked the King.

"Something like that." replied Livingstone.

"Poor Theodore, it will break his heart." said the King.

Livingstone thought the King was trying to trap him, but he could not tell how. He had spoken his mind very frankly.

"Livingstone, I called you here not to discuss Queen Victoria and Theodore, but to seek your help over a very grave matter. When I was told you are a doctor I thought you could help me," said the King.

"To the best of my ability, I will do my very best," said Livingstone.

"Monomotapa is in trouble. I have two sons, Ndovu and Taiwo. They were born twins. Ndovu who will succeed me is an idiot, but he was born first, so he is my heir. Taiwo on the other hand exhibits all the qualities of a great leader, but being second born, he cannot accede to the throne. Since they were born, the Queen has behaved in a most queer manner. It all adds up to the general suspicion that something went very wrong in the Royal Cave at birth. I have thought of killing Ndovu to give Taiwo the opportunity to rule Monomotapa after me, but I fear the wrath of the gods and the spirits who govern our lives. I need your help," the King pleaded.

"I am sure I can find a solution to the problem all in good time," said a beaming Livingstone.

"Take all the time you want, but remember, I am an old man; I do not have forever for a lifetime," said the King.

They looked at each other in the eye and each was satisfied that they had established bonds of trust, albeit for different reasons.

"You know, I have not slept well for a very long time and I will be most grateful if you can help me," said the King.

"I will help you in very many ways." With that, Livingstone opened his first aid kit and held two sleeping pills in his open palm. He told the King,

"After dinner, take these two magic tablets before you go to bed. In the morning, you will tell me how the night was." He handed the tablets to the King who placed them in an inner pocket of his robe.

"Take them with water," he instructed the King.

"What are they supposed to do?" asked the King.

"They will keep bad thoughts away and guard you from the evil spirits who disturb your sleep," said a beaming Livingstone.

"These two little things can fight evil spirits? Let's go for dinner, I need to go to bed early today!" said the King.

So they walked to the banquet hall and found people seated, waiting for dinner in honour of the special guests of the King from faraway lands where people were of a different colour, pale-faced and thin. For all they cared, they could have been aliens but then, they looked like the Portuguese.

When the King and Livingstone sat at the table, one thing was clear to all, there was warmth of friendship between them. They had struck a chord with acceptable resonance. They both wore broad grins and were relaxed. The people had not seen the King so happy in as many years. The atmosphere was electrifying with dancers on the floor and the musicians rendering catchy popular tunes.

Spread on the tables was an array of foods; the display and the smells whetted their appetite. There was meat galore, beef, goat, ram and eland, ostrich, chicken and fish. To go with it were arrow roots, cassava, mashed bananas, sadza and boiled maize. At the end of the table were many kinds of fruits. They ate to their fill in this wonderful atmosphere. Livingstone and Rhodes complimented the King and his people for laying before them the most delicious and sumptuous dinner they had ever had. They were genuine in their compliments.

"What is the favourite dish in England for the royal family?" the King asked.

"Fish and chips," replied Rhodes with a chuckle.

Livingstone was about to say "haggis" but he held back.

"What does it look like?" asked the King.

"It is just fish and fried potatoes," responded Livingstone.

"In that case, Queen Victoria would do well to marry Emperor Theodore, and then she can eat like a real Queen!" said the King. Neither Livingstone nor Rhodes made a comment.

The King made a speech in which he welcomed the visitors and gave them the freedom to mingle with his people freely throughout the full breadth and length of the Kingdom. Livingstone in response praised the King and his people for the warm welcome and wonderful hospitality accorded to them. He added that the great Kingdom of Monomotapa was admired all over the world and that Changamire, the just and magnanimous leader, was recognised as one of the greatest statesmen in the world. He was wildly cheered.

The King retired to bed early, to put to test the magic of the small pills which warded off evil spirits and brought soothing sleep unperturbed.

Livingstone and Rhodes mingled freely with the top brass in the Kingdom. Most important, they got the opportunity to engage Ndovu and Taiwo. In the end, they could not agree more with the King's assessment that Ndovu was an imbecile while Taiwo was one of the sharpest brains they had ever met, with the gaiety, stature and pride of a true prince, fit to rule an empire.

As they retired, Livingstone turned to Rhodes and said, "So far so good."

Rhodes replied, "For God and my country."

"For God and my country," echoed back Livingstone, but the reference to country was as different as it could be. One was thinking of England while the other was thinking of Scotland.

The next morning, the King sent for Livingstone. When he arrived, he found the King in a very jovial mood.

"Dr. Livingstone, your magic works! Hardly had I covered myself when sleep overtook me! I slept like the dead until morning without dreaming; no evil spirits bothered me. You are the greatest doctor on earth!" said the King.

"I am glad to be of help," said Livingstone.

"Now about the curse, what did you find from your gods and spirits?" the King asked anxiously.

"Like you, we have only one God and we reach Him through his son Jesus Christ and the Holy Spirit," said Livingstone.

"Go on, what did they reveal to you?" asked the King.

Livingstone remembered the conversation between Moffat and Rudyard Kipling in London. They had agreed that Africans are like children and you could manipulate them easily. He put it to test, with the great Changamire.

"Great one, there is a problem. They told me that they only intercede and help believers of which you are not. Like Emperor Theodore, you have to accept Jesus Christ as your personal Saviour and the rest will be easy," said Livingstone.

"Nonsense! I thought your gods were benevolent, kind and non-discriminatory, unlike those of the Portuguese and the Arabs who condone slave trade and the butchery of Africans," said the King, a bit agitated.

"It is so, Great Changamire, but every regime, whether religious or secular has its rules. These are the conditions of my God," said Livingstone.

"Ehe!" interjected the King.

"He is the Living God who commands the affairs of all things from Heaven," said Livingstone.

"Why do you call Him the Living God? Are there gods who are not living?" asked the King.

"Yes, there are those who worship idols as gods," said Livingstone.

"Go on," said the King.

"Jesus, His son, was born of a virgin called Mary," said Livingstone.

"No! No! No! Virgins do not give birth. Just now you told me He is the son of God, the Father, and the Mother was Mary. That ends the nonsense of born of a virgin," said the King.

"Mary was a virgin when she gave birth to Jesus. She was not conceived in the earthly way," said Livingstone.

"You are just like Theodore. You tell juicy stories which are good for little children, but I am not a child," said the King who was enjoying the exchange like he had enjoyed the same with Theodore some while back.

"Mary was conceived by the Holy Spirit," said Livingstone.

"That is even worse! God lays claim to a child conceived by someone else! The Holy Spirit made a cuckold of your Living God!" said the King dying with laughter.

"No! No! No! The Holy Spirit and God are one," said Livingstone.

"There you go again, even more confused. You see, if there was a tussle between God and the Holy Spirit about which of them impregnated Mary, all they had to do was ask her and the matter of who was the father of Jesus would have been settled! I hope this is not the way you are going to solve the problem of the curse. I want a straight answer and not a maze of things and stories which will not help anybody. By the way, rest assured that I was not cuckolded, so the issue of who my wife, the mother of the twins, conceived with, does not arise," the King said in an emphatic matter-of-fact tone.

"Mary was the wife of Joseph, a carpenter," continued Livingstone as the King fell into a fit of uncontrollable laughter.

"Livingstone, you are a comedian. Within the short period we have been sitting here, you have given Mary three husbands: two gods and a carpenter. Please let's stop there! And you say she was the mother of your Saviour?" asked the King.

When Livingstone opened his mouth to speak, the King told him:

"Relax David, don't get all muddled up. I will hear the story to the end. I hope it will be as exciting as the one I heard from Theodore about another character called Moses who cut the water of the Red Sea into two halves using a walking stick! Moses should come and drown the Portuguese in the Cubango River!" The King burst into laughter, tears rolling down his old cheeks.

"I am dumbfounded by your knowledge of the Bible! I did not know that Christianity had penetrated this far!" said Livingstone trying another approach.

"Abyssinia and Monomotapa have been friends for ages. We have often exchanged state visits. Theodore was here some time ago. It is my turn to reciprocate, but the attack by the Donyiros and the curse have put paid to the plans I had. It is through contact with the Abyssinians that we have learnt much about your God. Of course we do not share their beliefs. They believe they are a chosen lot through the Union between King Solomon and the Queen of Sheba.

"What intrigues me most is the fact that the Saviour in their religion, the one you call Christianity, was crucified when his abracadabra or miracles failed to save the Jews from the Romans. He turned water into wine and multiplied fish and chips to feed thousands and yet he could not save his own life.

"I asked Theodore whether a magician can be a Saviour and he said yes. I am not surprised he is now proposing marriage to Queen Victoria. You see, when you turn from your traditional beliefs and the spirits of your ancestors; you become the laughing stock of the world. You become weak and vulnerable. That is why for Monomotapa, we will always worship our God, *Mwari*, though of late, his messengers, the lesser gods and spirits have deserted us. This is the reason why I cannot get answers to the nagging questions in this Kingdom. What have I done to deserve this punishment?" asked the King.

"As I told Your Majesty, I can only help if you embrace the Christian faith." said Livingstone.

"You will have to come with a more convincing story. All the characters in your religion are phony and weak. We worship heroes not failures. I will see you later," said the King.

Livingstone was left with a feeling that as weak as Simba was, the religious card held no promise. He had to try another route to win Simba's heart. The sleeping pill had brought them together as friends but it was not enough. He went to consult with Rhodes on a new approach.

Livingstone and Rhodes spent the day visiting different parts of the capital. When they came to the barracks of the warriors, they were amazed to see how many well-armed and well-fed warriors protected the capital. The Commander boasted that no power on earth could break the defences of Matapa as the archers alone were capable of unleashing devastating blows from the walls surrounding the capital.

"Beyond the capital, we have very many battalions of excellent warriors. Monomotapa is impregnable, a lesson the Donyiros learnt too late," said the Commander. This was not an idle boast.

That evening, Livingstone had another meeting with the King.

"Have you found a solution to my problem?" the King asked.

"But Your Majesty, I gave you the conditions of my God and our Saviour Jesus Christ. Are you ready to embrace the faith?" asked Livingstone.

In as much as Livingstone and Rhodes had agonised on ways to sway the King, they had come up with no answer. Christianity, commerce and civilisation were sounding hollow, given that the Kingdom was rich, politically stable and spiritually strong.

The silence which ensued was broken by the King, "If we keep on pursuing one problem, we will lose sight of the other dangers surrounding us. The issue of my succession will come after I am dead, isn't it?"

"Indeed it will, but why bring up the matter of death now? You still have a long life to live," said Livingstone.

"I should worry about protecting the Kingdom when I am still King. The Kingdom will take care of itself when I am gone, isn't it?" repeated the King.

"Yes it will, but Your Majesty, I don't understand where this discussion is heading to," said Livingstone.

"You said Queen Victoria is a great ruler?" inquired the King.

"Indeed, she is. Britain is a powerful country," said Livingstone.

"How many battles has she won?" asked the King.

"We have not lost a single war. We have defeated the Spanish, the Portuguese and the French in past battles," said a smiling Livingstone.

"Is it true that your Kingdom was driven out of America by a rag-tag army of cowboys? Theodore told me that your Queen is still smarting from that defeat." said the King amused.

"It is true that the Americans won the war of independence. They are a strong breed of people, a cocktail of the worst lot from all over the world; and they love to kill, so we left them alone," said Livingstone.

"Do you have guns and cannons?" asked the King.

"Yes, we have them Your Majesty. All types of guns, pistols, rifles and cannons. Why do you ask?" asked Livingstone.

"When the emissaries of Emperor Theodore came to warn me about the impending attack by the Donyiro Sultanate, they also brought to me another message. That I must modernise the armed forces of Monomotapa, in view of the imminent threat from European powers that have evil schemes on Africa, worse that slave trade."

David Livingstone looked down. He had no wish to make eye contact with the King on this matter.

"Emperor Theodore is alarmist and as you pointed out yourself, he seems to be involved in many miscalculations or should I say hallucinations," said Livingstone trying to pour cold water on the subject of European threats to Africa.

"I could have agreed with you if it was not for the behaviour of the Portuguese in Angola and the Boers in South Africa. There is growing credibility to Theodore's assessment and Monomotapa will not be caught napping," said the King.

"What do you mean by that?" asked Livingstone.

"Theodore is modernising his forces and I intend to do likewise. I will send Taiwo to Abyssinia to study modern warfare in the company of Theodore's son Menelik who I gather is a great warrior and strategist. When Taiwo returns, he will be in a position to give Monomotapa the lethality it needs against any force on earth. I need pistols, rifles and cannons. Can your Kingdom provide them?" asked the King.

"Your Majesty, the guns will come later. Let us solve your nightmare first." pleaded an alarmed Livingstone who felt that his "divine mission" could be derailed by the plans of the King. A more powerful Monomotapa would not be an attractive target to any European power, especially Britain.

"Nonsense," said a smiling Simba, "your Christian stories are good and

they help to kill boredom. But, they are of no spiritual value to me. So, you keep your God and I keep mine. You talked about commerce and I want to offer you good business. I want guns, lots of guns, all types. And in exchange, I will give you silver, diamonds, gold and ivory. I need the guns urgently."

Livingstone pondered the matter for a while then said, "Your Majesty, your wish is my command. We will support you so that the Portuguese, the Arabs, the French or anybody else will never meddle in the affairs of your great and civilised Kingdom."

"Good man! I knew I could count on you," said a very happy Simba as he continued, "You tell Queen Victoria that if she agrees to marry my friend Emperor Theodore, I will invite them to Monomotapa for their honeymoon and they can camp by the Mosi-O-Tunya and enjoy the bliss of their love for as long as they like, all expenses paid! The United Kingdom, Abyssinia and Monomotapa will form a bulwark against aggression through a defence alliance pact!"

"I will carry your words to the Queen. I am sure she will respond to all your kindness in good time like I am sure she will respond to Theodore's proposal. With your permission, I will spend only one more week in your Kingdom and then I will rush back to London." said Livingstone.

"Take two weeks if you wish," said the King.

"One more thing, I would like to see the Casket of Benin," said Livingstone.

"How do you know about the Casket? It is the most valuable piece of art in the world!" "It is priceless!" said the surprised King.

"We have heard about it from travellers; I am interested in good works of art. They ease my soul," Livingstone lied.

"The Casket is in the custody of the High Priest in the Hill of the Holy and the Hill is out of bounds." said the King.

"Well, maybe someday I will have the luck to see it," said Livingstone.

"Never!" said the King.

"I have to retire now, Your Majesty," said Livingstone giving up.

"Yes, you may go but first, give me more magic pills. I don't know what I will do when you are gone," said the King.

Livingstone gave the King more sleeping pills.

"You can rest assured I will not be gone for long," assured Livingstone.

"Good man," said the King as he bade Livingstone goodnight with a friendly pat on the shoulder.

CHAPTER 13

FOR GOD AND MY COUNTRY

In the evening when Livingstone returned to the capital from daily tours of the countryside, he found King Simba waiting for him.

"Tell me, where did you go today and what did you see?" King Simba asked.

Livingstone responded by giving an account of the marvels of the Kingdom including the happy citizens, advanced technology in many fields, agriculture and the enormous herds of wildlife he had seen. He told Simba that he was adored by his subjects to which Simba responded, "I know. If it was not for this nagging problem of the birth of the twins, we would have embarked on a new phase of development. I had planned a great leap forward to quadruple production in all sectors."

The King continued, "It is many years since Emperor Theodore visited this Kingdom. Many of the stories he narrated to me from the Bible are hazy memories. Remind me of the King who was ordered by your God to slaughter his son, and he was going to do it before a ram presented itself for the sacrifice."

"Oh, that was Abraham; he was the leader of the Israelites," Livingstone responded.

"He is the same one who impregnated his maid because his wife could not provide him with a heir! I was told his wife afterwards became pregnant when she was over one hundred years!" Simba said and chuckled.

"Yes, it says so in the Bible," Livingstone confirmed.

"And you believe the story?" asked Simba.

"Indeed I do," Livingstone responded.

"Now tell me about the donkey that spoke like a man!" Simba continued as he broke into uncontrollable laughter.

"Now tell me about the wall which tumbled down in Jericho simply because Israelites walked around it a few times," Livingstone recounted the story of Joshua and the battle of Jericho.

"What about the man who wrestled with your God and almost won? Are these your people?" Simba asked.

"No, they were Jews but I am Scottish," Livingstone clarified.

"Then why do you so fervently believe in Jewish mythology?" asked the King.

"Because it was from among the Jews that the Lord our Saviour was born."

"The same one who was hanged by his people?" asked Simba, holding back laughter.

"No, He was crucified but he rose again on the third day," Livingstone expounded.

"He came from the dead, and arose from hell; that is why you believe in him..?" Simba laughed as tears fell from his eyes.

"And these are the people you want me to pay homage to spiritually, which you term as salvation?" Simba asked in a most serious tone.

"Yes, Your Majesty," Livingstone responded.

"Next time you come, I will tell you about our God, his messengers and the spirits, then you can judge for yourself who is more powerful, your God or my God. I strongly recommend that when you are here, you should pay homage to *Mwari* or else, you might incur His wrath by worshipping foreign deities such as Jesus Christ and the Holy Spirit," said the King.

"When I return, we shall see," said Livingstone as he concluded that his work as a missionary did not have a chance in Monomotapa or anywhere else. He was not born a preacher; neither could he master the art of being one. He was made for sterner stuff.

Livingstone's sojourn at last came to an end. The King gave him gifts to take to Queen Victoria. They included a huge piece of polished diamond, the biggest Livingstone had ever seen, gold, red garnets, blue sapphire, two massive elephant tusks, a big stuffed lion, horns of a giant kudu and a long shiny skin of a rock python. Livingstone knew the Queen would adore them, especially the diamond and the precious stones. He profusely thanked the King for the generous and most valuable gifts and pledged to deliver them dutifully.

"I am sure Queen Victoria will reciprocate your kind gesture, which will go a long way to opening lasting relations between our two great Kingdoms," said Livingstone.

"Tell her I want the guns urgently," was the reply from Simba.

Livingstone and his party were given armed guards to escort them to the port of Sofala on the east coast where they boarded a ship to England. It had been two long years since he left Bechuanaland. It was the year 1856.

The ship sailing to England came from Cape Town. On board, were all sorts of characters who had been engaged in all manner of activities and each had a story to tell about their exploits. Livingstone and Rhodes listened to recounts by hunters, gold prospectors, pleasure seekers and sailors who had travelled all over the world. All their stories had a common theme; that wild Africa was the new frontier for wealth accumulation and fun. Then one of the sailors provoked Livingstone,

"And you Scotsman, what have you to tell?" he asked.

Livingstone put up a stoic poise and in a very self-assured manner, he responded, "I came to Africa on honeymoon ten years ago. I landed in Bechuanaland and became a gold digger for one Dr. Moffat. I became a gold trader and ventured farther inland. My journey took me to Angola and finally to the Kingdom of Monomotapa, here I am heading back home." said Livingstone.

"Wait a minute, you have travelled from Cape Town to Bechuanaland, to Angola and to Monomotapa?" asked another.

"Indeed I have, and Cecil here is my witness. He was my companion." said Livingstone.

"Not that we doubt you, but it is the fascinating realisation that you are the first Briton to cross Africa from Angola in the west to Sofala in the East! You are bigger than Mungo Park!" said another.

It had not dawned on Livingstone that his long journey could be considered as an epic feat! If the world regarded it so, he was going to exploit it fully.

"Well, basically I am an explorer and a missionary, and in my disposition, distances are part of the game," he said with a smile.

"So how many savages did you convert to Christianity?" asked another.

"None," responded Livingstone.

"Your journey was a waste of time! How much gold did you find?" asked another.

"There is plenty of gold and diamonds in the interior, and as for the hunters, you have never seen such lions, kudus, rhinos, buffaloes, crocodiles and pythons as those massive beasts roaming the Kingdom of Monomotapa.

The fortunes in South Africa are a drop in the ocean compared to those abundant in Monomotapa," said Livingstone.

The crowd swelled around Livingstone, wanting to hear more.

"I met King Simba, an affable ruler. Although he would not confess it, Monomotapa is home to the fabled King Solomon's Mines. He confessed that his Kingdom has had relations with Abyssinia for years and to my mind, this is how the name Solomon came to Monomotapa. I believe the fortune is there for the picking when the moment is ripe. There is also the bronze Casket from Benin, the most priced piece of art in the world. He confessed it is hidden somewhere in the hills. Gentlemen, Britain has to take over Monomotapa before the Portuguese and others do, or else we will be biting our fingers and forever crying in shame over a golden opportunity lost," explained Livingstone.

For the rest of the trip, Livingstone was the centre of attraction. Every passing day, Rhodes noticed that, he exaggerated one aspect or the other of their "epic" journey. If the people on the ship could have found a way to turn back, they would have dearly loved to go to Monomotapa immediately, not later. Such was the frenzy whipped by Livingstone that it set many minds planning on a return journey to Africa immediately, with Monomotapa as the ultimate destination.

There was a journalist on the ship who had been sent to South Africa to cover the war between the Boers and the Zulus fighting over land. He abandoned that report and started on another; "*The Epic Journey of Livingstone across Africa*". Livingstone was most glad to fill in the details.

"When we confronted a whole battalion of Portuguese soldiers in Caprivi Strip, we warned them that should any ill befall upon us out of their hands, they would face the wrath of Queen Victoria and the British forces. They were scared to hear this and left us alone. It was then that I discovered the greatest waterfall in the world which I named Victoria Falls. The natives call it Mosi-O-Tunya, but such a splendour deserves a great and better sounding name, hence my decision. It is truly a marvel, one of the wonders of the world and to me the greatest. My mission is to put the facts before the British Government and the people, that time has come for us to take control of the enormous natural wealth of Africa, which will make us the most powerful Kingdom on earth," said Livingstone.

The journalist had his day made. He was going to write such a story as had not been seen in journals and papers for years. Arising out of interest shown by all on the ship, Livingstone decided to update his story to an epic journey motivated by his patriotic love for Britain and the need for a vast empire, to avert the disaster which Malthus had predicted.

Cecil Rhodes was considering the change of fortunes for himself. If the people on the ship were to be used as a gauge, then his dream of a business empire stretching from Cape Town to Cairo was going to be a certainty, but he had to be in control. He told Livingstone, "When we get to England, I will convince my father to set up a meeting between us and Queen Victoria. As you deliver the gifts from King Simba, we will talk to her about the riches of Africa. You have to fine tune your report to be most convincing. Here, these are the sketches I drew of Victoria Falls, the City of Matapa and some of the big game. Include them in your report." Livingstone looked at the sketches one by one and concluded that Rhodes was a very gifted artist.

"When did you do all this?" he asked.

"When you were talking with the King as well as when you abandoned me to write your report," said a smiling Rhodes.

"I am most grateful. For God and my country!" said a jolly Livingstone.

"For God and my country," responded Rhodes.

They hugged in warmth and friendship like brothers do, as the ship cut the waters heading for England.

Livingstone arrived in London full of himself. Having mesmerised the passengers on the steam ship, he hoped to extend the same throughout Great Britain. He was counting on Cecil Rhodes and the journalist friend he had met on the ship to do their bit too.

First, he went to Moffat's house for a reunion with his long lost family. The children had grown so much so that he could hardly recognise them. They looked at him like a stranger who deserved no love or respect. He tried to explain himself, but they showed no interest in his stories. His eldest son told him bluntly,

"You abandoned us!"

"No, you don't understand, I had an important mission to accomplish," he said.

"Are you done with it?" the son asked.

"Not yet," replied Livingstone.

"Then what have you come here for? Go ahead and finish your mission. We are doing fine on our own." And the young man banged the door hard behind him as he strode into the street, angry with his father.

It was not that the children had not missed their father. Far from it. Upon their arrival in London, Livingstone had asked his mother to help Mary with the children, as a nanny. She had obliged and moved to London from Scotland. She had no other obligations, her husband having died some years back and with no child left at home. They had matured and moved on.

Mary had not welcomed the idea of the intrusion, so they quarrelled day in day out. They could not see eye-to-eye on any issue and Mary blamed it on the backwardness of the "senile hag from Scotland." Mary loved her drink and every evening she visited the pubs. She always came back drunk, sometimes escorted by weird looking men. Livingstone's mother could not stand her wild behaviour which she termed "reckless".

During these awkward moments, the children wished their father was around to put the family in order. They had become the laughing stock of the neighbourhood, made worse by the fact that they were the only Scots. People said they spoke with an awkward accent. So, by and by, they came to accept their unenviable existence. They were ridiculed wherever they went, in school, in the parks and around the neighbourhood. They blamed their predicament on their father who had abandoned them.

Livingstone's mother, having failed to change Mary or cope with her, packed her bags and returned to her lonely life in Scotland.

Livingstone then realised that choices had consequences and the sacrifices he had to make in order to accomplish his mission were monumental. Aware of the dilemma he was in; he shed tears and swore, "I will not abandon my mission no matter what!" He cherished the idea that he would soon be meeting with Queen Victoria to sell to her the idea of the need for Britain to acquire territories in Africa before other European nations moved in. He was waiting to hear from Rhodes.

Rhodes sold the idea of meeting with the Queen to his father, the humble preacher who handled the spiritual affairs of the Royal family in Buckingham Palace. The humble request was met with a rage like he had never witnessed.

"Preposterous!" the Queen shouted in utter disgust.

"The black savage who calls himself the Emperor of Abyssinia, the Lion of Judah sends a message proposing marriage and before I can give him a befitting response, another savage King sends gifts in the hands of a Scotsman! What do they think I am, a harlot? I will teach them lessons they will never forget!" she fumed.

"Your Majesty, I gather the King of Monomotapa is not proposing marriage. He wants to do business with Britain," said Rhodes' father.

"Oh, is that so?" said a less bellicose Queen Victoria.

"Yes, it is so, Your Majesty. He wants to buy guns because the Portuguese and Arabs are threatening his rich and peaceful Kingdom. There is no harm in accepting his gifts which I gather are very valuable and beautiful," said the preacher.

"In that case, you will receive the gifts on my behalf from your son and the Scotsman, what is his name? Livingstone? Tell them I am most thankful, and about the guns, they should see John Kirk in the Foreign Office. He will assess the situation and file a report with me through the relevant minister," said the Queen with finality.

Livingstone and Rhodes were very disappointed with the Queen's reaction.

"Did you know that the Emperor of Abyssinia wrote to the Queen proposing marriage? She is still raving mad with the insult. It has poisoned her mind and that is why she will not receive you. However, she has accepted the gifts which I will take to her. For the arms' sale, she says you contact John Kirk in the Foreign Office." Rhodes' father reported to his son, who dutifully conveyed the information to a sad Livingstone.

The gifts were handed to the preacher who dutifully delivered them to the Queen. She was astounded and immeasurably pleased. To this day, the huge cut diamond, the massive red ruby and the blue sapphire adorn the crown of every British King or Queen, with no reference to their origin.

It was never the intention of Livingstone or Rhodes to press the matter of arming Monomotapa. It ran counter to their individual schemes. They never saw Kirk. They shifted their energy to Hyde Park where they told attentive crowds of the wonders of migrating to Africa. Their speeches mesmerised the crowds.

The King of Monomotapa impatiently awaited the return of Livingstone with the shipment of pistols, rifles and cannons. His desire was to use them to defend his Kingdom from the Portuguese, Arabs and anybody else who dared to threaten his mighty rich and powerful Kingdom. Though he had other issues to solve, at least the Kingdom's army had to be well-equipped, or so he thought. From the time he met Livingstone, he felt his life had changed for the better. And although the little magic pills were finished, he was still getting sleep without too much of an effort.

The main reason he was so relaxed was the fact that he knew his good friend Livingstone would soon be back with guns, funny stories and the white magic pills. He also prayed that Livingstone and his God would be less demanding and give him an answer to the curse of the cave in the Vumba Mountains, even though, he did not embrace the white God or His Son, the magician who performed miracles, but could not save his own life.

CHAPTER 14

AN UNSAVOURY PROPOSAL

My many years of observation since creation reveal that of all God's creation, the most powerful, the most wayward and the most reckless is called woman. When the creature sets on a course, no power on earth can alter it. Woe unto anything in her path if the course is destructive. The driving principle is known as emotions. Livingstone was painfully aware that the Mary Moffat he found upon his return to London was very different from the Mary Moffat he married. The Mary Moffat he found was on a course of self-destruction by way of alcohol – she was a drunkard. She had squandered the fortune he had given her and what else her father had added. He became painfully aware that the condition his wife was in could only be handled by a psychiatrist. But he was a surgeon, not a psychiatrist.

In London, the Livingstones were ostracised by their neighbours. Mary was described as a perfect specimen of the typical Scot, 'reckless and drunk'. They lived a recluse life, they loathed it. They recalled how they had been happier in Africa, and they could be more acceptable in Scotland, but Mary would not brook the idea of moving to Scotland.

"I will not live among those miserable people in Scotland," she had said. Livingstone repeatedly coaxed her with kindness to move to Scotland but she refused. "For what?" she would ask. He felt powerless and helpless. It is easier to overturn a government than to change the mind of a deranged woman. He could not understand the reasoning behind her actions, but then Shakespeare had written that "the whims of a woman are bound by no law". Like Adam and Samson in the Bible, he knew his fate would be sealed by Mary. She would destroy him just as Eve and Delilah had destroyed their husbands. He put the problem in the back burner as he had more urgent matters to attend to.

The journalist with whom he had sailed on the ship from Sofala published a long article on the epic journey of Livingstone and Rhodes. It was in the leading dailies. Livingstone became a much sought after celebrity. The Royal Geographical Society, the Church Missionary Society, Oxford and Cambridge

Universities, several professional associations and even foreign governments were seeking him through their Ambassadors in London. Realising what he had become, he moved into a suite in a posh hotel in Central London. If Queen Victoria was too proud to see him, he was going to show her that he was not a non-entity. Sooner or later, she would be compelled to seek him to lead the charge in the British conquest of Africa.

In the meantime, Rhodes who had the singular focus in furthering his knowledge and understanding of world affairs had drifted to the serene quietness of Oxford University. He left the showmanship and glory to Livingstone, but not for long.

When Livingstone's story appeared in the papers and magazines accompanied by the sketches he had drawn, Rhodes could hardly believe his eyes. The story was so well crafted and so much exaggerated that it was a perfect script for a great movie. The heroism of the two "great men" was said to have been "propelled by the nationalist desire to give Britain a vast empire on which the sun would never set", a great empire which would transform the lives of people in Britain. "The empire is a question of bread, butter and power," concluded the article.

Rhodes became the centre of attraction at Oxford. He did not hide the fact that he was extremely rich and he gave lavish parties. When he visited London over the weekends, he enjoyed the company of his hero and mentor, David Livingstone as they mesmerised crowds wherever they went.

It was through Rhodes' urging that Livingstone gave a lecture on "The Dark Continent" at Oxford University. From then on, Africa was referred to as the Dark Continent.

Livingstone and Rhodes addressed the public in Hyde Park over the weekends and public holidays. People from all walks of life came in droves to listen to the duo as they narrated the need for a vast empire in Africa. Those who had visited Africa and made a fortune swore that the duo was speaking nothing but the truth. To avert the prediction by Malthus about a looming revolution, Livingstone urged the British Government to conquer the wealthy and fertile lands of Central and Southern Africa, especially the Kingdom of Monomotapa.

"If we do not seize this God's given fortune, others will and they will overtake us economically and militarily through the great wealth they will

acquire in the Dark Continent. The Queen and the government should be told we do not have the luxury of time. The future and fortunes of Britain are stored in Africa. We must move there in large numbers as there are fortunes galore to be made by anybody and everybody," Rhodes would add most convincingly.

"Africa is our promised land," Livingstone would stress.

The two resembled saints on a holy crusade. Most intriguing to many was how a young Englishman and a Scotsman could have found convergence of heart and mind on an issue. "Patriotism…" many said, "is a very strong bond." So the duo continued to deliver their message with passion and precision. To the hungry and impoverished Englishmen, the two were harbingers of a new dawn which promised Heaven on earth. Farmers, hunters, bankers, industrialists, merchants, artisans, missionaries and harlots were coming to Hyde Park to hear the good news. Private dinners were arranged for Livingstone so that he could freely mingle with high members of the elite society in London, to clarify murky issues which caused great concern, like the fear of cannibalism in Africa.

At last, the invitation that Livingstone had been waiting for arrived. He was to be the key speaker at a special dinner organised by the Royal Geographical Society, in a prestigious hotel in London. He had written and polished his *Missionary Travels in Africa*.

Early that evening, Livingstone stepped into the hotel lobby to wait for his escort. He was immaculate in his dressing, in a custom made suit and shirt and with an expensive watch, tie and shoes to match. He looked more like a rich businessman or a politician than an explorer-cum-missionary. The only thing which gave him away was his customary hat which had been thoroughly weather beaten in Africa. He loved it. His hair was shaggy and long, but he still cut an impressive figure.

As usual, the gathering was made up of the elite in London. The government was well represented.

By the entrance into the hall was a long table on which was placed Livingstone's *Missionary Travels in Africa*. The booklets were going for free. He had considered the printing of the article as a weapon in the battle for the liberation of Scotland. The dignitaries walking in grabbed a copy each and guarded it as if their lives depended on it. It was regarded as a very precious gift, most revered.

The frenzy had taken deep roots in the imagination of many and so had the speeches by Livingstone and Rhodes in Hyde Park and Oxford. People came to hear about the New Canaan.

As I watched Livingstone walk to the podium, I could hardly believe my eyes. The sickly boy I had first encountered on the point of death; the resolute boy who had spoken so convincingly to his fellow students at the municipal park in Glasgow had now become a key player in matters pertaining to colonial imperialism.

I recalled the words of St. Peter and shuddered. Livingstone had just returned from the Kingdom of Monomotapa. And now in the hands of hungry wolves were copies of his "*Missionary Travels in Africa.*" The book detailed the riches to be made by British citizens who ventured to invest in Monomotapa in particular. But first, as he had pointed out, the ragtag army of Monomotapa warriors had to be pacified and disarmed as its nuisance value was not small.

Second, the land had to be effectively occupied because of the threat posed by Portuguese colonial expansionists who were threatening the weak African Kingdom. Time was of essence, so he had underlined in the booklet, but secretly for selfish reasons. The urgency in essence was the speed in which Scotland would arrive at the door of independence. The sooner the better, he thought, for his "divine mission" to be accomplished. While he took his high seat on the podium, no one could suspect he was an executioner, with the intention of leading Englishmen to the gallows of Monomotapa. He wore the smile of a saint under the guise of an explorer and a missionary. Deep down inside, however, he knew his true label "a terrorist fighting for freedom". Freedom fighters in Ireland had been labelled terrorists by the British Government. In the circumstances, he was the leading terrorist in Scotland. The disguised smile on his face was sardonic for those in the know.

Lord Richard Murchison, the President of the Royal Geographical Society, called the meeting to order. He introduced Livingstone as an extraordinary man, a man whose exploits as an explorer were about to give a new lease of life to the citizens of Great Britain and to take the Empire to new heights, heights in which the sun would never set. He continued,

"You have all read the article in our dailies which highlighted the extraordinary journey by Livingstone and Rhodes right from Cape Town to Bechuanaland, all the way to Angola and finally through the kingdom of Monomotapa.

Of critical importance to Great Britain are the natural resources such as diamonds, gold, copper, silver and gemstones found in Monomotapa. If the natives with crude tools and furnaces can grow rich upon their exploitation, imagine what we can get from the bowels of the earth with our advanced machinery!

"Second, and as Malthus had warned us, we need to offload some of our population to the fertile soils in the Kingdom to grow cotton, sugarcane, tobacco, wheat and other cash crops. The climate is good; there is no winter, so one can plant two seasons or more in a year. Our industries are hungry for more raw materials.

"The climate is as good as Rhodes has attested. He arrived in Africa with asthma and arthritis, but the warm tropical sun has cured him! We all could do with such wonders of nature.

"There is also dairy farming and ranching on a large scale. The reports say the land is sparsely populated. Can you imagine owning ten thousand acres of land!

"For those with an eye for hunting, the range of animals both in numbers, sizes and varieties are mindboggling. There are rhinos, lions, leopards, cheetahs, buffaloes, kudus, elephants, zebras, giraffes; you name it, beyond count! Why waste your time and ammunition hunting foxes and grouse?

"I know we all love golf, the game of gentlemen and fair ladies. I am informed that the plateaus in the kingdom can be turned into hundreds of eighteen-hole golf courses where you don't have to cross a valley between one hole and another. Besides, the land is even for a nice walk.

"When I read the article by the journalist, I was skeptical but when David gave me a sneak review of his own booklet, he stood by every word in it. I was left without doubt that what he and Rhodes have done for Britain will be remembered for generations to come as the birth of British colonialism in Africa. Livingstone, you are the mid-wife of our coming empire in Africa, especially in Central Africa, beginning with the Kingdom of Monomotapa.

"I know I am excited and I could go on and on. But I want you all to hear it from the horse's mouth. Livingstone, the floor is yours," he concluded.

The president sat down as Livingstone stood to address the audience. The moment he had been waiting for, for years had arrived, the beginning of the execution of his "divine mission".

As Livingstone approached the podium, he recalled words that had guided him in his "divine mission". They were from the book of Jeremiah in the Bible which read; *Before I formed you in the womb I knew you, before you were born, I set you apart, I appointed you as a prophet to the nations.*

At that moment, he felt very special. His mind specially focused on the part of the book where Jeremiah prophesied the fall of Judah to Babylon and that many of Judah's men would be held captive in foreign lands. Yes, he was God's instrument to deliver the English to foreign lands where they would die in their thousands at the hands of gallant Monomotapa warriors. And Scotland would be free at last. What a parallel!

I was shivering in awe of the Heavens and St. Peter's words through which I had received my orders! Indeed, my mission was well grounded, now I knew.

I recalled St. Peter's words, "*Momentous tidings on a global scale are about to be unleashed and Livingstone will be in the thick of it.*" These events would "move God to tears." Whether God knew him, before he was born or not, was not of any concern to me. That he had indeed become a prophet of some sort, there was no doubt, but it appeared to me like he was a prophet of doom. I couldn't wait to see.

Livingstone began his address, "The President of the Royal Geographical Society, my Lords, Dukes, officers from the Foreign Office, ladies and gentlemen…

"The opening remarks so eloquently delivered by the President of the Society have taken the wind out of my sails!

"He has truly captured the essence of my message which I want to convey to this great nation that God in His infinite kindness, which passes our understanding, has heard our prayers. He has given us a great opportunity to avert a revolution on this land, as Malthus has warned.

"My journeys through Southern and Central Africa were nothing short of a miracle. Under the guidance of the hand of God, and with Cecil Rhodes in tow, we braved many dangers until finally we arrived at the King's palace in the kingdom of Monomotapa. We were well received. The people are strong and hardworking; they can be converted into excellent farmhands and miners. But their customs and beliefs have to be addressed as they are primitive and backward. Preachers are needed to convert them to Christianity

as commerce takes root. I believe in the end, some modicum of civilisation can take root in them under our tutelage.

"As I have warned, the warriors of Monomotapa do pose a nuisance value to our dreams. However, the menace can be handled with a few muskets, cannons and pistols in a relatively short time. Immediately thereafter, the land will be ours to do whatever we want. The natives who will reject Christianity, commerce and civilisation should be pushed to the dry marginal lands. We can drive them into the Kalahari Desert where they will languish until they come to their senses!

"The second point I want to make is that the Portuguese who have long known about the wealth in the area are trying to capture the land starting from Angola all the way to the Eastern coast of Mozambique, which includes the kingdom of Monomotapa. They must be stopped by all means including the threat of war over Monomotapa.

"Gentlemen, God is on our side and Great Britain will rise to become a great world power. We will build an empire over which the sun will never set. I have captured all these points and more in my pamphlet. I thank you for your attention."

David Livingstone received a long standing ovation.

Speaker after speaker praised him for his courage and foresight and called him the biggest gift Britain had seen for years. They wished him a happy and long life. The president in his closing remarks challenged Livingstone to find the source of the River Nile to which he replied,
"It is on the cards."

The meeting drafted and adopted a resolution to speed up the work initiated by Livingstone. He was praised as a pioneer, a great explorer and a patriot of the highest order.

On his way back to the hotel, Livingstone was a very happy man. He could see the light at the end of the tunnel in the actualisation of his "divine mission" – "For God and my country" he muttered. His country was Scotland, not the moribund entity they called the United Kingdom.

In his hotel room, he wrote a note to Rhodes, "The meeting passed a resolution to speed up the presence of Britain in Africa. You have to move fast to secure your interests and be the linchpin in the operations. Best wishes," signed Livingstone. He had planted a bug in the mind of Victorian

England, one which was biting very deep across all sectors and above all, as a way out of poverty into the heights of world dominance. It came at a time when other European nations were thinking likewise. Many Englishmen regarded him as a prophet sent by God to save Britain, but Livingstone had a different mind-set. In his room, he gazed at the heavens and praised God, in supplication, for His guidance, on the road to setting Scotland free.

He prayed to God, "I believe that mine is a "divine mission". It was You who guided me to Monomotapa and back. Like You guided David in the struggle against the Philistines, I put myself at Your disposal to use me, to save Your people of Scotland from the tyranny of the English. I will go to any length following Your commands and guidance, Amen." He was a happy man, at peace with himself and with the Divine power which had selected him for the noble mission.

In a way, Livingstone knew that the passing of the resolution urging for the expansion of the British Empire to Africa had completed his mission. All he had to do now was to lie back and watch the English get entangled in wars with African Kingdoms before Scotland declared her independence. Then his sixth sense warned him that should he appear to hold back the passion for the empire, he would be regarded with great suspicion, that is, if things went wrong. He therefore had to remain in the thick of things to the end. It was a wise decision because on the same day, he received a note from the President of the Royal Geographical Society summoning him to an urgent meeting the following day.

That evening, the President of the Lloyds Bank paid him a courtesy call in his hotel. He told him, "When I read your article and heard you speak, I realised what a mistake we had made invading India, because Africa surely holds the key. The bank has decided to commit a huge financial outlay as venture capital for any Briton interested in plunging into Africa, for business, especially farming and mining. We believe the returns will be astounding."

The President, a short stocky man with a thick neck and a protruding tummy, threatening to burst out of his shirt, was a man of his words. He was a charming man with an Oxford accent, well-born and schooled, including in manners. He reminded one of Roman soldiers who had once occupied Britain, solid in mind, body and very resolute. Truly, the man could easily trace his genealogy from the days of the Roman occupation of England to some place in Italy. His interest in money matters pointed in the direction of Sicily, the home of the Mafia.

He continued, "Business is bleak in Britain and the recession is threatening many businesses with bankruptcy. We need a safety valve to save this country from social upheaval or God forbid a revolution! We have all agreed that you are a god-send to save the United Kingdom." He beamed with a broad friendly smile.

Livingstone reciprocated in kind, for a totally different reason.

"I am humbled by your kind words," said Livingstone.

"We will need you to chart the way forward for our business people," said the President of the bank.

"How so?" asked Livingstone.

"The President of the Royal Geographical Society will be talking to you about it."

"I will be calling on him tomorrow," said Livingstone.

"You must continue with your good work," said the President of the bank as he bade Livingstone goodnight.

So, when Livingstone visited the President of the Royal Geographical Society the following day, he had an idea about the meeting. He was going to play an active role in the expansion of British imperialism to Africa. The President went to the point, "I wish to thank you for your foresight and sacrifice in the service of the United Kingdom. As you know, for some time now, the government has been trying different policies and strategies to save the economy, but the recession is getting worse. Your approach has been bought by the government, but before we put it into action, we need details on the navigability of the Zambezi River, both for security and commercial reasons. The Royal Geographical Society has decided to mount an expedition to map the river and the surrounding areas. You have been chosen to head the expedition. The terms are generous and you are free to choose the team, although we also wish to add some experts. Will you accept the offer?" asked the President.

If Livingstone had a weak tummy, he would have thrown up at that point. This was more than he had bargained for in terms of commitment to building the empire. His role, he had thought, stopped with selling the idea, not in executing it. He considered suggesting that Cecil Rhodes should head the expedition, and then he remembered the inner counsel about the consequences of abandoning the scheme.

"I will gladly head the team," he said with a heavy heart.

"You don't appear too enthusiastic about it," commented the President.

"It is the timing Mr. President. I have a few family issues to resolve and some medical problems of my own to attend to," said Livingstone.

"I know, I know. Poor Mary, she should come to her senses. What are the medical problems you are facing?" asked the President.

"Minor problems to do with my bowels and my dentition, the treatment shouldn't take too long," replied Livingstone.

"Well, call on me when you are ready. I wish you quick recovery."

They parted company with a friendly handshake, united by a common purpose.

For some years, Livingstone had been suffering from a weak tummy which led to frequent trips to the toilet. At first, he had attributed the condition to the good diet in Africa, but eventually, he became aware that it was a condition which needed specialised attention. His teeth had also decayed and he had lost some in the process. His gum ached and bled.

As he went to the hotel, he thought of the other project he had hoped to embark upon; the discovery of the source of the Nile. He promised to give it urgent attention after the Zambezi Expedition, in honour of his uncle Mungo Park.

Livingstone was fully occupied trying to bring his broken family together. But besides Agnes, his daughter, who wanted to move to Paris, his sons loathed him. His wife, Mary, was too far gone to change. All they demanded from him was money and more money. He gave them, more out of guilt than necessity. It pained him more than the visits to the dentist who was treating his rotten gum and teeth using needles and knives.

He felt his life had become just pains and aches including being ensnared by the Royal Geographical Society. Funny, the only thing which did not give him pain was the dream of one day announcing to the world that he had discovered the source of the Nile, thereby solving the greatest geographical mystery in the world. It would be a gift to Scotland, an independent Scotland, he hoped.

CHAPTER 15

A MOST DIABOLICAL UNDERTAKING

Now that matters were taking shape in London, a hunch told me it was time to revisit Lisbon. I went to the Royal Palace. The King of Portugal was getting regular updates from his Ambassador in London. In the dispatches, he was warned that the clamour for an overseas empire had become a national frenzy. The heart and spirit of the thrust, he was told, was one David Livingstone who was said to have a wide knowledge of the people and wealth in Central and Southern Africa from Cape Town to the Zambezi and from Angola to Sofala, with special focus on the kingdom of Monomotapa. This new British thrust clashed directly with Portuguese strategic interests in the region.

The King called the war council and declared; "The stupid British are planning to deny us our gains in Africa. They took India from us and now they want to take Central and Southern Africa. We must stop them even if it means going to war."

Aware that he lacked the funds to fight the war alone, he sent a message to his friend the Pope in the Vatican warning him that the heretic protestant kingdom of Britain was planning to reverse the anticipated gains of the Catholic Church in Central and Southern Africa. The Pope, in response, invited the King to the Vatican, to seek a way forward in confronting the threat. It was a grave matter of mutual concern to both parties.

With the King went Cardinal Domingos, the head of the Roman Catholic Church in Lisbon.

Strategic alliances are meant to deal with matters such as these, when national, commercial, and spiritual vital interests are threatened. Such contests can give rise to war including holy wars. The King told the Pope and continued;

"It is with great concern that I have been following the activities of one David Livingstone, a Scotsman. He has convinced the British Government to occupy Central and Southern Africa. The loss of America and India were painful and I swore never to yield again without a fight. The British are closing our last window of opportunity. You and I owe it to the Catholic Church and to God to effectively counter the activities of these Protestant spiritual rebels. After we do away with Nzinga in Angola, I plan to move against Monomotapa, and then we will control all the gold and diamonds in the region. Now, we have a problem in our hands generated by the Scottish idiot," said the King.

"Why has it taken so long to deal with this woman Nzinga?" asked the Pope.

"Your worship, we had underestimated the strength of her forces and their capacity, tenacity and will to fight. Our losses have been considerable, but we are making headway albeit at a slow pace," confessed the King.

"What of Monomotapa?" asked the Pope.

"Monomotapa is the wealthiest and most powerful Kingdom in Africa. It is home to the fabled King Solomon's Mines. Whoever conquers Monomotapa will be richly rewarded!" said the King.

"Well, if you cannot defeat Nzinga, how do you expect to fight Monomotapa yet the Kingdom walked over the powerful Donyiros in a matter of hours?" asked the Pope.

"Your worship, I have a secret weapon."

The King explained the details of the secret weapon to the Pope and concluded as follows, "Then we will move in to mop-up the remains and effectively shut out the British."

"Well thought out! You have wonderful strategists! Where do I come in?" asked the Pope.

"I brought Cardinal Domingos with me because I want you to personally charge him with the execution of the mission. He must understand that this mission is a holy calling with your full blessing," said the King.

"Have him brought in," commanded the Pope. Cardinal Domingos entered. The Pope looked at him and with a commanding voice said, "You would not wish to see the Archbishop of Canterbury control the world, would you?" he asked.

"No, Your Highness, NEVER!" replied Domingos.

"A Scotsman by the name David Livingstone has been working on such a scheme in Central and Southern Africa. He's been working for the rebel church and the Queen. He is not your equal being of low birth, with a simple mind and he is a reckless weakling. On behalf of the Roman Catholic Church, I am charging you with the responsibility of countering his actions. The King will furnish you with the details of the operation," instructed the Pope.

"At your service Your Worship," said Domingos kneeling before the Pope and kissing his feet.

"I have always received good reports about you. That is why I have chosen you as the instrument of our church, with great faith, in the execution of this matter," said the Pope.

"I am greatly humbled, Your Worship," said Domingos.

And so it was that the ecclesiastical and secular interests fired by common greed, converged to claim the Kingdom of Monomotapa before the British made any move, in a pre-emptive strike.

Now about Domingos! In his earlier life, he was a pimp. In time, his fortunes changed and he established the most successful brothel in Lisbon which served the Royal Family, politicians, businessmen and the clergy. Then he was arrested for murder. His well-connected clients bailed him out. If you are rich and well-connected, getting away with murder is not a big deal.

Having come close to facing the gallows and going straight to hell, he repented and threw his lot with the Catholic Church, like all good and rich Portuguese did. He had seen the light at last and not only that, he joined the ranks of priesthood. The speed with which he rose through the order was breath-taking. He used his wealth and connections as a ladder to the top. But to his credit, his sermons moved congregations to tears. "I am a Saul who became Paul," he would always begin. Many sick harlots followed him to the church and wholeheartedly accepted Jesus Christ as their Saviour. They became nuns. They were all at the beck and call of Domingos for whatever he fancied. They let out wild wails and spoke in tongues during church services just as Domingos secretly requested them to do from time to time. The brothel had moved to the church and the pay package was good.

Domingos was a good example of the great work of the hand of the Lord, "a living miracle". It was the Roman Catholic Church which founded, "The Sacred Congregation of Propaganda, of which Domingos was a leading member. Its focus was missionary work in the dark places of the earth like Africa and Asia. With Cardinal Lavigeries, the Pope's representative in Lisbon (Nuncio), they had upgraded the outfit to, "The Society of our Lady of Africa" later to be renamed 'White Fathers'. After showing spiritual interest in missionary work, Domingos was now being called upon to demonstrate his physical commitment, in order to blunt the threat by Livingstone, the Protestant Church of England and Queen Victoria. He was on a dangerous mission.

On the eve of his departure for Monomotapa via Angola, the King gave him final instructions;

"It is with a clear conscience and the blessings of our Holy Father the Pope that I command the breaking of the will, pride and conscience of the natives of the land of Monomotapa. Their numbers must be drastically decimated to reduce their capacity for resistance. The experience in Angola has been a painful one and this time, a new weapon has to be deployed. Monomotapa has to fall as soon as possible with no casualties on our side. Their destiny is in our hands," the King boasted to Domingos.

Domingos knew that when he entered the Palace, he had been a free man, but he was leaving as a captive of conscience, not knowing what was in the sealed sachets the King handed to him. How this so-called unconventional secret weapon was going to work, he had not the slightest clue, but he had been warned to handle it with utmost care and great caution until it reached its destination, the Kingdom of Monomotapa. He felt like an animal caught in a snare.

"Why me...?" he asked himself. There was no answer. Somehow, he felt special that he had found favour with the King and above all, the Pope. The sachets formed what was termed as phase one of the attack. Phase two was to be handled by five carefully selected nuns. And there was going to be the final phase, to be executed by the armed forces of Portugal.

Domingos sailed from Lisbon to Angola with the five nuns. He was escorted to the Caprivi Strip, the No Man's land by Portuguese armed forces. Like Livingstone before him, he was confronted by Monomotapa frontier guards who demanded to know why he had strayed so far eastwards in the demilitarised zone. He told them that he was truly on course as his destination was the capital city of the Kingdom of Monomotapa. He had gifts and a special message from the Pope in Rome. Well, the last man to have come from the west had made the King a happy man. The guards saw no harm in sending a message to King Simba to inform him there was yet another foreign dignitary who wished to convey a message, and that he was accompanied by five beautiful women.

"It is not Livingstone?" asked the King.

"No, it is not. This one has a message from the representative of their God on earth, one they call the Pope," said the guard.

"Is he carrying pistols, rifles and cannons?" asked the King.

"No, Changamire, he has only brought gifts and a message," said the guard.

"Then their God has decided to answer my prayers for a solution to the "curse of the caves". Bring him to me. A man who comes accompanied by women is a peaceful man," said the King.

Like Livingstone before him, Domingos was lost for words when he saw the architecture, expanse and beauty of the City of Matapa. It was beyond belief.

"If this is native civilisation, then Africa should conquer Europe and teach us how to be civilised!" Domingos told his party.

"But then, orders are orders," he reflected within himself.

"Where are the primitive natives, the savages, and the cannibals walking naked in the jungle and living in caves?" asked one of the nuns. Nobody replied.

All around them were curious Africans who were dignified, proud, clean, well dressed and well fed, who wore broad smiles inviting friendship. They looked happy and contented. By any standards, their lives looked far much better than those of their counterparts in Portugal. In the midst of this friendliness, Domingos remembered his mission, "to destroy Monomotapa". He felt sad that he was the agent chosen to deliver the secret weapon. His was a diabolical mission. Every man has the right to enjoy long life, fulfil their potential, enjoy freedom, peace and security and above all, be happy. But this was what his mission was going to destroy! His conscience began to trouble him. Who was condemned? Himself or the people of Monomotapa; or were they all victims of nefarious forces who thrived on greed and caprice in the name of civilisation, the church, God and national interest, the agents of Lucifer wearing crowns and coloured garbs? He was a slave in the service of his masters and not supposed to query the motive and morality of decisions, so he marched on remembering the song "onward Christian soldiers..."

The gifts that Domingos gave to the Changamire had been well selected.

The Pope had donated a velvet tunic with golden embroidery which was the very stuff won by Kings and himself. There were silver sandals to complement. The items were very pleasing to behold. The King of Portugal had silently added to the King's wardrobe and that of the Queen silk shirts and dresses. The Changamire was pleased with the material and the masterly of the craftsmanship. The King of Portugal was not mentioned in the conversation. Domingos told Changamire about the Pope and the Vatican and the struggle between Catholics and Protestants, which was the entry point of his mission. King Simba concluded that the Pope was a benevolent old man, a harmless man who ruled a small village called the Vatican, but who pretended to have global interests of a spiritual nature. Since he did not possess an army or even pistols, rifles or cannons, he was of little or no use at all to the urgent needs of Monomotapa except perchance, as a chief priest, he might have an answer to the curse.

"So, what message do you bring me from your Chief Priest?" asked the King.

"The Pope, Your Majesty, he is referred to as the Pope," said Domingos.

"Whatever. What is in a title!" said the King

"I bring to you a grave message, Your Majesty," said Domingos.

"You have come all the way to bring bad news? So what is the curse all about?" he asked him.

"What curse?" asked Domingos.

"The curse of the Royal Caves in Vumba Mountains!" said the King showing signs of irritation.

"I know nothing about the curse, Your Majesty."

"Then what other bad news could there be?" asked the King.

"The Pope has sent me to warn you about one David Livingstone and the British Government. They are planning to invade your Kingdom and to occupy it."

The King laughed out loudly and said, "Listen, Livingstone is my very good friend and soon he will bring pistols, rifles and cannons to fight the Portuguese, the Arabs and anybody else who ever dreams of invading Monomotapa. The British will never dare attack Monomotapa. Even as I speak to you now, no force on earth can defeat our mighty army. Tell the Pope not to worry, we are safe."

Domingos opened his bag and produced cuttings from British periodicals, magazines and newspapers which carried Livingstone's stories including his visit to Monomotapa. Domingos read them to the King stressing the parts which called upon the British Government to occupy Kingdoms in Central and Sothern Africa, especially the rich Kingdom of Monomotapa!

"It cannot be!" shouted the King.

"It is the truth," said Domingos.

The King was quiet for a long while then he said,

"So this is the reason why the Scotsman has not returned as he had promised! But supposing he appears tomorrow with the guns?" he asked.

"Then I will bear my chest for your warriors to spear me to death!" said Domingos.

"You are an honest man, a man who can be trusted," said the King.

"And why did you bring only women with you as companions? Are they your wives? Are the pale-faced men of the Vatican polygamous?" asked the King.

"No, Your Highness. No single woman lives in the Vatican. It is a city of men only," said Domingos.

"So, you decided to bring many of them to make up for the time lost when you were in the Vatican?" asked the King in jest.

"No, Your Majesty, these are nuns who have devoted their lives to Jesus Christ and His word," explained Domingos.

"But I was told the Man was hanged many years ago. They certainly were not his wives?" asked the King.

"No, their work is to spread the gospel," said Domingos.

"I do not want to go into the Bible and religious matters. The last time I listened to Bible stories, I fell into a trap. I should have killed Livingstone. My Chief Priest and the Spirits have become powerless since our gods went away! They should have warned me!" said the King as he continued: "How do I thank you for the wonderful gifts and the kind message?" asked the King.

"We have been spellbound by what we have witnessed so far. Your Kingdom is like Heaven on earth. Allow us to tour as much as we can so that we can tell the Pope about your great leadership and the industry of your people," said Domingos.

"I cannot deny you such a humble request. My warriors will take you as far as you want to see. When you return, I will host a big feast in your honour. By the way, do you carry the pills which make one sleep without tossing and turning?" he asked.

"Sleeping pills? Of course!" and he gave the King a handful.

As the King slept, Domingos set to work.

For a whole two weeks, Domingos and the nuns roamed the Kingdom of Monomotapa as special guests of the King. They visited towns and villages and, slept in the barracks of the elite warriors. Domingos carried the sachets and everywhere they went, he emptied the contents in filthy dumps as he had been instructed. He noted that the stuff inside looked like broken rice mixed with ashes.

"Could this be a weapon of mass destruction?" he asked himself in doubt.

The last twenty sachets were to be emptied in the capital, Matapa. In as far as he was concerned; the first phase of his operation was almost over. The second phase was running concurrently with the first! The five women he had brought were not nuns. They were harlots; each had been selected because of the sexually transmitted diseases they carried including syphilis, gonorrhoea and fungus complications. They had been promised huge payments for their services in Monomotapa. So, wherever the team went, the women drank native beer and slept with as many warriors as possible who wanted a fling each night, and they were many all over the land. The leaders of the warriors and the most decorated soldiers always had the first priority. Domingos made sure that the women had many sexual encounters. He worked them overtime.

"You don't get paid well for nothing," he would warn the women who would in turn redouble their efforts. And so the second and most visible phase of the destruction of Monomotapa was effectively under way. The calculation was that since the warriors had several wives, and they also slept with women who had lost their husbands in battle, the sexually transmitted diseases would spread like bushfire.

Then came the eve of departure and as promised, King Simba hosted a huge feast for his good friend Domingos and the nuns. He praised him for divulging information on the callous scheming of Livingstone and the British. He decorated him with "The Roaring Order of Mosi-O-Tunya", First Class.

A big shining spear, a head gear made from a lion's mane and a coat from colobus monkeys were his for the taking. He looked spectacular in them. In addition, he was handed valuable gifts to take to the Pope.

When Domingos addressed the sitting, he heaped praise on the King for his leadership and the great progress in the Kingdom in all fields of human endeavour. He promised the King that next time he visited Monomotapa, which he had fallen in love with, he would bring him a special gift, a maxim gun, which could deal effectively with the wild scheming of the British! He was cheered endlessly by the people including King Simba.

Before the King rose to leave, Domingos excused himself pretending to go for a gulp of fresh air and went outside. Once there, he found the garbage dump and poured all the contents from the remaining sachets. His mission was now accomplished.

The following day, the team was escorted to the Caprivi Strip and warned to be careful of the Portuguese soldiers who might kill Domingos and rape the women.

The King called The War Council and ordered for fresh supplies of weapons to the warriors, especially the archers, in the face of the coming threat posed by the British as conveyed by Domingos.

"If Domingos is to be believed, and I have no reason to trust Livingstone, we will soon be fighting the British," King Simba warned the War Council.

It was in the midst of the war preparations that news began to spread that many commanders and top warriors were suffering from strange diseases. Their genitals were burning and they were oozing a smelly discharge. It was said that all of them had slept with the pale-faced women! No medicine man in the land could find a cure for gonorrhoea, a disease hitherto unknown. Increasingly, women who had slept with the afflicted soldiers came forward complaining of uncomfortable sensation, foul odour and smelly discharge from their private parts. The Kingdom was in panic. Was this the curse revealed to the Queen in the caves? Nobody knew.

"This thing will come to pass," the optimistic among the afflicted would say, but it did not go away, it kept spreading and very fast too.

Before the Kingdom could come to terms with the epidemic, rats in their thousands came out of their hiding places sick and dying, bleeding from the mouth, eyes, noses and ears. The sheer efforts of collecting and burying them became monumental. Then came reports of many people lying in their beds, immobilised with swollen glands and bleeding through their noses, eyes, mouths and ears. But they had not slept with the women with pale faces!

Death came to the Kingdom from all directions, in the villages, in the towns and in the capital. The symptoms were all similar.

The King called a special meeting of the Ruling Council. They agreed that Domingos and the nuns had something to do with the sexually transmitted diseases, but the rats and the bleeding, where did they come from?

Domingos and the nuns were not received by the party of Portuguese soldiers they had expected in Caprivi Strip. After many days of anxiety, they decided to return to Monomotapa instead of risking the hostile warriors of Queen Nzinga or King Lobengula. Unknown to them, orders had been given by Lisbon that they must not on any count return to Angola or Portugal after their mission. They were to be abandoned to perish in the wild. By the time they made contact with Monomotapa frontier guards, Domingos and the nuns were all bleeding from their noses, ears and mouths. The warriors told them they were suffering from the same disease which had attacked the Kingdom since their departure.

"It started with rats dying and then the people had swelling of glands and then bleeding and death," the warriors explained in agony.

Domingos let out a loud yell of horror.

"It is the plague! The sachets were laced with plague *bacillus*! Oh my God! We are all dead!" He knelt down in prayer:

"Dear heavenly father, forgive me for I did not know what I was doing."

The warriors lifted him up and told him to explain himself. He confessed to having been the agent who brought the affliction to Monomotapa.

"In the dumping sites in all the places we visited, you will find plastic sachets. They carried the disease. These women you see here are all very sick with sexually transmitted diseases. Monomotapa is in deep trouble and once you are weakened, the Portuguese army will attack. Now you may do with us as you wish," confessed Domingos, wishing for a quick death to escape the anguish in his body and soul.

The revelation was shocking. The head warrior asked Domingos,

"So you are Portuguese and not from the Vatican?"

"What is the difference? The two entities are working hand in hand," said Domingos.

The warriors thought of spearing the lot, but then decided against it.

"They are not worth expending an ounce of our energy."

The leader turned to Domingos and his party and ordered them in a harsh voice, "Face west and start walking. That is the direction of Angola and may the hyenas devour your carcasses one by one far away from our border."

Domingos and the nuns disappeared into the bush as ordered, walking towards the direction of Angola, without uttering a word. They were never seen again, by a living soul. The head warrior reported Domingos confession to the king.

Changamire summoned the Ruling Council to discuss the grave situation facing the Kingdom.

"I feel personally responsible for what has happened. I embraced the foreigners in the hope that they could help in solving the mystery of the curse. Instead, they betrayed my trust and brought more calamities upon us. From now on, I will not entertain any foreigners in the Kingdom."

As Changamire spoke to the council, his head was bowed in shame. He looked the worst he had ever been in composure, in recent times. He spoke slowly, in a low tone, tears welling in his eyes.

"To stop the spread of the afflictions, I order that except for the warriors on essential duty, the rest of the population must stay put in their locations until further notice." The decision was endorsed.

When King Simba told the royal household that it was prohibited to venture beyond the palace perimeter, Taiwo had a heavy heart. He begged his father, "The strength of our Kingdom is built upon your relations with our people, the warriors, farmers, herdsmen, miners and the artisans. While I understand the wisdom of your decision, it is at a time like this when the people need consolation most. I beg to be permitted to venture out to keep in touch with the people on your behalf," he requested.

The Changamire knew that Taiwo was right, and even if he wanted to, he knew he couldn't stop him once his mind was made up.

"My son, I marvel at the wisdom of your reasoning. So young and yet so wise, your wish is granted," said the King.

From that day on, Taiwo roamed the land consoling the sick and the dying. People were touched by this great act of solidarity and much appreciated his kind words. He assured them that all would be well soon, but alas, it was not to be. Within weeks of his excursions, Taiwo was afflicted by plague.

Upon the pronouncement of Taiwo's death, the Changamire let out a loud yell full of grief and said, "This is the end of Monomotapa. Without Taiwo, there is no Monomotapa."

The King summoned the High Priest to organise Taiwo's burial. His body was carried to the Holy Shrine in the Hill of the Holy. A plume of smoke was seen rising from the chimney in a straight line to the heavens. It was as if the wind had stood still to pay homage to the fallen legend. The High Priest, as instructed by the King, opened the Casket of Benin and put Taiwo's ashes in it. He had been cremated.

It was a sad, tired and haggard King who returned to the palace that afternoon after the cremation of Taiwo. He was speaking to himself, "Monomotapa is nothing but an empty shell without Taiwo," and for seven days, he mourned and fasted, at the end of which he summoned the Ruling Council once again.

"The plague has struck the royal palace. I order the evacuation of the capital. We shall build a temporary capital on the other side of River Mbuni and return to Matapa when the plague disappears."

In haste, a new temporary capital was built. In the circumstances, it resembled more an oversize slum than the seat of the government of a mighty kingdom. The King and his subjects yearned for the day they would return to Matapa. They named the temporary capital Harare or "the home of hope."

News of the atrocities visited on the Kingdom by the Portuguese in cahoots with the Vatican were making rounds across the world. It irked royalties in Europe especially those like Britain who had an eye on the conquest of the kingdom. No tears were shed for the deaths of thousands in the kingdom, but rather, there were lamentations for the human waste in labour for the mines and farms in the years ahead. The other reason for anger was the delayed colonisation of the kingdom; it had to be put on hold until the plague menace disappeared.

The holier than thou attitude of the British Government and other European powers ignored the fact that small pox had been used as a weapon to decimate Aborigines in Australia, to facilitate the occupation of their land by British citizens, including criminals. Equally so, fleas, bed bugs and jiggers had been unleashed upon South American-Indians who could not cope with the hitherto unknown menace. All these ungodly acts went a long way in reinforcing the truism that the creature called man is cursed; he is obsessed in the drive for fulfilment of selfish interests. He will stop at nothing including inflicting pain and suffering upon his own kind of the human race, including genocide to have his way! The condemnation of the Portuguese atrocities was therefore hypocritical.

However, just as much as fundamental changes had occurred in Australia and Latin America, from these massacres, the same would follow in Monomotapa. The pattern was the same; the actors were the same, hungry leeches driven by greed carrying the cross of Jesus to the lands of natives.

For Africa, this was the beginning of the scaring transition St. Peter had warned me about. The onset of momentous tidings, which would result in disasters of great magnitude that would sweep the mighty kingdom of Monomotapa away, with such acts of evil as would move God to tears, until kingdom come. In the carnage and pogrom, St. Peter had warned, Livingstone would play a leading role. But so far, it was Domingos and not Livingstone who had struck the devastating blow. Then it dawned on me that if Rhodes had to build his empire from Cape Town to Cairo, Monomotapa had to feature prominently. I braced myself for the foretold disaster to follow.

CHAPTER 16

UP THE ZAMBEZI

I could not tell when hubris entered David Livingstone's head, but it had become his second nature. Maybe it had been latent all along, exhibiting itself in modest measures in the form of infrequent displays of madness, and there were a few occasions when some could swear to it. It reached alarming proportions in the planning and execution of the Zambezi Expedition, which lasted from 1858-1863.

The mandate was to map out the navigability of River Zambezi and the natural resources in the surrounding lands which upon conquest, would be eventually used to beef up the coffers of the United Kingdom. It also included an assessment of the damage done to the Kingdom of Monomotapa by the Portuguese's unconventional biological weapons, the diabolical sexual onslaught, and the inferno which gutted the capital city, Matapa.

To the surprise of the Royal Geographical Society, which was funding the expedition, Livingstone, without consultations, placed an advertisement in London's leading daily, asking those who wished to invest in the new Heaven in Africa to step forward and join the Zambezi Expedition. It stated that he would provide free transportation. As Livingstone and Rhodes had laid the groundwork through private speeches, lectures and rallies in Hyde Park, the response was enormous. Livingstone single-handedly selected a hundred people from the lot. It was a diverse group representing a wide cross-section of society from Lords, Barons, entrepreneurs, hunters, ranchers, farmers, artisans and others with dubious credentials. The list included both men and women. They were united by greed for quick financial pickings with many yearning to mix business with pleasure.

Alarmed, the President of the Royal Geographical Society summoned Livingstone. He did not mince his words, "Livingstone, you have unilaterally expanded the mandate of the expedition before seeking my approval. I must warn you that the finances the Society provided were for a small expedition. Secondly, the British Government would not take it kindly if such a large number of its citizens were to come in harm's way. What is the meaning of this?" he asked.

"Mr. President," Livingstone responded, "I wish to assure you that my intentions are noble. Secondly, I have made a personal sacrifice to purchase a most seaworthy ship from the Scottish shipping magnate, Sir William Mackinnon, a man whom I know you hold in high esteem. Thirdly, having established wonderful working relations with Changamire, the King of Monomotapa during my visit, I assure you of the security and warm welcome of those on the expedition. My humble intention is to speed up the British occupation of Monomotapa before the Portuguese beat us to it."

"Well and good. As long as you know what you are doing, you may proceed with your plans," said the President.

"I have taken care of every minute detail," said Livingstone.

"Best of luck." said an unconvinced President.

"First, we sail to India for the investors to have a sound basis for assessing the difference to be made in fortunes between India and Africa. The latter, I can assure you, will carry the day," Livingstone said smiling.

"We shall see," said the President, in conclusion.

The President called senior members of the Society and briefed them on the matter.

"Apparently, Livingstone is sitting on a fortune. He has used his money to purchase a ship for the trip, starting with a tourist excursion to India! I hope the man is sane, otherwise we shall regret it."

When Mackinnon was contacted, he confirmed having sold a most seaworthy vessel to Livingstone.

"I would have gone on the ship myself if it was not for my prior commitments. Business in India is a lot of trouble for small gains. I have made up my mind to register a company, Imperial British East Africa. And, I intend to operate in the area north of Monomotapa in the region of the Mountains of the Moon and the Great Lakes," McKinnon, like Livingstone, was a scot.

The President was lost for words. Were the Scots out of their minds? Or did they know something the English did not? He would wait and see.

Grudgingly, Livingstone accepted to take John Klirk on the ship at the request of the President.

The departure of the ship appropriately named "Zambezi" was the greatest spectacle the United Kingdom had witnessed in years. Thousands of people came to witness the event which would herald the occupation of the new

Heaven and untold fortunes to be made by those who had the heart and guts to live with savages and cannibals. As the ship sailed away, there were mixed feelings of apprehension, fear and envy from the onlookers.

Those on board felt special, lucky and privileged. They included Mary, the alcoholic wife of David Livingstone, whom he had dragged along in the hope that she would drink less under his watch. His brother, a sheep herder in Scotland was on the ship with the hope of identifying a huge tract of land in Monomotapa for sheep farming. He was hoping to export mutton, wool and raw materials for leather products to the United Kingdom. He was happy to have a brother like Livingstone, "a man of great vision and a Saviour", as he used to say.

There was an Anglican Bishop who looked absolutely splendid in his purple robe and some sort of red cap resting on top of his head. As the waves heaved and the strong breeze swept the sea, it would only be a matter of time before the cap was blown overboard, but somehow, it remained there, as if fixed on the head with glue. The Bishop was representing the interests of the Church Missionary Society as well as the Church of England. Whether he was on board to take care of the spiritual side of the voyagers or to assess the convertibility of black heathens, savages and cannibals to Christianity was anybody's conjecture. Most conspicuously, he was in the bar having a drink with sailors and the general mob on the ship. A most liberal man of God, he was one who could easily fall prey to the temptation posed by the free women around him, as the liquor continued to flow, and with it, the unleashing of the spirit of liberty, and beckoning pleasures. He was known for his energetic commitment and devotion to pay nightly visits to the houses of widows, divorcees and single mothers, "to give solace and counsel." He was single and handsome, very prone to weakness of the flesh.

Livingstone's brother was seated next to a gentleman by the name Paul Smith, who had distinguished himself in credit financing, in the heydays of slave trade. He had been an employee of the Barclays brothers who had made a huge fortune financing English slave traders. The brothers took the human cargo, of those still alive, after the hazardous trip between Africa and the United States of America, to the slave market in New Jersey.

When the Barclays brothers relocated their business to America, Paul Smith declined to migrate. He considered himself a proud Englishman and a staunch nationalist, who felt his primary call of duty, was to create wealth for

the motherland. He was sponsored on the expedition by Lloyds of London to look into prospects of establishing insurance business. His first stop would be Cape Town, and then move onward to Monomotapa. Insurance would be good business, with the expected influx of investors in diverse fields.

As they played checkers, Livingstone's brother was briefing Smith, "My brother will finance my venture in sheep farming. Once I identify and take possession of the land, I will ferry two hundred ewes and rams on board his ship on the next trip. I will be the biggest exporter of mutton in the Empire."

"We will insure your business," said Smith.

On another table sat David Livingstone with Peter Humphrey. They were discussing philosophy, something to do with the essence of life, the frailty of the spirit and the ultimate destination of the human soul.

Peter Humphrey was a much travelled man. He had been to Palestine, India, Tibet and China in a quest to understand the meaning of the human soul and how it was nurtured by religion, be it Christianity, Islam, or Buddhism. He remained as empty as he had been before on the matter upon his return from the spiritual sojourn. He had adopted "simplicity, simplicity" as his totem pole. Not that he was disillusioned in life, no! Far from it, he was still full of vitality, but he needed a locus on which to anchor the spiritual basis of man. He came from a filthy rich family in Essex and thus could afford all sorts of mental and physical calisthenics without financial stress. He was sure of inheriting the Lordship upon the death of his ailing father. He was on the expedition to renew his vigour and spirit and to explore the potential of establishing pleasure and hunting resorts for the nobility in England.

"Tell me about the Caprivi Strip," he asked Livingstone.

"It is a No Man's land between Monomotapa, Bechuanaland and Angola. It is a piece of Heaven on earth. That is where the Kalahari Desert ends, and swamps and rivers emerge while mountain ranges rise to the east. It is not far from Victoria Falls," said Livingstone.

"Such contrasting topography should excite many tourists," said Humphrey.

"Yes, indeed. The variety of animals and birds in the area defy description. Did I mention that there is a salty lake nearby where people can "walk on water?" It is called Lake Ngami. You have to see it to believe. Of course with time, it will not be a No Man's land, it will be ours!" said Livingstone.

"No, it will be mine! I will build hunting and tourist resorts everywhere with the name "Caprivi Paradise Tours," Humphrey said beaming.

"You will not be disappointed Mr. Humphrey, and maybe one day, you will change the name to "Humphrey Pleasure Tours.""

"Brilliant! Let's drink to that!"

Sea gulls were circling the "Zambezi" and dolphins were giving a free acrobatic show to the passengers. Just then, a Baroness, a charming blonde lady in her late thirties walked to Livingstone's table, with the smile of a beauty queen and the gaiety of a fashion model.

"May I join you gentlemen?" she asked softly, in a disarming tone.

Humphrey shot up and pulled a chair for her.

"It is our pleasure to be honoured with such distinguished company!" he said.

As she sat down, hell broke loose. There was commotion at the bar counter. Women were hurling insults and threatening each other with all manner of calamities. Livingstone was alarmed. One of the high-pitched voices was from his wife, Mary, a lady who once had wild, sexy eyes, but they were now droopy from over-consumption of alcohol.

"Excuse me for a minute," Livingstone said as he stood up. He went straight to attend to the threatening doomsday scenario, which was threatening his family reputation or what was left of it.

A visibly angry Livingstone got hold of Mary by the hand and shouted;

"What the hell is going on?"

"She called me a pygmy, an alcoholic and a harlot," said Mary pointing at a woman with blood-shot eyes and an unkempt mop of hair. She was one of the women who had been smuggled into the ship by the sailors.

"Yes, I caught her in bed with my boyfriend. I will kill her!" the woman screamed.

"Mary, what is this?" asked a shocked Livingstone.

"No, I was not in bed with him. I opened a door thinking it was our room, only to find a sailor, who invited me in for a drink. We didn't do anything, honest, we didn't!" cried Mary.

"Liar! Liar! You had no panties!" shouted the woman prostitute with shaggy hair.

"I had not worn panties!" Mary defended herself awkwardly as the revellers shook with laughter.

"Enough of this!" shouted Livingstone as he took Mary away. She did not

protest but followed him meekly swaying from side to side, unsteady on her feet. Livingstone felt humiliated. His authority on the ship had been badly dented. He would henceforth be a subject of ridicule.

As Livingstone and Mary retreated out of sight, the Baroness commented; "Just like women!"

Shocked by the incident, Humphrey, responded; "I beg your pardon?"

"Women are trouble and much more so when drunk. Oh! We have not been introduced! I am Baroness Alice Wilkinson."

"I am Peter Humphrey," he said.

"I should have guessed so! There was something vaguely familiar about you. How time passes! I was a great fun of yours as a young girl. You played rugby for the London team, didn't you," she asked.

"True, but that was many years ago!"

"I had a crush on you! I am glad to meet you in flesh, at last!" said the charming Baroness.

And with that she extended her tender hand towards him, placing the fingers at the back of his hand, which was rested on the table. Her hand was covered with a soft white glove. Not knowing how to respond, Humphrey looked at her face. She had a warm and dazzling smile and as their eyes locked, she winked, tilting her head sideways. Her lips were parted and inviting.

Humphrey felt lost, confused and scared. He had married and divorced twice; he had not completely recovered from the experiences. Having just witnessed the ugly incident involving Mary Livingstone, the last thing he wanted to be associated with was a woman. Before he could recollect his thoughts, she spoke; "What brings you on this voyage to the wild and the unknown?" she asked.

"I am on a quest for earthly pleasures, as a master, not as a victim," he said.

"Exactly what do you mean by that?" she asked.

"Simply that I am going to open hunting and tourist resorts in a paradise called Caprivi."

"Funny, our two worlds seem to be united by a common destiny, only I did not know where to locate my business," she told him.

"What kind of business do you envisage?"

"Just like you, pursuit of earthly pleasures! Settlers, miners, hunters, administrators, tourists and the clergy will surely be looking for fun after a hard day's job. They will find gorgeous women waiting! Women seeking adventure will be taken care of as well!"

"You plan setting up a brothel?" Humphrey asked, almost with disgust.

"Not so, it will be a pleasure resort where both men and women will interact without inhibition. There are many rich women in Britain yearning for fun. Do you know that a lot of women in Britain have never experienced orgasm? They would give anything for an exciting experience in wild and sunny Africa! We could form a partnership, you know," she said in earnest.

Humphrey had never met such a candid woman, so free spirited and so charming. He was transfixed. Their night never ended. They woke up in the same bed the following morning, their quest for earthly pleasures having been initiated in a very practical and satisfying experience for both parties.

As the "Zambezi" approached the port of Bombay, Humphrey and the Baroness were standing on the deck, his arms around her waist. The wind was blowing her blond hair to his face; he was enjoying the teasing soft sensation.

"Tell me about your late husband, the Baron," asked Humphrey.

"Peter, I beg you one thing. Let's leave our past behind and enjoy each other until Kingdom come."

"Granted!" he acquiesced and kissed her lips tenderly, as the sea gulls continued to circle the ship.

Livingstone, who had remained recluse since the incident involving his wife, re-emerged. Visibly, he had hit the bottle hard as his eyes were red and swollen; his gait a lot less steady. The mention of the approaching docking in Bombay had jerked him out of his melancholy. Mary was nowhere to be seen in the cheering which echoed from the ship.

A contingent of British soldiers was at hand to welcome Livingstone and the passengers.

"We are here to assess the potential for investment and settlement in this colony, and to compare the same with Africa," Livingstone told the Commander of the British regiment.

"Here, the weather is very bad with high temperatures and devilish monsoons, not to mention the huge, lazy and starving population of beggars. I believe the fortunes of Britain should be charted elsewhere, except for trade in tea, spices and silk."

The visitors headed for the city of Bombay which was one hell of a massive overpopulated dirty sprawling slum. The stench and filth were horrendous.

The inhabitants were so thin that one questioned why they were not being blown away by the wind. They were arguably the most miserable human souls on earth.

"How do they survive?" Livingstone asked the Commander.

"Purely on small portions of rice submerged in a broth of hot pepper. They drink a lot of water to wash away the heat in their mouths and tummies. They all suffer from beriberi," narrated the Commander.

"And why does Britain want to conquer such a miserable lot of worthlessness?" asked Livingstone.

"Oh, they occupy a sub-continent of great strategic significance to us. Their handiwork in silk is also highly valued world-wide."

"That's all?" asked Livingstone.

"That's all," replied the Commander.

In the streets, rickshaws pulled by men, were running back and forth ferrying passengers and cargo.

"The rich don't walk, they are carried. They are the ruling class of Brahmins."

The rich wore colourful expensive silk clothing tied loosely around their bodies. The others wore simple attires comprising of cheap shirts and trousers which looked more like pyjamas than anything else. For whatever reason, everybody seemed to have a red dot on the forehead, maybe to ward off evil spirits.

Livingstone and a select few were guests of the Commander in the Senior Officers' Mess that evening. He had hoped to meet Speke and Burton, the upstarts who wanted to upstage him in the quest for the discovery of the source of the River Nile. Both were soldiers stationed in Bombay. When he enquired about them, the Commander responded, "They have already left for England to seek funding from the Royal Geographical Society. Personally, I am glad to see them gone. Besides acting like big bother, they have unrestrained appetites for the immoral. They are homosexuals, you know. They are very pompous and live in their world of beckoning grandeur through exploration."

Alarm bells were ringing in Livingstone's head. He was thinking to himself, "They are planning to upstage me! They have to be stopped. The work of Mungo Park must be completed by a Scotsman! Me! Not by some English hooligans!" He was seething with anger.

Discussions held between the soldiers and the fortune seekers led to the desertion of several English soldiers who hopped on the Zambezi when the time to depart came. They too wanted a piece of the pie in the new paradise.

The general conclusions made were that the Indians were ill-suited for hard work. Everybody gave thumbs up to the physique of the African man and his suitability as a work horse in farms, mines and factories. After all, had he not proved his mettle by building the United States from nothing to a great world power with his sweat and blood?

The ship was steaming to Sofala, the commercial port of Monomotapa, the targeted Heaven. As the voyage progressed smoothly, there were animated debates. Peter Humphrey and the Baroness were selling the idea of the Caprivi Paradise to all on-board.

"You will be most welcome on our paradise resorts to relax and enjoy yourselves." said Humphrey.

"Think of wife-swapping in your programme. Many of us are tired of our women," said Lord Graham, who was dreaming of establishing a huge ranch to export beef, milk, butter and cheese to Britain.

"Wives are also fed up with their husbands! A change is as good as new! I welcome the idea of husband-swapping or whatever with both hands." That came from a middle-aged lady, well attired. She looked like another lady of means. She was heartily cheered by the other women for her audacity in openly declaring fundamental feminine rights in the new world.

"There will be room for everybody and everything! It will be a pleasure paradise of unrestricted sex!" said the Baroness. The cheering that followed was deafening and electrifying.

"We will live like gods and goddesses!" shouted Raphael Bigwood, the head of a UK consortium dealing with mining of gold, diamonds and gemstones.

Livingstone had not recovered from the shame Mary had brought him. He was seated in a corner writing his report when John Kirk joined him. They had known each other for years.

"I want to commend you for your vision and sacrifice! I propose we form an investment partnership in gold and diamonds. I will do the donkey work once you show me how." John Kirk, the secret agent in M16 was genuinely

contemplating being a rich man, just like the rest, living a life of bliss full of fun and games.

"You work out the details," said Livingstone coldly, almost absentmindedly.

John Kirk did not take Livingstone's attitude kindly. He immediately shelved the idea of a partnership and withdrew quietly. His ego was wounded.

As the ship docked in Sofala, Livingstone bit his lower lip. His agreement with the Changamire was that he would return with pistols, rifles and cannons to fight the threatening enemies of the Kingdom, in particular the Portuguese and the Donyiro Sultanate. He had not brought the guns; neither had he intended to do so. He had to work out something convincing for the relationship to continue on a friendly footing. So much was at stake.

They disembarked in Sofala. At the port, he noted the imposing presence of Portuguese soldiers which had not been the case when he was there last. He wondered what had happened to warrant such a threatening boost of firepower. His curiosity would soon be answered.

Hardly had he settled in his rented room when a knock came on the door.

"Come in," he said.

In came Chuma and Sutsi, the slave boys he had rescued from the Portuguese. He had left them under the care of the Changamire.

"Master, master, we are glad to see you. We knew you would come back!" They hugged and hugged as the boys shed tears of joy.

"What are you doing here?" Livingstone asked them.

"We came on a caravan bringing ivory for export, but when it was time to return, we ran away. We have been working at the port waiting for you every day. Then today, someone told us the Englishman who had visited the Changamire has returned," said Sutsi.

"I always keep my promise," said Livingstone.

"We also kept ours. We waited for you!" said Chuma.

"We shall always keep our promise," said Sutsi.

"It is good we ran away before the big death," said Chuma.

"What death?" asked Livingstone.

"The death that the Portuguese priest and the nuns brought to Monomotapa," continued Chuma.

"The details we received in Britain before my departure for India were scanty. Tell me more," said Livingstone.

"They call it the plague. Haven't you heard the story? It was hell. Thousands of people died including Taiwo," said Sutsi then Chuma continued, "Everybody mourned the death of Taiwo for weeks, including the sick and the dying. Changamire remained in seclusion; he was very sad. For seven days, he neither ate nor drank anything. He was never the same after Taiwo's death."

"What are you talking about?" asked a shocked Livingstone.

"So many people died from the plague and the sexual diseases brought by the nuns. In the end, it was impossible to bury the dead because they were too many. It was then that Changamire ordered the evacuation of the great City of Matapa. Temporary makeshift structures were built in Harare," narrated Sutsi.

"Go on…" said Livingstone.

"Then the Portuguese soldiers came from Sofala and from Angola. They bombarded the city of Matapa with cannons; the mountains and valleys were shaking with the blasts and echoes of the cannons. For a whole day and night, they hurled bombs on the capital. Huge billows of flames and smoke could be seen from very far away. The smoke was so much that you could not see the sun during the day or the moon and stars at night. The inferno was too much to bear!

"Master, the Portuguese soldiers reduced the city of Matapa to ashes. No warrior ventured beyond River Mbuni to engage the Portuguese because their weapons were like thunder! The spears and arrows were useless against them. Finally, the bombardment stopped and the Portuguese went away. They did not enter the burnt city. Changamire lost the spirit to live when the Ruling Council told him point blank that it was his fraternising with foreigners which had ruined the Kingdom. He died a very sad man after all he had done for Monomotapa." concluded Sutsi.

"Changamire is dead?" mourned a disbelieving Livingstone.

"Yes master," replied Sutsi.

"What about the Portuguese soldiers?" asked Livingstone.

"Some returned to Angola and others are here in Sofala, waiting until the plague is gone and then they will take over Monomotapa," said Chuma.

"And who succeeded Changamire?" asked Livingstone.

"That idiot Ndovu! He is hated so much by the people that some regions have broken away and declared independence. There is chaos in the Kingdom or whatever remains of it," said Chuma.

These were some of the calamities St. Peter had predicted.

"But you know the saddest thing is that the Portuguese are accusing you of being the catalysts for their actions. Whatever it is that you told the British Government caused panic in Lisbon and in the Vatican. They say theirs was pre-emptive action to thwart the British occupation of Monomotapa," said Sutsi.

"Me? They call me the catalyst of their diabolical actions?" asked Livingstone.

"Yes master. They say you provoked their action," said Sutsi.

"I'll go to Harare; I must put the record straight. The people of Monomotapa must know the truth," Livingstone was pensive and there was silence for a while, then he said;

"Will you do me a favour?"

"All you have to do is to state it master," said Chuma.

"I want to send you to King Ndovu with a message. Can you make it?" asked Livingstone.

"Of course we can! The people of Monomotapa adopted us as their very own. Ndovu will be glad to see us and to receive your message," said Sutsi.

"When do we leave?" asked Chuma.

"As soon as we get to Ngorofa," replied Livingstone.

With that, Chuma and Sutsi retreated to their quarters. They were happy to be re-united with the man who had rescued them from slavery, the one they called "Master".

Livingstone wrote a report to the British Government giving details of the Portuguese destruction of Monomotapa and their planned occupation of the Kingdom as soon as the plague was over. He urged the British Government to unreservedly condemn the diabolical actions of the Portuguese in cahoots with the Vatican, and to lead the world in warning the Portuguese not to ever dream of occupying Monomotapa. "Evil must never be rewarded," he concluded. He sent a blind copy to Cecil Rhodes at Oxford.

When the report reached the Foreign Office, two things happened; the British Government led a vociferous crusade accusing the Portuguese of demonic atrocities and arson while warning that any further move against

Monomotapa would be met with equal force from London. In essence, the British Government was throwing its weight behind the independence, sovereignty and territorial integrity of Monomotapa, or was it?

The declaration confused Lisbon and the Vatican. They accused each other openly of the ill-conceived matter of the plague, the diseases and the destruction of Matapa. Be that as it may, the Portuguese could not move against Monomotapa for fear of direct confrontation with the British.

Satisfied that his message had produced the intended result, Livingstone was ready to sail up the Zambezi. The delay had been long and agonising; it had created uncertainty in the group.

The optimism and dreams of the passengers had waned with each passing day. The long wait had become an eternity. Hope had been replaced by disillusionment and gloom. Tempers were flaring and Livingstone had become the recipient of frequent taunts and insults.

It was Humphrey who finally declared;

"This stupid Scot is on an ego trip. I fear the expedition will yield no more than a catastrophe of an unknown magnitude," Many agreed with him.

"How the hell did we place so much trust on a man who brings a sick wife on such a trip? From now on, it is everybody for himself," declared the Baroness.

Livingstone had lost the control and respect of the group.

Many members of the party which had sailed with Livingstone from London and Bombay abandoned the expedition and headed for Cape Town which was cosier. Others stated that they wanted to do business in Sofala and would not venture into the hinterland. It was a whittled team, especially made up of hunters and miners which stuck with Livingstone. An enterprising Arab by the name of Tipu Tipu offered them his barge at an exorbitant price up to the inland port of Ngorofa. After much haggling, the barge was hired.

Tipu Tipu was the greatest slave trader in Eastern Africa. He had ivory, gold, diamond and rhino horn trade interests in Central and Southern Africa. He was one of the traders who had urged the Donyiro Sultanate to invade Monomotapa. The invasion had been a debacle, and so when Tipu Tipu received news that the Portuguese had destroyed the City of Matapa, he fell on his knees facing Mecca and said a prayer, "Allah Akbar" praising his Allah because the defeat of the Donyiros had been avenged, albeit by someone else.

"What lies beyond Ngorofa?" Livingstone asked him.

"Beyond there, the river winds and unwinds. The flow is punctuated by cascades and waterfalls, the greatest of which is the Mosi-O-Tunya. The source of the river is in the forest of the Congo, then it flows very fast tumbling upon itself on granite rocks and moving in a great hurry in search of a resting place, the Indian Ocean. But upon reaching Ngorofa, the river is so wide and tired that it flows steadily, gently and smoothly for the rest of the journey. This is the navigable section," said Tipu Tipu.

"I have never heard a river described that way, as if it is a living thing! Not even my friend Rudyard Kipling can describe a river in such a manner," commended Livingstone.

"Don't you know that rivers have lives? They eat careless swimmers, they give birth to life and when they die, they are buried in the ocean. Rivers have a beginning and an end, just like us," said Tipu Tipu.

"Talking about rivers, have you ever heard of the River Nile?" asked Livingstone.

"Of course I have. It ends in Egypt but its birth place is unknown," said Tipu Tipu.

"I am interested in finding its source," said Livingstone.

"My friend, not even the Greeks and the Romans could solve the mystery. Those who tried ended up dead. Like the secrets of the Pyramids, its source is protected by gods and spirits. Some say the source is east of here in the Congo forest, while others say it is up north in the Mountains of the Moon, who knows," said Tipu Tipu.

"Will you help me?" asked Livingstone.

"White man, I am not suicidal. Pay my fee for the boat and leave the Nile alone," said Tipu Tipu.

The barge was loaded and the journey to Ngorofa commenced as angry Portuguese soldiers looked on. They would have loved to finish the British expedition deep in the jungle of Africa, but they feared the consequences. It was an intrusion they loathed. Once again, they were being humiliated by the British, who had driven them out of India.

Everybody in the barge was once again in high spirits as the trip was taking them to the "Promised Land". Mary Livingstone sat in the bar chatting with anybody who cared to buy her another drink. Livingstone had given up on changing her ways as she had become incorrigible. He sat by himself putting pen to paper, writing another report of another epic journey in the Dark Continent. He had promised himself that after the Zambezi Expedition, he would immediately embark on the search for the source of the Nile, regardless of the interest expressed by Speke and Burton. He had the Herodotus map close by.

John Kirk eyed Livingstone and said to himself, "Poor fellow, so much effort expended for the right cause by the wrong man, for the wrong reason." He was referring to the quest for a vast British Empire, on which "the sun will never set", and Livingstone's misplaced ambition to liberate Scotland.

As the party moved upstream, they feasted their eyes on the splendid flora and fauna along the Zambezi Valley. Giants of elephants had tusks so huge; the party speculated how they carried them through the thick foliage. They saw a herd of rhinoceros with horns so long that each one was a hunter's dream. The hunters were begging that the barge be stopped so that they could commence their business there and then.

"This is why we came on this trip!" one of the hunters protested when the barge did not stop.

"You have not seen anything yet!" said Livingstone. "Shooting will commence in Ngorofa. I assure you, you will shoot until you run out of ammunition."

Livingstone turned to John Kirk and asked, "Have you ever dreamt of a paradise like this? Add diamonds, gold, precious stones, fertile land and a lovely climate and ask yourself, what is the British Government waiting for?"

"I could not agree with you more. We have been sleeping on our laurels. I should be appointed to administer this territory when we move in," he said.

"Then you will have a big fight in your hands. Cecil Rhodes has laid a claim on it and I support him."

They eyed each other for some time. Livingstone did not like the look in Kirk's eyes. He excused himself and retreated to a lonely corner where he continued writing his report. He had decided a long time ago that Cecil Rhodes was his tool for implementing the "divine mission". He was going to support him through thick and thin. They trusted each other and had done a lot together to incorporate Africa into the imperial scheme.

As soon as they came to Ngorofa, Livingstone called Chuma and Sutsi.

"I want you to proceed to Harare and tell Ndovu that I have brought the guns I promised his father the Changamire. Tell him the British Government stands by him in the struggle against the Portuguese. The expedition will be camping at the Mosi-O-Tunya. I want you to bring me his response there."

"Yes master..." they replied in unison and dashed off to prepare for the journey. Livingstone had calculated that having lived with the people of Monomotapa, the two could easily return to the capital and gain access to King Ndovu, and they had assured him so.

With the help of the locals and his previous experience, Livingstone mapped the area from Sofala to Victoria Falls. The journey from Ngorofa to Victoria Falls was made on foot; the hunters were confused as to whether they should shoot on their way going or on their way back. They were short of porters. It was surprising how many local people approached them with ivory, diamonds and gold, in exchange for any valuable item they fancied including blankets and sheets of cloths.

Victoria Falls was a sight they could not describe, so picturesque. The area around it was abounding with wildlife. They hunted and ate to their fill.

"This is paradise. I could live here forever!" commented an excited John Kirk. Then came the surprise from Livingstone; "I intend to visit the old capital of Matapa before visiting the new capital Harare. From here, the party will break into two. Those who wish to come with me and those who will return to Ngorofa, especially the hunters. We should leave Ngorofa for Sofala in a month's time."

Then hell broke loose. It was John Kirk who led the charge. He did not want to visit the city of the plague nor did he want to return to Ngorofa without Livingstone. He was not supposed to let Livingstone out of sight.

"I am totally opposed to the plan. Our mission is very clear, which is to map out the navigability of the Zambezi and the natural resources of this land. I believe we have accomplished our mission. Your plan to visit Matapa is a side show, ill-conceived in light of the plague, and badly timed because the British Government is urgently awaiting our report. Any deviation from our mandate will not be looked upon kindly." Kirk's words were met with shouts of "Hear! Hear!" All the people were in agreement with him. Livingstone's brother shot up,

"We came here as one party and we must stick together. Since none of us wants to visit the city of plague, we should all, including yourself, return to Ngorofa.

You cannot abandon us in the middle of nowhere," he said. He was wildly cheered.

"The mandate to map the natural resources gives us the right to visit anywhere and everywhere. In terms of time, the Portuguese will not dare occupy Monomotapa as they had planned. Thirdly, I intend to have a word with the new King because his cooperation is vital, if we are to avoid too much resistance when we occupy the Kingdom," Livingstone argued.

Kirk shot up.

"Your words sound hollow. We do not need anybody's cooperation to occupy Monomotapa. Secondly, the King has no army as his forces have been decimated by the plague and gonorrhoea. There is also rebellion in the Kingdom, so what resistance are you talking about?" he probed further.

"Gentlemen, any short-sighted decision on our part or that of the British Government will lead to loss of life. Our duty is to smoothen the way for occupation. Sleep over the matter and we will deliberate on the best course of action tomorrow," pleaded Livingstone.

Clearly, Livingstone was alone; his reasoning did not change things. The hard positions taken could not be bridged. Livingstone was hell bent on his plan while the others were opposed to it. The party had arrived at an impasse.

The following morning, Livingstone woke up late because he had drunk too much whisky with his wife Mary. He had a huge hangover. When he summoned the members of the expedition to a meeting, only John Kirk, the bishop, his brother and Mary showed up. The others had gone seeking fortunes in the name of game trophies, gold and diamonds.

"It is your fault. Your new course of action is totally disapproved by all. I suggest that we all head back to Ngorofa," proposed Kirk who talked with clenched teeth and a sneer.

Just then, news came in that Chuma and Sutsi accompanied by Monomotapa warriors were approaching. Livingstone went to meet them. After exchanging greetings, Chuma announced that King Ndovu was waiting to receive the guns from Livingstone. Livingstone was in a fix. He called John Kirk aside and told him, "I did not buy any guns for Ndovu and yet I must meet him. Since there are a number of spare guns with the hunters, I could take a few and pay the owners later. What do you think?" he said pleading his case.

"Why don't you wait and discuss the matter with the hunters when they return!" retorted Kirk.

"Because I want to leave immediately," said Livingstone.

"So what are you suggesting? That I endorse your plan to steal guns from the hunters and help you when they raise a stint later?" complained Kirk.

"Precisely…" said Livingstone.

"You are truly out of your mind. I will do nothing of the sort!" said Kirk.

Livingstone left with Chuma and Sutsi without one more word. They returned shortly with an ox-driven wagon they had purchased from a local trader. Kirk, the bishop and his brother watched as Livingstone loaded the wagon with goods including gifts for Ndovu. Then came the ultimate move! Livingstone hurried from tent to tent collecting hunting rifles and pistols from the absent owners! All in all, he took five pistols and three hunting rifles. He commanded Mary to mount the wagon; she did so obediently. To her, life had become a circus, so anything was just fine. He turned to Kirk and the other two and asked them, "Coming or not..?"

It was his brother who rushed forward and confronted him. "David, you are stark mad! You have stolen guns and now you are heading to the city of the plague? Do you want to take the disease to Britain? I will not let you go!" And his brother stood in front of the wagon, his arms outstretched, blocking the way.

"You do not understand the sacrifices I have made for the sake of Scotland; and nobody will stop me!" shouted Livingstone. But he at once regretted his outburst, because of the presence of John Kirk. He had not told his brother that he was pursuing the dream of liberating Scotland.

His brother did not understand. Livingstone tried to pull him aside, and then a fight ensued. By the time Kirk managed to separate them, Livingstone was bleeding by the nose, the worse off of the two in the scuffle. Once again, his brother stood in front of the bulls. This time, Livingstone drew his pistol.

"If you don't move, I will shoot you dead!" Livingstone said to his brother, very angry and humiliated.

John Kirk went to Livingstone's brother and pulled him away gently, then turned to Livingstone and said, "You may continue with your madness!" The venom in his voice was scaring.

Livingstone without another word signalled to Chuma and Sutsi that it was time to leave. They jumped on the wagon and moved in the direction of Matapa, while the warriors walked on foot some distance behind. In his inner self, Livingstone felt something had gone awfully wrong. Whether it was his sense of judgment which had gone awry or whether the divine powers willed him a personal disaster, he could not tell. There comes a time in a crisis when matters get very hazy. Such it was for Livingstone. All he could count upon was Mary and the two ex-slaves, Chuma and Sutsi. Mary's wild eyes had become droopy with drink. He felt his once mighty world was shrinking and disappearing very fast. He wished Cecil Rhodes had been with him, but then heroes are made in times of crisis.

Livingstone moved on, not quite sure of himself. Worst of all was the news that the mighty army of the kingdom had been decimated by the plague and some units had deserted to serve breakaway regions. How then was his "divine mission" to be accomplished if the British Army was going to have a walk-over? Was the "divine mission" still on course? He deliberated in alarm. How could God let him down after guiding him this far? But then, God always worked miracles for his chosen when times were most desperate. He needed his miracle now and not later. He lifted his eyes to the heavens and he was blinded by the glare of the scorching sun. He did not pray as he had intended.

"Perhaps later." he consoled himself as they moved on.

CHAPTER 17

DISASTER IN THE BUSH

Chuma and Sutsi did not understand what had happened to the happy party of foreigners who had left Sofala. What they had witnessed at Victoria Falls had informed them that all was not well. They had assured Livingstone that they would keep their promise to stand by him; therefore, they were determined to do so no matter what. They did not ask questions and Livingstone did not offer any explanation. The party was solemnly heading to the burnt city of Matapa, like a funeral procession; it was a sad sight indeed. Mary was holding an open bottle of whisky, sipping it dry, with uncontrollable hiccups which had come to bother her in recent times. They would come and go of their own accord, but they did not stop her from drinking.

The warriors marched behind watching the strange spectacle of a people without tongues. They had seen Livingstone before, a very jolly man who made the Changamire happy. This was a different Livingstone, looking very angry, ugly and very distant. The behaviour of the woman with him was even stranger. They wondered if she was carrying diseases like the Portuguese nuns, but Livingstone, they believed, was an honest man; not like Cardinal Domingos. They would deliver him to King Ndovu and maybe there would be laughter again in the palace which had come to resemble a graveyard.

Up the hills and down the valleys they went. They did not meet a single living soul. All they saw were skeletons of the dead, from the plague, and they were in the thousands.

In the circumstances, all was going well, as well as could be until the bulls pulling the wagon came to an abrupt halt. With their nostrils flaring, their ears pulled backward flapping wildly, while they let out wild snorts. Before questions could be asked, Livingstone saw a pride of lions emerge from the bush. Then in a flash, they came charging full flight at the wagon with their cubs in tow. There were yells of panic, all except from Mary who was too drunk to fathom what the alarm was about.

The oxen, in the confusion, took off cutting a sharp angle to avoid the lions. The cart overturned and those on board were thrown and strewn all over the place. Some oxen cut loose as the cart disintegrated. The lions chased the loose bulls as the passengers scampered in all directions for cover. Livingstone climbed up a tree as fast as his legs could carry him, and so did Chuma and Sutsi. Before the party of warriors regained their composure to deal with the menace, Mary let out a yell and her voice was heard no more. The lioness with the cubs had found her where she had fallen, bleeding profusely. Since the plague, wild animals had become accustomed to cheap meals, what with so many human bodies dead in the bush! Mary had become just another easy prey for the lioness and the cubs, while the other lions went for the bulls. She had screamed with the first bite on the shoulder before the lioness went for the jugular. Against such a big pride, the warriors had learnt never to confront the lions as it would be suicidal. It was therefore everybody for himself.

What remained of Mary was her blood-stained white flowing dress and her hat. Frustrated with the inadequate meal, the cubs vented their anger by tearing the dress into shreds. The shreds were blown by the wind only to be caught by the bushes where they remained fluttering vigorously as though they had inherited the miserable and troubled soul of Mary. When Livingstone looked down from the tree and saw what had happened, he cried,

"Oh, my God! Oh God, the lions have killed Mary, they have eaten her body. Oh God, please help!" It was too late for God to intervene.

The lions feasted on the bulls and thereafter took a rest in the shadows under nearby trees waiting for the sun to go down before they could go to the river to quench their thirst. In the meantime, vultures descended from the skies and cleaned up the carcasses including that of Mary. Before sundown, hyenas appeared and carried away the bones. Soon, the place was as clean as it had ever been except for the rags of what was Mary's dress, in shreds, dancing in the wind. Again, Livingstone remembered the conversation between Moffat and Rudyard Kipling. Moffat had invited Kipling to visit Africa to write a poem on the eating habits of animals, the pecking order and how they always left the jungle clean. Livingstone had not paid much attention to the matter then, but alas! He was now a witness, with his Mary and her wild eyes in the mix.

Much later after the lions had gone, the group reassembled. They were shaken to the core of their bones, mourning the death of Mary. The party consoled Livingstone although he did not appear to have any tears to shed for his dead wife. They lit a fire by which they spent the night. Livingstone recounted to them how Mary had studied archaeology and had dreamt of tracing the link between man and the ape. Now that would have to be left to someone else. The party could not comprehend what he was talking about. In their understanding, both a human being and an ape were made different ways. Therefore, there never could have been a linkage between the two. They then concluded that Livingstone and his wife suffered from some disease close to hallucinations and that they enjoyed distorting reality.

It was going to be a solemn, frightful and long journey to Matapa and then to Harare for Livingstone.

"Am I doomed or am I not?" he kept asking himself.

The answer always came back to him, "You are on a "divine mission". " If it was so, he thought, then divinity works in very mysterious ways. He recalled the story of a character in the Bible called Job. God brought to Job leprosy, poverty, death of his children and all forms of unbearable hardships just to test his faith. Poor Job held on to his faith and in the end, he was rewarded a hundred fold of his lost wealth. This brought Livingstone cheers. He thought of himself as the leader of Independent Scotland, as a reward for his suffering!

"And what a story it will be!" he said to himself smiling. But supposing his was only a wild dream as the Scottish Liberation Movement had warned him, then what? He thought.

They came to the ruins of the old capital Matapa. There, Livingstone stood before the ugly remains of the once majestic and beautiful city. He was in anguish and crestfallen. Years of immaculate planning, ingenuity in architecture and craftsmanship, worthy labour expended and the pride and joy of a great Kingdom had been reduced to rubble. Memories, tears, dislocation and desolation were all that remained. He shed tears and cursed the rot in the human soul that so heartlessly destroys for selfish ends. Remaining still standing – tall and defiant – were the walls that had surrounded the city. The cannon balls had been lobbied over them in the bombardment. But the beautiful patterns and figures still on the walls were beckoning and inviting all who wanted to draw nearer to do so without fear.

It was as if they were mocking the authors of the heinous crime. Livingstone knew in his heart that these walls would forever still remain standing, long after the human race was gone, just like the Pyramids of Egypt. They would defy war, fire or any other force, natural or manmade. There was something heavenly and eternal about them. They would speak about the destruction of a black civilisation and move both God and man to tears. Livingstone heard himself asking,

"Savages, who are the savages?" to him, the answer was clear, the Portuguese. His heart shuddered. He wondered how many other Kingdoms in Africa and other parts of the world would be destroyed by the rampage of European savages as they fulfilled their selfish ends in the name of national interests couched in philanthropic jargon and invoking the name of God. He recalled the demise of the Incas, Mayas, Aztecs and other kingdoms and wondered how God could stand such tyranny. In a way, he felt relieved that Scotland was still intact and it could be salvaged from the ravages of the English. He was saddened when it dawned on him that he was the prime agent of this destruction which had only begun. He was the mastermind!

"If Africans don't get their act together, they will suffer the fate of the Neanderthals. Some must perish for others to live, ah! The survival of the fittest!" he concluded without any feeling of guilt.

That he was to all intent and purposes associated with this dark march against Africa, did not bother his conscience. However, he consoled himself that he would address the moral part of it when Scotland was free and make amends by being a good friend to all Africans. He would then extend aid to them from guns, to infrastructure projects, agriculture and even balance of payments. And then God would look upon him kindly on the Day of Judgment but send the King of Portugal, the Pope and the Queen of England straight to hell.

The bestiality of the Portuguese brutality had not helped his cause though since the British Government was now eyeing Monomotapa as its exclusive preserve to be acquired cheaply as the backbone of its military power had been broken. It was a question of when not if for firm action to be embarked upon to occupy the land. The great army of Monomotapa which he had counted upon to furiously engage the British was a pale shadow of itself with deaths, defections, rebellion and the disintegration of the Kingdom.

However, since the appetite of the British imperial machine was insatiable, he hoped that Lobengula, the Zulus, Mirambo and others would fill in the gap as the empire expanded in all directions. His plan was still on course or was it?

"Let us proceed to Harare," said Livingstone.

After a long tiresome trek, they crossed the river Mbuni. Far in the distance, they could see the sprawling slum of makeshift huts, the new temporary capital, Harare, which was threatening to remain permanent after the destruction of the old beautiful city, and the death of the Changamire. The spirit of the empire was dead.

Finally, they arrived in Harare and met the head of the royal guard who told Livingstone,

"King Ndovu says I take you to him immediately."

"Let us go," said Livingstone.

Seated on a big traditional three-legged stool which must have been specially carved out of a giant tree just for him was the massive figure of King Ndovu, looking plump, lazy and stupid.

"Welcome old friend, welcome," he said.

"I am glad to be back in your great Kingdom," said Livingstone.

"I wonder how great she is now after all the bad things which have befallen her. I would have loved to inherit a jovial and prosperous Kingdom, but I inherited death, poverty and despair. My mother says you don't have to bother yourself with solving the "curse of the caves" because it is now behind us. She must have seen the destruction of the Kingdom, but she never warned my father, the Changamire. If she had, he would not have let in the Portuguese priest and the sick nuns."

"Maybe the gods and spirits told her not to talk," said Livingstone.

"She is relaxed now, but she is not the same. Something still bugs her. I am very scared. Could you find out from her whether there are other disasters to come?" he asked Livingstone. He could remember, Livingstone had a jovial relationship with Changamire, and he was going to exploit the goodwill to the possible extent.

"I will try," promised Livingstone.

"Where are the guns?" asked Ndovu.

David Livingstone instructed Chuma and Sutsi to bring the three hunting rifles and the five pistols.

"These are not the big guns which destroyed Matapa! Where are the cannons?" asked Ndovu.

"The cannons are coming. I brought these for training before the big consignment arrives. Your warriors must learn how to handle the smaller calibre weapons first before they learn how to shoot with the big ones," said a smiling Livingstone. His reasoning pleased Ndovu.

"And when does the training begin?" asked Ndovu.

"Tomorrow morning," said Livingstone.

If anybody had said that Livingstone was an evil man, like Domingos had tried to paint him, Ndovu would not have believed him. Here he was, with guns to train the warriors to ward off any threat to the Kingdom.

"First, I will teach those generals who have deserted me a great lesson and then I will bring back all the break-away tribes who have left Monomotapa! Now, tell me, I hear you had a great misfortune coming here and you lost your wife?" asked Ndovu.

"It is so Your Majesty," said Livingstone loathing the "Majesty" bit. Ndovu looked too commonplace to bear such a dignified title.

"We were attacked by a pride of lions which killed my wife," said Livingstone.

"But you had guns, why didn't you shoot them?" asked Ndovu.

"When we fell off the wagon, we had no time to think about guns," said Livingstone.

"So, where were you when the lions were devouring her?" Ndovu asked; Livingstone loathed the question.

"I was up on a tree," he replied

"Don't tell me you scampered up a tree leaving your wife defenceless! And now you tell me you will help us fight the Portuguese? One moment you are so helpless and the next, you are so powerful?" Ndovu sneered. Livingstone hit back.

"Your warriors were supposed to protect us! Where were they? The cowards ran as fast as their legs could carry them," said an irritated Livingstone.

"It is true, it is true. You do not mess up with a pride of lions. If it is a

solitary lion, we can deal with it, not a pride. Do you know I killed a lion just before I was circumcised?" asked Ndovu.

"Really? All by yourself?" asked Livingstone.

"Yes, all by myself!" but the King was looking down as he lied. "Next time, do not leave your gun in the wagon. Africa is not a place for cowards and the careless. You must walk with your eyes open and your ears to the ground. There are too many dangers," said the King.

"I will remember that," responded Livingstone.

"Now you must tell me those stories which you told my father, the ones that made him so happy. Like him, I am also a sad man. You have seen the state of the Kingdom, but even worse, every time I try to make love to my wife, I hear owls hooting, bats shrieking, hyenas laughing and jackals barking. Strange thing is; she never hears them! When the noises begin, I become disturbed and scared; I cannot make love to her. Do you think it is another curse? You know, at this rate, I will never sire an heir or even agree to another reed dance? If I cannot deal with one woman, how can I deal with two or three? I am finished! Please give me a cure, make me happy, and make the evil noises go away. Tell me the stories and give me the medicine you gave my father to make him sleep, then give me a solution to my problems," said the King.

"Like I told the Changamire, my God only helps those who believe in him. If you accept Jesus as your personal Saviour, the miracle of a solution will be found," said Livingstone.

"OK, tell me about Him."

For once, Livingstone got very serious about converting someone to Christianity. He narrated the story of Jesus to Ndovu as convincingly as he could. There was a huge bowl of roasted peanuts and cashew nuts in front of the King. As Livingstone spoke on and on, Ndovu kept on munching and mumbling, "Ehe..., ehe..." as the story got thicker and thicker. He looked more bored than attentive. Finally, and to Livingstone's great surprise, he said, "I believe." There were no more nuts left to chew!

Livingstone eyed him curiously and said,

"Then you must be baptised!"

"I am willing, only it has to be in secret. I do not want the Chief Priest and the Ruling Council to know about it," he pleaded.

"But there has to be a witness who will give the name," said Livingstone.

"My mother can help," said the King.

"In that case, we can finish with the matter immediately," said Livingstone.

The King sent for his mother. After pleading with her, she consented saying, "If this is the way to end the curse, then it is a small sacrifice."

"What name do you choose for him?" asked Livingstone.

"Since he was young, I always identified him as the big boy because of his size. You call him Big Boy."

Livingstone asked for water and made the sign of the cross on the King's forehead as he said,

"I baptise you Big Boy in the name of Jesus." Then he placed both his hands on the King's head.

"Is that all?" asked the mother who had expected an elaborate ritual.

"That is all," said Livingstone.

"When do I get the answer from your God?" asked the King.

"I will talk to Him tonight," Livingstone replied.

With that, Livingstone gave Ndovu sleeping pills and said, "Take two". They agreed to meet the following morning at the shooting range in the big grazing field outside the huge slum city.

Livingstone, Chuma and Sutsi came with three guns, two hunting rifles and a pistol. When all were assembled, he told the warriors to get two bulls and place them at a distance of two hundred metres away. He took the hunting rifle with binoculars and let go a slug. It homed on one of the bulls' head. The animal was thrown in the air and when it fell down, it lay motionless, dead! The sound of the gun scared the crowd, but when the bull was hit, they marvelled at how noise from a stick could kill a bull so far away. The other bull had moved a few steps and stopped. Livingstone turned to Ndovu and said, "Your turn". The King protested and refused to touch the evil thing which made so much noise and killed so quickly. He suggested that the leader of the archers' brigade has a first go.

The big warrior stepped forward. Livingstone put a bullet in the chamber and showed him how to hold the gun.

"After aiming, pull this lever backwards, it is called the trigger," he instructed.

Like Livingstone before him, the warrior was on his belly searching for the bull in the binoculars. He had been told to press the butt tightly on his right shoulder. Immediately he saw the animal, he excitedly pulled the trigger. Not only did the bullet leave the chamber and head to the rocks in the distant hills, but the butt kick broke the warrior's collarbone. He threw the gun down in pain.

"He has shot himself, "a soldier cried.

"No, he did not press the butt hard against his shoulder like I had instructed him. He has only broken his collarbone; he will be alright," said Livingstone. There was only one bullet left as Livingstone had managed to steal only three.

"Anybody else who wants to have a go?" he challenged the warriors.

There were no volunteers. He went down again and shot the other bull. He had honed his shooting skills while hunting animals with Cecil Rhodes in Bechuanaland; he was quite a marksman.

"As I told your King, the gun is a very dangerous, but necessary evil. It defends a nation by its ability to kill fast and from a distance. When the big consignment of weapons arrives, I want the warriors to have the courage to handle them in defence of Monomotapa." He was cheered wildly.

The King stood to address the gathering: "You have all seen what the gun can do. Soon, Monomotapa will be very powerful and we can shoot the Portuguese and the Donyiros from very far. Livingstone is our friend and Saviour. He has been sent to us by God." He too was loudly cheered.

When the demonstration was over, Livingstone and the King went into a private conversation. Livingstone told the King,

"You have found favour in God. Last night, He gave me a way out of the curse." said a beaming Livingstone.

"Ooh! Thank heavens, our troubles are over!" said the King.

"I was told the key lies in your mother's heart. I was instructed to speak to her in private. God has softened her heart and she will speak to me if you make the necessary arrangements." said Livingstone.

"Tonight, you will dine with my mother in a private chamber and exorcise the demons from the Kingdom," said a beaming King Ndovu.

"It will be my humble duty, honour and pleasure to do so," said Livingstone.

They locked hands and walked away chatting most happily, exchanging niceties.

Ndovu's mother was glad to see her son so confident and jolly.

"For lack of someone better, he is our King and he is beginning to behave like one. The load in my heart is made much lighter. I thank Livingstone for his divine transformation," she said to herself.

Later in the day, Ndovu conveyed to her mother the request for a private conversation with Livingstone, pleading, "Mother, please do this for me and save Monomotapa. He will exorcise the evil spirit which has been devouring us."

She was silent for a long while and then she said, "The spirits want to release me through Livingstone, I can feel it. I will talk to him."

Livingstone prayed hard the whole day asking God to open the heart of the Queen Mother so that she could open her heart. If she did, he too could have the power of the knowledge of the "curse of the caves", which had devastated the Kingdom. He waited impatiently for the night, for such sensitive information could be very useful as a powerful weapon to blackmail.

CHAPTER 18

THE "CURSE" IS REVEALED

Livingstone and the Queen Mother were in a private chamber in the palace. Dinner had been served, but neither seemed to have much of an appetite. The business at hand was sensitive and the matter weighty.

"Your God is very powerful," said the Queen Mother.

"Indeed He is. Why do you say so?" asked Livingstone.

"Because he goes with you wherever you go, He gives you power over the lives of people and beasts. I saw you make thunder with a stick half the size of a spear, and you killed animals at a distance twice beyond the range of arrows! With your thunder, the Portuguese and the Donyiros will never dare attack Monomotapa, and we can build a new capital in peace," said the Queen Mother.

"I have been sent by my God to help your people," said Livingstone.

"Our gods either died or disappeared. This is why we are suffering so many calamities. Does your God ever tell you what happened to our gods?" she asked.

"There is only one God, the God I worship. All other gods are figments of the human imagination. Your gods will never return. They never existed," said Livingstone.

"That is not true! Anyway, is your God willing to help us?" she asked.

"He helps all those who put their trust and faith in him. When the King, your own son accepted Him, I was commanded to intercede to end the 'curse of the caves', but only on condition that you confess what you know. God helps only those who help themselves," he said.

"So, once again, I am called upon to say what happened in the caves?" she asked.

"Yes, indeed," replied Livingstone firmly.

What followed shocked Livingstone to the core of his bones and tested his faith and manhood to the limit. The Queen Mother sat back in a most relaxed pose and said, "Do you know I never made love to the King again after the birth of the twins?"

"No! Not at all! Why didn't you?" he asked her.

"Because I could not bring myself to confess the curse I witnessed in the Royal Caves. But I have to inform you that, our customs demand that you make love to me to ease my mind and spirit before I share the secret. That is the order if it is between a man and a woman. However, if it is between men, they cut themselves in the arm and twin their blood," said the Queen Mother.

"I suppose customs are very strong," said Livingstone.

"Are you carrying the diseases which the Portuguese nuns brought to our men?" she asked.

"No, no, no! My mission is very different," said Livingstone pondering the direction the conversation had taken.

"Show me your dick," she said as she shot up unexpectedly.

"Why?" A surprised Livingstone asked.

"Because every man carrying the disease has a crying penis; oozing with pus! I want to confirm for myself that you are not sick." she said.

"A man does not go around exposing his private parts to strangers! I find your request most preposterous!" he protested.

"Before we share the secret of the caves, I must ensure that all is well," she said.

Livingstone gave it deep thought. Then he reasoned that if this was what it was going to take to unravel the truth, then it was a small sacrifice to make. He unzipped his trousers and exposed his penis to the Queen Mother. After touching and squeezing it gently, she exclaimed,

"Eeee-mama-yoo!" she continued, "it is very small, but it will do." It was much like talking to herself than addressing Livingstone. Livingstone felt like an animal caught in a snare. What was the woman up to?

"Your dick is not leaking. I am satisfied that you do not have the strange disease. Now, take off your clothes and make love to me!" she said in a matter of fact way, as she undressed.

Livingstone could not believe his ears. Was he dealing with a deranged woman? Was he being enjoined in the curse? He was most apprehensive.

"This has gone too far. I will not do such a thing," he said in a most unfriendly voice indicating change of mind.

Age had caught up with the Queen Mother, not to mention the pain of harbouring in silence the secret of the caves. But since the death of Taiwo and the King, she had become more relaxed and vibrant. She was still attractive to behold. The body was very well contoured and her skin appeared smooth and soft, most appealing.

"Pale face, it looks like we are not communicating! I told you that no secret can be shared between a woman and a man until they make love to interlock their souls and spirits as their body fluids mingle. This is a custom I dare not break, and as you yourself agreed, customs are very strong. I have been the victim of one curse. I will not wilfully invite another upon myself. Don't you know that I am making a difficult sacrifice? Or you think I am doing this for pleasure? If I had desired a man, there are many young and strong warriors out there who I would have lured to quench my thirst. They would have come to me running. This is a necessary ritual without which, we say goodnight to each another, and forget about the matter," she said resolutely.

David Livingstone was shaking and sweating. He was lost for words and motion. The Queen Mother, stripped naked, was lying on the bed waiting.

Livingstone went down on his knees and began to pray, "Lord, lead me out of this mess…save me from the temptation…" But before he could say Amen, he heard the harsh voice of the Queen Mother.

"Are you coming or should I dress up and go?"

Livingstone heard himself pleading, "Please don't dress up. Please don't go," he said with a shaky voice.

"Then hurry up," she said. He stripped post-haste, another victim of the glowing magnetism of the creature called woman.

And he made love to her.

When they sat to talk, the atmosphere was one of relaxation and new-found familiarity. There was a meeting of minds and purpose.

"Now that we have established the basis of trust, I will tell you the truth about the birth of the twins in the Royal Caves in Vumba Mountains," she began.

David Livingstone was truly lost in the surprises, mysteries and marvels Africa had to offer besides its natural wealth and beauty. He had made love to his late wife Mary with wild eyes, but he could swear that she had never made him feel the way he had felt with the Queen Mother. He had never thought that making love was an art, mesmerising, one that had to be learnt. Now he knew better. He wondered how it would have been had the woman been younger. He promised himself that all in good time, he would find out. Then he heard the voice of the woman again and this time, she had his full attention.

"When news came to the King that the Donyiro army was about to attack Monomotapa, he ordered the evacuation of the royal household to the safety of the secret Royal Caves in the Vumba Mountains to the east of the Kingdom. The King had five wives and ten daughters. I was his youngest wife. I was in the last stages of my pregnancy. On account of the size of my tummy and the troubles I had been experiencing with the pregnancy, the kingdom had high hopes that I would bear a son, the heir to the throne. All indications were that I had a big healthy boy on the way.

"The procession that headed to the east was very impressive. We rode on ox-driven wagons with warriors marching on all sides, front, back and sideways. The lead wagon in which I rode was colourfully decorated with a canopy of zebra, giant kudu skins and bright feathers from the birds of the wild. I had opted to take my sister with me because you never know among co-wives who might become jealous in case of the birth of a boy. I had also chosen the head of my security detail, a giant of a warrior with bulging muscles and searching eyes, who hailed from my native village. He remains a close friend to this day. The caves were not just holes in the hills. It was a marvellous masterpiece in architecture. There were many chambers connected by a labyrinth of passages. The caves housed more than three hundred people including warriors and workers. I was comfortably settled in the great suite reserved for the King himself. The Kingdom had several such bunkers to accommodate the royal household and top state officials in the event of a security threat. Each chamber had a secret exit.

"A few days after we settled in, I gave birth to twins, both boys, without any complications. I was very lucky in that several seasons before, the King had reversed the old custom which had demanded that in the event of the birth of twins, the younger of the two had to be put to death by suffocation. He had argued rightly that slave trade and the increasing threats from faraway lands called for the preservation of the life of every child born. "A nation cannot decimate itself through the murder of baby boys and hope to survive invasions," he had argued.

"The attack by Donyiros and actions by the Portuguese in Angola had vindicated him. We needed more, not fewer warriors. It had been decided that to distinguish the babies, in the event of the birth of same sex twins, especially boys, a bracelet should be placed on the wrist of the first-born, and in my case the heir to the throne. Every household purchased a bracelet, just in case. The King had a wonderful golden bracelet made for the royal family. In the haste to evacuate the royal family to the Royal Caves, the bracelet was left behind. My sister and I sorted out the matter by tearing a strip from a cow hide and placing it on the wrist of the boy who came out first. It would be exchanged for the golden bracelet once we returned to the capital.

"Custom further demanded that new-borns should not be exposed to the sun for seven days. On the seventh day, all new-borns were taken outside and their heads shaven clean in a special ceremony. The ritual was marked with a feast and a sacrifice to the gods for the gift of a baby or babies in case of twins.

"On the fourth day after their birth, I was breastfeeding them in sequence as my sister held the one or other. She was singing my praises that at last, I had given an heir to the Kingdom and guaranteed the future of Monomotapa. My thoughts were in a different direction. My main joy was that none of my babies was suffocated to death. I would have grieved to no end to see my baby killed in fulfilment of a stupid custom. Changamire was a truly wise man, I said to myself. I loved them both so dearly, like a mother loves all her children. The baby I was holding was suckling with vigour as I ran my hands along his plump arms. Then I said to my sister that it was the one without a bracelet.

"Imagine they would have suffocated this little beauty, had it not been for the wisdom of Changamire."

"No, it is this one who would have been suffocated," contested my sister referring to the one she was holding.

"No, no, this is the one without a bracelet," I corrected her.

"Funny, this one doesn't have a bracelet either!" she replied.

"Let me see." I told her, and sure enough, none of the two had a bracelet on the wrist. I let out a shriek in horror.

"What is the meaning of this?" I cried in fear.

"Shhh... Shhh... Don't panic. We will sort out the problem." my sister assured.

"What shall I do, what shall I do? I am in trouble," I cried.

"Let us move closer to the fire and examine the wrists. There must be some tell-tale marks indicating which arm had the bracelet," suggested my sister. But the light was not sufficient to yield a clue.

"Put more firewood," I suggested.

In the glowing flame of the fire, we searched and searched but again, there were no visible marks.

"We are in a crisis," I told her.

"I will tell you what, only sunlight can help," she told me.

"But this is the fourth day and the babies are not to be exposed to the sun until the seventh day. That is the sacred custom," I warned her.

"Look, get hold of yourself! This is no time for fear. Unless you are clear-headed, you cannot solve the problem. And if you don't, you will be in deep trouble!" cautioned my sister.

"We have to sneak out through the secret exit if only for a moment. In a time of crisis, custom can be broken," she said.

Quietly, we sneaked outside through the secret exit. Aided by sunlight, we examined the wrists of the twins for any tell-tale mark that could have indicated which baby had a bracelet. There was none. We gave up and returned to the chamber undetected.

"We have broken the custom!" I cried.

"It is only a custom not a curse. We are in a grave crisis, more so you than I. We have to find a solution," she told me.

"But what shall we do?" I asked in despair.

"I will tell you what; we will cut another cord and put it on the wrist. You suckle the babies and we will place it on the hand of the one who suckles the hardest. First-borns are said to be aggressive and the hard pulling is a sign of aggression," averred my sister.

"And supposing we get it wrong! Then what?" I asked in distress.

"So be it! Who will ever know?" concluded my sister. The operation of replacing the bracelet was executed. The boy with the bracelet would be called Ndovu, and his younger brother, Taiwo.

"I know it is not for nothing that the gods and the spirits commanded the placing of the bracelet on the first-born of the twins. It is even more important for the household of the Changamire. The heir to the throne is chosen by the gods and the spirits. I now bear the heavy responsibility and burden of living with the actions of this day, for the rest of my life. I trust that the gods and the spirits will understand my actions and judge me kindly," I said in supplication.

"I am sure they will," my sister consoled me.

"Promise me you will keep your mouth sealed forever about the events of this day," I pleaded, looking at my sister straight in the eye.

"May my breast swell to the size of giant pumpkins and may my nose grow to look like that of a pangolin if I ever squeal," she swore.

We embraced each other and shared the relief of a huge burden taken from our hearts. I prayed to the gods and spirits to assent to our action in their kindness," The Queen Mother paused to recollect herself because she spoke like one in a trance.

Here, I will digress a bit. I was a witness to all the above. I could have helped, but as you recall, my instructions were to observe and not to interfere. As I looked at the two sisters, I pondered whether their action was indeed a solution or high treason. You know, the choice of a solution to a problem can be wrought with all sorts of dangers, if it does not please the gods and the spirits. I also know that heirs and kings are anointed by gods and spirits, not by some underhand action by desperate women.

I know that gods detest conspiracies which undo their will and their retribution is harsh and swift. Had the Queen and her sister betrayed Monomotapa? Was I witnessing another reckless Eve destroying the Garden of Eden? I mused. By then, I could have sworn that what I had witnessed had no connection with my mission. I could not conceive how a birth in the caves could ever be connected with David Livingstone. But I was wrong and so, here we are.

The Queen had expected Livingstone to say something but he did not. Livingstone was absorbing every word the Queen spoke, like a sponge.

After a heavy sigh, she continued,

News of the birth of an heir had been received with jubilation throughout the Kingdom. It was a proud King Simba who rode in a long procession to the Vumba Mountains for the shaving of the heads ceremony. Again, the rite had been delayed because of the war. The Chief Priest conducted the ceremony.

The King had brought with him the golden bracelet, but as he placed it on Ndovu's wrist, a dark cloud hovered over me. I began to sweat and shake uncontrollably as my conscience was screaming. Had I placed the bracelet on the wrist of the right heir or had I made a mistake? I neither enjoyed the feast nor the dance which followed. The only person I wanted to keep company was my sister. Although the King was heaping praises on me, it fell on deaf ears. I could not reciprocate his kindness, but he was too lost in joy to pay attention or notice my moods. I guess if he did, he must have concluded that he would attend to my moods once the celebrations were over.

When we returned to Matapa, he tried many times to find out what was wrong with me, but as much as he tried to coax me, I could not bring myself to tell him the truth. He became sad, melancholic and a recluse out of frustration. As the twins grew up, the one I had declared the younger, Taiwo turned out to be sharp, strong and a legendary in his time. His brother Ndovu the heir to the throne became a cry baby, a dullard and an idiot. The gods and spirits kept an accusing finger pointed at me and the dark cloud never left me.

It was obvious to all that something dreadful had happened in the Royal Caves in Vumba Mountains which was detrimental to the future of the Kingdom. First, the dreadful thing made the King weak and insecure. And as a result, he succumbed to the machinations of Portuguese manipulators and their weapons of mass destruction. Secondly, it killed Taiwo, the greatest hope for Monomotapa and thirdly, it gave the Kingdom an imbecile for a King. I feel like I am responsible for all these misfortunes. But tell me, if it had been you in my shoes in the caves, what would you have done?" she asked Livingstone.

"I guess I would have done the same thing, but confessed my actions to the King. You know, the truth sets you free," Livingstone opined.

"What? And what do you think the King could have done, killed me and Ndovu?" she asked.

"Maybe or maybe not," said Livingstone.

"So you see I saved two lives with my silence," she defended herself.

"But then, your action led to the death of thousands including Taiwo, the destruction of the capital and the near destruction of the kingdom," said Livingstone accusingly.

"I know, I know. Is it too much to ask you to work with Ndovu and your God to save and rebuild the Kingdom?" she asked.

"No, indeed it will be my honour and duty to grant your wish," he said.

"Good man, I knew I could count on you. Now that I have confessed, the dark cloud hanging over my head has been lifted," she said.

"I am glad I have been of help to you. You will inform the King about our pact of cooperation in saving and rebuilding Monomotapa. First, I will go back to England to get the guns and a helper to assist me in the difficult task. His name is Cecil Rhodes, the young gentleman who accompanied me on my last visit. Do you remember him?" he asked.

"Ooh, I remember him well, tall and handsome. I have always had a soft heart for tall and handsome men, I suppose because my husband was tall and handsome," she said.

"Why didn't you get married when the King died? You are still very attractive. Dare I say full of vigour!" quipped Livingstone.

"Well, the head of my security detail is a close friend. He is the same man who guarded me in the Royal Caves. He has kept me happy," she said with a girlish cheeky smile.

"I can tell from the glitter on your face that you are in love with him!" said Livingstone.

"Yes, we are deeply in love," she said.

"God bless your relationship," said Livingstone satisfied that it was all he wanted to hear.

Well, well, well, when the Portuguese nuns went on a rampage with the warriors, the Queen's head of security detail had not been spared. He did not suffer from gonorrhoea or the plague, but unknown to him, to Livingstone and the Queen, he had contracted syphilis, which takes months or even years to manifest itself. On this day, the disease had just claimed another victim, David Livingstone.

Livingstone then hurriedly left the Queen Mother with King Ndovu so as to put on paper the confessions, leaving out certain details which he hoped would remain secret forever. He was also going to write to Cecil Rhodes to inform him that the hand of the Lord had delivered the Kingdom of Monomotapa on a silver platter. He was doubtful whether his divine mission had taken any concrete shape. This was not the original script. He was going

to exploit the Achilles heel of the Kingdom by bringing Ndovu and his mother to their knees by blackmail when the right moment so demanded. The warriors would then rise to defend what was left of the kingdom, or would they? something was amiss.

It was time for Livingstone to pack up and return to Ngorofa for the reunion with the other members of the Zambezi Expedition. The death of Mary had perhaps expedited good fortunes. He would have felt inhibited to yield to the Queen and the demands of a native custom, had she been around.

Her death had been a release and a springboard to freedom, which had worked wonderfully well towards the dream of independence for Scotland, albeit with an awkward personal sacrifice. He had enjoyed it though!

Let me tell you, whatever is done in the dark will come to light one day and choices have consequences, some of them most dire, all in the course of time.

CHAPTER 19

THE RETURN OF THE SAVIOUR

The departure of David Livingstone from Harare was quite a spectacle. The King and his mother were on hand to bid him farewell. After a chat with King Ndovu, the King embraced him like a brother. Livingstone promised he would return very soon to help in the security and rebuilding of the Kingdom.

"Big Boy, take it from me, I always keep my promise," he assured the King.

"I don't doubt you. Thank you for making my mother so happy," the King said with a big smile.

Livingstone blushed as he turned to the Queen Mother. He embraced her and impulsively kissed her on both cheeks. Though she looked most surprised, she did not protest. She had never been kissed before.

"Promise me you will return soon," she implored him.

"I will return before you miss me," he told her.

Livingstone was escorted by a team of warriors and porters who carried gifts that the King and his mother had given him. They included game trophies, diamonds, gold, gemstones and works of art, worth a great fortune. All went very well until the party arrived in Ngorofa, the inland port on river Zambezi. The barge had arrived and left. John Kirk had decided they wait for Livingstone who was late in returning to Ngorofa.

The party under John Kirk had arrived with many missing including the Bishop who had succumbed to malaria and was buried at Victoria Falls. Other members had simply vanished, maybe eaten by animals or crocodiles. Livingstone received a most hostile welcome when he showed up.

"We have been waiting here for days! You never sent a word that you would not arrive as scheduled! What kind of leader are you?" asked John Kirk.

"Too many things happened in Matapa and Harare..." said an apologetic Livingstone. But he was cut short by his brother. "David, where is Mary? Why did you leave her behind?" he asked.

For once, Livingstone shed tears for Mary as he narrated to them how they were attacked by lions which devoured his wife.

"Why didn't you shoot them?" asked one of the hunters.

"I had climbed up a tree to save my life; the rifles were in the cart which had overturned."

Instead of sympathising with him, they burst out into laughter, ridiculing him.

"You stole my rifle and my pistol, you are a thief!" one of the hunters accused him suddenly.

"Mine too." said another.

"I can explain; I can explain," pleaded Livingstone.

"Admit it, you are a thief and an irresponsible coward!" said his brother.

"I will pay for the guns and the bullets," Livingstone offered.

"That is not the issue. First admit you are a thief then the rest will fall into place," said Kirk with a lot of venom.

"Yes, I am a thief," submitted Livingstone.

"Well then, when we get to London, you will answer to the charges in a court of law," said Kirk.

"Gentlemen, I said I will pay for the weapons. I had to bribe King Ndovu to believe in me. I left the guns with him," he pleaded.

"You fool; he will use them against us some day," Kirk opined.

"No, he won't, he has no ammunition, and none of them has ever handled a gun. They are scared of them," Livingstone reassured them.

The hunters whose guns had been taken whispered among themselves, then one of them asked Livingstone, "How much are you willing to pay for the guns?"

"Name your price," Livingstone quickly replied.

When the matter was finally settled, Livingstone had paid more than ten times the value of each of the weapons.

"We have screwed the Scot," said one of the hunters. He was English. There were fortunes to be made in Africa, left right and centre.

After a long wait, the barge returned and they headed to Sofala loaded with gold, diamonds and game trophies. When Livingstone announced that the final destination of the "Zambezi" would be Zanzibar from where they would take another ship to London, there was a near riot.

"You brought this party from Britain to dump them on some Arab infested Island? Are you out of your mind?" censured Kirk.

Livingstone tried to explain that the ship had other more important functions, without elaborating. In the end, each and every member of his party, except Chuma and Sutsi found alternative means out of Sofala. Some headed to Cape Town, others to Aden and others back to London directly. Livingstone, Chuma, Sutsi and the crew headed for Zanzibar. There, he was going to make arrangements for his next trip to Africa in search of the source of the Nile. But first, he had to file his report about the navigability of River Zambezi and the natural resources in the surrounding regions. His doubts on the "divine mission" had become very real. He needed something else to hold on to for his own sanity. That he found in the search for the source of the Nile.

Livingstone was very pleased with his report on the Zambezi Expedition, save for the part which talked about the missing members of his party. He had explained that they were responsible for whatever fate had befallen them. In any case, he wasn't there to protect them because higher national considerations had taken him yonder to explore the fate of the Monomotapa Kingdom after the attack by Portuguese. While on this noble mission, he stated, he had lost his wife Mary. He confirmed first-hand that the great city of Matapa was no more.

He explained in the report that the population had moved eastwards en masse, leaving huge swaths of unoccupied fertile land. This land could be seized by British farmers and ranchers. Further, the land had deposits of gold, diamonds, copper, iron and gemstones.

Turning to the navigability of the Zambezi, he confirmed that a length of 800 km could accommodate large barges and already, there were some plying the route. One was owned by an Arab slave trader, who could easily be dealt with. He talked about the plight of the people and how despondent they had become. "They are like sheep without a shepherd," he wrote. With the death of the Changamire, his imbecile of a son was in no way capable of holding the Kingdom together. "It was time for Christianity to take root," he wrote, "deep in the broken hearts of the savages." It was also time for civilisation to be introduced through hard labour and taxation. And that would only be effective through the colonisation of the territory.

He warned that the Portuguese had not lost hope of securing the land between Angola and Mozambique Channel. "And once they are entrenched," he concluded, "it will be difficult to dislodge them." He therefore called for immediate action to seize, "this golden opportunity before it is too late."

Livingstone hoped to present the report to the full house of the Royal Geographical Society. He would also give a copy to Cecil Rhodes who in turn would give it to his father to sneak it into Buckingham Palace. The report was completed in Zanzibar. He bade goodbye to Chuma and Sutsi and promised to return very soon and embark on the Nile expedition. The "Zambezi" was left behind, in a dockyard under care for a fee. The "divine mission" had taken a most unpredictable course. It was now in the back burner.

* * *

On arrival back in England, Livingstone was surprised that none of the Royal Geographical Society dignitaries was there to receive him. The lone figure of Cecil Rhodes was the simple reception he got.

"Welcome back," said Rhodes in excitement.

"I am glad to be back," replied Livingstone smiling.

"How were things there?" asked Rhodes.

"How so?" asked Livingstone.

"They say the Zambezi Expedition was a debacle, a total failure, in other words, a disaster! You should read the report by John Kirk. It has received wide coverage in the media. You have to counter-attack," implored Rhodes.

"I am sure the Royal Geographical Society will bear me out after I present my report," said Livingstone.

"I don't think so, the mood here has changed. They say the building of the empire is purely the preserve of the English; others have just to follow," said Rhodes.

"Damn! Damn! After all I have been through, they now discover I am a Scotsman and expendable! Do I deserve this? Tell me, do I deserve this?" asked Livingstone raving mad with anger.

"You should understand that the affairs of state are not run by reasonable men. Wise are those who learn how to accommodate the tyranny of statecraft. You can be sure of one thing; I will stand by you through thick and thin. Don't do anything silly," advised Rhodes.

"Like what?" asked Livingstone.

"Like taking the state head-on," warned Rhodes.

Rhodes' words played in Livingstone's mind like a broken music record, repeating itself over and over again: "Like taking the state head-on…Like taking…" *ad infinitum.*

"Let's go to my house, you need some rest. We have a lot to discuss. I plan to return to Africa soon as I have completed my studies," said Rhodes. He had become a fine, mature and serious gentleman.

David Livingstone followed Cecil Rhodes to his house like a man in a trance. Later, when Livingstone called on the President of the Royal Geographical Society, he was told to his face that he was a disgrace. "How could you behave so recklessly?" the President shouted at him.

"I did not!" Livingstone shouted back.

"No need to raise your voice, it will not help the matter. John Kirk is a senior member of the Foreign Service and he cannot lie. Did you lose five members of the party and the Bishop?" asked the President.

"They went hunting and prospecting but didn't return on time. As for the Bishop, I had no command or control over mosquitoes!" retorted an angry Livingstone.

"You abandoned them! That is why the Board has arrived at a unanimous conclusion that you do not possess the qualities of a leader. You acted irrationally and irresponsibly. How will you face Moffat on account of the death of his daughter, your wife?" asked the President.

Livingstone was silent for a while then he burst out;

"I have had enough of this. I want a chance to address the Royal Geographical Society to give my version of events of the expedition," said Livingstone.

"The Royal Geographical Society as I said has already received the report. I suggest you find something useful to do; something simple within your faculties," said the President in a very harsh voice full of sarcasm.

Livingstone took this as an insult. He threw his report at the President and stormed out of the office, as mad as a charging bull. Once outside, he felt the world caving in. Slowly, he returned to Cecil Rhodes' house and drank himself silly. In that state, he contemplated suicide, but he could not reason well enough to choose the means. "May be I am very stupid after all," he concluded as he drifted into deep sleep.

For weeks, he chatted with Rhodes about the building of a business empire stretching from Cape Town to Cairo. He let him into details of the curse of the birth of twins in the Royal Caves, omitting the embarrassing details. The curse, Livingstone had told him, was a most powerful weapon Rhodes would resort to at a time of his own choosing.

"I have gone over the masterpiece of my plan many times and I will execute it. Together, we can control the continent from north to south under the protection of Her Imperial Majesty's government. We will mine, farm, hunt, set up factories and God knows what the limit will be! Forget about your other dreams, whatever they may be, this is the real deal," said an excited Rhodes.

Later, news of the arrival of the five missing members from the Zambezi Expedition greatly cheered Livingstone. They told of a heroic story of how they had found gold and silver mines deep in the mountains. The hunters narrated how they had buried many trophies because they were too heavy to carry, because they could not hire porters. The natives did not want to work for white men.

"Their warriors trailed us everywhere we went, like guardian angels. But whenever we looked their way, all we could see were the feathers of their head gears and their long spears protruding out of the bushes. They did not bother us and we did not bother them. When we came to Ngorofa, we found that Livingstone had abandoned us. We waited for the return of the barge to take us to Sofala and here we are. We will return to Africa to settle there. It is the promised land, the land of milk and honey," said one of them.

"As for Livingstone, I forgive him, but I am wiser not to be led by him ever again," said another.

"You know he almost shot his brother!" another interjected. And the image of Livingstone suffered with every detail revealed. It was a happy party of the lost and found; except for Livingstone's ruined reputation. Still, he told himself that these were temporary setbacks. Armed with this personal reassurance, he honed on Cecil Rhodes.

"Monomotapa is a pale shadow of its old self. If I could penetrate Ndovu the way I did, you can do better. In case of any problem, ferry, people from Cape Town in my ship. I left it in Zanzibar for your use if need be, for mounting an attack through Sofala. The vociferous, sustained and orchestrated British Government attack on the Portuguese genocide against Monomotapa is bearing fruit," Livingstone continued. "The Pope has distanced himself from

the Portuguese and called the use of the plague as a weapon a heinous crime. Without the Pope to bankroll their ambitions and bogged down in Angola, the Portuguese cannot afford to open another war front. The *bacillus* plague dies quickly. By now, the area must be uncontaminated for occupation. Seize this opportunity to achieve your dream. If you need more assistance from me, I will provide," assured Livingstone.

"You have done more than a brother can do...I will be forever grateful for your sacrifice and counsel...For God and my country!" said Rhodes.

"For God and my country," responded Livingstone, in a tone which betrayed disappointment.

Cecil Rhodes left for Zanzibar to collect the "Zambezi" with which to embark on his mission. Livingstone left for Paris to visit his daughter Agnes.

After a two-week stay in the city of light, fashion, architecture and great food, Livingstone went to Scotland. That did not augur well either with the British Government or the Scottish Liberation Movement. On learning that Livingstone had returned, the Chairman of the Scottish Liberation Movement summoned him to a meeting with the party luminaries. Livingstone strode to the venue happy to seize the opportunity to demonstrate to them how his "divine mission" was still on course, albeit with a few hiccups. To his disgust, he was met with very cold faces.

"Livingstone, you have brought disgrace to the whole Scottish nation! You have given the English an opportunity not only to ridicule you but also our whole nation as unworthy of positions of responsibility! They say you conducted yourself most irresponsibly on the Zambezi Expedition; deserting your team, Mary's death and abandoning five men in the bush! They say you bought a ship and abandoned it in Zanzibar for Arabs. What madness is this? You were once a senior member of the Movement and a lot was expected out of you. Can you explain yourself," said an agitated chairman.

"You are victims of English propaganda," Livingstone started in response to the accusations. "If we are not careful, it will destroy the Movement. Yes, there were accidents along the way, but everybody is now safely home. I need not dwell any more on that. What is important is that I have single-handedly coaxed and cajoled the English to expand the empire into Africa. Soon, their sons and daughters will be involved in wars of conquest, just like the Portuguese. They will get bogged down and when they do, we shall declare our independence! Simple! The English cannot battle India, Africa, Ireland

and also fight against us. They will let us go believing that Africa is a richer and bigger prize than Scotland," concluded a beaming Livingstone.

"But Monomotapa, they say, is a pale shadow of its former strength. It has no capacity to put up a fight," stated the Chairman.

"True, true, but it will still offer stiff resistance; plus, there is Lobengula and Mirambo farther north and among others, the Maasai and Donyiros between Cape Town and Cairo. The English cannot win," said a self-assured Livingstone.

"And if they do? You know they say, 'The English plan meticulously and in the end, they always get what they want'. Where will that leave us? All the same, we have carefully debated your conduct and decided to strip you of your membership of the Scottish Liberation Movement. Henceforth, whatever adventure or misadventure you undertake, please, regard it as a personal endeavour. It is also our sincere hope that whatever you do should not be associated with Scotland to avoid ridicule. Do I make myself clear?" asked the Chairman.

"These are cruel words and a harsh decision as well. I meant well for the motherland. I will not appeal against the judgment of the Movement, but it is hard to imagine I can abandon my 'divine mission'. Let us put it this way, the end will judge who was right and who was wrong; the Movement or myself. I will fight for the independence of Scotland until I die," Livingstone concluded solemnly.

"No one questions that you are a true nationalist, none whatsoever. It is the manner and the damage which is the problem. Please heed my warning; we do not want to denounce you openly like the English have done. Keep a low profile and all will be well," concluded the Chairman.

Livingstone stared at the Chairman for a long while, turned around and walked away, a murderous expression on his face. He never uttered another word.

"I am compelled to throw my weight behind the conclusions of the English that this man is indeed an incorrigible fool," the Chairman observed after Livingstone had departed. "And I dare add that he is a vagabond on a suicide mission. Well, *those whom the gods wish to destroy they first make mad*," he concluded with the classical quote.

Livingstone's world had caved in. It had crashed, tumbling upon his "divine mission", or had it?

"From here to where?" he asked himself. His feet wobbled as he walked.

The future looked bleak, unpredictable, hazy and uncertain. All his children had left home. He kept in touch with his mother and his daughter, Agnes, who was living in Paris. Of his other three children, Albert had sailed to America under a pseudonym. Oswell and Anne-Mary could not be traced. He assumed they too had migrated, running away from the shame and uncertainty brought to the family by his abandoning them. If only they had waited for him to explain, they would have understood his "divine mission" which was to liberate Scotland. He was alone and very sad. The Saviour needed someone to save him and not a Saviour of the religious kind. His life was losing meaning, but still there was Cecil Rhodes. He prayed for Rhodes' misadventure to conquer Africa from Cape Town to Cairo, to succeed a mission he greatly hoped would bring hell to Britain, when it backfired.

It was about that time that he read in the newspapers that two brave Englishmen, Richard Burton and John Speke had landed on the Island of Zanzibar. They were on their way to the heartland of Africa in search of the source of the Nile. Livingstone was devastated. Supposing they found the source, what else was left for him to live for? And if indeed the English succeeded in subduing the Africans? "I am the successor to Mungo Park and the glory of the discovery of the Nile has to be mine alone," he swore.

Knowing that the Royal Geographical Society would never finance him again, he contemplated approaching the French government for assistance. But, he soon dismissed the idea arguing, "The government will think I have joined the Irish in rebellion." He remembered the words of the Chairman of the Scottish Liberation Movement that counselled him to tread with caution.

Out of the blue, he received a letter from Cecil Rhodes. It informed him that after the mutiny of the British Army in India, many British soldiers had deserted and arrived in South Africa. Rhodes had harnessed them and others into two well-equipped battalions ready to march on to Monomotapa.

You will be glad to hear that your ship is in top condition though the Arabs demanded too much money for guarding it. By the way, I have been elected to Parliament in Cape Town and I intend to exploit the position fully to further the imperial policy in the direction you already know.

More next time.

Signed

Hon. Cecil Rhodes

Livingstone's life had become a yoyo; grief one moment and joy the next. He had found a Saviour amidst the villains. The villains included Richard Burton and John Speke who were trying to upstage him in discovering the source of the Nile. He immediately left for London to get more details on the two characters.

Richard Francis Burton was, Livingstone found out, a lieutenant in the British Army, serving in India. Burton was an educated and well-travelled explorer. He had visited Saudi Arabia (Mecca), France, Italy (Sicily), Egypt and Somalia. His one desire was to write a great book on travel which would immortalise him. His passion for immortality through the pen was driving him crazy. He had told his superiors that he had a higher IQ than most of the British Army generals, which was partly true. However, his assertion did not go down well with officers within the higher ranks.

Many times, Burton would leave the base to visit brothels where he frequently contracted gonorrhoea and finally syphilis. While on leave, it was always a relief for his superiors any time he asked for permission to visit weird places such as Tibet. He made one such visit to Cairo to enjoy belly dancers while still suffering from syphilis. He had the time of his life! He was also a confirmed homosexual; many young recruits had reported him to the superiors when he made passes at them. He had been nicknamed "Ruffian Dick"; not an honourable tag by any standards!

On Speke, Livingstone found that he was also a Sergeant in the British Army, serving in India. He was barely literate, but with a great gift as a cartographer. He had explored and mapped Tibet while enjoying bear hunting. He had great passion for hunting. He too had a weird side. He was heterosexual. Unlike Burton, he was not am imperialist, but he hated the dull life in England.

The two had met in the Crimean War and struck lasting friendship. Their love for adventure took them to Somalia where they were lucky to escape with their lives. Speke had saved Burton's life. The adventure yielded a book entitled *First Footsteps in East Africa*. It was a non-starter.

Out of failure, Burton decided to go for something bigger and juicier. And so it was that first he subjected himself to circumcision, polished his Arabic and disguised himself as an Afghan Moslem. He made pilgrimage to Mecca and Medina! The two volumes he published on the two voyages gave him more pain than fame. He was accused of being a fake and an outright liar. He did not give up. He approached Lord Murchison, the President of the Royal

Geographical Society, for assistance to search for the source of the Nile. Both Lord Murchison and Burton were confirmed imperialists; so the request was granted. Burton invited Speke to join him in the expedition as deputy leader; Speke gladly obliged. The two were almost inseparable, maybe because they were lovers!

These were the good-for-nothings in Livingstone's eyes, who were threatening to derail his cherished mission of solving the world's greatest geographical mystery, the source of the Nile. They were giving him sleepless nights; he agonised on how he could stop them in their tracks. He was lonely, sad and madly looking for a way to revenge against the loathful English. Speke and Burton became his prime targets. And the honour for the discovery of the source of the Nile became more than a race of time for Livingstone. It gave him reason to live instead of taking his own life as he had contemplated.

CHAPTER 20

THE NINE LIVES OF A CAT

I pondered whether my mission was over. David Livingstone had become a recluse shuttling between Scotland and London, thinking about how to embark on the mission of the discovery of the source of the Nile. He was bitter with himself about the manner in which he had squandered his fortune financing the Zambezi Expedition which had in many ways only yielded pain. While he did not miss his wife, for the shame she had brought on the family, he wished he had had the opportunity to explain to the children why he had been away for so long. The only one with whom he kept in touch, Agnes, was as cold as ice towards him. She did not wish to discuss the past.

He kept himself abreast of the development in the colonies in the hope that one day he would read of the big battles between the British and the colonial subjects in India, Africa or anywhere else. The news he received did not cheer him. The British were expanding their reach all the way to the Malvinas in the Southern Hemisphere which they had renamed Falkland Islands. The expanse of the empire meant that at any time of the day or night, the sun was ever shining somewhere on the vast empire. The English were boasting that "the sun never sets on the British Empire", which was a fact in that context.

One of the most interesting developments overseas had nothing to do with the building of the empire. David Livingstone was to learn that indeed the Emperor Theodore of Abyssinia had actually sent a marriage proposal to Queen Victoria. After a very long wait, Theodore became angry with the Queen for not responding to his request. He then arrested the British Ambassador in Addis Ababa and had him locked up in jail in the hope of forcing a reply from the Queen. The British Government responded by sending a huge military force to Abyssinia. As the foreigners approached the capital, the Emperor had the Ambassador released before committing suicide to avert arrest or humiliation. The British force withdrew.

Livingstone was disappointed that the British Government had not seized the opportunity to colonise Abyssinia. The Emperor's forces were said to be strong.

In his usual folly, he wrote an article in the papers castigating the government for the wasted chance.

Livingstone was reprimanded with such vitriol by the Foreign Office that he wished he had never written the article. He was reminded that the reckless miscalculations for which he was known had no business in shaping foreign policy. He was told that he was a surgeon and not a tactician in political and military matters.

Both in London and Scotland, he had no friends, and the little money he had was dwindling fast with the medical bills taking the lion's share.

When all seemed lost, he received an invitation to address the French Parliament Committee on Defence and Foreign Relations. The fee was handsome. Seizing the opportunity, he drifted to Paris, well-prepared to demonstrate to the French that the future of Europe lay in acquiring territories in Africa, a fact the British were taking too long to understand. At the back of his mind, this trip was connected with the "divine mission". He hoped the British and other European powers would clash in Africa over the spoils.

"I have tried to open the eyes of the British to the great wealth in Africa, but I have come to the conclusion that as the Bible aptly says, they have eyes but do not see and they have ears but do not hear," he told the French.

"I urge all European powers that have the political will to change the lot of their people from a life of squalor to a life of prosperity and bliss, to colonise Africa without further delay."

Livingstone was convincing; he was handsomely paid. He was also invited to dine with the Emperor.

When the leading French daily reported about the meeting, Livingstone became an instant celebrity in Paris. He found himself in the company of businessmen, academicians and politicians. Not only that, he received an invitation from the Chancellor of Prussia Otto von Bismarck to which he obliged. The message was the same. He received an invitation from King Leopold of Belgium which he declined, arguing that Belgium was too small to play in the big league and it could in no way contribute to the "divine mission". He wished to see the British, the French and the Germans lock horns in Africa and add to the speeding up of independence for Scotland! He knew his disappointment with the capability of African armies to resist

could be more than adequately compensated by European armies fighting over territories in Africa.

The reports on Livingstone's activities in Continental Europe alarmed the British Government. He had to be reined in somehow. "The crazy Scot has become an agent of confusion. How can he fraternise with our enemies?" asked the Foreign Secretary especially in relation to France which was aiding the Irish resistance. "A way must be found to silence him," he told John Kirk, the Intelligence Officer attached to the Foreign Office.

On his part, Livingstone was not satisfied with his newly found fame in Continental Europe. He did not know how long it would take before clashes between European powers in Africa took shape. He was impatient. His quest for the search of the source of the Nile had been blunted by the hostile relations he had with the Royal Geographical Society. He therefore prayed for Cecil Rhodes to make fortunes quickly and return his kindness in a manner which would facilitate one more expedition.

In the meantime, he seemed at home living in Paris where he rented a studio, occupying himself with writing his memoirs and fraternising with journalists and writers, in peace. The ambience was more than he could expect in England or Scotland. His renal and dental ailments were being managed, although the long delay had exacerbated their condition.

Livingstone believed that the state of limbo he was in was temporary and that sooner than later, like before, a miracle would happen to shape his mission especially towards the discovery of the source of the Nile. There was nothing left to do for the independence of Scotland as he had played all the cards. All he had to do was to wait for the glorious day.

In the meantime, his arch rivals Richard Burton and John Speke had arrived at the Port of Mombasa in their drive to find the source of the Nile. First, they sought two German Explorers, Dr. Ludwig Krapf and Johann Rebmann. The duo had travelled farther into the interior of East Africa and made the preposterous claim about discovering two snow-capped mountains on the equator which they had renamed Mt. Kenya and Mt. Kilimanjaro, respectively.

"Next they will report of snowballs in hell," the President of the Society had remarked most sarcastically.

The Germans assured the British upstarts that they stood by their claims and that farther to the west, there were other snow-capped mountains known as Mountains of the Moon. They suggested these could be the source of the Nile as Mt. Kenya and Kilimanjaro were not. They were advised to circumvent the route to avoid the warlike, proud and no-nonsense tribe called the Maasai who dealt ruthlessly with intruders into their territory.

"When you see any large herd of cattle grazing side by side with herds of wild animals, you are in Maasai territory. The Maasai are mysterious, elusive, and dangerous, but somehow, they live in peace with wild animals," advised Dr. Krapf and Rebmann. Unknown to Speke and Burton, Krapf and Rebmann were charting German imperial interests. The duo was in Mombasa awaiting the arrival of the Chief German architect of imperialism known as Karl Peters.

Speke and Burton went to Zanzibar and followed the slave route to Tabora on Lake Tanganyika. The mosquitoes in Tabora took a liking to Burton's blood, syphilis and all; he in turn contracted malaria. He became too weak and delirious, and could not travel anymore.

Speke had always played second fiddle to Burton in their previous excursions. When he was informed about a huge mass of water to the north of Tabora, he abandoned Burton and headed there. After a few weeks, he came to the shores of a massive lake which he renamed Lake Victoria. If Livingstone had renamed a mere waterfall after the Queen of England, he thought it more befitting to rename the lake after her. It was majestic. Speke had not been decorated, but he knew, given the size of the lake, he would be. Then he went to Jinja where he saw for himself waterfalls which then became a gigantic river flowing in a north-westerly direction. He excitedly asked the locals where the river flowed to and they told him into another lake called Kyoga. "And then?" he asked them.

"We don't know," they replied.

"Does the river flow northwards?" he insisted.

"No, never, all rivers flow either eastwards or westwards, but not northwards or southwards," they replied.

"But the Nile flows northwards!" he said in exasperation.

"That one is a big joke," said the lead sailor. He forgave the Africans for their ignorance.

"Eureka!" he shouted, "I have discovered the source of the Nile."

Joyfully, he returned to Tabora to find that Burton had recovered. When Burton heard the claim by Speke, he was not amused.

"Who gave you the authority to travel north?"

"You looked too weak, so I decided to do some exploration on my own while you recuperated."

"And you claim that, just because you found some water flowing to the north-west from a lake, you have discovered the source of the Nile? Did you follow the body of the water?" asked an angry Burton.

"No, I did not," Speke replied in haste.

"Then in that case, your claim is no more that the figment of your own imagination. I am the leader of this expedition and I never want to hear such nonsense repeated ever again. Do you want to bring this expedition to disrepute like Livingstone's Zambezi?" asked Burton.

"No sir, but the lake is huge; it is like an ocean and the waters flowing out must surely be the Nile, hence the source! After all, the river flows northwards," pleaded Speke.

"No more of this nonsense. The malaria has made me very weak; even my eyesight is impaired. We return to London at once!"

* * *

Once in London, Speke the cartographer laboured to write a separate report. He carefully drew the area where he had found the lake and claimed that he had discovered the source of the Nile at last. Burton wrote a counter-report describing Speke as a liar. There was no doubt that in the contest, Burton enjoyed several advantages. First, he had been the leader of the expedition and therefore, he had the final say on the outcome.

Second, he hailed from the elite class – the Lords – while Speke was just a commoner. Theirs was therefore a master-servant relationship. And of course, a slave's voice can never be superior to that of the master.

Third and related to the second, Burton was an educated and forceful writer. He had always dreamt of immortalising himself through the pen. He had made several unsuccessful attempts, not because he could not write, but his self-glorification did not meet the threshold of credibility. And that included his unbelievable pilgrimage to Mecca disguised as an Afghan. All that notwithstanding, he continued to have good relations with the Royal

Geographical Society because of the high standing of his family. Speke, the commoner, the barely literate cartographer could only offer tears and anger in the contest. Speke and Burton were lovers no more.

With glee, Livingstone sighed with relief as he observed the contestation. He had prayed for the expedition to fail and it seemed his prayers had been answered. When he finally sought audience with Richard Burton, he was surprised at the speed and warmth of their quick rapport that hitherto seemed unlikely. It was centred singly on destroying Speke.

When the duo wrote a joint article in which Livingstone poured out his wide knowledge of Africa to discredit Speke, the damage was total. Livingstone pointed out that the source of the Nile by all accounts lay much farther west of Speke's claim, in the region of Lake Tanganyika. This was the position held by Burton. Livingstone, the seemingly dead had just re-invented himself; he enjoyed every moment of it. It gave him hope of one day returning to Africa to settle the impasse once and for all – for the glory of Scotland and himself. He was fixing the English just as he had promised himself he would – and then he returned to Paris.

Speke and Burton's accusations and counter-accusations flowed in the press, embarrassing the Royal Geographical Society. To put an end to the acrimony, the Society ordered Speke to return to Africa accompanied by one Captain Grant to settle the matter permanently.

The duo followed the same route from Zanzibar and eventually arrived in the Kingdom of Buganda. The Kabaka told them they could not go any farther to the north as he was at war with the neighbouring Kingdom of Bunyoro led by one Kamurasi. He asked them for military assistance to which Speke declined. Still, the kind Kabaka gave Speke a Tutsi wife who later protested that the man was impotent and incapable of making babies.

Speke returned to England a very frustrated man, having not proven his claim. Soon thereafter, he shot himself dead while on a hunting expedition. At the time of his death, he had submitted an article to the Scottish *Blackwood* Magazine knowing well what influence Burton had with the English press. It was just as well he had died because Burton upped the campaign to vilify him. So cruel was the campaign that Speke must have tossed and turned in his grave. He wrote in the end that "Speke's death was certainly suicide, unable to live with his own lies."

The one person who was getting a great kick out of this great battle between the two Englishmen was David Livingstone. His desire to unravel the world's greatest geographical mystery remained, if only he could get a sponsor.

In the meantime, Cecil Rhodes had written to the Foreign Office asking for back up to outmanoeuvre the Portuguese and take over Monomotapa. He detailed how he had two battalions of seasoned soldiers and capable volunteers ready to sail to Sofala and then march into the interior. The response was swift. It came in the form of a message from the Foreign Office:

HMS Furious has been ordered to sail from Zanzibar to give you escort to Sofala and to render any assistance you may stand in need of. Good luck. Signed,

Foreign Secretary

In a high-handed action, Cecil Rhodes had written to the Portuguese Viceroy in Angola, warning him that Britain, on behalf of the international community was sending a reconstruction team to assess the situation in Monomotapa "following your barbaric attack. Any interference with the mission," he warned, "will be deemed as an act of war against Great Britain and the international community."

Still reeling from the scathing attack after the plague debacle, the Portuguese government told its Viceroy to assure Rhodes that the reconstruction mission would not be interfered with. Rhodes had pulled a fast one. His dream was beginning to take shape, of a business empire stretching from Cape Town to Cairo, with the centrally located Monomotapa as the key. He secretly thanked Livingstone for opening his eyes to the world and charting his path to glory. Nothing could stop him now.

Rhodes did not hire the barge from Tipu Tipu, he confiscated it accusing the Arab of dealing in slave trade after it had been abolished. When Tipu Tipu protested, he was put in jail in Livingstone's ship anchored in Sofala. The barge ferried Rhodes and his troops to Ngorofa in several trips as the Portuguese looked on. Once assembled, the troops began their march to Harare, the temporary capital of Monomotapa. They were surprised that they met no challenge or resistance all the way to the capital as Livingstone had prepared the way. The Kingdom was waiting for guns and Livingstone.

Young King Ndovu received Rhodes with open arms. He had been informed that the man who had visited the old capital with David Livingstone was back, carrying many guns for the defence of the Kingdom and with plans for reconstruction as promised.

"I am glad you have come to keep the promise Livingstone made. How much do I owe you for the guns?" asked the young King.

"Nothing, you owe me nothing," said Rhodes.

"Your arrival could not have come at a more opportune time. Since we buried my father, generals and warriors have deserted. I am facing a rebellion. They claim I am not fit to rule or defend the Kingdom. They have gone back to their tribes where they are declaring themselves Chieftains! Some rogue generals and warriors have been raiding their neighbours for women, cattle and land. Can you imagine? Warriors of Monomotapa are now engaged in killing their own people! You will teach the remaining royal warriors how to use guns. Though diminished in numbers, they are equal to the task of holding the Kingdom together. I will teach those renegades a lesson!" said the young King.

"Don't worry, I will teach your soldiers how to use the guns and bring order to your Kingdom," said Rhodes.

"Thank you, I knew you were a good man the very first time I saw you," said Ndovu.

"But there is one more thing. Before I give you the guns and commit my instructors to teach your warriors bow to defend the Kingdom especially from the Portuguese, you need to sign an agreement of cooperation. Since we are now your guardians, the Kingdom will be known as a protectorate of the British Government," said Rhodes.

"No, no, no. Friends help one another without elaborate formalities. It is so between us and Queen Nzinga and also with Abyssinia. You are our friends," protested the King.

"Our government is different. Without the agreement, there will be no cooperation," warned Rhodes.

"Well then, give me time to consult my mother," said the King.

"I would like to meet her to deliver gifts and greetings from Livingstone," said Rhodes.

"We meet over dinner this evening," said Ndovu.

It was a lie. Rhodes did not have greetings or gifts from Livingstone, but he had bought expensive items for this purpose. That evening over dinner, Rhodes put on the table the same terms for cooperation. When the Queen Mother protested, Rhodes took her aside and told her:

"Remember the 'curse of the caves?' My God told me to warn you that the legitimate heir was Taiwo. You are to blame for the disasters which followed because you put the ribbon on the arm of the wrong boy! Had it not been so, the King would not have been miserable and weak in the head. Taiwo would have inherited the Kingdom and Monomotapa would have grown from strength to strength. The gods have sent me to warn you that Ndovu is a King by default and there are more disasters on the way, unless you agree to our protection, which will help to exorcise the evil spirits through the intervention of our God. It is up to you," concluded Rhodes.

"What is he talking about?" Ndovu asked his mother who was in tears and shaking like a reed in the wind. The Queen Mother did not want Ndovu to know the truth. She wanted to interrogate Rhodes further, but she could not do so in the presence of Ndovu. Rhodes saw that he had touched a raw nerve.

"Sign the agreement and save yourselves and the Kingdom," he cajoled them.

"Sign the agreement," the Queen Mother said eying Ndovu in despair. Ndovu who always obeyed his mother did not question her wisdom and judgement. He put his thumb on the ink pad as instructed by Rhodes and placed it firmly on the agreement.

"Well done Big Boy," said Rhodes.

"So, Livingstone told you about my new name?" asked the King.

"Yes, and a whole lot more," said Rhodes fixing his gaze on the Queen Mother who in reaction looked down, feeling like a caged animal ready for slaughter. A new king had arrived on the scene; his name was Cecil Rhodes. He held secrets enough to dismember whatever remained of Monomotapa or to remould it to his fashion and taste, thanks to David Livingstone.

Rhodes demanded a meeting with the Ruling Council and it was granted. In the presence of the King, his mother and the Chief Priest, he informed them about the agreement with the King to co-govern and reconstruct the Kingdom. Not knowing what the new arrangement would entail, the Council endorsed it. In next to no time, Rhodes had set up his administration to govern the territory. Military expeditions against rebel generals were mounted. In time, all were defeated or pacified with pistols and rifles. Soon, Rhodes was boasting that he had established order, security and peace which were necessary for the spread of Christianity and for commerce, development and civilisation to thrive.

To further cleanse the Kingdom of the "curse of the caves", the territory was renamed Rhodesia. British citizens arrived in hoards and carved for themselves all the fertile land they wanted at the expense of Africans who became marginalised, serfs and despondent. The introduction of cash crops especially tobacco, cotton and coffee denied them even sufficient basic foodstuff. Civilisation, Christianity and Commerce arrived alright, for the benefit of settlers who praised their own God. The gods of the Africans had disappeared, but the natives prayed and did not lose hope that one day, their gods would return. Until then, servitude and pain would be their constant companions.

Ndovu, the King was swallowed by the new force. He became a figurehead, a drunkard and the laughing stock of both natives and foreigners alike. His mother, like Mary Livingstone, became an alcoholic.

When Livingstone received the story of the great success by Rhodes without much of a fight, he was very angry with himself.

"What went wrong?" he kept asking himself.

"What happened to the furious and ruinous battles between the British and the natives that I had seen in my vision?"

Painfully, he remembered the question which the Chairman of the Scottish Liberation Movement had asked him, "Suppose the English succeed in subduing the natives; where will that leave your 'divine mission?'" And that is exactly what had happened in India, Ghana and now Monomotapa. Where did that leave his dream? In tatters. Not even with the slightest chance of independence for Scotland! So, the gods had toyed around with his life and soul, or had they? Was he like Job to be tortured first then handsomely rewarded in the end? But how? He felt his head spin round and round.

Livingstone took his sleeping bag, surrendered the studio and went to see Agnes, his daughter. Agnes could hardly recognise her father. He was so haggard, emaciated and unkempt. He walked with a droop.

"I want to stay with you for a little while. I want someone to talk to," he beseeched her.

In a day or so, Agnes was already averse to her father's habit of scratching his arse uncontrollably. It was not amusing; she really detested it. Second, he could not brush his teeth on account of his ailing dentition. She longed for the day he would leave and go away for good. And soon, Livingstone discerned that he was no longer welcome. But who else could he turn to? He could not think of anybody. His world was caving in inexorably.

CHAPTER 21

THE POISONED CHALICE

I could not fathom how Livingstone's future would be. His life in Paris had become an intolerable mess. There was a cafe by river Seine; a favourite meeting place for philosophers, and there were many in Paris. It was not an organised group as such, but they drifted there all day to discuss ideas on the essence of life, liberty and governance. They shared both convergent and divergent views. Livingstone who had gone to great lengths to study the French language, showed up often, more of a listener that a participant. There were conservatives, liberals, socialists and communists who at times came to blows upon disagreement.

It was not that the discussions were helping shape his ideas or the way he viewed the emerging and cruel order of life in Europe of which he had been a victim. But, he agreed with the disciples of Jean Jacques Rousseau and Voltaire. They postulated that what the so-called civilisation had done was to corrupt the natural goodness in man and that excessive emphasis on private property had created a class of the bourgeois who controlled insensitive governments. That, they argued was an evil that had to be destroyed.

Livingstone drew a parallel with the English who had enslaved the Scots. He thought of himself as a philosopher whose ideas were crystallising. Their final shape would revolve around the absolute need for the freedom of nationalities to determine their own destinies without outside interference. It was in this light that he saw the future of Scotland as an independent and egalitarian society. He resolved to put his ideas on paper like Rousseau and Voltaire. That would add another feather to his cap. In this equation, he did not have African nations in mind as they were too backward, too primitive to be of any significance in the new world order, so he thought.

Across the river, opposite the cafe were big willow trees. There foliage often hovered above the water. They were giants by their own right. Nobody could tell whether the cluster had been planted or the seeds had drifted to rest on this fertile spot on the bank of river Seine, to germinate and grow into giants. They had seen the river handle trade and transport for years, before the railway stole the limelight as the main means of conveyance. Only barges and leisure boats remained.

The giant willow trees missed the heaving and swaying of the tides created by the ships which had plied up and down for ages. They had witnessed a transformation most unkind to nature. The industrial effluent and raw sewage polluted the river threatening their very existence. The smoke from the engines and factories settled on their leaves, suffocating them.

As the willow trees swayed in the agony of modernisation and civilisation, they could not agree more with the old philosophers. The world was indeed hurtling into the unknown; the future of many on earth looked bleak. The creature called Man had crassly embarked on a course of self-destruction threatening, his fellow men and life around them with death and decay. And majority were cheering him on in the name of commerce, civilisation and modernity! Only a few benefited, but for how long? The giant willow trees seemed to ask as they stooped towards the waters of the river in discomfort, weeping. It was the duty of the philosophers to find a solution soon before it was too late; and in this mix sat David Livingstone. Malthus' proposal was to them not the solution to the problems. The thinking of the philosophers was radical but abstract. Theirs, I discovered, was in essence, an exercise in futility!

One late evening, his daughter Agnes entered the flat they were living in and threw an English newspaper at him before sitting down with a heavy slump.

"What is it?" he asked her.

"The Queen's list of honour! They are decorating explorers and those who have been in the forefront of building the empire. Your name is not there!" she said amid tears.

"It can't be!" he hissed as he rummaged through the pages. Then he came to the list. Under the title "Exploration and Empire Building", there were several names. On top of the list was Cecil Rhodes, followed by Richard Burton and Samuel Baker. That was the end. There was no David Livingstone!

"This is utter rubbish. Rhodes yes, but Burton and Baker are no more than wayward vagabonds! I have been betrayed," he cursed.

"Father, you have told me countless times that you are the greatest strategist and tactician that Scotland has ever produced; something like a modern day

Robert the Bruce who became King of Scotland. You told me you would send the English to death in their thousands in wars of conquest, especially in Africa. And then Scotland would declare her independence. That is why you abandoned your family, for the sake of Scotland. The way I see it, the English must have read your mind and followed another route! Are the French and the Germans not complaining that the English have gobbled much of Africa; and that without too much of a fight? You prepared the way for them, so the papers told us, but they have now abandoned you. Is Scotland free? No! Is Scotland ever going to be free? Never! And what do you have to show for it? Nothing!" fumed Agnes.

"Child, don't talk like that..." Livingstone tried to assuage her. Recently, he had confessed a lot to Agnes when he felt he was about to die. She had listened more out of pity than duty, interest or respect.

"Father, if nothing else, you must go back to London and protest that by not making it to the Queen's list of honour, your efforts have been ignored. You must do this, not for Scotland, but for yourself and your family. Otherwise, how will history judge you?" asked Agnes in tears.

Livingstone had not been blind to his daughter's irritation with his overstayed visitation. It had now run into years. He thought she was seizing the moment to throw him out.

"I have nowhere to stay in London," lamented Livingstone.

"You have money in the bank, don't you? Use it."

"I am saving what is left for you."

"I don't need it! Use it to rent some place."

To Livingstone, this was a goodbye message from his daughter.

"Give me a few days to think about it. I agree with you, I have to fight to ensure my efforts are recognised and honoured," he said unconvincingly.

Secretly, Agnes desired that her father would be gone sooner than later. He was a hindrance to her freedom and enjoyment. Like her mother, she had embraced alcohol as a never failing companion. In distress, Livingstone wished he could share his unenviable predicament with someone. But he had no close friend, not even among the philosophers in the cafe by the Seine. He felt like an old willow tree, helplessly hanging on to the loose banks of the river, sickened by the all-around pollution. It was a matter of time before it fell to be washed by currents to the unknown.

Then he reasoned with himself, "God does not walk with the faint hearted. He chose me like he chose David and Moses because we are a special breed of men. I will face the English and tell them off to their face!" he resolved. Then he entered the cafe by the Seine to listen to philosophies on life, not feeling any more like a weeping willow tree about to fall. He decided to stay in Paris until after the Queen's ceremony of presentation of honours was over. He had long been warned about confronting the government head-on, and the matter was of a sensitive nature.

When the honours list was read, there were murmurs and grumbles. Those who had been honoured were people with high political connections, many with very questionable credentials, including Richard Burton and Samuel Baker.

The papers carried scathing attacks on Samuel Baker. His father was a banker and the co-director of London Railways. He owned huge sugar plantations in Mauritius and tea plantations in Ceylon; he was also a high ranking member of the Royal Geographical Society. Samuel had a wild nature; he was spoilt brat and a playboy who not satisfied with the ordinary, had purchased a beautiful slave girl in Eastern Europe as a sex object. Eventually, she became his wife in a secret wedding. He renamed her Florence.

He settled for hunting elephants in the Sudan and made a fortune. His father talked him into "doing something sensible" to which he agreed. He was to search for the source of the Nile while hunting elephants. With funding from the Royal Geographical Society, he travelled to Sudan and went as far as Lake Albert out of which flowed the Nile northwards. He established that the lake was not the source of the Nile as a huge river from God knew where fed the waters of the lake from the east.

However, he could go no farther because the kingdoms to the south and to the east were at war. He picked his bags and went to Ethiopia to hunt. While there, he discovered a huge river which he named the Blue Nile.

Upon return to London, he wrote an interesting article by the title *The Albert Nyanza Expedition* in which he laid no claim at all to discovering the source of the Nile. He concluded that there were two Niles; one from the south and the other from the east. Both converged in Khartoum to form the river which flowed to Egypt. The larger one was the White Nile from the south whose source remained a mystery. He swore he could have resolved the age-old mystery, had it not been for the wars in the region between savage chiefs. He therefore called for the "taming of the warring creatures" through British occupation of the fertile land they inhabited, and which in his judgement was the pearl of Africa. For this simple effort, he had been knighted!

Button's knighthood was also questioned. Many protested that Speke and above all David Livingstone had done a whole lot more than Burton. Speke had been to Africa three times, one more than Burton. He had discovered Lake Victoria, the largest lake in Africa.

Finally, an article in the dailies boldly accused the British ruling class of favouritism, bias and nepotism. An accusing finger was pointed at Lord Murchison, the President of the Society. Most damaging was the observation that Speke was not knighted because he was a commoner by birth and Livingstone simply because he was a Scot! This was the truth. Lord Murchison in response called for calm and patience as there would be honours awarded in the years ahead and he assured the public that more explorers, missionaries and empire builders would be considered all in good time. The omission of Livingstone and Speke stuck out like sore thumbs; it was embarrassing the integrity of the Royal Geographical Society and the British Government.

Cecil Rhodes had sailed to London from Monomotapa to receive the honour personally. He was the star attraction. Upon arrival, he protested the omission of the name of his friend Livingstone. But he was warned that the state has its yardstick for assessing who deserved what and when. He raised the matter with his father as the family and friends were celebrating his honour. His father warned him:

"Livingstone is a Scot, pure and simple; such a lot does not carry favour with the Royal family. Furthermore, the man has a split personality. At one time, he is the champion of the empire while at the same time he is in the forefront for the dismemberment of the Union! Without flinching, he wines and dines with British mortal enemies, the French and the Germans. And he is more at home in Paris than in London. Such men of unstable minds with dubious national loyalty are a danger to themselves, to those around them and to the state. They can easily be bought and manipulated to cause chaos."

"But father, I have known Livingstone for years since you trusted him with my life on my first journey to Bechuanaland, where he became my big brother and mentor. I owe what I am to him!" Rhodes argued.

"Never trust a Scotsman. Probably he was moulding you to use you." disputed the father.

"Never! Never! His heart is pure and free from malice and evil. You do not know him at all and yet you judge him so harshly! You are a man of God!" protested Rhodes.

"My son, when you put your trust in a Scotsman, it demonstrates that your reasoning is impaired. You are a self-made, strong Englishman. You do not need anybody's backing to achieve your dream of building an empire – except the blessings of the British Government of which I guarantee you," objected the father.

"It is going to be hard without Livingstone. He is the spirit behind my dream, in a way the chief architect of the British Empire in Africa!" Rhodes retorted.

"My son, in dealing with the natives, all you have to learn is the art of deception; charming, mesmerising and cajoling. If these don't work, use the stick, the gun or whatever force that is at your disposal. Where does this Scot come in in all this?" asked the father.

"Livingstone had promised to provide a shipload of missionaries to help dismantle the bonds which so tightly hold the natives together; their customs, beliefs, culture and solidarity..." Rhodes had not finished when his father butted in:

"Cecil, am I not a highly rated clergyman second only to the Archbishop of Canterbury? Is the Church Missionary Society not at my beck and call? I will send you English preachers to take care of English settlers, administrators, and soldiers. As for the natives, I will dispatch Scottish and Irish missionaries for being equally dim-witted as the savages, they will soon come to an understanding without too much of a hustle. At your bidding, they will turn the natives into zombies, dunderheads, and scatterbrains; empty shells that will labour like donkeys without grumbling and sing songs of praise and salvation on Sunday!" his father said beaming with joy.

"Charming, mesmerising, cajoling and use of force, these are great weapons! Thanks Dad, you have opened my eyes yet wider! I can see the future clearly like a man using binoculars! I see large clear images of sweating labourers producing food for my motherland to feed its people. The empire is a question of bread!" proclaimed Rhodes with a wide grin on his face.

"To hell with Livingstone!" concluded the father.

"To hell with the Scotsman!" agreed Rhodes.

"Let's get on with the party," said the happy father holding his son by the shoulder as they marched to join in the merriment.

* * *

The chorus on how Livingstone has been short-changed reached a crescendo. The grumbles spread from England to Ireland and Scotland. It was said Queen Victoria was under siege from greedy Englishmen who were putting their interests first at the expense of national interests. If they continued unchecked, they were going to be the sole beneficiaries of the fortunes of the empire while the nation bore the burden of protecting their wealth. They were referred to as goblins. It was argued that Livingstone had preached a message beneficial to all, but had suffered humiliation by being left out of the awards list. If such injustice was extended to the colonies, then there was no hope for the common man. It was indeed a huge price to pay.

Queen Victoria summoned Lord Murchison and demanded damage control measures. "A single miserable Scot should not be the centre of such an acrimonious vitriolic national outburst. You must put a lid on this matter," commanded Queen Victoria.

"Your Majesty, I have spent miserable sleepless nights thinking of a solution. Thank God, I have now found one," replied Lord Murchison.

"Good! Then get on with it!" ordered the Queen.

"Yes Your Majesty," said Lord Murchison humbled.

That evening, Lord Murchison learnt that Livingstone had landed in London from Paris. He was for once afraid when he pictured the angry Scotsman at Hyde Park denouncing the unfairness of the selection to the Queen's list of honour and getting support from the press and the workers. Then again, he was hopeful that he could offer Livingstone a deal he could not resist and thereby kill the matter. He immediately sent an agent of the Royal Geographical Society to deliver a message to Livingstone inviting him to a special meeting with key members of the Society.

After reading the message, Livingstone had a mind to tear it into shreds in front of the agent to demonstrate his disgust with the Society and everything it stood for. However, on second thought, he agreed to attend the meeting

and use the opportunity to pour his chagrin on the President and the "goons" who ran the society.

"Tell him I will be there tomorrow, first thing in the morning," he told the agent. Livingstone had hired a single room in a run-down hotel in Soho, in the backstreets of London.

"Either Livingstone is very sick, half-mad or both or he is the master of disguise. He looks weird, almost unrecognisable. But it sure is Livingstone alright," the agent reported back to Lord Murchison.

"I will see for myself tomorrow. Thanks a lot," said Lord Murchison not keen to discuss Livingstone further.

That night, Lord Murchison and his deputies met over dinner in a hotel to devise a strategy on how to contain and tame Livingstone. Someone suggested giving Livingstone a good financial package because as had been reported by the agent, he looked haggard, unhealthy and in a poor financial state, or why else was he putting up in a decrepit hole?

"With what we know about Livingstone, he would like to make political capital out of the issue. He wants to ride on the present charged mood in the Union. He will claim to be a champion of the oppressed, the workers, the Irish and the Scots. This is what we must avert at all costs. The Queen has charged us with the responsibility of dealing with the threat," said Lord Murchison.

"What do you have in mind? asked a senior member of the Society.

"Leave it to me! Tomorrow, I have a great surprise in store for you and Livingstone as well! Do I have your mandate to execute my plan, whatever it may be?" Lord Murchison asked with a wicked smile.

"We have never doubted your capacity for wisdom and brilliant solutions to irritating problems. You have our full mandate," said his deputy.

"Thank you gentlemen for trusting me; we meet again tomorrow morning," said Lord Murchison when dinner was over.

In his dealings with the philosophers in the cafe by the river Seine, Livingstone had lost all pretensions of a well-dressed gentleman like all the other philosophers. It is in this improbable manner that he arrived at the office of the President of the Royal Geographical Society; scruffy, unkempt, with a trail of stench from accumulated filth following him.

Besides the President, those waiting to receive him were among others, Cecil Rhodes' father and the father of Sir Samuel Baker. Sir Richard Burton had declined the invitation as he was indisposed. His syphilis was now at an advanced stage.

"David! Welcome! It has been a long time!" the President ushered him in stating in a jovial mood.

"The last time I was here, we did not part on amicable terms. I find it hard to understand the excitement," retorted an angry Livingstone.

"There must have been a misunderstanding!" shot back Lord Murchison.

"Indeed a misunderstanding that has led to my public humiliation! Why was my name not on the Queen's list of honour?" asked Livingstone with a sneer.

"Calm down David. The world is full of people with small minds. The Queen's list of honour is a purely local event! You are bigger than that. You deserve more!" the President pampered him.

"I don't understand you," said Livingstone surprised.

"You are a man of high standing; both in the Union and internationally. The honour you deserve is world recognition!" said the President in a serious tone.

The others in the room were as lost as was Livingstone. Nobody had any idea as to where the discussion was leading to.

"Get to the point," said an irritated Livingstone.

"The biggest honour in the world awaits the man who will discover the source of the Nile! His name will reverberate around the globe among the names of the greatest explorers since the days of the Greeks and the Romans! The Queen and the Royal Geographical Society are of the opinion that nobody deserves this special honour more than you do. Are you willing to take the plunge? Do you have it in you to be the most decorated man in the world?" asked the President.

David Livingstone looked at the President in a daze.

"David, are you alright?" the President asked. Livingstone was shaking and sweating, his mouth half open, exposing a dentition with some excavated teeth awaiting replacement. That would have been possible, but for lack of money. His chest was heaving as trapped air in his lungs arrested his voice. His brain raced back to his youth days; he had sworn to accomplish two things; first the "divine mission" which would lead to the independence of Scotland. That had almost fizzled out, save for a miracle. The second was the accomplishment of Mungo Park's dream of finding the source of the Nile.

The offer from the President sounded like another miracle. He had to seize it. "It is a big personal honour that you offer. What are the terms?" he asked, just to be sure.

"Most generous; let us know when you are ready. Then we will assist you in all ways," said the President.

Livingstone, with a beaming face stood up and excitedly shook hands with those present saying, "Thank you, thank you..." countless times. Then he left.

"I couldn't stand the stench any longer," said Cecil Rhodes' father.

"Mr. President that was a master stroke!" said Sir Richard Burton's father.

"In that state of health, David will be lucky to survive the voyage to Zanzibar, let alone the journey into the wild," commented another.

"And so finally, I can report to the Queen, good riddance!" and they all cheered heartily.

"It is a master stroke!" concluded Rhodes' father.

As I watched, I felt pity for Livingstone. At this point, I wished I could get guidance from St. Peter as to where the plot was heading to.

CHAPTER 22

THE MONKEY'S DILEMMA

The folly of the creature called Man knows no bounds. There is a saying that goes, "The day the monkey has to die every branch becomes slippery." Livingstone felt that his fate and that of the monkey were similar. But in his case, he knew he had one more dry branch to cling onto; his last journey to Africa, with the source of the Nile as his prize.

Unlike the Zambezi Expedition, he was wiser this time, to travel solo. He did not want antagonisms and bad reports. The Royal Geographical Society did not oppose his plan. They provided all that Livingstone asked for both in money and gear. He was further informed that the British Consul in Zanzibar had been instructed to keep him supplied should he fall short of provisions.

I was very exhausted and uncomfortable, but I could not let Livingstone out of sight. I followed him.

As he left England, he was confused. He found it hard to believe that he was abandoning the "divine mission" of liberating Scotland from the Union. On the other hand, events had conspired to derail his strategy so much so that it could not be salvaged. Being of a non-violent disposition, he knew he could never throw his weight behind the elements in the Scottish Liberation Movement who were calling for a war of liberation. He needed to refocus on another solution to the problem, if time permitted. But for now, the source of the Nile beckoned with urgency.

"I will never abandon Scotland, never! Not for fame or all the money in the world," he swore to himself.

"Pitiable soul," I said to myself as I watched him fumble.

He resolved to give the matter much attention before his return. He felt at ease that the twin missions were not incompatible and while he embarked on one, he could still keep the other alive. While preparing for the journey, he had sent a message to Cecil Rhodes who was busy building his empire from Cape Town to Cairo.

The message read: "At the request of the Royal Geographical Society, I will be landing in Zanzibar soon on an expedition to settle once and for all the question of the source of the Nile. Arrange for Chuma and Sutsi to meet me in Zanzibar."

The letter was clearly dated. The year was 1866. Rhodes was puzzled when he received the message. His father had told him Livingstone was an enemy of the State and he should cease all dealings with him. They had both agreed, "to hell with the Scot". How was it that the position had been reversed? Why was Livingstone reinstated to serve the interests of the empire if he was untrustworthy? There were more questions than answers on the matter; the more he pondered it, the more puzzled he became. The request by Livingstone was modest; he had no qualms about sending his loyal friends to Zanzibar, and giving them the name of the ship bringing their master. As instructed, they left with the assistance of Rhodes.

A month later, Livingstone's ship docked in Zanzibar. Chuma and Sutsi were at the port to receive their liberator and master. They trained their eyes on the passengers disembarking, but they couldn't spot Livingstone. Then, a rather elderly man who looked out of sorts approached them with a broad smile. He wore the same kind of hat Livingstone was fond of wearing.

"Oh! How mighty glad I am to see you again! I am so happy you got my message," the old man told them. He stretched out his arms and hugged the hesitant men, each in turn. They wondered what the strange apparition had to do with their friend David Livingstone. But they deduced a remarkable semblance between the haggard figure and Livingstone, especially the hat and the eyes. The rest, they were not sure.

"Master, is it really you? Chuma finally gathered courage and asked.

"Yes, it's me!" responded Livingstone.

"You have grown very old!" Sutsi observed.

"Master, you don't look well," said Chuma.

"Yes, it is true. I have been unwell for quite a while," confirmed Livingstone.

"Then why have you come back? It would have been better if you had waited to regain your strength. Long journeys are not kind to the weak," said a very concerned Chuma.

"I have urgent matters to settle," said Livingstone.

"More important than your life?" asked Sutsi.

"Yes," replied Livingstone.

There was a heavy sack among Livingstone's luggage.

"Master, are you carrying stones?" asked Sutsi.

"No, those are potatoes. I will make fish and chips for you, and the rest we will give out for planting. Fish and chips are very special in England. It is the food for the rich. I want Africans to eat like the English Lords," said Livingstone with a smile.

"It must be very special – this fish and chips – for you to carry such a load all the way from England!" said Chuma.

"Without potatoes, the Irish will be dead and the English will go hungry too. It is a wonder crop," said Livingstone.

"Well, thank you for bringing this wonder to Africa. I guess we will never go hungry again and we will be eating like English Lords," said Sutsi.

"Perhaps," said Livingstone.

"Why the doubt?" asked Chuma.

"The English...the English, never mind, let's go and settle in," said Livingstone.

Chuma and Sutsi would have loved to hear Livingstone complete what was on his mind. The English had taken all the fertile land in Monomotapa and left Africans in the least fertile parts of the land where even potatoes could not grow. Perhaps, he was going to warn them that the English would not allow Africans to grow potatoes and feed like Lords. They did not pursue the matter further. They had detected a tone of anger or alarm in Livingstone's voice... "The English..."

So far, Livingstone was oblivious to the gory details of Rhodes exploits in Monomotapa and South Africa, yet they were moving God in Heaven to tears. They included burning of villages, flogging, taxation, forced labour and genocide.

"We are going to undertake a long journey into the interior, to find the source of the River Nile." Livingstone told his faithful servants after dinner.

"What for?" asked Chuma.

"It is of vital strategic interests to the British Government," said Livingstone.

"How?" asked Sutsi.

"Whoever controls the Nile, especially the source, controls Egypt and the Sudan," Livingstone informed them.

"You discovered the Zambezi and now the English have taken over the kingdom of Monomotapa, especially all the fertile land. Is that what you mean by vital strategic interests? What will happen to the people of the Sudan and Egypt?" asked Chuma.

"Sadly more or less what has happened to the people of Monomotapa," said an apologetic Livingstone.

"And you told us you do not believe in slave trade. Do you know the people of Monomotapa are working for the English by force? Your friend Rhodes has used lies, the whip and gun to cow the natives. Monomotapa is lost forever, to the English. They are worse than Arabs and Portuguese," said Sutsi.

"It is the same in Scotland. We are fighting a common enemy," said Livingstone.

"Then why give the enemy more land to control?" asked Chuma.

"So that when we rise against him, there will be many fronts to fight and we will weaken them that way. We will win together," said Livingstone.

"Then let us go and find the source of the Nile and let the English spread themselves thin. We shall finish them together," said Chuma.

"God willing, this is my dream," Livingstone said beaming.

The following day, Livingstone went to pay a courtesy call on the British Consular Officer in Zanzibar. He wanted to affirm the promise by the President of the Royal Geographical Society of constant supply of provisions until his mission was accomplished.

The British Consulate had been recently established to safeguard British strategic interests along the Eastern African Coast especially the protection of shipping lanes from Cape Town to Aden. Increasingly, the British were supplanting Arab interests along the coast, with imperial designs on the mainland. A new Consular Officer had just arrived.

When Livingstone knocked on the door, a very familiar voice answered. He opened the door and entered. To his shock and dismay, John Kirk sat behind the desk, his roommate from the University of London and the man who had written a most damning report on his handling of the Zambezi Expedition.

"You are here?" a surprised Livingstone asked.

"As you can see, I am!" replied the cold voice of Kirk.

"The world is never short of surprises. We meet again in the most unlikely of places. I am embarking on another expedition," explained Livingstone.

"I am aware. What can I do for you?" asked a curt Kirk.

"Besides reporting my arrival, I wish to inform you that my plan is to sail south to river Ruvuma as the starting point for the search of the source of the Nile. From there, I will travel northwards towards Lake Tanganyika. If and when the need arises, I will be requesting for provisions including medicine. I was assured of your full cooperation," said Livingstone.

"You have my word, and such are my instructions," assured Kirk without looking at Livingstone. He busied himself filing his finger nails, seemingly most distant in thought.

"Well, I have to go now," said Livingstone.

"Best of luck old man; I hope this time, the outcome will be commendable," said Kirk.

Livingstone was very angry with the comment which he felt did not dignify a response. With the memory of Kirk's betrayal being rekindled, he stood up slowly and left without another word.

As Kirk continued to file his nails, his feet relaxed on top of the table, the only words which left his mouth were "poor chap, so misguided by demons. I hope I will never see his face again."

He scribbled a message to the Foreign Office in London:

Confirming arrival of Livingstone in Zanzibar. Will keep you posted of subsequent developments.

John Kirk had been specially posted to Zanzibar to monitor David Livingstone. He had instructions on how to manage "further developments", which he was going to execute without feelings. He closed his eyes and dozed off, trying to cope with the hot and humid weather.

Livingstone believed that the source of the Nile was connected to Lake Tanganyika. He was going to start from the south and work his way, if possible, to Cairo and that would settle the issue once and for all.

Sailing up River Ruvuma, he came to Lake Nyasa and made enquiries from the locals whether a river flowed northwards from the lake. "No, there is no such a river flowing northwards, but farther north, there is Lake Bengwelu with a river flowing northwards," he was told. He hastened there but found

Bengwelu too small to be the source of the Nile. "The biggest lake in this area," he was told, "is Lake Tanganyika and it has a river flowing northwards."

For information, protection, escort and porters, Livingstone was parting with a fortune daily. He travelled by boat where he could, but most of the journey was on foot. By the time he approached the southern shores of Lake Tanganyika, his health had deteriorated. Porters and thieves had also carted chests of provisions and medicine. From then on, he relied on slave traders for supplies and company.

What remained of his teeth was giving him excruciating pain; chewing food was quite an ordeal. He survived on fruits and milk, but the acidity level in his body gave him a burning sensation and an itch in his seat which he kept scratching even in the public. The locals nicknamed him "Mr. Itchy". Some would imitate the action when talking about him. It was at times like these that he wished he had a potato plantation close by, but the potatoes had disappeared as well.

"Master, we should abandon the expedition and take you to Zanzibar. You have to go back to England for treatment," concerned, Chuma and Sutsi told him. Livingstone looked at them and understood their worries. They did not want their master to die in their hands.

"Chuma," replied Livingstone, "this is only a temporary setback. In the Bible, God tested Job with death in his family, the destruction of his property and finally with leprosy, just to see how much faith he had. Not once did Job curse God. The Almighty, satisfied with Job's steadfastness rewarded the man a hundredfold. I am like Job. Since the day I embarked on my mission, I have been tested many times. My faith will not waver, no matter what; I will be rewarded a hundredfold."

"What sort of reward do you expect?" asked Sutsi

"I can't tell. The ways of the Lord are very mysterious," said Livingstone

"I hope whatever you get, you will share it with us. Haven't we been faithful to you?" asked Sutsi.

"Whatever I get, your share is guaranteed," Livingstone said smiling.

"But suppose things get worse?" asked Chuma.

"I don't see the situation getting any worse than it already is," said Sutsi.

"Gentlemen, enough of this; God will take care of us all," concluded Livingstone.

Things did get worse. As they were planning to sail northwards onto Lake Tanganyika, Livingstone suffered from a bout of malaria. He would have died had it not been for local herbs administered on him. Malaria was common in the region and the natives had learnt how to deal with it. The disease left Livingstone very weak. How long they stayed there was anybody's guess as time had ceased to have meaning.

By the time Livingstone was back on his feet and ready to move on, all the provisions he had bought from slave traders were exhausted. He crossed the lake to the eastern side and camped in a fishing village named Ujiji. It was infested with Arab slave traders and ivory dealers. He found a slave caravan heading for Zanzibar and for a fee he sent a message to John Kirk, the British Consul, to urgently dispatch provisions and medicine.

As he waited for the supplies, he occupied himself building a shack with two bedrooms, one for himself and the other for his faithful servants.

While Chuma was ever at Livingstone's side, Sutsi found a way of occupying himself by assisting slave raiders as a mercenary. The money he earned fed the trio and some he spent on drink and women. Livingstone did not know the source of Sutsi's income, but he hoped he was earning it honestly. He did not ask questions.

Once in a while, when Livingstone was asleep, Sutsi would drag Chuma along to the dens where beer and women ruled the night. They did not feel guilty of their nocturnal escapades. Moreover, they were always there in the morning when Livingstone needed them. Livingstone had rescued them from slave merchants, but in a way, they were never really free. Although they were in a position to run away from the sick man, never once did they contemplate it. It was as if their fate was so interlinked with that of the sick man that only death could make them part.

Livingstone kept on sending messages to John Kirk which were never responded to. He could have gone to Zanzibar to confront John Kirk, but he preferred to send messages. He was aware that a direct confrontation might not be very pleasant. He was civil in the wording of the messages, almost to the point of begging.

He also felt that a journey to Zanzibar and back would sap too much of his energy. He had made up his mind to save whatever was left for the final leg of the journey. He could feel it – the source of the Nile was at the northern end of Lake Tanganyika, and Richard Burton had said as much. He felt they were both right.

His quest for glory beyond the Queen's list of honour was within grasp, if only Kirk responded, and he hoped, sooner than later. In the meantime, he also killed boredom by writing his report and talking to anybody who cared to engage him, on any subject matter. Although he was not among sages in a cafe by the Seine, there were many fascinating things about life to discuss with the natives and Arab slave traders. Since they did not understand his strange mission of finding the source of a river, he instead engaged them in talks about the lucrative trade in slavery, ivory, gemstones and game hunting.

"He is a queer man," some opined.

"He is a homosexual. Chuma and Sutsi are his lovers. See how they have messed up his backside. He stinks and he is forever scratching himself," others would gossip.

The story of "Mr. Itchy", the poor old white man who lived in Ujiji spread around the villages along the lake. There were those who swore he was a ghost, a spirit, but of the benevolent kind. The stories kept Livingstone, Chuma, and Sutsi amused as they waited for provisions. His "divine mission" was now in the back burner.

On day while they were relaxing in the house, a young man came bursting through the door. "Master," he said panting, "there is a white man to see you." he told Livingstone. Livingstone's mind raced to John Kirk. Had Kirk thought it fit to bring the provisions and medicine personally? He could have sworn that Kirk was too heartless to make such a sacrifice.

"How does he look like?" Livingstone asked.

"Tall, with a huge beard; he says he is a German," said the young man.

To Livingstone, the issue was getting more complicated. Unable to fathom why a German would be looking for him in Ujiji, Livingstone turned to Sutsi, "Go and bring him in." Sutsi left with the young man. Livingstone and Chuma sat on stools outside their shack to await the surprise visitor.

A white man of a remarkable physique and sporting a most imposing beard and an accompanying moustache came plodding alongside Sutsi. When he reached Livingstone, he stretched his arm and greeted him with a lot of familiarity.

"My name is Karl Peters, don't you remember me?" he asked Livingstone.

"I will be damned if I have ever met you," responded Livingstone.

"Then you are damned! We met when you came to see Chancellor von Bismarck in Berlin. I see you never took note of me, but it doesn't matter. After all, there were many important people."

"Yes, I now vaguely remember! You are the one who booked me into a hotel! But...! My, oh my! How you have changed! It is the moustache and the beard!"

"I can hardly recognise myself in the mirror either! I did it for a purpose."

"What purpose?"

"To impress Africans!"

"I am sure they have never seen anybody with such a mass of hair on their face. What brings you to wild Africa?"

"Adventure! When you talked about the Dark Continent, I was completely mesmerised. I said to myself, if a man has courage to venture into the unknown, then he must, and here I am. We have met purely by chance and what a pleasant coincidence!" said Peters.

"But adventure must be pegged on a cause, a hobby or something, otherwise it is related to madness," teased Livingstone.

"Let us say mine is related to madness. Nonetheless, Bismarck has asked me to do for Germany what you are doing for England, that is, to map out the natural resources and the fertile areas. As you told us, the future of Europe lies in the conquest of Africa. We are true believers in the new creed. Most of all, I want to experience raw nature in its perfect form. Africa is so unspoilt!" said Peters.

"You have come too late! Virgin Africa is no more. The Arabs and the Europeans are messing up the place. The Boers, the Portuguese, the English and soon the Italians, the Germans and the French will dismantle what good remains," said Livingstone.

"Isn't it what you wanted?" asked Peters.

"Yes and no, but mine is a long story. Come in, you must be tired," said Livingstone.

Peters was Livingstone's guest for two weeks. The kind German provided them with provisions and medicine. The man, Livingstone thought, had been sent by God to save his life, in another act of divine mercy, a miracle from Heaven.

He told Peters everything he knew about Africa. Peters took notes and plotted places on his *Mappo Mundo*. He was going to give a first class report to Bismarck. The German colonisation of Africa would truly be on course, thanks to Livingstone.

"Old chap, I have to move on. Thank you for all the information. Perhaps we will meet again in Berlin or some other place. Life is full of surprises!" he said to Livingstone.

"That is so. You have been very kind to me. I owe my life to you. Give my warm regards to the Fuhrer," said Livingstone.

"So long..." said Peters.

"So long..." Livingstone replied.

Peters, the amiable majestic and mesmerising German with a generous hand for expensive gifts hurried to sign treaties with Chiefs throughout Tanganyika and Uganda. He secured the countries for Germany, for which Livingstone was later blamed by the British Government.

The public in Britain had been told that Livingstone had gone to Africa on a big mission which would elevate him higher than the Queen's list of honour. Several years passed. The journalist who had travelled with Livingstone from Sofala wrote an article which asked the question; "Where is Livingstone?" He hinted at the possible death of Livingstone, stating that perhaps the British Government was too ashamed to break the news to the public. He demanded that at least, Livingstone be given the honour he deserved posthumously.

The government asked John Kirk to shed some light on the rumour of the death. He responded that Livingstone was alive and well according to reports reaching him from the hinterland. This response was not convincing, but the government did not wish to sacrifice an Englishman, a top spy to undertake a journey to the interior to verify first-hand that the Scotsman was well and kicking. Of the two, Livingstone was expendable. John Kirk was of a higher breed.

While the public waited for proof that Livingstone was still alive, articles from the Royal Geographical Society started hitting the press, describing Livingstone as the greatest explorer that ever lived. He was described as a trailblazer, a frontier man and the soul and spirit behind the acquisition of territories in Africa. He was, it was reported, the mentor of Cecil Rhodes who had dismantled the mighty kingdom of Monomotapa without firing a single shot, owing to the fine groundwork laid by Livingstone. He was hailed as a great strategist and tactician. His stature was greatly elevated by these articles. Had Livingstone read them himself, he would have been amused.

Not to be outdone, the Church Missionary Society published articles on Livingstone hailing him for his work in Africa. It was reported that he had saved many from slave traders, but most of all, he had baptised the King of Monomotapa following which the crumbling kingdom had embraced Christianity and civilisation. As a result, the savages had humbly accepted the tutelage of their new master Cecil Rhodes. They called Livingstone "a saint".

The articles were meant to pacify both the living and the dead so that the British Government would not face a backlash in the event that Livingstone was never heard of again. The articles talked of how the government was making great efforts to reach Livingstone deep in the jungles of Africa and assist him in all ways possible to achieve his life-long ambition of solving the mystery of the source of the Nile. A deviant editorial in a Scottish daily challenged the stories in the English press. It concluded, "Livingstone is dead, but the British Government does not want to admit it. Just like Mungo Park disappeared in mysterious circumstances, Livingstone has disappeared too. How many more Scottish great men will be sacrificed by the English to satisfy their insatiable greed for power and wealth?" the article posed.

The matter had come to a head and the British Government had to find Livingstone dead or alive, to put an end to the damage the debate was inflicting on the cohesion and harmony of the Union.

Living on alms does not only reduce a man's self-esteem, it also reduces his will to live. Livingstone, "the stinking man" was a subject of derision among locals and slave traders. He earned the term 'white stinking beggar' from Arab slave traders and ivory merchants.

Like King David, Livingstone wondered, "How the mighty had fallen." With his chances of finding the source of the Nile reduced to wishful thinking, given the state of his health, he began to think of the unthinkable, death! The warmth of the African sun which had rejuvenated him now appeared oppressive to his eyesight and his soft white skin. The native herbs he was consuming were working only partially. He was withering fast like any living thing whose time span had come close to the end.

His faithful friends, Chuma and Sutsi were very concerned. They did not want their "master" to die under their care.

"It is better we take you to Zanzibar where you can get treatment," pleaded Chuma again.

"Or better still, you can go back to England and come back when your health is better." added Sutsi.

"No, no, no! I will be fine in a short while. Furthermore, I do not think I can undertake the long voyage to England until I find the source of the Nile. I would rather die trying than return empty handed," he argued with finality.

"But supposing you get worse? What shall we do?" asked Chuma in a voice full of concern.

"I have been thinking about that. You know, I promised my mother that whatever happens, my heart will be buried in Scotland, and that is how it should be, God forbid, if I die here," confessed Livingstone.

"That will not be possible. If you die here, you will be buried here," said Chuma.

"We have been together for a long time. I owe you a lot; you also owe me a lot. I have a small favour to request of you, maybe the last one I will ever ask," Livingstone continued after a hearty laugh.

"Your wish is our command," said Chuma waiting in anticipation.

"If I die, you will bury my body here, but you will take my heart to Zanzibar for onward shipment and burial in Scotland."

Perplexed, Chuma and Sutsi looked at him the same way one looks at a mad man; first with pity, but wishing to be at arm's length.

"You heard me, right," said Livingstone.

"Yes, but pray it does not happen," said Sutsi.

"But should it happen, how do we carry your heart to Zanzibar. It will be rotten on the way!" said Chuma.

What happened next was beyond belief. Livingstone took them through the anatomy of the human body.

"Human organs can be preserved in brine. You will open my chest here. The heart lies here. You will cut it out and stitch the chest back. Put the heart in a container with brine and seal it. It will change colour but it will not rot. In that form, it will be delivered to my mother for burial, see? Simple!"

Livingstone finally completed the explanation.

"It will be a most sad and difficult day should that come to pass. But one thing we promise you, we give our word of honour, never to let you down, in life or in death," affirmed Chuma. The assurance seemed to please Livingstone to no end. With a warm smile, he hugged each one of them in turn.

"I knew I could always count on you," he said. He asked them to go to the village to relax as he wanted to be alone for a while.

Livingstone could not explain why he had rescued Chuma and Sutsi from the slave traders. All he knew was that he would be eternally thankful to the inner voice which had led to the kind act. He wondered how life would have been without them. They were not his slaves though they called him master. The relationship was more like between a father and his sons. They trusted and loved one another and above all, each could count on the other in times of need. Right now, he was counting on them for survival. And if the worst came to the worst, he was still counting on them to perform his last rites, including keeping the promise he had made to his mother.

"Where on earth can one find friends as kind and trustworthy as these?" he asked himself.

It occurred to him with shock that he was contemplating the unthinkable, death! Was life playing tricks on him? Had God selected him for a noble mission then abandoned him? And if so, why? His "divine mission", he was sure, had been on course until the Portuguese destroyed the kingdom of Monomotapa, or who had destroyed the kingdom? No, it was not the Portuguese, but Cecil Rhodes who had put the last nail in the coffin.

And who was Cecil Rhodes? He had actually created the monster to use him as a cog in the plan to liberate Scotland. The British had occupied the land with ease because he handed Rhodes the key to success; the secret of the curse. Rhodes was fulfilling his dream of building an empire full steam, a national hero. But for himself what did he have to show for all his efforts? Nothing! Absolutely nothing!

Livingstone regretted that he had lost his family in the process, he had no friends, and in Scotland, he was thought a traitor. Why had he not thought of an alternative strategy to liberate Scotland, a non-violent way, perhaps a referendum? Now here he was, in the middle of nowhere, preoccupied with thoughts of death!

"What kind of God is this who leads one to self-destruction?" he wondered. Was his God the same as the God of David, Moses and Job? No, that was the God of Israelites, he was a Scotsman. Then who had sent him on the "divine mission"? Another god or, or...

"Oh my God, have I been at the service of Satan, the devil himself?" he asked himself. The answer came to him in a blinding flash, screaming before his eyes in capital letters "YES!" Then he pondered, why had the devil sent him to search for the source of the Nile? Was it another trick – and the answer was the same, "YES!"

Livingstone went on his knees and prayed fervently, "God, save me from this evil spell. Shame the devil by showing your humble servant the source of the Nile..." Before he could finish the prayer, he was startled by a man who came bursting in unceremoniously.

"Master, master, there is another white man looking for you. He is standing outside the door." David Livingstone summoned all his strength and walked outside very slowly. The white man was not John Kirk, but a total stranger. Livingstone was relieved because the last person he ever wanted to see again was Kirk.

Before Livingstone could offer greetings, the stranger spoke and said, "Dr. David Livingstone I presume?"

"Yes, my name is Livingstone and who are you?"

"My name is Henry Morton Stanley, a journalist with the *New York Tribune*. I have been mandated by the British Government through the Royal Geographical Society to look for you," said the stranger.

"Come right in, you are on the right track," said Livingstone. The man had a strange American accent. They had sent a foreigner, not an Englishman to look for the worthless lost Scot. Stanley was Welsh in fact, but he had migrated to the USA.

I had anticipated that my orders from Heaven would engage me for a relatively short period of time. It was now over forty five years since I had first encountered Livingstone. Not that I was complaining, no, it had been one hell of an adventure beyond anything I had ever dreamed of. Somehow, I had yearned for Livingstone to return to Monomotapa to check on his misfired dream. The English were not dying. If anything, they were killing Africans at will.

The natives had been dispossessed, dehumanised and brutalised. Those who were engaged in labour in the farms of settlers were paid peanuts and forced to pay taxes. Those who had run away found out that the dislocation of their cohesion as a society meant the death of individuals. They were malnourished and lost. How would Livingstone's conscience live with the hell he had created? And for this, he was asking for knighthood? I longed for answers. I now knew why St. Peter had given me the mission. Man, the frail creature, is indeed incorrigible, blind, insensitive, cruel, self-destructive and therefore doomed, both heroes and villains, and there is a very thin line between the two.

CHAPTER 23

GOD'S ANGEL

Henry Morton Stanley was a well-built man. Tall and stately in stature, he carried himself with an easy demeanour which endeared him to almost anyone at the very first contact. Added to his athleticism were his good looks and extreme intelligence. To the women, he was magnetic, an Adonis. If looks were a yardstick to judge a man's standing in society, then he certainly fitted in the nobility! But nothing could be further from the truth. As a journalist, standing out easily served him well, and he could not ask for more.

At once, I opened the pages of recent history to find out who exactly this new character was in the plot. Stanley was the son of a Welsh barmaid, Elizabeth Perry by name, who had no recollection as to who exactly had impregnated her. Her lovers or customers were many, but from the looks of the boy, she had the vague memory of a man who had migrated to Australia since. She could not remember his name. The veracity of the matter was never established and it was of no grave concern to anyone. She named the boy Rowland and gave him away to a relative as she could not cope with the responsibilities and demands of parenthood. It was not that the relative cared much either, but she had the luck of acquiring a free farmhand, and she worked him like a workhorse.

At the age of fifteen, young Rowland could not stand it anymore. He ran away and found a job as a butcher's delivery boy. Judging that his life would remain miserable if he had no education, he enrolled for evening classes. It was here that he came across Livingstone's book, *Missionary Travels in Africa* which he not only enjoyed reading, but it also fired his imagination, and triggered a craving for foreign travel.

One day, as he delivered meat to a visiting American ship at the harbour, he said to himself, "It's now or never". By the time the ship docked again in New Orleans, in the USA, he was still on board, as a stowaway! He had fulfilled a lifetime dream of travelling to foreign lands, and he felt that was only the beginning.

He changed his name to Henry Stanley and later adopted Morton after a kind gentleman by the same man. He had changed his name, his identity and his nationality. He was now an American, not a Briton. He undertook further studies while working as a cook and in the end landed himself an enviable job, as a clerk to a judge.

When the American Civil War broke out, he enlisted under duress. It was as a conscript that he met Livingstone's son, Albert who was also fighting for the Union. Soon thereafter, Robert was killed in the battle of Gettysburg.

Fearing for his life, Stanley deserted and went to the mountains to prospect for gold and made a small fortune with which he enlisted to study journalism. He hoped that he would one day have the good fortune to travel to Turkey, India and China and write such masterpieces that would elevate him to the pinnacle of the trade. For a start, he made a pilgrimage to Jerusalem and filed a story with the *New York Herald* as a freelance journalist. The piece was so detailed and so well written that it landed him a job with the newspaper. He was commissioned to cover the opening of the Suez Canal.

The series of articles he filed on the history and the geo-political importance of Egypt mesmerised the American public, so much so that they craved for more. He was an instant sensation.

He predicted that the opening of the Suez Canal had heightened the strategic importance of the region and that it was bound to antagonise its co-owners, namely Britain and France. He reiterated that whoever controlled the source of the Nile controlled both Egypt and the Sudan, but the source still remained a mystery.

The American public had never been taken on such a tour-de-force by a journalist. Stanley was hailed as a genius, a strategic thinker and a bright son of America. The man was basking in his new found glory and he was thoroughly enjoying it. Truly, America was the land of opportunity. He wondered what he would have become had he remained in Britain. The answer was not hard to find – just another non-entity. Unknown to him, the British Government secret agents had unravelled his true identity.

Taking advantage of his newly acquired fame and status, Stanley requested the *New York Herald* for funding to unravel the mystery of the source of the Nile. To his utter dismay, he was told America had no interest in the geography of far-flung places without a bearing on its national interests in the short or long-term period!

Summoning his great resolve, he decided not to give up. He went to London and knocked on the door of the President of the Royal Geographical Society with the same request. He could not have arrived at a more opportune moment. The Society was desperately looking for anyone eager and foolish enough to go into the jungles of Africa, to establish the status of Livingstone, dead or alive, but not an Englishman. Stanley was Welsh and therefore expendable.

"We have been keenly following your reporting on the Suez Canal and Egypt. By and large, you seem to have a keen eye on details for an American," the President of the Royal Geographical Society told Stanley.

"Thank you sir, I take my work very seriously," said Stanley.

"No doubt; no doubt; however, while the search for the source of the Nile remains a key focus for Britain, the most urgent concern for now, is to find the whereabouts of Dr. David Livingstone. The public is accusing the government of having abandoned him in the jungles of Africa to be devoured by wild animals, but nothing is further from the truth. John Kirk has assured us that the man is well and kicking, but he is too busy in Zanzibar to venture into the interior for first-hand information on the man's whereabouts. Are you willing to undertake the mission?" asked the President.

Stanley needed no persuasion. In as much as he wanted to visit Turkey, China and India, he felt the search for the missing Scot in the jungles of Africa, would be a great adventure, an epic journey, one which would yield a fantastic story.

He was so excited that he filed a story with the *New York Herald*, on his new assignment to the unknown. He chided the American government for its lack of enthusiasm, in the new creed of imperialism, which the Europeans had embraced wholeheartedly. His article must have pricked the conscience of someone somewhere, because the owner of the paper wrote to him personally and offered American co-sponsorship of the trip.

"America fully associates itself with your new adventure, and the paper offers continued collaboration in publishing your findings for a special fee. The state of affairs in that part of the world is of general and particular interest to the American public. Best of luck!" the newspaper owner wrote.

Stanley could not fathom how "the geography of far flung places" had all of a sudden become a part of American national interests. Like Livingstone

had led the charge in enticing the United Kingdom to grab a huge chunk of Africa, he felt he was pioneering the same for his adopted home, the United States of America.

Stanley knew he had become very powerful. The world was bending over backwards to be associated with a bastard, the abandoned and neglected son of a barmaid and a harlot who was now becoming a prime mover in the new order of things in the world.

"How quickly fortunes change for those who dare!" he said, looking up to the sky in supplication.

"Thank you God for your mercies. Give me strength to write articles and books about the uncivilised savages of the Dark Continent. I pray that the cannibals have not eaten David Livingstone. Give me power to expose the English vagabonds who have paraded themselves as explorers and philanthropists, while all they sought was personal glory and wealth. Give me the weapon to make those who called me a bastard come begging for mercy. Open the eyes of the American government. Amen," he concluded the prayer.

Stanley was not happy with his past in Britain and the humiliation he had suffered. He had promised himself he would hit back when an opportunity presented itself. Somehow, he thought, the search for David Livingstone yielded a wonderful platform. In the meantime, he had a strong desire to seek out his mother, before leaving in search of Livingstone.

Under his new name, he left London for Wales to seek out his mother. He went to the pub where she had worked all her life and made enquiries. He was taken to task to explain who he was and why he was looking for her. At last, the bar owner told him she had migrated to Australia with her lover of many years standing.

"I don't know what the sailor saw in her, but whenever he was around, they were inseparable. They even had a child, a boy, who vanished." It was late at night and the customers were few. The bar owner did not mind a chat.

"You said the child simply disappeared in thin air?" Stanley asked.

"Something like that. The mother gave the boy to a relative, an aunt I believe, to look after him. It was from there that he vanished."

After another round of drinks, the bar owner asked Stanley: "You said Elizabeth was your auntie? From which side, your mother's or your father's?"

"From my father's side," he lied.

"And who was your father? I thought I knew the family well," said the man. Stanley excused himself and went to the toilet. When he returned, he got the shock of his life. The bar owner after fixing a long gaze at him pronounced: "I don't know whether it is the drink or the dim light, but I can swear there is an uncanny resemblance between you and the sailor who took Elizabeth away!" Stanley was by now quite alarmed. After putting two and two together, he knew he could not fake his identity any more. The conversation had to be terminated.

"I think it is the drink and fatigue. I have to retire to bed. I will see you tomorrow," he said standing up.

"Good night," said the bar owner, still looking at Stanley with a lot of curiosity.

In the end he said: "I will be damned if this young man is not Elizabeth's boy who vanished!"

Very early in the morning of the following day, Stanley left Wales in a hurry. He was not going to return there any time soon. He was glad to board a ship bound for Zanzibar to look for Livingstone.

* * *

"So, the British Government and the Royal Geographical Society are concerned about me?" Livingstone asked Stanley. They were seated under a palm tree in Ujiji.

"I beg your pardon? You are their most valued asset abroad, well, besides Cecil Rhodes," said Stanley.

"I see. Rhodes has become a big name, has he?" asked Livingstone.

"You have been away for too long! Cecil Rhodes is the biggest giant of imperialism in Africa! His star has risen to the zenith. They worship him!" said Stanley.

"What of the natives of Monomotapa? I gather they have lost all their fertile land and livestock," said Livingstone.

"It is the same all over the world when a people are conquered. The rights of the natives, if any, should not be an impediment to our fortunes. It happened to the Red Indians in America, the Aborigines in Australia and the Indians in Latin America! Africa is not any different," said Stanley.

"And they cannot resist the occupation?" asked Livingstone.

"The cannons, rifles and pistols dictate that resistance would be a foolish thing," said Stanley.

"So Rhodes is busy building his business empire from Cape Town to Cairo?" asked Livingstone.

"The man is in complete control," said Stanley.

"You will tell me more about him all in good time. Now tell me about yourself."

So, Stanley told Livingstone about his life, after which Livingstone said:

"Imagine two Celt vagabonds meeting in the jungles of the Dark Continent, to fulfil the whims of the English! I can swear it is not by coincidence. What are we, their objects or slaves?" asked Livingstone.

"I think the Celts were made either for adventure or war. We fought the Romans and now, we are in the forefront in the efforts to resolve mysteries of the world. Do you think we are in the same class as Mungo Park?" asked Stanley.

"It is immaterial whether we are there or not, the truth is we are all instruments of the English. We are wayward vagabonds made to suffer, both at home and abroad," said a bitter Livingstone.

"You know I never saw it that way, but then, why did they knight Samuel Baker, Richard Burton and Cecil Rhodes and forget about you?" asked Stanley.

"Now you have the answer, they are all Englishmen from the nobility, are they not?" said a bitter Livingstone.

"So we are both here in God forsaken land, doing the bidding of selfish Englishmen, who will discard us like valueless trash in the end! I thought of you as a great missionary, a philanthropist, a great explorer and the chief architect of the expansion of the civilisation in Africa. You are my hero, my role model, my mentor!" said Stanley.

"Fie, fie as Moffat used to say. Life is more complicated than meets the eye at a glance!" said a very relaxed Livingstone.

In the search for meaning in their existence, they were getting closer and closer, to each other's heart as soul mates. There was no doubt that Stanley held Livingstone in high esteem, and the feeling was mutual.

"I am worried about your health. I suggest we leave for England as soon as possible. My chest of medicine will last for only a while," suggested Stanley.

"I thank you for your kind suggestion, but as soon as I am on my feet again, I will be on the march. The search for the source of the Nile is very dear to me. A Scot has to finish the work of Mungo Park. I am doing it for me and for Scotland, not for the English. I believe I am very close to solving the mystery. I can bear the pain for a year or so. I am of the Celtic stock, remember!" said Livingstone.

"Well, old man, I am of the same stock too! As soon as you get better, we will go in search together. I cannot abandon a fellow tribesman to suffer alone," said Stanley.

"Thank you son! You will not be disappointed. A lucky turn here and a lucky turn there and voila…! The source of the Nile! You and I will go down the annals of history, as the men who defied all odds and solved the world's greatest geographical mystery. The English can go hang!" said Livingstone.

"Do you think we will be knighted?" asked Stanley.

"Never! Did they knight Speke? No! He was a commoner though of English stock. Burton came from a big family and so did Baker; from the nobility. Speke, you and I, are non-entities no matter what we do. The English snobs who rule the Kingdom and the empire will make knights out of English idiots through arrogance and falsehoods. We are expendable objects," said Livingstone.

"I know why they sometimes glorify you as a saint and a legend. If the drive for imperialism in Africa turns out to be a nasty experience, they will blame you. They will say yours was the work of the devil," said Stanley.

"And if it works? asked Livingstone.

"Then, you will forever be presented to the world as a saint, the man who brought Christianity, Commerce and Civilisation to Africa. In other words, the architect of the downfall of Africans, but you will never be knighted. Yours will remain a mysterious and mind boggling story in the big book of history, and it will neither alter nor dent the English pride. It will always remain another of their tools to confuse Africans," replied Stanley.

"So what have I been working for? If the English have the temerity and impudence to treat me like trash, how will they treat the Africans? How will they treat Ndovu and the Queen Mother?" asked Livingstone.

"Simple, worse than they have treated the Scots, the Welsh, the Irish and the Aborigines! Africans will be beasts of burden on their own land, hence the abolition of slave trade! Like America was built on slave labour, Britain will prosper on the sweat and blood of Africans, working on their own land!" said Stanley.

"My plan was different. I wanted the Africans to rise up against British imperialism and teach them a lesson they would never forget. If the Africans didn't do it, I expected Europeans to fight among themselves in Africa with Britain as the main enemy," said Livingstone letting off his guard.

"In aid of what?"

"There is a big story to tell, one I might tell you some day."

"So you were not sincere when you urged Britain to conquer Africa?"

"I was, but it was not meant to benefit the English. It was meant to bring them down, on their knees!" explained Livingstone.

"For whose benefit?"

"For Scotland," replied Livingstone.

"How?" asked Stanley.

"It is not a simple matter. As I said, when the moment comes, I will tell you about it. Now tell me about Cecil Rhodes," said Livingstone.

"Well, your friend conquered the Kingdom of Monomotapa without firing a single shot. He signed an agreement with King Ndovu making the Kingdom a protectorate, and then took over. He is the Governor and has renamed the country Rhodesia, after himself! Such hubris!

"Ndovu and his mother have been reduced to alcoholics; they have an insatiable appetite for Scotch whisky. People say they are being consumed by the "curse of the caves". Ndovu is impotent and it looks like the Royal lineage is finished for good.

"The Europeans have taken the fertile land and planted cash crops: tobacco, cotton and coffee. Others have huge cattle ranches. The natives have fewer rights than wild animals. Funny, many disillusioned natives have turned to Christianity because there is nowhere else to go. To them, it is a catharsis. You should hear them on Sunday as reports have it, singing songs and saying prayers in Latin! It is most pathetic and quite comical. They have been dispossessed of their dignity and their souls. They have been brainwashed and turned into zombies; dehumanised. By the way, the Protestant and

Catholic churches have taken as much land as the settlers! The game is grab, grab and grab more! The natives can go hang or sing this world is not my home," said Stanley.

"And people say I am the architect of all this?" asked Livingstone.

"Remember your great oratory in Hyde Park, 'The Empire is a question of bread' and your articles and books, *Missionary Travels in Africa* and *The Zambezi and its Tributaries,* remember?" Stanley explained further:

"I am afraid yes. You were the sole mastermind of British colonialism in Africa. Rhodes was your creation, was he not? You were the architect, the prime mover and the spirit which guided British Imperialism into Africa."

"Listen Stanley, it was not me who did it. I was only the obedient servant of the divine spirit which controlled and guided me," said Livingstone in self-defence.

"I am afraid you are wrong David! No divine spirit can design such a diabolical scheme. By its very nature, it was evil! To my mind, it was hubris, your own quest for greatness and immortality which was the driving force, with the devil at the helm!" replied Stanley.

Livingstone sat still, his hands clasping the knees, weighing the words of Stanley, who nevertheless continued;

"How could you think of such a scheme after all the pain we have been through in Scotland, Wales and Ireland at the hands of the English? Did you have to export misery? Did you think that Africans were immune to pain or what on earth did you have in mind?" asked Stanley.

Livingstone did not answer. He just sat there, like some dead matter, transfixed, Stanley's harsh voice ringing in his mind... "It was hubris, with the devil at the helm". He realised that Stanley's judgement was true and a most painful revelation. He was weighed down by guilt and grief, both of which he could not bear. He felt like an executioner who had cut short the life of an innocent man, an executioner who was feeling more pain than the victim.

He began to sob, at first slowly and then uncontrollably. Stanley laid a hand on his shoulder and consoled him: "Listen old man, what had to be had to be, and don't you ever shed another tear about it," he consoled him.

"How then do I explain my "divine mission" if it was the work of the devil?" asked Livingstone.

"Let's put it this way. It was destined that Judas had to betray Jesus for the Saviour's life to have meaning. The British Empire needed a forerunner to

set the pace. For you, it was hubris which was the driving force. A goblin! Remember Satan told Jesus to worship him and he would give him a kingdom to rule. Remember he coaxed Him to throw Himself down from a multi-storey building and angels would rescue him from the fall, because the scriptures said so! Did Jesus yield to the temptations? No, certainly not! In both instances, the Devil was quoting the scripture as if his was a "divine mission", ordained from high above."

Ask yourself, just as Jesus stopped to think and rationalise, did you stop to think? Did Judas stop to think? No! The devil dangled a carrot by offering you independence for Scotland in return for your work on his behalf in Africa! You did not stop to think, did you? Do you think if God was with you? Would he have abandoned you holed up in some godforsaken place without provisions, sick and dying? In there lies your answer," concluded a most philosophical Stanley.

"Come to think about it, did I ever stop to question the command? No, I did not! I just marched blindly trusting in…in…I don't know what!" said Livingstone.

"Now, tell me, which Lord would send his faithful servant on a "divine mission" only to abandon him to fate in the middle of the jungle, in a dark continent? Which one?" asked Stanley.

"Yes, now I see it. It was all diabolical from the very start, but how could I have been so blind?" asked Livingstone.

"It is called blind faith. The final outcome is pain, chaos and damnation." Stanley did not understand where he was getting the words or the courage to spew them out. He was scared he might have been possessed by an evil spirit, and so, he did not want to pursue the discussion any further.

He however felt the need to get to the root cause of Livingstone's dilemma, if only for keepsake. But who knows, perhaps in some future article, he would put in proper context the truth, and nothing but the truth, the life and tribulations of David Livingstone.

"Tell me about the "divine mission" and maybe together we can decipher the meaning of your dream and where it went wrong," said Stanley. He waited most eagerly for Livingstone to speak. It was going to be a big scoop!

After a long spell of silence in which it appeared as if Livingstone was on another wavelength, communicating with another world, the old man said almost inaudibly:

"That will have to wait for another day. I am the author of pain and misery, am I not?" asked Livingstone.

Stanley did not answer. He was disappointed with the response.

Stanley had always regarded Livingstone as a great missionary, the greatest explorer and a saint. Now he feared Livingstone was going mad right before his eyes, and like the Queen Mother in Monomotapa, he was keeping the truth of the curse to himself.

"Cheer up! When the Lord closes the door, he opens a window. You have to hold on to your one dream which remains intact and within reach – the discovery of the source of the Nile – remember! The Lord wanted you to complete the work of your uncle Mungo Park. All others were side-shows, the temptations of the devil! If you accomplish this one great mission, which defied ancient Egyptians, Greeks, and Romans; and even Speke, Burton and Baker, you will have more than justified your long years of pain. Your suffering will not be in vain; the world will remember you as the most focused and resilient man in history, with an endless capacity for taking pain without grumbling. You will be canonisced, you will be immortalised! I promise you, I will stand by your side until you accomplish your glorious mission," Stanley assured him.

If Livingstone had used Cecil Rhodes to achieve his selfish ends, he was now the target of the sweet talking Welsh-cum-American. Everybody would like a big thing to happen in their life and for Stanley, he had just found it. He had to hold on to it. It was David Livingstone, whose story he knew, would propel him to immortality.

"You still believe in me?" asked Livingstone.

"As sure as I believe in God," said Stanley, despite his very little faith in the existence of the divine, in whatever shape or form. His life was charted by pragmatism and what was possible from day-to-day, within his very high ambitions of making it one day, even though, he wasn't quite sure what it was he was aiming for. "From a jack to a King," was the rationalisation of his great drive."

"Trust me! Who on earth would pass an opportunity like this, to be associated with a legend, even if it was in small measures, a footnote perhaps, it would suffice," said Stanley.

"Ooh Stanley, you breathe new life into my aching body. You are God's angel to take away the pain in my soul," said Livingstone hugging him. Stanley responded enthusiastically in alike manner.

"I have enough provisions to last us for an expedition, if it doesn't last too long," declared Stanley.

"I feel much stronger now. We shall soon be on our way and as I told you before, a turn here and a turn there and we will find the source of the River Nile!" said a rejuvenated Livingstone.

"You are on your way to immortality!" said Stanley.

That night, both men slept most soundly each assured they were going to make history. As fame and glory beckoned, all else was forgotten. Cats have many lives, they say nine! This special aspect of felinity had become second nature to Livingstone, and Stanley was not far behind.

While Livingstone and Stanley slept, I was restless. In my estimation, the big picture in my mission had been completed with Rhodes occupation of Monomotapa, which brought with it great suffering for the natives. Still, the spirit urged me to hang on and follow Livingstone's sill. To what end, I had no clue. I dozed off too.

CHAPTER 24

THE LAST STRAW

The recovery of Livingstone was remarkable, thanks to the ample supplies of foodstuff and medicine courtesy of Stanley. His camaraderie with the Welshman helped to uplift his spirits a great deal. Above all, there was the certainty of immortality around the bend with the discovery of the source of the Nile, which he felt was within an arm's length. His scratching of the behind had gone down considerably, but there was nothing to be done about his dentition. Many teeth had fallen off of their own accord, and this would remain a permanent feature of his decaying anatomy.

Stanley spent time talking to the locals and traders and updating his diary. Even if they did not discover the source of the Nile, he knew he had a great story to tell, a scoop with the riches and wonders of the continent in detail! Maybe, like Cecil Rhodes, he too could build himself an empire with the support of the American government.

"Master, are you not interested in diamonds and gold?" Chuma asked Stanley one evening.

"I would be interested if there were any for the picking," said Stanley, savouring memories of the small fortune he had made in America, in gold.

"Supposing we seal a good bargain for you, how much will you give us as commission?" asked Sutsi. This was serious talk, so Stanley put his diary away.

"It all depends. Let's put it this way, for anything I buy, I will give you ten percent of the purchasing price. Is that a fair deal?" he asked.

"Most generous Master! This evening, Banyamulenge traders will arrive from across the lake. They live in the Congo where they mine diamonds and gold. Do you want us to bring them here or would you rather we meet them at the port?" asked Chuma.

"We will meet them at the port," he said after some consideration.

"Carry with you a lot of valuable items for exchange. They bring plenty of gold and diamonds, gemstones and ivory," said Sutsi.

Stanley had heard the gossip in London about how young Cecil Rhodes and David Livingstone had made a fortune in diamonds and gold, but surely it had to take some effort to find precious things! He was surprised at how casual the conversation with Chuma and Sutsi had been. Gold and diamonds is serious business between rich people, not the subject matter of a casual conversation between acquaintances. He wondered whether he was being led into a trap. Moving from the shade of the palm tree where he had been seated jotting notes, he went inside the house to find Livingstone busy looking at the *Mappo Mundo* by Herodotus.

"I can see you are piecing together the loose ends on the source of the Nile. I have had a very interesting conversation with Chuma and Sutsi about gold and diamonds from the Congo. They tell me that traders called Banyamulenge will be here this evening. Do you know anything about them?" he asked.

"It is true; there is plenty of gold and diamonds in the Congo, more than in Bechuanaland. In my earlier days, I made a fortune out of the trade, but what joy did the wealth bring me? Save for what I gave my daughter Agnes, I squandered the rest. Easy wealth is evil; it can only bring you misery," said Livingstone.

"Well, I do not have the time to become a merchant of gold and diamond, but at least, I have to find out how true the claims are. That there is plenty of gold and diamonds in the Congo, even if it is for curiosity's sake," said Stanley.

"Then go and find out. You can trust Chuma and Sutsi," said Livingstone.

When the boats arrived from the Congo, Stanley and his party were at hand to meet the traders. There was an uncanny physical resemblance between Sutsi and the traders. They were all tall in stature, with long noses. Sutsi used to swear that he was a Tutsi by origin, but he could not remember from which village in the Congo. Maybe that was the reason why his name was close to that of the tribe he came from, the Tutsi – Tutsi and Sutsi were pretty close. Anyway, that did not matter anymore as he did not speak or understand a single word spoken by the Banyamulenge.

Chuma equally claimed that in as far as he could remember, after the slave raiders killed his parents, burnt the houses and captured many slaves including himself, it took one week walking before they came to Sutsi's village, where they spoke a language exactly like his. The difference was that,

his people were shorter and they had broad noses like all Bantu-speaking people. Speaking to the Banyamulenge, he was told that he had the features of a Hutu. The word rang a bell, but of a long lost distant past.

Now, they were brothers, servants of their master, David Livingstone, with no other attachment except to each other. They were united by fate and they were the best of friends. Stanley, the nice tall and handsome gentleman was a most welcome additional new member to the party. They took him as a brother, as Livingstone was like a father to them all.

In a town called Tabora, a week's march east of Ujiji, Tipu Tipu the old slave merchant was waiting for the Banyamulenge gold and diamond dealers from the Congo. The abolition of slave trade and the taking over of Monomotapa by Cecil Rhodes had disrupted his trade in gold, ivory and rhino horns. He had shifted his base to Tanganyika which had plenty of wildlife. He longed for the day he would penetrate a special area called Serengeti, which had more animals than all the animals of the world put together. Unfortunately for him, the area was in the heart of Maasai land and they had refused to do business with anybody, first in slave trade and then in ivory and other game trophies. They protected the animals as if God had charged them with that responsibility.

Tipu Tipu cursed the failure by the Donyiro Sultanate to capture the Kingdom of Monomotapa before Cecil Rhodes. He had hoped that before he died, the Islamisation, Arabisation and colonisation of Africa would have been extended from North Africa to the Limpopo River in Southern Africa, and then came Cecil Rhodes! He detested the intrusion of white men in Africa. Recently, he had sent an emissary to the Kabaka of Buganda warning him that he should not allow the Germans, the French or the English to penetrate his Kingdom, or else, it would suffer the fate of Monomotapa. Soon thereafter, an Englishman, Bishop Huntington had left Mombasa for Buganda to preach the gospel. He was speared to death when he crossed into Buganda territory. The news of the murder pleased Tipu Tipu to no end.

He had tolerated the presence of Livingstone in Ujiji because by all accounts, the man was sick, old and non-antagonistic. But he was not so sure of the new arrival Henry Morton Stanley; he was keeping a close watch on him. What he was not going to tolerate was any man: black, white or yellow interfering with his gold, diamond and ivory dealings with the Banyamulenge. He was gratified when the German, Dr. Karl Peters told him

he was not a trader but a tourist. Old and not able to move much, his only desire was to amass easy wealth, for the sake of it. Tipu Tipu had no dreams left after the one of an Arab conquest of Africa died. He had become senile, his mind bordering on the deranged. He thought himself a demi-god.

It was a happy Stanley who returned to Livingstone in the night loaded with the treasure.

"I offered them twice the price of the Arab trader! They offloaded everything on me, gold, diamonds, rubies, sapphires, the lot, but I did not take the ivory. I told them to take it to the Arab in Tabora." said an excited Stanley.

"Let me see the loot!" said Livingstone.

Stanley opened a heavy leather bag. In it were items wrapped in bundles. One by one, he opened them and laid them on the table. With every successive exposure of the contents to light, the room became dazzlingly brighter. In the end, all sorts of colours seemed to play with each other dancing around the lamp in the room. It was like a microcosm of Heaven itself, with many stars, each displaying its splendour, like they were in contest with one another.

"Put them away, put them away, they are blinding my eyes," said Livingstone.

"I could not imagine anything more dazzling! They are worth a great fortune, maybe the greatest collection of natural preciousness outside New York City!" said Stanley.

"You are now a stinking rich man, but as I warned you, easy wealth has its undesirable and dire consequences," said Livingstone.

"I will not let it get into my head. When do we embark on the expedition? You are now strong enough to march a thousand miles!" said Stanley.

"Don't worry there will be no much marching, most of the journey will be by boat. We will cross Lake Tanganyika and follow the Lualaba River. If it is not the source of the Nile, I will be damned! I have looked at the maps and the reports by the wayward vagabonds Speke, Burton and Baker. The only missing link is the area west and north of Lake Tanganyika. We are almost there and history is ours to conquer! But one caution, Tipu Tipu is a man of vengeance. You have wrenched a treasure from his grasp. Watch your back and watch mine too!" warned Livingstone.

Livingstone need not have worried. When the Banyamulenge took the ivory to Tipu Tipu, he demanded to know what had happened to the rest of the treasure. The Banyamulenge told him that since he had been fleecing them over the years, they had found a better deal. At once, he knew it was Stanley. Tipu Tipu went raving mad.

"You and your English dog will suffer my wrath. If these were the days of slave trade, I would have you frog-marched to the market in Zanzibar!" He was fuming, with foam coming out of his mouth.

"You call the white man a dog and what are you?" asked leader of the Banyamulenge. He had escaped capture by Tipu Tipu and his slave raiders purely by the speed of his lanky legs, only to return to the village to find death, destruction and pillage. He had never forgiven Tipu Tipu and his raiders who took away his entire family."

"You are a slave trader, a murderer, a thief, a dog and a pig!" he shouted at Tipu Tipu.

"You call me a pig? A Kaffir like you has the impudence to insult me?" and he reached for his rifle. Before Tipu Tipu could touch the gun, three Banyamulenge spears were deeply lodged in his chest. He fell on the side, blood streaming in gashes from the gaping wounds and from his mouth. The Banyamulenge took the guns and ammunition from his house. Firing in the air, they left towards the direction of Ujiji in great celebration. They left the still body of Tipu Tipu lying on sacks of ivory, his lifeless eyes staring at a void which seemed to stretch to infinity, with twitches of muscle spasms on both cheeks. The huge world of the master-tyrant had been reduced to a small space surrounded by eternal silence.

On their way to the port, the Banyamulenge sought out and found Livingstone and Stanley. They reported that they had executed Tipu Tipu in revenge for his insults, and to exact justice for the thousands of natives he had displaced, killed and taken as slaves. It was at that point that Chuma and Sutsi spoke.

"The Arab is the one who sold us to the Portuguese, but because Livingstone is a man of peace, we did not want to raise the issue with him. We thank you for executing him, and our hearts are now at peace that justice has been done," said Chuma.

"In fact, I had thought of killing him myself. But I did not want to cause trouble for master," said Sutsi.

The Banyamulenge told Stanley it had been their pleasure doing business with him, and inquired if he would like to do more business.

"Definitely," replied Stanley with excitement. "But I have a mission to accomplish first."

"What mission?" the leader of the Banyamulenge traders asked.

"We are looking for a huge river which flows north," said Livingstone.

"Ah, that is not a problem, the Lualaba flows northwards," said the leader.

"Out of Lake Tanganyika?" asked Livingstone.

"Yes," said the leader.

"I told you! I had no doubt in my mind that that is the missing link." said a joyful Livingstone.

"What are we waiting for?" asked Stanley.

The following day, Livingstone's party and the Banyamulenge crossed Lake Tanganyika together.

"After you accomplish your mission, come back and we will do big business," the leader of the Banyamulenge traders told Stanley.

"What else do you have to offer?" asked Stanley.

"There is also copper, chrome, mahogany, ebony, teak and rubber. We are not interested in trading with the Portuguese; they are as bad as the Arabs," said the leader.

"Give me a couple of months, maximum one year and I will be back," assured Stanley as they parted. Stanley was serious about his desire to go to the Congo, the land of endless fortunes.

They parted ways as great friends. Sutsi had a throbbing desire to accompany his people to the Mulenge hills in the Congo, but his loyalty to Livingstone was more compelling. He was sad to see them go.

Soon, Livingstone and Stanley were in three boats heading north, hugging the western shore of Lake Tanganyika looking for River Lualaba.

"Damn the English!" shouted Stanley who broke into a song,

> *We shall not*
> *We shall not be moved*
> *We shall not*

We shall not be moved
Just like a tree
That stands by the water side
We shall not be moved.

Livingstone liked the tune, especially the message that the actions of the English snobs could not deny them the glory they deserved. The worldwide recognition for solving the world's greatest geographical mystery!

At last they came to the spot where the Lualaba begins its journey out of Lake Tanganyika, in a northerly direction.

"How far north do we have to sail?" asked Stanley.

"Until the Lualaba meets the river from Lake Victoria, which I guess should take us no more than a few days," answered a joyous and rejuvenated Livingstone.

After sailing for four days, they got a rude shock as the river changed course, turning sharply westwards. They disembarked and engaged the locals:

"How far does this river flow westwards before turning northwards?" Livingstone asked them.

"It does not turn northwards, it flows westwards forever, until it joins river Congo, which feeds the big ocean to the west."

"Are you sure it does not turn northwards?" asked a shocked Livingstone.

"Sail on and prove me wrong," said the native.

"And do you know of another big river which flows from around here to the north?" asked Stanley.

"None that I know of. All rivers in this area flow westwards, from the Mountains of the Moon, they all join River Congo and on to the big ocean to the west."

They consulted other people including hunters, herdsmen and pygmies. The story was the same. Their journey had come a cropper.

The euphoria of instant glory and assured imminent immortality with which Livingstone and Stanley had left Ujiji was overtaken by a heavy gloom, with the sombre realisation of a barren quest.

The dashed expectations were greeted by a painful lengthy silence, in which the gravity of the debacle was slowly digested. The scene resembled a funeral party, for the burial of hopes and dreams, in which eye contact between Livingstone and Stanley was avoided.

The suicidal instinct has a staying power. It never dies. It can hibernate, but by and large, it will come back again like the plague *bacillus*. Livingstone thought of releasing a life boat from the ship for the mission. He would peddle down the Lualaba until he hit the rapids, to die like Mungo Park. Then he remembered Mungo Park had not committed suicide, and he shelved the idea. He walked to the big boat and sat, face down, tears welling in his eyes.

Stanley felt a daze. Momentarily, all he could see was darkness. When it cleared, he became aware of giant trees surrounding him, deep in the Congo forest. Some were so huge you could cut a road through them.

"Which trees are in this forest?" he asked a guide.

"There is cedar, podo, mahogany, oak, teak, ebony, rubber and many others; beautiful, mature hardwood. The Portuguese say the forests of the Congo are a gold mine!" said a guide.

Stanley made a simple calculation and concluded that with the hardwood, gold, diamonds, ivory, precious stones and big rivers for waterways heading to the Atlantic Ocean, it was a most profitable territory to colonise. He walked to the ship to join Livingstone smiling and saying to himself, "Cecil Rhodes has his Monomotapa, Congo will be mine!" He pledged himself to return, but not in the service of the British Government. Never!

It was a forlorn team that changed course for Ujiji. When they reached Ujiji, Stanley looked at a dejected Livingstone and said;

"Old man, it is time to return to England."

"You go back alone. I will never abandon the search for the source of the Nile, even if it takes the rest of my life." Livingstone said in a firm voice.

"Where will you go from here?" asked Stanley.

"I have a hunch that the elusive source of the Nile is somewhere to the south of here. There must be a river which enters Lake Tanganyika in the south, and another which leaves the lake in the north. The mistake we made was to believe that Lualaba was the only river which flowed northwards out of the lake. We should have sailed to the northern tip of Lake Tanganyika. But then, where does the lake get its water from? I do not want to return with a conjecture like John Speke. My discovery will be based on the full flow of the river, from the source to Cairo. Don't try it, no amount of persuasion will make me return to England until then," said Livingstone.

Stanley looked at Livingstone with great pity. The man had determination and willpower. Did he have the strength in his feeble frame to trek the

African continent for another couple of years? The answer was definitely in the negative. He had a feeling that Livingstone did not wish to see England or Scotland ever again, he was on a suicide mission. The English had ridiculed him for being a bad decision maker, and Stanley could not agree more.

"You see, my first mission in Africa was not accomplished and to a large extent, I feel I am a failure," Livingstone told Stanley.

"No, no old man, you have never been a failure. You are admired the world over, for your work…" said Stanley.

"You will never understand, but being of Celtic blood, perhaps you can appreciate my position. I came to Africa on a "divine mission" to liberate Scotland," said Livingstone.

Stanley sat upright and eyed Livingstone with great concern. Was he looking at a man who was about to lose his mind? Was he suffering from syphilis which had gone to his head? He wondered.

"You came to Africa to liberate Scotland from the English? Are you sure you are feeling alright David?" asked Stanley.

"You see, I had this hunch that the Scots, unlike the Irish, would never take up arms against the occupying force, so there had to be another way to liberate ourselves. This is when the 'divine mission' kicked in. I figured that if the English, the masters of the so-called United Kingdom established a vast empire throughout the world, with time, trouble would start brewing just as was the case in America. With wars in India, Africa and elsewhere, the English would be spread too thin and weakened. I reckoned it might also provoke wars with several European colonial powers. You see, the war in the Crimea was too short and other European powers fought alongside the British forces. The American war of independence rather than teaching the English a lesson left them bitter about losing a colony. They wanted to make up for it. I chose to be the architect of imperialism in Africa, with Monomotapa as the linchpin, and thus lead the English into a snare. In the middle of the ensuing pogrom, Scotland would declare independence and the English would be presented with a *fait accompli*!

"Now I have come to the agonising conclusion that my strategy was faulty. There was a grave categorical miscalculation bordering on the absurd, this I admit. The British Empire continues to grow, but the resistance is weak. I have been betrayed by fate. The Portuguese dismembered the strongest Kingdom

in Africa, the Kingdom of Monomotapa with hideous biological weapons. Thanks to their new imbecile of a king, Cecil Rhodes has established himself in Monomotapa without a fight. If only Taiwo had lived! But that is now wishful thinking. So, my first and most cherished mission has gone up in smoke. And now, I have to prove to myself that I am not a mad man and that God is on my side, by finding the source of the Nile. It is God who led Burton, Speke and Baker through the blind alley, so that they could not snatch the glory of the great discovery from me. Like David in the Bible, I carry favour with God! I have been selected as his instrument to solve the world's greatest geographical mystery, and with it His name will be exalted, and the name of Scotland will be elevated above all other nations since the times of the Greeks and Romans, at least in this one aspect. I owe this to my motherland.

"I thank you for showing great concern over my health. You have been like a son and a very kind one at that. But as you can see, I will not return to England until my mission is accomplished," stated Livingstone in no uncertain terms.

Stanley looked at Livingstone like one looks at an apparition with awe and fear. He did not know whether to pity or sympathise with him. "Incomprehensible!" he concluded in silence. The following day, they had an emotional parting.

In the short period they had been together, they had developed a deep liking for each other. Somehow, they knew they would never meet again. They looked at each other for endless moments, tears welling in their eyes. They were imprinting each other's faces in the brain, in the hope the picture would last until Kingdom come, for whatever it was worth. Livingstone felt his heart lighter now that he had told the purpose of his mission in life to a fellow Celt, for safe keeping and posterity.

"If you find time, pass through Paris and give my love to Agnes. Tell her I am doing fine," said Livingstone.

"I sure will," said Stanley as they embraced.

Henry Morton Stanley left Ujiji with a heavy heart. He felt he had abandoned a dear friend in dire need. At the same time, he felt very sorry for David Livingstone whom he did not know how to describe. Was he a nationalist, a saint or a fool? He did not doubt Livingstone's sincerity about the "divine mission", but he had issues with the "divinity" which had authorised such an impossible undertaking. He recounted how Livingstone had compared himself to the David in the Bible, who had simply laid down cold a giant, with a sling and a pebble. Well, not all miracles are assured of a good ending.

Livingstone's miracle had gone awry. If he did not discover the source of the Nile, how would he end? Then he reflected on how the English had painted Livingstone as a great explorer, a missionary and a saint when the clamour to find him reached high pitch. His own journey to Africa to find Livingstone was to appease the population, to put a lid on the issue!

"Damn!" he said in anger.

When he found him, Livingstone's pathetic state of health was a reflection of premeditated official neglect on the part of the British Consular office in Zanzibar, and by extension, the British Government. Why had John Kirk not answered Livingstone's appeals for provisions? Was there a conspiracy to abandon Livingstone to fate and sure death in the middle of Africa? What was the urgency by the Royal Geographical Society, and by implication, the British Government in sending an invalid on an arduous journey, one they knew he could not survive!

The more questions he asked himself, the more the picture became clearer. Livingstone was a thorn in the flesh of the British Government, but why? At once, it dawned on him that the British Government had known all along that Livingstone's ruse of a vast empire in Africa had been conjured as a trap. It was a trap which snared the hunter. The British Government had benefitted tremendously from the efforts of Livingstone as an explorer or a trailblazer.

The British intelligence network in Scotland having long uncovered Livingstone's inclinations towards the independence of Scotland, a decision had been made to use him to further imperial interests. Consequently, he became a beneficiary of generous donations from the Royal Geographical Society. Although he had covered a lot of ground in Africa, there was no way the Queen could have given a national award to a traitor. The public could holler and rave, but the truth would remain a state secret. It was also seen as desirable, for Livingstone to perish far away from the British Isles, because in this way, news and circumstances surrounding his death could be manipulated to suit the interests of the state, as was the case with the death of Mungo Park.

"Then what am I doing here? Am I not party to a conspiracy to distort history? In my stupidity and lack of judgement, am I not betraying a friend? Am I unconsciously not a tool in the hands of the British Secret Service?" Stanley asked himself and shuddered with the revelation. The realisation of the truth made him very angry. When he reached Zanzibar, he went straight to the office of John Kirk.

"Why have you abandoned Livingstone?" he asked John Kirk.

Unguarded and full of pomposity, Kirk retorted that Livingstone was an incorrigible fool, destined to perish like Mungo Park, chasing shadows.

"Livingstone is not a man of a sound mind. That is why he is a member of the clandestine Scottish Liberation Movement, whose singular focus is to dismember the Union. He should thank his stars, that instead of facing the gallows, he was given a scholarship, a honeymoon in Bechuanaland and paid for expeditions. He has now outlived his usefulness," said Kirk, his legs resting on the table, smoking a pipe.

"Is that why he never received the Queen's award of honour like Rhodes, Burton and Samuel Baker?" asked Stanley.

"Of course, how do you decorate a rebel, a traitor? Would you?" asked Kirk.

"No, I would not. But what of Speke?" asked Stanley.

"Let's put it this way, you don't go around decorating every Tom, Dick and Harry," said Kirk.

"He was too much of a commoner you mean?" asked Stanley.

"The words are yours, not mine," said Kirk.

Henry Morton Stanley stood up and with anger in his voice, addressed John Kirk:

"I am most glad I am American not Welsh. As a reporter, I will be free to tell the world how the British Government misused a Scottish half-wit by the name David Livingstone and then abandoned him to die in Africa. I will also put a good word for John Speke. You thought you were using me as a tomb stone to cover the rotting remains of Livingstone, but I have a story for you! If I ever come back to work in Africa, I will work for the Germans, the French or the Belgians, but never for the English…You have rotten minds and you are bereft of a soul, the lot of you English bigots!"

Kirk was taken aback, alarmed by the venom in Stanley's voice. He also knew what harm he could do with the pen, having unmasked the truth.

"Look Stanley, American, German, English or whatever, there is nothing that good money cannot fix. By the time you get to London, there will be a handsome offer for your story. Secrets must remain secret, at whatever cost. Think about it, for your own good," said Kirk, taking great care to conceal his fear.

Stanley stormed out of Kirk's office not knowing whether he had been threatened or offered a bribe, to cover up the truth. Even though he had written many stories, he now knew that the "Livingstone Affair" would have to be handled with a lot of care, leaving out sensitive details. He calculated that Livingstone, the toughest wayward vagabond of them all, was worth a fortune. He was going to trade the story for a lot of money with the British Government. He knew the Royal Geographical Society would eventually release an adulterated version, full of falsehoods. His conscience bothered him but he concluded:

"One day, the world will know the truth about David Livingstone. That he was not a philanthropist, an explorer, a missionary or a saint, but a self-created chimera. A robotic wayward vagabond, remotely controlled by the English ruling class, and he didn't even know it until it was too late!"

The questions I had asked myself as to whether Livingstone's mission was divine or not were being answered. God's chosen heroes throughout History had special powers, like David, Samson and others. Livingstone was no more than a sad character for derision. I would wait to see how Henry Morton Stanley was going to avenge his good friend or betray him for a fee. The character called Man never ceases to amaze, and greed is a powerful tool in shaping decisions.

I left Zanzibar and hurried back to Ujiji to see how Livingstone was faring.

CHAPTER 25

NEVER SAY DIE

I found Livingstone in Ujiji on the shores of Lake Tanganyika, a forlorn man. He had begun to doubt his own sanity. Had he been wrong all along, while everybody else had been right? He vividly recollected the words of the Chairman of the Scottish Liberation Movement. The Chairman had said that his plan to scatter the British troops throughout a vast empire, thereby creating conducive conditions for the declaration of independence for Scotland, was no more than a pipe dream or the illusion of a deranged mind. The Chairman had been proven correct by subsequent events. British troops were firmly in India and Ghana and some were with Cecil Rhodes in Monomotapa, but the big backlash of resistance had not materialised.

He recalled his quarrel with his brother on whom he had drawn a pistol. He deeply regretted his irrational behaviour. He had watched as his wife was eaten by lions. If this indeed was not madness, then what was? And why did he squander a fortune purchasing a ship, just for the heck of it? Then there was his hunch, that River Lualaba eventually became the Nile, and this he had painfully discovered was not so. Was he to give up now, and if he did, what would be his legacy?

Sure, the British had given him high sounding names, the greatest explorer, the missionary, the saint. But the English could never be trusted. The same mouth which called you a saint today would label you a villain tomorrow with great vehemence. He had been left out of the Queen's list of honour. No, he had to put his reputation beyond reproach, and the only way left, was to find the source of the Nile. This alone would vindicate him.

Livingstone, Chuma and Sutsi could not fathom what happened next. While they were away at the port, Arab slave traders came to Livingstone's house. They broke in and carted away most of the provisions left by Stanley. They left a message that they had come to avenge the death of Tipu Tipu and they would return at a time of their choosing. That night, Livingstone and his two servants left for the safety of Tabora. Once there Livingstone sent a message to John Kirk in Zanzibar that he needed provisions to proceed on the last leg of the expedition. A long time passed and there was no response. The drugs were running low and so were the other items.

Livingstone knew it was not only his body which was fast withering, but so was his will power. He had reached the point where death was a welcome release. He fought the feeling with prayers in which he begged the Divinity above to intervene. In this half delirious state, he told Chuma and Sutsi to prepare for a journey southwards to Lake Bengwelu. The year was 1873.

"We will follow the river which flows from Bengwelu to Lake Mwero. I believe we can establish that the river flows into Lake Tanganyika. We will then follow Lake Tanganyika to the northern tip because as Richard Burton had claimed, there is a river which flows from there, to Lake Albert, which as Baker found out, opens its northern shores to release the Nile to flow to Egypt. There is no other way. That is the sequence of the flow, but I have to prove it."

Obediently and without asking any questions, the two servants prepared for the journey which took them to a point on Lake Tanganyika south of the dreaded Ujiji. They went by boat to the southern tip, and then hired ox-carts to Lake Bengwelu, where the greatest adventure ever known to man was to begin. Livingstone was not himself anymore, as they took a boat to sail around Lake Bengwelu. When they arrived at the southern port of Chitambo, he ordered a rest. He was looking very pale, weak and sick. Supposing this final leg does not yield the source of the Nile, then what? He now understood why the Greeks and the Romans, Speke, Burton and Baker had given up the search.

"The source of the Nile is a secret well-guarded by African gods." he said to himself. For once, he yielded to the power of the gods of the primitive natives.

"Please, *Mwari* and others let me into the secret," he prayed to the gods of the pagans beseeching them. One night while in deep asleep, the ghost of Taiwo appeared to him.

"Wake up miserable old man," said the ghost.

"What do you want?" asked Livingstone.

"I have come to warn you that your suffering will never cease," said the ghost.

"Why do you come to torment me?" he asked.

"Because St. Peter in Heaven has heard the cries of the people of Monomotapa; it was you who unleashed the demons upon them. Now, their most fertile land has been confiscated by Cecil Rhodes and given to settlers to grow cash crops, establish ranches and mines. My people have been forced to work like slaves and to pay hut tax and poll tax. They have been driven to marginal lands and their livestock confiscated. Is this the civilisation, commerce and Christianity you promised my father? Is it the protection from Portuguese and Arabs you lied about? Speak!" said the ghost of Taiwo.

"I will tell you the truth. I was on a quest to liberate my people from the English. I had thought Monomotapa would fight and defeat the English, and then came the Portuguese with their biological weapons. That changed the whole equation. Please, understand my predicament," pleaded Livingstone.

"I was myself a victim of the plague. But you are the one who prompted the Portuguese to use underhand means when you took your imperialist crusade to London together with Cecil Rhodes, remember?" asked the ghost.

"Sometimes ill-fortune and fate conspire to play tricks on you," said Livingstone.

"When you laid down a strategy for the suffering of my people, in order to save your own, you brought upon yourself a curse. You elevated yourself to a level worse than that of a slave trader. You plotted for Africans to be dispossessed of their fortunes, natural resources, to work as slaves and finally to lose their souls to unscrupulous preachers. Do you know that the church has grabbed as much land as the settlers? That there is no difference between the duo in greed, cruelty and lust! Do you know many children have been born by our women to preachers, some from rape? Why did you plot these evil acts?" asked Taiwo's ghost.

"Please forgive me. I did not know the end would be like this," said Livingstone.

"It is not me to forgive you; it is for the people of Monomotapa, the people of Ghana and elsewhere who have been consumed by the evil fire of colonialism that you lit. By the way, when you die, do not attempt to ask for forgiveness from St. Peter. He has said loud and clear that unless you are forgiven by the people of Monomotapa first, you will not enter the Kingdom of God. I will always be with my ancestors in the holy vapours of Mosi-O-Tunya, if you ever feel the need to repent before the guardians of our people."

And with that, Taiwo's ghost disappeared.

David Livingstone woke up with a start. He was sweating profusely and hissing like a man with an asthma attack. Chuma was the first to stir.

"Master, master, are you feeling ok?" he asked.

"I have had a strange dream. How far is it from here to Victoria Falls, to the Mosi-O-Tunya?" he asked.

"That's an impossible journey from here. Sleep, we will talk tomorrow." And Livingstone slept.

Chuma did not sleep again. If Livingstone now thought the source of the Nile was the Zambezi, then he had gone mad! In the morning, he talked to Sutsi about the matter, before Livingstone woke up.

"There is no way we are going to Victoria Falls! It is time we took charge of what happens next, otherwise we will be meandering all over the continent purposelessly," said Sutsi. A pact was drawn between the two. They would assist Livingstone only if he made sense. After breakfast, Livingstone summoned his two faithful servants and said: "I am now a man tormented by the living and the dead. The people of Scotland have forsaken me even though I spent all my life trying to set them free. My family has deserted me except for Agnes. But even for her, I guess she is more relaxed when I am away than when I am with her. I saw relief in her eyes when I told her I was leaving Paris.

"The English make mockery of my Nile expedition which, I now believe, was a ruse to force me into self-imposed exile. Their calculation is that I will meet death sooner or later, in the hands of cannibals, malaria or while overshooting a waterfall, deep in some godforsaken place. And that my body will be devoured by hyenas, crocodiles or vultures.

"They are mollifying their guilt by giving me all sorts of high sounding accolades, a saint, the greatest explorer, a philanthropist, but in the end, I will always remain the stupid Scot! Ask yourselves, why didn't they mount a rescue party when I went incommunicado for five years? Why didn't Kirk respond to my messages? I will tell you what! They wished me dead sooner than later! The Celts are a strong lot like Africans. Our resilience knows no bounds. They can kill Livingstone today, but another one will be born to torment them until we are free! What do they say "comrades" may die but cause continues!"

"I hasten to add that someday, hard times will befall Cecil Rhodes, the settlers and concessionaries, who are stealing the wealth of Africans. If not them their descendants; another Taiwo will rise and wage a *Chimurenga*, war of liberation, and the land and wealth will return to its rightful owners. I wish it would be sooner than later. But when the gods of the natives return to assist them in the war of liberation, what shall they say of me? They will say I was the architect of the calamity which befell them through colonialism.

"Last night, Taiwo's ghost came to me in a dream. He warned me that my soul is bound for hell, unless I seek forgiveness from the people of Monomotapa. In my current state of health, I find it an outrageous request. You two belong to all nations since you do not belong to any tribe or state. When I left you with King Simba, you enjoyed the hospitality of Monomotapa as equal citizens to her nationals. Therefore, it is to you as true representatives of the people of Monomotapa in my eyes, that I make the apology. I ask for forgiveness for what I did, in urging the English to occupy the Kingdom of Monomotapa. I plead to the ghost of Taiwo, to set me free, with this solemn confession, so that I can face St. Peter at the Pearly Gates with a clean conscience. Say you forgive me on behalf of the people of Monomotapa," Livingstone pleaded with Chuma and Sutsi.

His two faithful servants looked at each other in confusion. The litany of things they had heard was hard to digest. However, they had been said by a man in complete control of his faculties, with a seriousness which could not be doubted.

"Don't you want to help me?" he asked them in a pleading tone.

"We forgive you on behalf of the people of Monomotapa," came the chorus in reply.

Livingstone was elated like one who had been relieved of a heavy burden. He took his medicine and returned to bed. Late in the evening when he woke up, he called Chuma and Sutsi again.

"When we were in Ujiji, I made a special request to you, the only special request I ever made. Can you recall?" Livingstone asked.

"Yes master, you sought our assurance that if you die, your heart will be buried in Scotland," said Sutsi.

Livingstone reached under his bed and fetched a pouch, in which he kept his valuables. He unzipped a leather wallet and took out a bundle of papers.

"This is the money used in England. I do not trust John Kirk to take my heart to Scotland. I am therefore entrusting you with the task. You will go to Zanzibar and board a ship to England. Inform John Kirk of your mission and tell him that I ordered it. Tell him I said if he cannot help me in life, he should not deny me in death. Tell him to inform my mother and the Royal Geographical Society of my wish, that my heart be buried in Scotland. There is enough money for the journey, your upkeep, and the return journey.

"I am lost for words to thank you for your devotion and dedication to me. It is my guardian angel who brought us together. I have suffered untold sorrow and pain in life. But in your company, I have known comfort, care and love. I could never have imagined that people from such a wide divide in life, could find such solace in one another's company. Now I know why Baker could never let go the slave girl he purchased in Eastern Europe, and why he married her. It was out of genuine love, one he could never find in an English woman. You have given me more joy than my own children ever did, and you did not desert me, even when I was sick and worthless. I wish you the blessings of prosperity, happiness and wisdom. When you return, you must get married and enjoy a happy family life," said Livingstone.

"Master, don't talk like that, you still have many more years to live," said Chuma.

"That is your wish. But I am afraid it is not the wish of the gods. I see bright lights beckoning me to a new world. I have fought the good fight and lost. I am now a worthless wayward vagabond in Africa."

Chuma and Sutsi had their heads bowed as they listened warily to Livingstone. It was true that the old and sick man had become a burden, but they did not wish him death. No good son ever wished his father death, but how else were they to be set free?

"Master we are scared of making the journey to England. It is a strange place and we know no one," said Sutsi.

"I am sure my mother and the Royal Geographical Society will take good care of you. Tell them you have enough money to take care of yourselves, if expenses should become an issue," said Livingstone, even though, he knew at the back of his mind that he was being irrational, irresponsible and unreasonable. If members of the Royal Geographical Society had betrayed him, how were they going to treat savages in London!

But then, how else was he going to keep the solemn promise he had made to his mother? He felt he had been misused by the English, but on his part, he was only using the services of trusted friends. He felt disturbed and uneasy and once again, helplessly caught in another trap, from which there was no escape. Fate had been most unfair to him, he admitted.

"We are all victims in life, one way or the other," he rationalised.

"We have the diamonds and the gold Stanley gave us as commission for the Banyamulenge deal. Can we sell them in England?" asked Chuma.

"Tell my mother to get someone to assist you. You will get a good price and you can buy a lot of things. You will be happy that you went to England! Remember, my body will be buried right here. Where is the jar in which to carry my heart?" he asked.

"Right over there in the bag," said Chuma.

"And the salt to make the brine solution?" asked Livingstone.

"They are together," said Chuma.

"Good, then that is settled. You should not think of me when you perform the surgery. Think of the promise you made, of our friendship, our deep solidarity," said Livingstone.

"We understand," said Sutsi while shaking from head to toe.

Dinner was served, as a heavy atmosphere of unease prevailed in the room. It was Sutsi who broke the silence, "Father, what would have happened to us, if you did not rescue us from the Portuguese?"

"You would have been shipped to the Americans as slaves! You would have been worked to death for nothing! With the abolition of slavery, and if you were still alive, you would have become second rate citizens, segregated, with no civil rights. Thereafter, you would be engaged in a struggle for equality and freedom, just like other oppressed people around the world," said Livingstone.

"It is good you rescued us. We are free men! When you go, we will miss you; we will tell the world about your kindness," said Chuma.

Livingstone looked at them and asked himself, "Free men? Who is a free man?" Then he told them: "The world is deaf to good things. It is the bad news which make headlines and history. Most of the good stories kept alive are all lies, to mask the truth, like David Livingstone, the greatest explorer, the greatest missionary and the saint! Was I ever a free man? How many people did I convert to Christianity including you two?" Livingstone asked.

"None that I know of," answered Sutsi with a chuckle.

"You see! And the English have the impudence to call me a great missionary! They are serving their own purpose, and they will struggle to keep this lie forever. They have moulded a false image of me like a statue! Those who will come later and read history will be fooled to think the British Empire was about philanthropy and civilisation, with David Livingstone at the helm! You now know better. Tell the world the truth," said Livingstone.

"We will," said Chuma. This was not a commitment as they would not know where to begin. It was meant to put Livingstone at ease. They said a prayer, embraced and retired to bed.

Late that night, the ghost of Taiwo returned. Livingstone half awake, half asleep recognised the presence:

"Taiwo, you have come to haunt me again?" he asked.

"No, old man, I have come to share with you a story. You should not fear death, only the aftermath, including your soul's final resting place.

"When the Portuguese bombarded and set Matapa on fire, they did not hit the Holy Shrine, which housed the oracle and the High Priest. You know, my body had been cremated, and that was not the end. Over the years, my father King Simba had received many precious gifts from the Emperors of China, India and Abyssinia, but most valuable was the gold and bronze Casket from the King of Benin. It is a marvellous and exquisite piece of art. It has figurines depicting life in Africa like faces of Kings, dancers, artisans, warriors and animals, so well done that one wonders if it was not made in Heaven!

"The hand of man cannot match such a glorious feat. On top, it has the bust of a prince, made from pure gold. His eyes are two huge diamonds which give a kaleidoscope of colours when exposed to sunlight or fire. On his neck hangs a garland made of gold, diamonds, rubies, pearls, green and red garnets, blue sapphire and emeralds. If you expose the bust fully to light, it is like a fire ball, with many colours dancing in harmony, a marvel beyond words.

"In the foot of one of the figurines is a hidden key hole. When you turn the lock, a flap at the top of the bust opens and the colours are even more dazzling. The key is made of silver. This is the Casket which has been talked about by the English, Arabs and Portuguese as priceless. The information about it reached England through Aden. They termed it an object of worship,

which they longed to own someday, by whatever means. To cut a long story short, the Casket was in the custody of the High Priest and locked in a safe in the Holy Shrine.

"When I was cremated, my father directed the High Priest to put my ashes in the Casket, and it was done, by opening the flap. The High Priest died of the plague. He was buried with the key to the Casket…" said Taiwo's ghost.

"Why are you telling me all this?" asked Livingstone.

"Because as I told you, your resting place in death is very important; don't interrupt me until I finish. Where was I…ooh yes. Your man Cecil Rhodes and his moths and wasps, as we call the English invaders, visited the old capital last year. They went to hunt for King Solomon's treasure, which they believed was left buried in Matapa. They did not find the treasure, but they stumbled upon the Holy Shrine.

"After ransacking the place, they found a safe which they broke, and right there before them, was the priceless Casket. They held it each in turn, awed by its beauty. It was Rhodes who killed the temptation to sell it and share the loot. It could have been sold in the New York auction of art, for the biggest price the world has ever known."

"Priceless booty belongs to the state. We will surrender it to the Queen," Rhodes told the party of greedy fortune hunters.

"And so it was that the Casket bearing my remains arrived in Buckingham Palace. The Queen was awed and thrilled. She summoned the curator of the British Museum and ordered him to create a special space in the Museum, with elaborate security measures, for the highest gem in the whole world. She said the Casket uplifted her soul, inspired her and it was an item of worship. There it sits to this day, in the section marked, "Top security, total silence" for revered objects. On the bullet proof glass surrounding it, there is an inscription, "priceless". Its value is estimated to be one hundred times more that of Mona Lisa.

"It stands on a table made of ivory, and the whole framework is wired to an alarm system, connected to Scotland Yard and Buckingham Palace. I tell you, it commands awe greater than the mummies of Egypt, in the Cairo Museum. The short history inscribed says 'Gift to Queen Victoria from Sir Cecil Rhodes, conqueror of the Kingdom of Monomotapa.' Imagine, there I am buried in a foreign land! Someday, when our gods return and we liberate our land, my people will demand the return of the Casket to Monomotapa, and I will rest in peace in my motherland. Tell me, have you ever been to Buckingham Palace?" Taiwo's ghost asked Livingstone.

"Never!" replied Livingstone.

"Do you think your heart in brine, in a jar, will seat next to me in the British museum?"

"Never!" he replied.

"You know why? Those whose hearts are full of vice and malice never receive favours from the gods, in life or in death. Your mission was diabolical," said the ghost.

"Please, I beg you, how do I get rid of this curse upon my life?" asked Livingstone.

"I will tell you what; the other day, Cecil Rhodes and his henchmen visited Mosi-O-Tunya. When they came to the big drop to the extreme west, the one with many levels of stones which break water into mist and froth as it tumbles down, they named it 'the Devil's Cataract'. One of them quipped that its wild and turbulent nature resembled the life of Livingstone. They gave it the nickname 'Livingstone's Cataract'.

"To my mind, when you die, make this the resting place for your soul. Our ancestors' spirits reside in the calm and serene eastern side of Mosi-O-Tunya. Maybe you will be able to make contact and seek dialogue. You might have some credible mitigating circumstances to fall back on for forgiveness. My people are reasonable, unlike your people," said Taiwo's ghost.

"But why don't you intercede on my behalf, for I fear the weight of my case is too much to bear?" asked Livingstone.

"Nobody can. You tried to mislead Chuma and Sutsi to intercede on your behalf. They are not of the blood of the people of Monomotapa. Once again, you missed the trail like you missed the source of the Nile. This time, you must get your act right, or else you will have no chance to see St. Peter. You will be on a one way ticket to hell, to everlasting perdition.

"Pray hard for the salvation of your soul. Every man must carry his own cross to the end, both in life and in death. I don't envy you old man. You have been a reckless fool in life, try to be wise in death, for there lies the key to the salvation of your soul, otherwise..." and Taiwo's ghost disappeared in a whiff.

Livingstone got out of bed and knelt, while resting his head between the

palms of his hands, his elbows on the bed supporting him. He felt very tired, in his heart and his spirit. He could not bear the heavy burden any more. He went into prayer:

"Oh God…" he did not know whether to pray to the God of David with a sling in the Bible or to *Mwari*, the God of the people of Monomotapa, or other spirits who resided on the calm and serene eastern end of Mosi-O-Tunya. He decided to pray to any supernatural power that cared to listen.

"All you spirits who look after the affairs of men, please give me a hearing…" he could not find the right words. His heart was pounding faster and faster as the words of Taiwo's ghost rang in his head. "Pray hard for the salvation of your soul. Every man must carry his own cross to the end, in life and in death," Livingstone cried:

"I can't carry my cross any longer, it is too heavy!" Just as he had abandoned his "divine mission" and the search for the source of the Nile, he abandoned the prayer and gave up the ghost. In the morning, Chuma and Sutsi found the master kneeling down, dead cold.

Chuma sharpened the knife and Sutsi the axe with which to perform the surgery; removing the heart, from Livingstone's chest. Painstakingly, they took out the heart and placed it in a jar, filled with brine. It was a very small heart indeed.

They buried the body and set off on the journey to Zanzibar, two hundred miles away. Thereafter, they were to proceed to England, thousands of miles away, to deliver the small heart to the Royal Geographical Society and Livingstone's mother, as instructed.

"Supposing it had been the other way round?" asked Chuma.

"Which other way round?" asked Sutsi.

"I mean, supposing he had asked us to bury his heart here, and to take his body to England!" said Chuma.

"Don't be ridiculous!" replied Sutsi.

* * *

As I watched the two marching heading to Zanzibar, I said to myself, "that sums it all!" Livingstone's life was a cursed misadventure and the journey of his two faithful servants was another ridiculous misadventure. How on earth seemingly sane minds are caught up in a whirlpool of idiosyncratic madness

will always remain a mystery to me. But this has remained a permanent feature of the feeble creature called Man since creation, and it will remain so to the end of his tenure on earth.

Livingstone's body had been buried in Africa and his heart was in a jar full of brine heading to Zanzibar and eventually to Scotland. I had no heart to follow Chuma and Sutsi on their journey to England, which I considered misguided.

Satisfied that I had successfully seen the end of my assignment, I took off to Kuzania to write the report, which would be used as evidence against Livingstone on judgment day. It was a painstaking undertaking as I did not want to leave out any detail. It took many years to complete. Just when I thought I was enjoying a well-earned rest, at the end of it all, a voice from Heaven warned me that I was neglecting my duty.

"How?" I asked

"Where is the soul of David Livingstone?" the voice of St. Peter demanded to know.

I woke up and pondered the question. Then it dawned on me that the ghost of Taiwo had advised Livingstone to take refuge by the Devil's Cataract on Mosi-O-Tunya as his soul sought forgiveness from the people of Monomotapa.

"Get on with it," said the voice from Heaven.

I did not need further prodding, I took off.

CHAPTER 26

TRIAL AND EXECUTION

For very good reasons, God gave Man a lifespan of three score years and ten and no more. Indeed, it is more than enough for the irresponsible creature to cause great havoc, in all directions, and to move his creator, to endless streams of tears. It began in a botched experiment codenamed "creation and cloning" in the Garden of Eden. Livingstone lived for sixty years only, and forfeited ten, for he went overboard, post-haste!

On a massive granite boulder by the Devil's Cataract, surrounded by mist and a rainbow, sat the ghosts of David Livingstone and Taiwo. They were engaged in a conversation. Livingstone, seated in an ungainly crouching posture, still looked unkempt, haggard, and melancholic, like he had come to be, in most years of his life.

Next to him sat Taiwo, his real life characteristics still preserved. He was tall, stately, majestic, charming, radiant, composed and self-assured. He sat in an upright posture, most alert.

"When I sent the swallow, to convey to you my invitation to this meeting, I was not sure you would come. Thank you for honouring the invitation. Of late, I have come to accept rejection, betrayal and disappointment, which have accosted me with frequent abandon," said Livingstone.

In response, Taiwo, sounding most impatient told him, "Cut the crap and come to the point. What do you want?"

"When we last met, I begged for forgiveness as I cannot face the Creator on judgement day, with this heavy burden weighing on my soul. Once again, I am begging for forgiveness, from the people of Monomotapa," pleaded Livingstone.

"Look old chap, after what Rhodes has done to my people, forgiveness is out of the question. Do you know he confiscated livestock, and dished out all the fertile land to British settlers? Do you know that my people are forced to work on farms and mines, to pay taxes for services they never receive? On their behalf, I would rather add to your misery, than help you to face St. Peter," said Taiwo.

"Taiwo, don't be so harsh. I regret what I did to Monomotapa, and if I could reverse it, I would. Two wrongs don't make a right, so please have pity on my soul. You were a witness to the final stages of my life, which had become miserable, deplorable, despicable, and most pitiable. Do I not deserve pity, from men, ghosts, spirits and gods? Who has ever suffered, more than I?" asked Livingstone.

"Oh, the answer is quite simple, black slaves and colonised Africans. Your lamentations remind me of the man you told my father about, what was his name? ...Job, the man who lost everything except his faith in God. But for you, you wilfully lost everything; dreams, faith, family, fortunes and lastly your soul!" Taiwo paused for a while then burst into laughter.

"You even lost your teeth! You need divine intervention to rehabilitate what is left of you!" said Taiwo.

"Don't judge me so harshly. I was a victim of evil, not a willing servant of Lucifer," said Livingstone.

"Oh Heavens! Listen to him! The chief architect of hell in Africa claims he was a victim! You, the master designer of colonial imperialism, who coached Rhodes how to conquer Monomotapa! How can you ask for forgiveness? If you want to know how victims look like, visit my people as they toil under the yoke of your evil scheme. Their plight moves your God and *Mwari* to tears!" said a visibly angry Taiwo.

"They are the victims of British imperialism which only serves the interests of the English," said Livingstone.

"And who was the sole mastermind of British Imperialism in Monomotapa?" asked Taiwo.

"I must confess; I was," said a sad Livingstone.

"Yet you claim you were a victim?" asked Taiwo.

"The force that compelled, propelled and controlled me was very powerful. It was most cunning and diabolical, camouflaged in the guise of some form of divinity. I did not stop to question or rationalise my action. I marched blindly, to doom and damnation, and carried with me to hell a happy and powerful kingdom. Do you know that Lucifer confused many angels and almost overthrew God's rule in Heaven?" asked Livingstone.

"Old man, I am not interested in your biblical stories. You confused my father in life and I have no inclination to listen to your preaching in death. Can you think of any single good thing you ever accomplished in life?" asked Taiwo.

"I am afraid, I can't think of any," said Livingstone.

"I would have given you credit for saving Chuma and Sutsi from slavery, but then, by sending them to Britain to deliver your heart, you have sent them to death," stated Taiwo.

"Oh no! God forbid!" cried Livingstone.

"They will be robbed of their valuables and end up in the European Circus, with animals from around the world as objects of scorn, mirth and derision, thanks to you! That is the gratitude they will receive, for being your most obedient servants!" said Taiwo.

"I am the most despicable and ungrateful wretch that ever lived. I sent my greatest and true friends to death just to keep a promise I made to my mother. Was my heart in a jar worth their wonderful lives? Oh! I am ruined beyond redemption and condemned before the Day of Judgement..." and on and on continued the self-admonition of Livingstone's ghost.

Then there was stillness and silence. Livingstone lifted his eyes and asked Taiwo:

"I want to be forgiven for what I did to Chuma and Sutsi...and don't interrupt me...one day, the people of Monomotapa will pick up arms and in a fireball of *Chimurenga* fight for their land and dignity. I will be there to fight with them, and to share in their victory and glory. This you cannot deny me, and I will do it for Chuma and Sutsi as well. I wish this victory more than I wish independence for Scotland or my ticket to Heaven. Heaven can wait!" said Livingstone.

To Livingstone's surprise, Taiwo put his hand on his shoulder. Calmly and with a smile, he asked Livingstone: "Do you believe in what you have just said? About the victory of my people against the invaders or is it just another of your dirty tricks?"

"My mind has never been clearer, " replied Livingstone.

"For once, you have conquered Lucifer, and there is a glimmer of hope for your salvation!"

"Thank you Taiwo! Please ask your people to forgive me," said a hopeful Livingstone.

"Not so fast old man. Not so fast. Now tell me, before we seal the deal, do you have anything else to confess?"

Livingstone thought for a while and then said, "Just one more small thing."

"Go ahead."

"It is about your mother and the 'curse of the caves' in the Vumba Mountains," said Livingstone trembling.

"Leave my mother out of this," said Taiwo harshly.

"I can't, I have a confession to make," said Livingstone.

"Speak then..." said a most attentive Taiwo, looking at Livingstone straight in the eye.

Livingstone lowered his eyes as he began the confession:

"All I had wanted was the truth about the curse, which your mother had kept secret. I thought it would be a powerful weapon against the kingdom..." then Livingstone paused.

"There you go again. Get to the point!" shouted an impatient Taiwo.

"Before she confessed, she forced me to make love to her, because she said, that was what custom demanded...and..."

"My mother did what?" Taiwo demanded wondering whether he had heard Livingstone right.

"You heard me clearly. She said it was out of custom," said Livingstone.

"You slept with my mother?" asked Taiwo, tears welling in his eyes.

"Yes. She left me with no alternative..." said Livingstone.

Taiwo's face was now covered with sweat, his chest heaving up and down and veins in his muscles bulging to bursting point. In a flash, he slapped Livingstone so hard on the face that the old man was lifted in the air and thrown back quite a distance. Taiwo was on him, murderous and furious. He grabbed Livingstone by the neck and squeezed him so hard, that his eyes, boggling, popped out of the sockets.

In panic, Livingstone pleaded in a whimpering voice: "Taiwo please understand." but Taiwo was blinded by fury. Placing Livingstone's face in front of his, he hissed a tornado of hot air which uprooted Livingstone's beard and hair and blew them into the rapids.

"You haggard stinking creature, you half construct of a scarecrow, you agent of Lucifer, how could you defile the royal household of Monomotapa? How could you?" Taiwo's voice was rising higher and higher, his eyes burning like furnaces.

"You contaminated my mother with your filth...You cuckolded the great King Simba, my dear father..." his voice was now reverberating like thunder.

"Your father was dead by then," pleaded Livingstone.

"Dead or alive, you had no business poking your nose into the secret affairs of the Kingdom!" roared Taiwo.

Livingstone could see the situation was getting out of hand. Taiwo had cautioned him to be wise in death. He had blown it! He regretted his fool's courage to tell it all. He had come very close to forgiveness, half way to the salvation of his soul, but that was now gone. He remembered the words of Shakespeare that, "Whoever tells too much truth is sure to be hanged". He cursed himself for having sealed his own doom. If his life had been one long catalogue of mistakes, one riding on top of the other, he knew this one was the gravest of them all. It had shut the door to the salvation of his soul.

"Please, Taiwo, Taiwo..." he continued to plead.

Taiwo opened his mouth and like a dragon, blew hot air and fire in Livingstone's face; it contorted it to shapelessness. The Scot was in unbearable pain.

"On this day, all your stories and tricks will come to an end. Forget about Heaven, the spirits of Monomotapa will judge you right here and now, you crazy filth!" said Taiwo.

As Taiwo spoke, a roaring thunder was heard across the whole of the vast Zambezi Valley. It shook everything for miles around. The voice reverberated in the forest and over the surrounding mountains. The roar dislodged mighty boulders from the sides of high cliffs along the Zambezi Valley. The monsters, hurtling down wildly, uprooted giant trees.

The stones and trees made spectacularly high fountains in turns, in quick succession, as they hit the water in the river far below. Wild animals scampered in all directions and birds took to the skies, as shrieking bats flew out of caves and snakes slithered out of holes in the ground. There was fear, stampede and mayhem everywhere. It was like the Armageddon had begun, to herald the coming of the Day of Judgment. Taiwo, his grip still on Livingstone's neck, waited for the great force which was moving, heading in their direction.

It was the ghost of King Simba, furiously marching on water with great strides, his nostrils flaring his eyes red in anger.

From a distance, he commanded Taiwo, with an angry booming voice:

"Tighten the grip, don't let him escape!" and Taiwo tightened the grip around Livingstone's neck another notch.

Livingstone was very scared. Having undergone torture from Taiwo, he knew that ghosts were more than capable of inflicting pain on each other. He feared for his soul, the only thing of value which remained of him, but even that was now in doubt.

"Mighty Changamire the magnanimous and the just, please give me a hearing…" pleaded Livingstone.

"Pale face, I trusted you and treated you with honour, kindness and respect. I listened to your funny stories even when they did not make sense. How did you pay me back? You lied to me and made a fool out of me with your offer for guns to protect my kingdom. You cuckolded me and gave the kingdom to Rhodes, on a silver platter!

"The punishment for committing adultery with the Queen is death. Let me tell you, it does not matter whether you are caught when you are alive or dead. Nobody escapes punishment for defiling the royal household."

With that Simba gave Livingstone a mighty blow on the jaw. It knocked out the remaining teeth. This was Simba of old, the strong towering warrior who did not spare his enemies. He was exacting revenge with no mercy for the wrongs done to his people, the kingdom and to himself.

"When I heard your confession on how you extracted the secret of the curse from the Queen, I felt a cold shiver in my heart. Most unforgivable was the reason why you sought the information, to blackmail the kingdom, for easy conquest!

"Admittedly, you have suffered much in life through your own folly no doubt, and because you are an incorrigible fool, you shall continue to suffer in death, for the same reason. By conjuring a plan to subject others to misery and pain, for whatever reason, you planted the seed for your own destruction. What did you tell me the Good Book says – "Do unto others as you would have them do unto you." Well the spirits of Monomotapa have charged me with the responsibility of giving you a practical lesson in your Christian teachings! As you would have Monomotapa destroyed, I am he who is to execute the evanescence of your soul, with great pleasure!"

Livingstone did not understand the punishment Changamire was talking about. "And what are you going to do with my soul?" he asked.

"I had hoped that one day, I would have the chance to preach to you about the might of our God *Mwari*. You never gave me the chance and this is not the time. You lost a great opportunity to be saved, and that is why you went messing around. As civilised as you claim to be, your people have never learnt how to harness the powers of the spirits like us. We call it voodoo. We possess the power to vaporise a human soul, and this is going to be your punishment," Changamire said smiling.

"What are you going to do to me?" asked Livingstone, looking at Changamire like one would face a gorgon, paralysed with fear.

"It is simple! Your soul will be evaporated and totally destroyed, beyond reconstruction, so that you will never enjoy reincarnation or resurrection like other souls. It means total annihilation, or total erasure of your spiritual existence. You will be rendered worthless, non-existent! For you are filth and a scum," responded Simba.

"Then how will I face St. Peter and the Creator on the Day of Judgement?" asked Livingstone.

"Either you are hard at hearing, or you do not have the capacity to understand complicated issues! You are a dimwit, a nincompoop, a simpleton! May I repeat myself for your comprehension of the gravity of the matter?" Changamire asked.

"Yes, please do," said Livingstone.

"By the time I am through with you, David Livingstone will be erased from the spiritual worlds, both on earth and in Heaven. You will only exist as bad memory. You will be worth less than cow dung. Do you understand me now?" asked the Changamire.

"You mean I will not have a chance to defend myself on the Day of Judgement?" asked Livingstone.

"Think man, think! What is there do defend? When Taiwo asked you to remember a single good thing you ever did in your entire life, you could not remember any. Your life has been a series of evil acts, incomprehensible and unforgivable. Now, brace yourself for the punishment, for it is going to be painful beyond life in hell," Livingstone started crying.

Changamire teased him further: "Not yet old man, not yet. It is not yet time to cry. You will have enough time to holler and yell as tears stream down your face before it is over. I am going to give you a taste of the pain and agony my people are going through, in the hands of Cecil Rhodes. It is going to be unkind, harsh, long, unendurable, then you can fully fathom why you cannot be forgiven or allowed to exist anymore."

"Taiwo," Simba commanded, "hold this creature tightly. We shall shred his skin and flesh into thin ribbons and smash every bone to smithereens before we work on his soul!" And with that, they started working on Livingstone from the head down. He screamed and writhed in unbearable pain.

"Now old man, sing the song you sang with Stanley by the Lualaba River, the one which goes:

> We shall not
> We shall not be moved
> We shall not
> We shall not be moved
> Just like a tree
> That stands by the water side
> We shall not be moved."

But Livingstone could not sing as he moaned and yelled in excruciating pain. At first, his cry had a high pitch like the repeated yelp of a puppy dog in great pain. It excited bats, jackals, hyenas and monkeys to join in, with renditions of their own versions of cries. Towards the end, the cry of Livingstone became guttural and crocodiles, rhinos and elephants joined in the chorus of the weirdest cacophony ever heard on earth since creation. The only thing missing was Scottish bag pipes. Then the noise began to die down, progressively drowned by the sound of the roar of the Mosi-O-Tunya. Even the animals were glad the weird noise had come to an end.

What remained of Livingstone was a blob; Taiwo was working on it furiously with a grinding stone, with the intention of destroying it completely. It would not yield to blows; or rather it was behaving like mercury. With each blow, it broke into tiny particles only to regroup and assume the same shape. For Taiwo, it was a most curious and frustrating waste of time and labour.

"Daddy, this thing seems indestructible," he told the Changamire, who was looking at his son with great amusement.

"It is not easy to destroy the soul," said the Changamire.

"You mean this is the soul of David Livingstone?" asked Taiwo full of curiosity.

"When you warned Livingstone, you would destroy his soul with voodoo, did you mean it?" Taiwo asked his father.

"Yes indeed. I was never a man to make a promise in jest." And Simba reached for a silver necklace around his neck with a round and shiny object attached to it.

"This is a secret weapon. It is called the Vaporiser! It is the preserve of the gods and spirits of Monomotapa; not any other kingdom, Hell or Heaven, has any defence against it. When you hold it against the light of heavenly bodies, the stars, the moon or the sun, a razor beam appears. It is the beam which destroys the soul. That is why we call it a soul vaporising glass. There is only one in the whole universe, this one," said Simba proudly.

"May I hold it?" asked Taiwo.

"Take it! From this moment I bequeath it to you. Avenge the rape of Monomotapa through the evil acts of Livingstone, Cardinal Domingos, the 'nuns' and do likewise when Rhodes and the leeches die. Intercept them before the Pearly Gates and give them the ultimate punishment," said the Changamire.

"Father, you have done me great honour. I never had the opportunity to do anything for Monomotapa in life, but in the execution of this new mandate, I will make our gods proud!" said Taiwo as he adjusted the weapon to focus the beam on Livingstone's soul. It was still lying on the black granite rock, wobbling.

While I gazed with great awe and mesmerisation at the unfolding drama, the soft swish of wings and an approaching light diverted my attention. The object of my fresh attention came and settled next to me and I heard the voice of St. Peter: "How have you been old boy?" he asked me.

"As good and obedient as I can be," I replied.

"True, true. The Heavens are pleased with your patience and commitment to duty. You are worthy of a reward, the celestial knighthood! An assignment which lasts fifty years is not a mean task. Fifty years following a reckless vagabond and you did not grumble or deviate from your mission. Congratulations!" said St. Peter.

"You mean I now carry favour with the Almighty for my obsequious conduct?" I asked in excitement.

"Of course old chap, of course!" he replied smiling.

"The only snag is that I am not yet done with the report on Livingstone, if that is what you have come for. My recollection is that you requested me to make it ready for the Day of Judgment when it would be used to nail the vagabond," I told St. Peter.

"Don't get jittery old chap. The instructions have not changed. I came to witness the vaporisation of Livingstone's soul! Heaven is interested in the weapon," he informed me.

"Why?" I asked.

"There are a lot of people we would like to vaporise instead of sending them to hell. The place is full. The German general who killed over five million Hereros in Namibia and Henry Morton Stanley who cut limbs, noses, ears and breasts of Congolese natives top the list," he said.

"Henry Morton Stanley? The same one who came to Ujiji?" I asked.

"That very one; he has killed over ten million Congolese on behalf of a half-pint size idiot called King Leopold II of Belgium, a most deceitful and shrew ruler. Stanley sold the idea of Congo to the king for a fat sum, revealing the immense wealth in the land," he revealed to me.

"I don't understand," I pleaded ignorance.

"While you were writing the report on Livingstone, you missed many things. Propelled by the reports by explorers and missionaries, European rulers embarked on a scramble for Africa. They were coming to blows over claims and counter-claims. When common sense prevailed, they assembled in Berlin in 1884-85 and divided Africa among themselves. To them, the continent was a *terra nullis, a tabula rasa* on which they could write anything they wanted with the blood of the natives as the ink!

"Stanley was made the administrator of the Congo by King Leopold II on the understanding that he would deliver tons of ivory, rubber, gold, diamonds and hardwood.

"In the Congo, Stanley set quotas for each chief to deliver. If the quota fell short, Stanley and his henchmen chopped limbs, ears, noses and breasts of women to enforce compliance. It has been reported that he cuts one hundred and fifty arms per day. Even children are not spared. He has also killed over ten million natives! By our estimates and as collaborated by German reporters, soon there will be no labour force left! It is genocide. The world since creation has never witnessed such cruelty driven by greed. It moves God to tears," St Peter shed tears too as he spoke.

"So missionaries and explorers were the devil's agents?" I asked.

"Yes, each and every one of them, from Mungo Park, Livingstone, Speke, Burton, Baker, Karl Peters, Rhodes, the whole lot – French, Italians, Germans and Belgians. No nation ever civilised another, they only exploit, maim and kill – driven by greed.

"Once we master the weapon, we shall vaporise them all. But first let's see how it works," said St. Peter.

Livingstone had thought that the Changamire's intent to vaporise his soul was just an idle boast, until he felt the sharp sting of unbearable heat and began to evaporate. The blob tried to shift, but it could not move of its own accord.

As the pain increased, Livingstone cried out: "Oh you good for nothing savages…you pagans…heathens…creatures of a Dark Continent…ouch… God in Heaven will strike you…you servants of Lucifer…Ouch! You are destroying my soul…Ouch…St. Peter help! Oh God help…!" but nobody answered. In fact, St. Peter was fixated, fascinated and mesmerised with the powerful weapon, wondering whether he should borrow it to vaporize Lucifer, to end his menace for good.

Livingstone's voice became dimmer and dimmer as the last drop of the blob was vaporised. The powerful voice that had proclaimed the urgent need for a vast British Empire on which the sun would never set, died in a whisper, drowned by the roar of the Mosi-O-Tunya.

"What does a vaporised soul become?" Taiwo asked his father, who was grinning in triumph, with great satisfaction.

"It becomes foul air, odoriferous fumes which are scattered in all directions by the wind. You see, every soul longs for a return to life in reincarnation or resurrection, but an evaporated soul is worth less than the soul of a dog. It is nothingness forever. It is a painful realisation, is it not?" asked Simba.

"You have done well to erase Livingstone for good. Who knows what harm he could be up to if he ever came back, for example as a snake," said Taiwo

"That is the point. Extreme evil must be totally destroyed for the sake of man," said Simba.

"I long for the day I will vaporise Cecil Rhodes, Domingos and the 'nuns' and anybody else who has brought injustice and suffering to our people," said Taiwo

"Oh how I wish you had succeeded me as king of Monomotapa, our people would have been assured of a bright future. Your idiot of a brother sold his soul and the future of our kingdom. I have a dream that someday, a great son of the kingdom will start a *Chimurenga* and drive out the leeches. He will claim back our independence and dignity and give back the land to its rightful owners. I hope his name will be Taiwo," said Simba.

"I left behind a son, you remember? Your lineage is not dead! I know he will lead the fight. Rest assured father, my soul will know no rest until our

day of glory comes. I will warn our people not to listen to foreigners as all who come from foreign lands only come to line up their pockets," said Taiwo.

"It is a lesson well learnt," concluded Simba.

Father and son hand in hand walked majestically on water, back to the eastern side of the Mosi-O-Tunya, their mission accomplished.

St. Peter put his hand gently on my shoulder and said: "Sorry old chap we have taken you through a lot of trouble for nothing; fifty years with a reckless vagabond was one hell lot of a long ordeal."

"It could have been worse had it been three score years and ten remember? But what do you mean my ordeal was for nothing? The report is almost ready," I reminded St. Peter.

"The man has been vaporised and Heaven has accepted the trial and judgement by *Mwari* and his 'faithful agents' said St. Peter. I did not quite comprehend what he meant.

"I beg your pardon! What do I do with the report?" I asked him.

"You heard me. Case closed. You can shred it, burn it or do whatever you want with it," said St. Peter.

Full of pain and anguish with the realisation that my painstaking efforts for all those years were not worth the papers they were written on, I closed my eyes. And at that moment and most involuntarily, I heard myself say, "Goddamn it."

I opened my eyes to apologise to St. Peter for my foul language, but he was gone.

To ease my pain of years wasted in labour, I thought of revealing it all in a book someday. May be I will, maybe I won't.

Adieu.